THE
SILENT
HOUSE

BOOKS BY LAURA ELLIOT

Fragile Lives
Stolen Child
The Prodigal Sister
The Betrayal
Guilty
The Wife Before Me
The Thorn Girl

THE SILENT HOUSE

LAURA ELLIOT

bookouture

Published by Bookouture in 2020

An imprint of Storyfire Ltd.
Carmelite House
50 Victoria Embankment
London EC4Y 0DZ

www.bookouture.com

ISBN: 978-1-80019-085-6
eBook ISBN: 978-1-80019-084-9

The Silent House is dedicated to my beloved grandchildren,
Romy and Ava Flynn, and Nina and Sean Considine.
I love you all to the moon and back.

PART ONE

CHAPTER ONE

Southern Stream FM

This is Gavin Darcy opening Morning Stream with an exclusive news flash.

An emergency call was received in the early hours of this morning from a young girl who claimed she was being held at gunpoint by a dangerous gunman at an unknown location. The connection was broken before she was able to reveal her whereabouts and it's believed a shot was fired before her call abruptly ended.

Gardai were tracing the call to find out if it was genuine or a hoax. Unfortunately, as listeners know, hoax calls, whether to the gardai or the fire service, are regular occurrences and we have been awaiting confirmation from the Garda Press Office, who, as yet, are not prepared to comment. It's not known if there are others at the location with her. We'll keep you up to date as further information is released so stay tuned to Morning Stream for coverage of this unfolding situation.

CHAPTER TWO

Six months earlier

Sophy

The rooks had arrived before them. The shriek of rusted hinges when Isobel opened the entrance gates had startled them from their roost and they had risen in clamorous protest to wheel above their nests before scattering into the evening air. Now, they had settled like an ominous, black cowl over the chimneys and roof of Hyland Hall. Silent and unmoving, their sharp, beady eyes watched Sophy as she left her car and took stock of her surroundings.

She had imagined moving into a 'great' house. One that had weathered the centuries and stood stately and proud at the end of a long, tree-lined avenue. The bumpy, narrow lane leading to the entrance gates had worried her but the avenue had been as leafy and wide as she had hoped. Her spirits had risen as she drove under a canopy of overhanging branches towards her destination. The trees, she now realised, had been a deceptive lure that did nothing to prepare her for the shock of seeing her new home for the first time.

Hyland Hall would once have been a magnificent dwelling but decades of neglect had carved fissures into the red brickwork, flayed the paint from the front door and tarnished the brass horseshoe-shaped knocker. The courtyard was equally run-down, the flagstones barely visible beneath a wilderness of weeds and overgrown shrubbery.

She did not need to look at her daughters' expressions to appreciate their shock. They must be waiting for her to break; to turn on her heel and leave this eerie house to the rooks and the two stone lions perched on either side of the high steps. She shared their desire to run but she could not turn back now. Too much was at stake. This house, whatever its flaws, would shelter them and that, for the time being, was enough.

The musty smell of abandoned spaces rushed up to greet them when Sophy unlocked the front door. Isobel stepped back, her nose wrinkling in disgust, and Julie, after an initial hesitation, asked, 'Is this *really* the start of our exciting new adventure, Mammy?'

'You're right, Julie, that's what it is.' Taking their hands, she ignored Isobel's resistant pull and drew them forward into the wide entrance hall. Its glory days were well past and the embossed wallpaper had faded to an indistinguishable beige. A pall of dust covered the furniture – a large wooden trunk with a curved lid, two antique chairs, and a long-legged console table positioned under a gun cabinet. A carving of a horse's head was displayed on the marble pillar and portraits of horses hung from the walls. A tall grandfather clock sent out six startling, sonorous booms, as if acknowledging and welcoming their arrival.

Isobel clasped her hands over her ears and Julie, unable to hide her fear, ran back to the car where she had left Cordelia. She carried the mannequin back into the hall and propped her against the grandfather clock. Crooning softly to her, she straightened Cordelia's wig and adjusted her arms.

'What's this supposed to be?' Isobel stood at the bottom of the stairs and stared at a steel rail with a stairlift attached. It ran along one wall and followed the curve of the staircase until it wound out of sight.

'It's a stairlift that's been installed for Mr Hyland,' Sophy replied. 'Remember what I've told you. You are *not* to climb these stairs under any circumstances. Do you understand, Isobel? Julie?'

'Yes.' Isobel nodded. 'No way are we to bother The Recluse.'

'His name is Mr *Hyland*.' Sophy frowned. 'I've told you to stop calling him by that ridiculous name.'

Julie pressed her foot to the bottom step then withdrew it. 'It's weird,' she whispered. 'Him not wanting to see anyone. I'd hate that.'

'He has his own reasons for demanding his privacy,' Sophy replied. 'He's been very ill and is still recuperating. We must respect his wishes at all times. Come on, let's check out the downstairs rooms. We have two bedrooms. Decide which one you want to take and I'll use the other one.'

'Does that mean I'll have to sleep with Julie?' Isobel sounded outraged.

'The rooms are large. There's plenty of space for the two of you.'

'Three of us,' warned Julie. 'Cordelia also needs her own space.'

Sophy sighed as she opened the door of the larger room. The dark, cumbersome furniture was such a stark contrast to their bedrooms in Park View Villas and Isobel, staring in horror at a four-poster bed, its canopy speckled with blue mould, shuddered.

'That's *disgusting*.' Her finger shook as she pointed at the bed. 'No *way* will I sleep in that… that *thing*.'

'It'll have to do for now,' Sophy replied. 'I promise I'll organise separate beds once we've settled down.'

'Settled *down*—' Isobel began but Sophy was already entering another room. The high ceiling was discoloured yet faint, intricately designed mouldings of musical instruments and musicians were still discernible on the cornicing. Sophy imagined the

Hyland family gathered there in the evenings to play music but all that remained of its former purpose was an out-of-tune grand piano and an elaborate piano stool. The overgrown courtyard was visible through two long windows at either end of the music room. The frames of their six-over-six sashes were flaking and encrusted with mould.

'Cordelia thinks this house is *really* eerie.' Julie opened the lid of the piano and struck a few chords. She winced at the discordant notes and carefully closed the lid. 'But she'll get to like it soon.'

'How do *you* feel about your new home?' Sophy asked.

'It's… okay. Kind of nice, I guess?'

'*Nice*.' Isobel rolled her eyes. 'It's only nice if you like living in hell. You can't possibly expect us to live here, Mum. You *can't*.' Her truculence had disappeared and she sounded on the verge of tears.

'We made a promise to be brave and share this new adventure,' said Sophy. Understanding her daughter's distress was not the same as acknowledging it. To do so would undermine her composure. What purpose would it serve if she wept and huddled into a mass of anxiety? Her daughters needed to see her strength, not the weakness that threatened to overwhelm her at times.

Once past the staircase the hall narrowed into a corridor that led them down three steps into a spacious kitchen. A long, wooden table ran along the centre of the room and an old-fashion dresser filled with crockery stood against one wall. The fridge, washing machine and dishwasher were new but a wood-burning stove seemed to be her only means of cooking. A dusty space with wires hanging from the wall showed where the original cooker had stood. She spotted a note on the table and read it. Charlie Bracken apologised for the delay in the delivery of the cooker and hoped she could manage with the stove until it arrived.

Jack Hyland had mentioned Charlie in his correspondence with her and referred to him as his friend. He had been asked to organise the delivery of electrical goods and had succeeded in doing so except for one of the most important items. After they had carried in their luggage and chosen their bedrooms – because of its size, the girls agreed to sleep in the four poster bed – they returned to the kitchen to eat.

'The stove shouldn't be too difficult to light…' Sophy pointed resolutely to a stack of old newspapers on the floor. 'Roll the pages up as tight as sticks and we'll have a fire going in no time at all.'

The girls did as they were told. As the spirals of paper piled up and began to burn, she added logs from a basket. The fire went out immediately. She set more newspapers alight and shrieked when flames lashed across her fingers. As she splashed cold water over her hands, she realised that smoke was billowing from the chimney and filling the kitchen. She coughed and ushered the girls outside into the backyard.

The setting sun cast an eerie glow over the blackened remains of the burned-out stables that had almost killed Jack Hyland. They reminded Sophy of pyramids; the roofless walls bleakly angled. The corrugated frame of a larger building with a domed roof was visible beyond the stables. That must have been the barn where the fire started. One of Jack's stipulations was that the girls were not to go near the ruins in case they collapsed. They nodded glumly when Sophy reminded them that the stables and barn were out of bounds.

'Let's forget about a hot meal for tonight,' she said when the smoke had cleared and they returned to the kitchen. 'I'll make sandwiches instead?'

'Can me and Cordelia have cheese and onion crisp sandwiches?' Julie had taken the mannequin from the hall and settled her into a rocking chair by the stove. 'They're our best favourite food.'

'I want *proper* food,' Isobel snapped. 'I'm not going to sleep in the same bed as Julie if she smells like a stinking onion.'

Sophy sucked in her cheeks and buttered bread. Losing her temper was not going to help matters. She was weary of arguments. Weary of understanding her daughters' grief, worries, loss. So many emotions expressed, and she had listened to them, determinedly positive, while she battled her own inner conflict. Selling her boutique and then her house, the proceeds of both running like water through her fingers, had numbed her too much to feel true pain but it swept over her now, raw and raging against the circumstances that had led them here.

'Don't start arguing again,' she said. 'We're all tired after our long journey. Everything will work out if we just give it time.'

'No! It *won't*.' Isobel smashed her fists off the table. 'You know it won't get better, not in a million years. We can't stay here. It's *horrible*. I don't want to live with The Rec— with Mr Hyland. There has to be another way. There *has* to be.'

'What do you suggest we do, Isobel? Where will we go?' Sophy stared at the blisters rising on her hand.

'You're crying.' Isobel made it sound like an accusation. 'You're crying yet you keep pretending everything's going to be all right.'

'It's all your fault, Issy Kingston!' Julie yelled. 'You keep spoiling our exciting new adventure. Cordelia hates you—'

'Cordelia is a fucking dummy—'

'You said a *curse*.' Julie rose on her toes with self-righteous shock. 'Mammy, Issy said the *F* word.'

'Stop it this instant, both of you,' Sophy shrieked. 'I'm tired listening to the pair of you bickering. You never stopped for the entire journey and I won't put up with it for a moment longer. Do you hear me? Eat your sandwiches then go to your bedroom and unpack.'

'I'm never going to unpack—'

'You heard me, Isobel. Do what you're told for once. I don't want to hear another word out of either of you for the rest of the night. Is that understood?'

Isobel, her eyes downcast, bit hard into a sandwich and nodded.

'Don't worry, Mammy.' Julie leaned her elbows on the table and cupped her face in her hands. 'This is going to be the best adventure ever.'

'I know it is, my darling.' Sophy released her breath, in and out, deep and slow.

When the girls were asleep, she entered her bedroom and loosened her hair, allowed it to fall to her shoulders. She stared at her reflection in the dressing table mirror. Tears had traced furrows on her soot-stained cheeks and her eyes were red-rimmed from lack of sleep. Too tired to undress, she lay on the bed and stared at the ceiling. A series of faint cracks radiated across the once-white surface. She watched the slow sway of a cobweb hanging from the lampshade. How long had that dreary, grey smear been suspended above the bed? Decades, probably. Sounds reached her from the bedroom next door. The thump of something falling – a book, perhaps. Books had become Isobel's defence, her weapon of choice to keep her parents at bay. Sophy considered going in to check on her. She would gather her eldest daughter into her arms and reassure her that everything was going to be okay. A wasted effort. At fourteen years of age, Isobel recognised a lie when she heard one, but Sophy continued to repeat the same platitudes every time they discussed their future. What else could she do? Isobel might demand the truth but did she want to hear it? No, Sophy decided. Reality needed to be doled out in bearable doses.

The high pitch of Julie's voice reached her. The sound of the voice that Julie used when practising her ventriloquism skills set Sophy's teeth on edge. Julie's affection for Cordelia, the child mannequin who had once stood in the window of Sophy's boutique, was just another problem to be tackled when life settled into a new normality, whenever that would be.

Was Luke sleeping, she wondered, or was he also lying awake and tormented by thoughts of their broken marriage? He had only ever laid his hands on her in tenderness and passion, yet when he walked from their home, she felt as if her body had been bruised beyond healing. He had never betrayed her with another woman yet when she uncovered his lies, she was as duped and humiliated as any wife who had ever been deceived by an unfaithful husband. He adored their two daughters yet he had recklessly steered their future onto the rocks.

She continued staring at the ceiling. Like palmistry, it seemed as if her two lives – the one that had been heedlessly destroyed, and the new one that was being forced on her – could be read in the lines. The crack that ran in a straight direction until it broke into a tangled network was the present. There had to be another line, a newer one, and she eventually found it. This one had the sharpness of a recent fracture; a quavering uncertainty in its run towards the centre of the ceiling. Her future. It hadn't taken shape as yet, but the forward momentum was unstoppable, and the past, where happiness once reigned, was seen for what it was: a deluded ideal filled with false promises and empty kisses.

CHAPTER THREE

Isobel

On the evening before he left them, her father mowed the front lawn for the last time. Isobel sat on the garden wall and watched him making lines of light and shade. Daisies spun in the air as the blades of the mower sliced through their fragile stems and the twilight air was filled with the scent of crushed grass. She wondered how something severed could smell so sweet.

He had been sitting tall and straight in an armchair on the day everything changed. He hardly spoke at all when Sophy — sitting just as stiffly, but away from him, far, far away, her arms tucked against her waist, her fingers locked together — said that they, their parents, no longer loved each other. They had made a decision to live separate lives.

Julie, huddled close to Isobel on the sofa, kept asking questions like, 'Why can't you just forgive and forget, the way you're always asking me and Issy to do when we fight?' She squeezed Isobel's hand and said, 'Tell them, Issy. Tell them it's easy to say sorry.'

Isobel held her sister's hand just as tightly but she didn't plead with them. The sad, set expressions on their faces told her that nothing she or Julie said would change their minds.

'But why… *why* are you leaving us?' she had asked her father that night. Unable to sleep, she had gone downstairs to find

Peeper. Her cat normally slept in the kitchen but she needed his fluffy warmth beside her. No longer sitting straight, her father was slumped over the kitchen table, his face in his hands.

'Oh, my darling girl,' he said when he saw her. He held out his arms to her and his mouth twisted in an attempt to smile. Ignoring him, she picked up Peeper, who nuzzled his nose into her neck and calmed her down. She was then able to sit down opposite him and listen as he explained what it was like to have a gambling addiction. That was what he called what he did, his terrible need to spend money and gamble his family's happiness away.

She had always thought addiction was about drugs. It was about drinking too much or eating disorders. How was spending money an addiction? He said it was an addiction when the money didn't belong to him. When winning was never enough to make him stop. Their mother had sold Kid's Chic to help pay his debts and he no longer owned his business, Kingston Fountains, where he used to design incredible water fountains for gardens and parks.

He was going to a special place called The Oasis of Hope to be cured from his addiction. Afterwards, he would begin again, only in a new way, and be a better father to them.

Isobel had no memory of what she said to him. All she could remember afterwards was the hurt on his face, as if her words were bullets sinking into his skin. Her own skin was wet with tears. How could she cry so much and still have tears to spare? He had traced his finger over her cheek, as if, somehow, that could stop the flow, and begged her to be brave.

'One day we'll be together again,' he said. 'I promise with all my heart it will happen.'

She wanted to believe him but her mother had said that that was *never* going to happen. Never, *ever*.

Two months had passed since then. How could so much in her life have changed in such a short space of time? At first, her anger had no target, or so she thought. Was it directed at her father with his big plans and fine promises? Or the families who came to view their house and tramped through the rooms as if they'd already moved in? Or the removal men who took away the furniture she thought they owned but didn't? Or the men who loaded her father's silver BMW and her mother's Range Rover onto two trailers and drove them away? Or her mother for pretending that moving in with a recluse was such an exciting adventure when everyone knew it was just an alternative to becoming homeless? Isobel guessed it was all of those things rolled up together, but most of all she blamed her father. He had cast them adrift from the safe, happy world they once knew and she would never forgive him. Never!

At breakfast this morning before they left Park View Villas, her mother had once again insisted that they were at the start of an exciting new adventure. 'We're walking away from here with our heads held high,' she said. Her voice had sounded shrill and unfamiliar, as if she knew how fake she sounded but was unable to stop. 'I know this is difficult for you both but it's also a wonderful opportunity to begin again.'

Beginning again was not what Isobel wanted. The plans she had made with her friends, the beach trips and the sleepovers, the long summer evenings doing nothing except hanging out together in the park, that was exciting and adventurous, but the move to Hyland Hall was a tragedy, plain and simple. She hated it when her mother tried to pretend otherwise. They had held a farewell party for her in Joanne's house, so much hugging and crying and so many promises to keep in touch. It should have helped Isobel to feel better but her mood was mutinous as she left her bedroom for the last time. Her footsteps clattered off the wooden stairs. She hadn't even left and, already, her house sounded empty. Like her memories were evaporating into the stillness she was leaving behind.

They had already said goodbye to their neighbours. Her mother had asked them not to wave goodbye in case it got too emotional but Isobel knew they were watching from their windows. Julie knew it too. The pink feather boa she wore for dressing-up games had fluttered like a swarm of butterflies around her neck as she ran down the garden path. She flipped it from side to side, then curtsied to their invisible neighbours before climbing into the back of the car.

Two enormous rubbish skips filled with all their belongings they had dumped from the attic and the garden shed were parked in the driveway. The leaky garden hose hanging over the edge of the first skip reminded Isobel of an elephant. A grey hunkering beast waiting for them to depart. She took her rabbit's foot and glass horseshoe out of her pocket and flung them over the edge. What use were good luck charms when they had failed her utterly?

The car was already packed with boxes and plastic sacks of stuff they still *actually* owned and was so tiny compared to the one her mother used to drive. Mrs Gordon from next door had insisted she was too old to drive her car anymore and Sophy must take it as a 'thank you' for all her kindness over the years. Isobel had never noticed her mother being kind to Mrs Gordon. Just as she had never noticed her parents getting ready to begin their new lives without each other.

She was fourteen, almost an adult and old enough to under-stand that marriages broke up. Old enough to understand that divorce, although terrible, did not destroy lives. Old enough to cope with the fall-out. Or so she kept trying to convince herself. But words like 'new beginnings' and 'it's no one's fault' were just that — *words*. They weren't a cure, weren't magical potions that could make her feel any better. She had lifted Peeper down from his favourite spot against the back window where he was dozing and ran her fingers through his fur. His purring had rippled against her lap as her mother started the engine on a car that must have been designed for hobbits. Looking out the window, it seemed to Isobel as if Park View Villas, where she had lived since she was born, was holding its breath until the Kingston family disappeared around the corner and life could return to normal.

CHAPTER FOUR

Sophy

Alone at last once the girls had gone to bed, Sophy tidied up the kitchen and opened a second door at the far end of the room. This led into an annexe that had been added to the original building and gave the back of the house an L-shape. It must have been used as a changing area for the jockeys and grooms who once worked in the stables. Shower stalls were discoloured and broken, as were the urinals, and the toilets in a smaller bathroom where the sign *Ladies* was barely visible. This space had become a hoarding area for old furniture that had broken and been deemed beyond repair.

Returning to the kitchen, she switched off the light and was heading towards her bedroom when she heard a noise from outside. She tensed, her fear rising as the isolation of her surroundings bore down on her.

She hurried towards the music room. Peering out, she watched as headlights swept over the bushes in the courtyard. An engine was cut and the courtyard was plunged into darkness. An automatic outside light switched on and revealed a figure walking swiftly towards the steps. She glanced around the room for a weapon. Her eyes lit on the companion set beside the old-fashioned fireplace. She grasped the poker and carried it out to the hall. The intruder had a key and was intent on entering the house. She was standing with the poker raised when the hall door opened and a man entered. He looked equally startled to see her.

'What are you doing here?' Sophy spoke with an authority she was far from feeling.

'I could ask you the same thing,' he replied. 'But I'll afford you the courtesy of answering your question first. My name is Victor Coyne. My uncle is Jack Hyland.'

'I'm sorry.' Feeling foolish and embarrassed, Sophy lowered the poker and propped it against the grandfather clock. 'Mr Hyland didn't tell me to expect you. I'm Sophy Kingston, his nurse.' She held out her hand then quickly withdrew it when she noticed it was covered with soot.

'Are you from the hospital?' he asked.

'No, I'm a private nurse, hired by Mr Hyland to look after him.'

'Really?' His dark eyebrows lifted. 'When was this arrangement made?'

'Two weeks ago.'

'I see.' He nodded, obviously perplexed. 'Do you mind if I sit down?' Evidently familiar with the layout of the house, he walked ahead of her into the kitchen. Dressed casually in a pale blue, open-neck shirt, indigo jeans and ankle boots, he lounged back on one of the kitchen chairs and crossed his feet. 'I've been keeping a regular check on Hyland Hall ever since my uncle was admitted to hospital,' he said. 'I was convinced vandals had broken into the house when I saw your car outside.'

'Your uncle didn't tell you to expect me?'

'No, he didn't. To be honest, Ms Kingston, I've absolutely no idea what you're doing here.'

'I told you already. I'm here to look after your uncle when he's discharged from hospital.'

'But that isn't going to happen. My uncle is being transferred into a specialist nursing home.'

'That's not possible.' Her fear had been replaced by a growing uneasiness. It was always there, the feeling that something had to go wrong. She had expected their departure to be fraught with difficulties but it had all been too easily organised in the aftermath of her meeting with Vivian Ford. 'Mr Hyland made no mention of that when he interviewed me.'

'Interviewed you. How was that possible?'

'We spoke by phone.'

'Were you able to communicate with him?' His puzzled expression deepened.

'I'd some difficulty initially but I was able to make out what he needs. We've exchanged letters. Everything was made perfectly clear to me.'

'Yet he never mentioned that he was going into a nursing home?' He tapped his fingers on the table. They were long and slender – musician's fingers – the nails short, practical, well-tended. 'I'm afraid you've been deceived, Ms Kingston. There is no vacancy for a nurse here. Sadly, my uncle suffers from delusions. It was not only his body that was severely damaged in the fire, his mind was also affected. I can't imagine how he contrived to make this arrangement with you but I'll ensure that you're properly recompensed for all the inconvenience you've suffered.' He spoke politely and with certainty. 'Mr Hyland is a wealthy man. I'll speak to him and agree a settlement.'

She heard a sound from outside, a sneeze, quickly muffled. Hardly surprising with all that dust around. Moving swiftly, she crossed from the table and opened the kitchen door. Isobel stepped to one side and said, 'Sorry, I'm trying to find the bathroom.'

Sophy closed the door behind her and spoke quietly to her daughter. 'Go back to bed, Isobel. I'm having a private conversation with Mr Hyland's nephew.'

'He said we shouldn't be here.' Unable to disguise her hope, Isobel added, 'It's all for the best, Mum.'

'I know what's best for you and that's your bed. Now scoot.'

Returning to the kitchen, she said, 'Sorry about the interruption. Where were we. Ah, yes, you were telling me about your uncle's delusions. Unfortunately, it seems that I'm one of them.'

'It's most unfortunate,' he agreed. 'I can only offer you my sincerest apologies for the misunderstanding. I take it you've a child here with you?'

'Two daughters.'

'I see. Well, it's too late to settle anything tonight but I'll return tomorrow with an offer from him. You won't have to make contact with him again.'

'Thank you, Mr Coyne—'

'Victor, *please*. There's no need for formalities.'

'Victor, I don't think my departure will be that straightforward…' She picked up her backpack from the floor and removed an envelope. Opening it, she handed a sheet of paper to him.

'This contract of employment which I signed was drawn up by your uncle's solicitor,' she said. 'It was then witnessed by my own solicitor and it stipulates that I must care for Mr Hyland in Hyland Hall for the next twelve months. Why would his solicitor draw up such an agreement if he believed Mr Hyland was incapable of coming home from hospital?'

He read the contract then turned it over, as if expecting to find an answer on the blank side.

'How did you hear about my uncle's accident?' he asked.

'Word of mouth,' she replied.

He waited for her to elaborate and when she remained silent, he left the contract on the table and stood, as if undecided whether to leave or stay. His black hair, lightly gelled, was brushed back from his forehead, and his eyes, an intense cobalt blue, were his most arresting feature. Her gaze followed the smooth plane of his forehead, the slant of his nose and flat cheekbones, the taut line of his jaw. His chin was square but not aggressively so, and there was a slight swell to his bottom lip. He was, she thought, startlingly handsome, but that was an abstract thought that went as fast as it came.

'Jack is not in any position to enter such an arrangement,' he said. 'How can he return to this heap of rubble? Look at the condition it's in.' He banged his fist against the wall and a lump of plaster landed on the floor. She could feel the dust at the back of her throat, a dryness that caused her to cough before she could reply.

'I agreed to come here under those conditions.' She ran her finger under the clause that stipulated the length of time she could stay at Hyland Hall. 'I have two options. I either leave here and render myself and my daughters homeless or I stay here until my term of employment expires. Thank you for offering to help but I am determined to fulfil my side of this agreement.'

'You're within your rights to stay here, of course,' he agreed. 'Obviously, I need to report what's happened to my uncle's medical team.'

'Whether or not Mr Hyland returns here is immaterial.' She slid the contract back into the envelope. 'If he's discharged into my care, I'm ready to assume my duties. If he's moved into the nursing home, I'll visit him and provide him with the companionship I promised when I signed that contract. Now, if you don't mind, I've had a long, stressful journey and I'm tired.'

'I apologise for taking up your time.' Once again, he glanced around the kitchen then shook his head, bemused, she guessed, by her refusal to accept his offer to organise a financial settlement.

She walked with him towards the front door.

'I hope you manage to sort everything out to your satisfaction.' He handed a business card to her. 'I live next door and if you need any assistance, please call me.'

'Thank you. I didn't realise there were any other houses nearby. Hyland Hall seems so isolated.'

'It's further along Marsh Road and built on land that once belonged to Hyland Estate. My uncle was considering moving in with me when the fire broke out. Sadly, that changed everything. Goodnight, Sophia.'

She couldn't remember the last time anyone had used her full name. The syllables swayed towards her, his soft emphasis on the 'a'. The headlights of his jeep swept across the courtyard as she watched him drive towards the tree-lined avenue.

In the bedroom, she loosened her hair and allowed it to fall to her shoulders. She stared at her soot-streaked face in the mirror. What must he have thought of her? Not that it mattered. She was hardly likely to see him again. *Word of mouth*, she had replied when he asked her how she had heard about his uncle's situation. Why hadn't she told him about Vivian Ford? Her ship in the night who had left no forwarding address or contact number. All she knew was that Vivian had offered her a light in her darkness and Sophy was determined to keep it burning.

Shortly after Luke's departure to the Oasis of Hope, Vivian had called to Park View Villas. Unaware that she was about to shape a new future for herself and her daughters, Sophy opened the door to an elderly woman, who smiled apologetically and gestured towards the *For Sale* sign in the front garden.

'I appreciate that viewing your house is by appointment only,' she said. 'But I'm hoping you can make an exception in my case and show me around now. I'm going abroad for two weeks and no doubt your lovely house will be sold by the time I return.'

Sophy's first inclination had been to refuse her request. Breakfast dishes were still on the kitchen table and every bed in the house was unmade.

'The house is not ready for viewings,' she began. 'I haven't had time to tidy—'

'My dear, you don't have to worry about that.' The woman stared back at her through an over-large pair of red-framed glasses and waved aside Sophy's excuses. 'Tidiness is an overrated virtue, I always think. My name is Vivian Ford – and I know exactly what I want to buy. Your house looks ideal.' Her thick, grey hair was cut short in a no-nonsense style and the authority in her voice suggested she was used to being obeyed.

They entered the living room, which, for once, was tidy. Vivian walked to the French windows and stared out to the back garden where a bronze sculpture of two children dancing together, hands joined, was visible. 'What a beautiful piece,' she said as she opened the doors and stepped outside. 'May I ask the name of the sculptor?'

'My husband,' Sophy replied. 'He specialises in garden sculptures, mainly fountains. Occasionally, he makes standalone pieces like that one.'

'A gifted man. Do you mind if I take a photograph?'

Unable to stop her, Sophy waited while she photographed the figures.

'He loved those children.' Her keen glance at Sophy was somewhat unnerving. 'Do you mind if I ask who they are?'

'My daughters.' She walked back into the living room and waited for Vivian to join her. 'I'll show you the rest of the house.'

Entering Isobel's bedroom, she closed her eyes at the sight of the scattered clothes on the floor, the books, nail polishes and empty hairspray can making it almost impossible to walk across the carpet.

'I remember that phase so well,' Vivian laughed as she surveyed the disarray. 'I'd one daughter whose room was in a permanent state of chaos yet you could eat your dinner from the floor of my other daughter's bedroom.'

'It's much the same here.' Sophy ushered her into Julie's bedroom. 'Julie likes everything to be tidy and organised.'

'My goodness, who's this?' Vivian stared at the mannequin on the bed.

'That's Cordelia.' Sophy smiled at her astonished expression. 'I used to own a boutique and she was my display model.'

'She looks so real. I thought for a moment she was breathing.'

'It's a common mistake. Children often pinched her to see if she'd react.'

Sophy lifted the duvet and covered the mannequin. Cordelia's garish, red smile was a painful reminder that Kid's Chic was in the process of being transformed into an Indian restaurant. 'My daughter insisted on "adopting" her when I sold my boutique. I suppose I shouldn't have been surprised. I bought Cordelia ten years ago, the same year Julie was born.'

'A close attachment, obviously.'

'I guess so.'

'And a link with Julie's past.'

'That, too.' Sophy was already regretting her decision to allow Vivian into the house.

When the viewing was over, Vivian sighed and shook her head. 'You'll have no problem selling your lovely house, Sophy. Unfortunately, it's not suitable for my needs. It's bigger than it looks from the outside. I live alone you see, so it's far too spacious for me.' She removed her glasses and rubbed them briskly with a tissue. 'My husband died last year. I'm trying to rebuild my life without him so I want walls that are close to me. Small spaces that I can manage easily.'

Without her distinctive red-framed glasses, her face looked vulnerable, older, her mouth crushed with grief. Sophy was only too familiar with the signs of loss. They reflected back at her every time she caught a glimpse of her face in a mirror.

'I was just about to make coffee when you arrived,' she said. 'Would you like to have one before you leave?'

'Thank you, my dear. You're very kind.'

They sat together in the kitchen and talked about her husband, Eoin Ford, who had battled cancer and lost. Vivian's son and two daughters lived abroad. She was retired from a career in human resources. A dull, dutiful career, she said, and she had no regrets about her decision to retire.

'Where will you live when your house is sold?' she asked Sophy. Her question forced their easy-going conversation to a standstill.

'I'm looking at options,' Sophy said when the silence had reached breaking point.

'Options?' Vivian considered the glib reply. Her glance was sharp, concerned, and Sophy, her eyes brimming with tears, realised that she was about to unburden herself to this stranger.

Quicksand. That was how she described the foundations on which her marriage had been built. A relationship built on quicksand that shifted and buried the life she believed she and Luke had been sharing for fifteen years. The tears came then, angry and scalding. She would be without a home when the house was sold. What was left after paying off the mortgage would wipe out his debts but it would leave her and her daughters without a roof over their heads. Homelessness... the thought chilled her. She had made enquiries about rented accommodation and been shocked by the exorbitant rents charged for houses in the vicinity of Park View Villas, where the girls were desperate to continue living.

'Can I make a suggestion?' Vivian asked. 'Do you have any experience of nursing?'

'I used to be a nurse before I opened Kid's Chic. But I haven't practised for years.'

'That shouldn't be an issue,' Vivian said. 'A friend of mine is looking for someone to take care of him. He was seriously injured in a fire six months ago. Actually, injured is too mild a description for what he's gone through and will continue to endure. He should have died in the flames but, somehow, he survived it. He's coming to the end of a rehab programme but he's going to need ongoing treatment and physio. He'll be discharged from hospital soon. He's made a good recovery but, sadly, he's badly disfigured and has become quite reclusive. He's determined to live independently rather than enter a nursing home. That's been suggested as a more sensible option but he's stubborn and won't hear of it. He's single, no family, and his house would be large enough to accommodate you and your daughters.'

'Where does he live?'

'On the outskirts of a town called Clonmoore, which is about an hour's drive from Cork city.'

Vivian had brushed aside Sophy's concerns about her lack of up-to date nursing experience, her human resources skills coming to the fore as she outlined the benefits of moving to Hyland Hall.

'I'll ring him now and see what he thinks of my idea,' she said. 'He may be somewhat difficult to understand but you'll get used to his way of speaking in no time at all.'

Jack Hyland spoke to her from his hospital bed. His deep, rasping voice suggested that smoke inhalation had damaged his vocal cords. Sophy, after some difficulty, had been able to separate his mashed words and understand that he was offering her and her daughters a home. He had certain stipulations that he would outline in a letter to her and he needed her to be installed in his house by the beginning of June when he hoped to be discharged from hospital.

By the time Vivian left, Sophy had decided to place the sale of the house in the hands of an estate agent and turn her life upside down. She would transplant her daughters to Hyland Hall and live with a reclusive man, whose words were as hazy as the smoke that once clogged his lungs. Weighing up the positives and negatives before taking the next step had always been second nature to her. Not any longer. When love had been squandered and faith destroyed, risk-taking no longer felt like a leap into the unknown.

CHAPTER FIVE

Isobel

In the dictionary a recluse was described as, *One who lives retired from the world*. Surely, if someone retired from the world, they should be dead? Not so, Sophy said when Isobel argued this point with her. People could be reclusive for all sorts of reasons. Some wanted a direct line to God and lived as hermits in caves or rocky islands with only seagulls for company. Others never left their homes because they were too nervous or too shy to mingle with people. Then there was The Recluse who was dead and came back to life. Three times his heart stopped in the ambulance and, later, at the hospital. Three times he had been revived. Just thinking about being dead and coming back to life again made Isobel shudder, especially when Victor Coyne had admitted to her mum on the night of their arrival that his uncle suffered from delusions. She had been convinced her mother would be ready to leave the following morning but, instead, she had figured how to light the wood burning stove and was making pancakes for breakfast.

So much of Hyland Hall scared Isobel. The dark corridors and spooky furniture, the gun on display in the hall that was, Charlie Bracken claimed, strong enough to fell a bear. She was convinced that dead bodies must once have been laid on her sagging bed. She imagined their waxy corpses, the pennies on their eyes. Were they watching her? Ghosts had to exist in this eerie house. She heard them at night when she was trying to sleep. Her mother insisted that the sighs and groans and creaks were just the sounds of the old day settling but that information did nothing to calm Isobel down. She thought about her bedroom in Park View Villas and how her father had painted smiley faces on the ceiling so that she would laugh first thing in the morning. And she always did, no matter what kind of mood she was in when she opened her eyes. Now, all she saw was a mottled canopy with a dangling fringe.

Julie started school on the Monday after their arrival. Unlike Isobel, who would be attending Queen of Angels Secondary in September, she had another month to go before her school holidays began.

In her absence, Isobel set about exploring her new surroundings. So far, all she had discovered were trees. Hyland Hall was surrounded by them and wandering between one trail and another, all of them indistinguishable, only added to her sense of having landed on an alien planet. She spent most of her time reading in the den and joined the local library in Clonmoore where she used the computers to keep in contact with her friends. Broadband at Hyland Hall was non-existent and even mobile phone signals were unreliable.

The room she and Julie had chosen as their den must have been a posh drawing room in the olden days. The musty armchairs had lost their spring but the sofa was still comfortable, and Julie immediately claimed the fancy chaise longue for Cordelia. The Recluse was still in hospital and her mother, along with a woman called Ellie, were busily preparing the house for his homecoming. Charlie Bracken came and went at different times of the day and did odd jobs like chopping wood or weeding the courtyard. He drove a hearse with *Brackens Funeral Home* written on the side.

The letters were almost obscured and the hearse had bumps and scratches all over it. Ellie said he was a retired undertaker and Isobel shuddered every time she saw him driving his hearse up the avenue. Her mother had managed to persuade The Recluse's medical team that she was perfectly capable of looking after him and the thought of living with someone who came back from the dead three times was the scariest thought of all.

On the Saturday after their arrival, she carried her breakfast into the den and braced herself for his return home.

'Mr Hyland will be arriving shortly,' her mother said. 'I don't want you staring out the window at him. His only request is that you respect his privacy. Be quiet and stay in the den until I've settled him into bed.'

She smoothed down the front of her uniform and brushed her hand over her hair in case a few strands had escaped from her ponytail. Gone were the skinny trousers, high heels and dresses that used to float around her knees.

Gone were the curls that fell to her shoulders and the eye make-up that made her look like a sphinx. Instead, she wore a white uniform and flat shoes that made no sound as she left the den and closed the door quietly behind her.

'Don't spy,' Julie warned when the sound of an engine reached them from across the courtyard.

'Just a quick look, that's all,' said Isobel but it was Charlie, not The Recluse, who was parking his hearse in the courtyard. He stepped down from the driver seat and walked erectly to the back of the hearse. Isobel was never able to see him without imagining him walking in front of a coffin. She glimpsed a swirl of yellow fur when he opened the hatch at the back of the hearse and released a dog, who immediately ran towards the window where Isobel was standing. For a horrified instant she thought the dog would crash through the glass but he stopped in time and planted his massive paws on the windowsill. Streaks of black and yellow hair covered his face. Saliva dripped from his open mouth and his fangs glistened as he stared at her through smouldering eyes. She could hear him barking, sharp, staccato sounds that had a terrifyingly dangerous pitch. Julie dived towards the chaise longue where she had left Cordelia and covered their faces with a rug. Peeper crawled from under an armchair and stared calmly out at the dog, who barked even louder. When Charlie whistled at him, he dropped to the ground and followed him up the steps. Was it possible that a dog who looked capable of ripping out her throat was about to enter the house? Her mother answered the door and Isobel's question was answered when she heard the dog padding across the hall.

'Is he a werewolf, Issy?' Julie's muffled voice came from behind the rug.

'What else could he be?' Isobel replied. 'But don't worry. He won't go mad until there's a full moon.'

'He's going upstairs to Fear Zone.' Julie had decided on a name for The Recluse's quarters and Isobel was not going to argue with her choice. The dog appeared to be in the room directly above them and Julie, holding tightly to Cordelia, said, 'What do werewolves do, Issy?'

'What's all this talk about werewolves?' Their mother had returned unnoticed to the den.

'There's a werewolf upstairs,' Julie replied in her pretend Cordelia voice.

'Where did you get that idea?' Their mother sounded amused. 'Caesar is a German Shepherd, not a werewolf, and he's Mr Hyland's pet. Have you been filling your sister's head with nonsense again, Isobel?'

'Why are you blaming me? I never said anything—'

Her protests were interrupted by Victor's arrival in his fancy, silver jeep. He had collected The Recluse from hospital and the moment Isobel had been dreading was finally here. Sophy closed the curtains then hurried from the den with a final warning to Isobel not to spy.

'Can you see The Recluse, Issy?' Julie whispered when Isobel twitched the curtain on the nearest window ever so slightly. 'Can you?'

Isobel nodded and put a finger to her lips as Victor helped his uncle down from the passenger seat. Apart from a grey scarf that hid his face, The Recluse was dressed in black: a black hat with a wide brim and a black coat that swept the ground when he hunched forward. His body seemed fragmented by the panes of glass as he straightened slowly. Isobel was reminded of a puppet being pulled upward by invisible strings. He thumped his walking stick off the courtyard as he walked stiffly towards her mother, who was waiting to greet him at the bottom of the steps.

When he reached the stone lions he stopped and stared towards the den. Dark glasses covered his eyes yet Isobel felt as if he was staring directly at her. A moth flew free from the folds of the curtains and fluttered its shivery wings against the window as her mother supported this man, who was dead but came back to life *three* times, to walk up the steps and into their lives.

They listened to the thud of his walking stick on the hall, followed by the bleep of the stairlift as it glided him towards Fear Zone. A crescendo of barking broke out, along with a frantic skitter of the dog's paws on the Fear Zone floorboards. The arrival home of The Recluse was even more dreadful than Isobel had anticipated.

She was still in her pyjamas when Victor came into the den. This was his third time to visit Hyland Hall. Yesterday, he spent ages in the kitchen talking to their mother about The Recluse and how best she could *manage* him. He made it sound like chains would be needed.

'Don't mind the noise from above,' he said. 'It'll settle down soon enough. How are you two adjusting to your new home?'

'Three.' Julie flapped her hand towards Cordelia.

His eyebrows shot up when he saw the mannequin sitting on the chaise longue in her stripy leggings and yellow T-shirt.

'Forgive me.' He made a slight bow towards Cordelia. 'Who have we here?'

'My name is Cordelia Kingston,' Julie squeaked in her Cordelia voice.

'Delighted to make your acquaintance, Miss Cordelia.' He shook the mannequin's hand and smiled across at Isobel. He was about the same age as her father and, though she was reluctant to admit it, he was better looking.

'Well, Isobel, how are you?' he asked.

She inspected her bare feet. There was fluff between her toes. She'd never had fluff between her toes until now. Soon, she'd have fungus growing there, mushrooms sprouting.

'I hate living here.' She answered him truthfully. 'I'm never going to get used to it.'

'Moving house is a huge challenge,' he agreed. 'It's not surprising you feel that way after saying goodbye to your friends and all the places that were familiar to you. What about you, Julie?'

'It's nice,' she said. 'I like it here. It's a new adventure. Ask Cordelia's opinion?'

'I will indeed.' He grinned and said, 'Tell me, Miss Cordelia, are you happy in your new home?'

'Hyland Hall is a horrible dump,' Julie sounded as if she'd been sucking air from a helium balloon. 'I'm just as upset as Issy.'

'Don't you dare compare my feelings to that *turnip head*.' Isobel was finding it harder than ever to listen to the Cordelia voice.

'You're the stupid turnip head.' Julie's forehead scrunched with annoyance.

'I saw your lips moving,' said Isobel. 'I *always* do.'

'Squinty eyes!' Julie chanted. 'You've got squinty eyes. Squinty eyes.'

'Girls… girls, I didn't want to start an argument.' Victor held up his hands, palms out. 'Try not to worry too much about the future. Believe me when I tell you it has a way of working itself out.'

He sounded just like their father. *Lies*, Isobel wanted to shout. Things would never work out, not as long as they were forced to stay here.

When night time came they discovered that The Recluse's bedroom was above the one they shared. He coughed and moaned, and his bed creaked every time he moved.

They spooned against each other in the four poster bed and tried to ignore the sounds from Fear Zone. 'Do you think Daddy will come and live here with us when he's better?' Julie whispered.

'He'll come back to us but he won't live in the same house.'

'But there are lots of rooms here…'

'That doesn't matter. Mum would never allow it.'

'Cordelia says—'

'Cordelia can't talk.'

'Yes, she can. She thinks it's for the best.'

'Stop pretending she can *think*.'

'She can so. She says…' Julie paused and chewed her bottom lip.

'Says what?'

'That he's gone forever.'

'Dad will come back to us again but it won't be the same as before. He's going to live somewhere else and visit us. But it'll be all right, Julie. You'll get used to it. We both will.' She didn't want to talk about her father or to think about him anymore.

Julie drifted off to sleep but whenever Isobel's eyes closed, she was startled awake by a noise from The Recluse's bedroom. She needed to pee but the thought of going outside into the dark corridor and searching for the light switch made her hold on until that became impossible. She turned on the bedside lamp and almost tripped over Cordelia when she stepped onto the floor. Since she and Julie had started sleeping together, Isobel had refused to allow the mannequin into their bed. Cordelia spent the nights in a sleeping bag on the floor, just a stretch-down hand reach away from Julie.

Isobel's fear reflected back at her from the dressing table mirror as she walked past it. The mirror was angled in three sections of glass and another full-length mirror was attached to the door of the wardrobe behind her. She was trapped in glass, framed in multiple images that grew smaller and smaller, like Russian dolls that fitted inside each other until there was nothing left except a tiny figurine, almost a dot. A dot that was ready to explode every time she thought about her father and how he had changed their lives with the toss of a coin.

Julie was kneeling on the floor beside Cordelia when she returned from the bathroom.

'What are you doing?' she asked.

'Cordelia's lonely and scared.' Julie's voice shook as she tried to slide into the sleeping bag beside the mannequin. 'I'm keeping her safe from The Recluse.'

One part of Isobel wanted to leave her sister there. It would serve her right for preferring to sleep with a stupid shop dummy. But another part of her was ashamed of being jealous of Cordelia. That was the part that made her persuade Julie to climb back into bed – and to bring Cordelia with her.

CHAPTER SIX

Sophy

Victor was correct when he told Sophy that his uncle would not be an easy man to nurse. Charlie had installed a monitoring system that linked Jack's rooms to the downstairs floor but his usual summons when he needed Sophy was to bang his walking stick on the floor. His monosyllabic replies and occasional outbursts of impatience were upsetting but she could cope with them. What she found most distressing was his lack of expression. What must it be like to be unable to convey emotion, to live with a face that was stretched, frozen and immobile? His eyes, one saved and one blinded by the fire, were hidden behind dark glasses. She understood what he was saying, his yes's and no's, the wave of his hand, the lift of his shoulders. Even the curve of his finger conveyed meaning to her. What she was unable to decipher were his outbursts when his frustration turned his words to babble.

Physically, he was growing stronger, though he moved with difficulty. If he was capable of expressing pain, it would have been etched on his face, yet his determination forced one foot in front of the other as they walked together around the courtyard.

Outwardly, he was so damaged by the fire that it was difficult to believe he was capable of such willpower and determination. She had been conscious of his inner strength from the first time she sat down at his bedside with his medical team to discuss his future care. None of those present, including Sophy, could doubt Victor's concern for his uncle but Jack had overruled and upended the health plan that had been organised for him.

At times, Sophy was overwhelmed by the responsibility of caring for him. Ellie came three times a week to tidy the house but Sophy, Charlie and Victor were the only people he allowed to look upon his blemished features. Sophy never knew when to expect Charlie but each time he came he was ready to tackle an outdoor chore like fixing the leaking roof on one of the outhouses or cutting back the overgrown bushes in the courtyard. Sometimes he just sat with Jack and talked to him about old times.

In his own gruff way, Jack was anxious for Sophy to settle into his home. He suggested they call each other by their first names. His difficulty with words gave his questions an abruptness she found unsettling yet as she began to relax in his company, she was happy to talk to him about her life before she came to Hyland Hall. She was selective about the information she shared with him. He knew her mother had died when she was six years old and that she had lived with her father above his greengrocery shop until she married Luke. She told him about her experiences working in the accident and emergency department of a city hospital and how she had given up nursing when she was expecting Julie.

It had been a stressful pregnancy that occurred just before her father suffered a fatal heart attack. In the grief-stricken months that followed, she had continued working in the emergency ward but that ended abruptly when she was attacked by a drug addict during her final trimester. Forced into an early labour, Sophy believed she had lost her baby but Julie survived and thrived in the weeks that followed.

Too traumatised to return to nursing, it was Maddie, her mother-in-law, who charted a new future for her. Her father's greengrocery had been empty since his sudden death and Maddie, a successful childrenswear designer, was tired of travelling and constant deadlines. She was still not ready for full-time retirement and it was her idea to design a special collection of childrenswear for Sophy, who turned the greengrocery into Kid's Chic. The *Maddie* and *Laddie* labels had been an immediate success, as had their business partnership. They had worked harmoniously together for over eight years until Maddie was diagnosed with cancer.

The shock of the prognosis had hardly been absorbed before she was gone from them and the slow corrosion of Sophy's marriage began. Not that she had been aware of the cracks. She loved Luke and refused to heed the maxim that love was blind, deaf and incredibly credulous.

In her nightly conversations with Jack Hyland, she never discussed her husband or her broken marriage. If she did so, she would dissolve into tears, as she had done when Vivian Ford sat in her kitchen and asked her about 'options.' But the grim journey that led her to Hyland Hall was always at the forefront of her mind.

Luke was now coming to the end of his second month at the Oasis of Hope. He rang once a week to speak to the girls. Julie was always thrilled to hear him but Isobel took his calls reluctantly, and kept their conversations brief. Sophy had spoken to him only once on the phone since he entered the Oasis and their conversation had quickly deteriorated into an argument. A one-sided argument, she had to admit to herself afterwards. Luke had taken her refusal to engage with an intervention therapist quietly and had listened without arguing back to her angry reasons for her decision. She had neither the time nor the inclination to make the long journey back to Dublin to discuss the issues that had destroyed their relationship. Her hard, angry voice could have belonged to a stranger. These days, she had difficulty recognising herself. The sense of being adrift on feelings she was unable to understand was so crushing that the only way to relieve her inner turmoil was to muffle her cries into her pillow at night.

June came to an end and Julie's school holidays began. She would be company during the day for Isobel, who had resolutely refused to adjust to Hyland Hall. Her clothes remained unpacked and those she wore were washed and ironed before being folded back again into her suitcase. Her dislike for Hyland Hall turned to disgust when she discovered that fly tippers were dumping rubbish on the estate. Charlie organised a clear-up but admitted that it had become a regular problem in recent months, despite the formidable entrance gates.

'They'll always find a way,' Victor admitted when he called one evening on his way home from work to visit his uncle. 'The estate has as many openings as a sieve.' Since that first awkward night when he had entered the house so unexpectedly, he was anxious to help Sophy and the girls to settle down. He suggested they join the summer drama school and the pony club in Clonmoore. Julie had enrolled in both. She was determined to perfect her skill as a ventriloquist and had been an instant hit when she introduced Cordelia to the group. She was learning to ride a pony called Golden Eye and seemed to have adjusted completely to her new life.

Sophy's days were uneventful, the evenings broken by Victor's visits to his uncle. Sometimes, as she climbed the stairs with Jack's medication or his evening meal, she would hear them talking. They always fell silent when she knocked and entered. The atmosphere while she was in the room was tense, as if they were anxious for her to leave so they could resume their private conversation.

She had found framed photographs of the two of them in one of the cabinet drawers. She'd had no idea what Jack had looked like before his accident but there was no mistaking his dark blue eyes or his tall, slim stature. In one of the photographs, they were standing outside Hyland Hall. Another had been taken when they were fishing on a lake. They were older in the third photograph which included a row of empty stables in the background. The stables were derelict, doors hanging from hinges, ivy crawling over the walls. Jack had his arm around Victor's shoulder and there was no doubting his affection for the younger man.

On impulse, she dusted the photographs and displayed them on the piano. Ellie had polished it to a high gloss and Sophy had booked a piano tuner to tune the keys. It would soon be restored to its former glory. Charlie had helped her to move armchairs, a sofa and a cabinet with book shelves into the music room and she had turned it into her own sanctuary.

Victor came one evening as she was preparing dinner. His dark blue suit was bespoke tailored, she could tell by the fit, and his white shirt was still crisp and pristine after his day at work. She was conscious of his gaze. It caused her to work faster, chopping onions and peppers, slicing tomatoes, adding slivers of garlic to the Bolognese sauce.

'I've a swimming pool at the back of my house,' he said. 'The girls are welcome to use it any time they wish.'

'Isobel loves swimming. As does Julie. That's a wonderful idea.'

'I'm delighted to help. The pool is empty most of the time and there's also a tennis court that hasn't been used for years.'

'That's even better. Thank you so much.'

'Have you had any time off since you arrived here?' he asked.

'I don't need time off,' she replied. 'My work load is easy to manage. Charlie looks after Jack when I go shopping or drive the girls into town.'

'Sounds fascinating.' He smiled, as if amused by her reply. 'It's a wonder you've time to draw breath when you lead such a frantic social life.'

'It's the life I've chosen and it suits me fine,' she replied shortly. Did he pity her? She should be used to it by now. Her friends hosting farewell gatherings, their sympathy blunted by their amazement that she hadn't seen the signs, hadn't read the runes Lady Luck left in her wake.

'God never lays a burden on a back that is not strong enough to carry it,' Mamie Gordon had said when she handed over the keys of her Honda Civic. It had seemed impossible to imagine squashing everything they possessed into its cramped interior but Sophy had done so and, now, she had grown used to its smallness. Just as she was becoming used to a life that grew ever smaller with each passing day. Jack had insisted that she drive his BMW, which had been unused since his accident, but the little Hobbit car, as Isobel called it, had become symbolic of how her life had changed.

'I'm not trying to upset you...' Victor paused, as if uncertain how to continue. 'I'd like to invite you and the girls, and my uncle, of course, to my house for Sunday lunch. It's time he started going out again. I know he's afraid his appearance will frighten the girls but he can't continue hiding in his room forever.'

Sophy agreed. Jack's reclusive behaviour was having an impact on the girls. Despite her efforts to explain to them that he was self-conscious about his appearance, and that there was no reason to be scared of him, they were unable to let go of their fears. They flinched and looked upwards at the ceiling every time he made a sound.

Isobel claimed it was like living with a phantom and Cordelia's recent utterings concerned full moons, Caesar and werewolves.

'Let me think about it.' She hoped he would ascribe her flushed face to the steamy kitchen. She was being overly sensitive, seeing pity where none was meant. How tempting he made it sound. 'But I've no idea if Jack will accept your invitation.'

'It would be better if the invitation came from you,' he said. 'He still hasn't forgiven me for thinking he should go into a nursing home. If I'd known you were a miracle worker, I'd never have agreed with his medical team that that was the right decision to make for him.'

'I'm far from being a miracle worker. It's Jack's own determination that's helping him make such progress. Now I need to bring him his medication. He needs to take it before his evening meal.'

She found Jack sitting in his living room at an old-fashioned bureau, writing in a hardback journal. The windows were open yet the balmy evening breeze had failed to cool the air. His heat intolerance affected his mood. She switched on two fans and handed him a glass of iced water. He had taken off his dark glasses and the glint in his sighted eye warned her to be gentle with him. She was still learning to read the different signs he made. Gradually, his shoulders relaxed as cool air flowed through the room.

'Do you feel like a visit?' she asked. 'Victor is downstairs.'

'Not tonight,' he said. 'This heat wearies me.'

'He's invited us to lunch on Sunday,' she said.

'Has he indeed?' He half-stood, then sat down again. 'And who has he included in this invitation?'

'All of us. He thinks it's time you went out, even if it's only for a few hours. I agree with him. It will give you an opportunity to meet the girls.'

'*No.*' His hands trembled so violently she was afraid he was about to have a seizure.

'Jack, what's wrong?'

'I've no intention of ever leaving my house.'

'But his house is only up the road—'

'I said *no*. You go with your daughters and enjoy his many amenities. Charlie will keep me company while you're gone.'

'I can't do that—'

'Yes, you can.' He closed the journal and rose stiffly from his chair. 'You need time off from looking after a cantankerous old man. Help me into my bedroom.'

'Won't you have something to eat first?'

'I'm not hungry. Don't fuss, Sophy. I've no intention of starving to death. I simply don't feel like eating tonight.'

Afterwards, when Sophy had reported the conversation and Victor had driven away, she walked Caesar as far as the avenue. The bats were flitting in the gloom and the trees rustled as the rooks gathered to roost on the branches. The woods spanned out on either side of her. The weight of her desolation slowed her footsteps as she called the dog to heel and returned to Hyland Hall.

CHAPTER SEVEN

Sophy

The sensation of moving between two different worlds was breathtaking as Sophy stepped from the oppressive mustiness of Hyland Hall into the opulence of Victor's white-walled house. It stood at the end of a flag-stoned driveway and was fronted by an ornate portico and four Palladian columns. The name *Mount Eagle* was carved into the boundary wall and two bronze eagle sculptures were perched on the gate posts. Their outspread wings suggested they were resting briefly before taking to the skies again.

Victor greeted them at the front door and guided the girls across the marble-tiled hall towards the downstairs bathroom where they changed into their swimsuits. Outside, water lapped gently against aquamarine walls, lilos floated just out of reach and a pink rubber flamingo bobbed in a sedate circuit around the oval-shaped swimming pool.

Diving straight in, the girls disappeared under the water and surfaced in a cascade of bubbles. Their excited cries reached Sophy as she sat under a parasol and sipped a glass of chilled white wine. The contrast to Hyland Hall could not have been starker. She had forgotten what it was like to just relax and allow herself to switch off. The patio doors were open and she was able to watch Victor as he moved around his bright, modern kitchen. She was free to stare at him for a change as he set the finishing touches to their lunch.

They ate outside. The sun could not go to waste, he said. He had ordered it for the day and it would not stop shining until they left.

After lunch, when the girls rushed back to the pool, Sophy walked through the garden with him. On the lower level, steps led down to a tennis court. A hot tub murmured suggestively when he lifted the top to show it to her. This was something Luke had considered installing in their garden at Park View Villas. At night, when the children were in bed, they could relax together and watch the stars. One of his many promises that never came to anything. Her lips tightened then relaxed. She wasn't going to let bitterness seep into her day and spoil it.

A wide terrace with sun loungers gave way to a copse of trees.

'How much further does the garden go?' she asked.

'It's a wilderness beyond the trees,' he admitted. 'As I mentioned before, this land was once part of Hyland Estate. It's where my grandmother grew an orchard and market garden. She was quite an entrepreneur for her time. After she and my grandfather died in an accident, the estate was broken up. My mother inherited part of the land and the twins got the other two-thirds.'

'Twins?'

'Yes. Didn't you know Jack was a twin?'

'I'd no idea. Is his twin still alive?'

'Sadly, no. Laurence died last year.'

'I'm sorry to hear that.'

They turned back when the terrain became too dense to penetrate. The girls had changed back into their clothes and were playing tennis on the court.

'It's a long time since I've seen them so happy,' Sophy said. 'Thank you for today, Victor.'

'It's my pleasure. Come on back to the house and I'll show you around.'

The rooms were filled with light and the slant of sunshine spilling through the conservatory reminded her of Park View Villas. No ancient wood creaking, or shadows falling before her in unnatural shapes that stirred long-forgotten superstitions.

'Have you enjoyed yourselves?' Victor asked the girls when it was time to leave.

'I loved it,' Julie replied. 'I wish Cordelia could have seen your beautiful house.' She cast a reproachful glance at Sophy. 'Mammy said I had to leave her in the den.'

'Miss Cordelia is more than welcome to visit anytime,' he said. 'In fact, she can move here, if she likes.'

'Move here?' Julie glanced from him to Sophy. 'Do you mean *just* Cordelia?'

'Of course not. All of you, including my uncle. What do you think, Sophia?'

Sophy was shocked by the unexpectedness of his suggestion. Angry, too, that he made it in front of the girls when she was still trying to settle them into Hyland Hall.

'Oh, Mum, can we?' asked Isobel.

'I think Mr Hyland should be the one to ask,' Sophy replied. 'I don't have the right to discuss it without his permission.'

'Why not?' Isobel's eyes were fixed on the swimming pool. 'Just think what it would be like.'

'She'll unpack her case if we move here, won't you, Issy?' Julie's eyes shone with anticipation. 'Would we have our own rooms, Victor?'

'Even Miss Cordelia can have her own room if she wants one,' he replied and laughed as Julie spun in a circle, her arms outstretched.

'Victor, that's enough.' Sophy cast a warning glance at him.

'Okay… okay.' He smacked his hands together. 'Give us a minute, girls. You'll find some board games in the conservatory. Take what you want back to Hyland Hall. There're also some books you might like to read, Isobel.'

'Cool.' Julie was already moving towards the conservatory, closely followed by Isobel.

'You shouldn't have suggested something that I'll be unable to deliver.' When the girls were out of earshot, Sophy spoke more abruptly than she intended. 'I don't know what's going on between you and Jack, and why he refuses to visit you. It's none of my business but it becomes so when you involve my daughters.'

'I didn't mean to put you in a difficult position,' he said apologetically. 'But *do* think about what I've suggested. Jack has improved enormously under your care but he won't survive the winter in that house. The heating stopped working years ago and the dampness is an ongoing problem. You've seen the rooms, the mould on the walls, not to mention the loose plaster. This house is big enough for everyone. The downstairs rooms are wheelchair accessible if his mobility becomes a problem. But, apart from his physical health, I'm more concerned about his mental state. Have you noticed any deterioration?'

'No, I haven't. He's stubborn at times and testy, but his mind is still sharp. I can't see him moving from Hyland Hall.'

'He's on borrowed time, Sophia. I want to make the last few months of his life as comfortable as possible. I'm also thinking of you and the girls, and what you've been through—'

'We don't need your pity, Victor.' She was sick of pity; it stuck to her, suffocated her.

'Believe me, Sophia, this is not about pity or charity. It's a practical solution to a problem that affects us all. Talk to Jack. You've earned his respect. That's not an easy thing to do.'

'You overestimate my powers of persuasion.'

'On the contrary, you're a very determined woman. You have the right conditions to continue looking after him here. He can't go on living in that mausoleum.'

'What's a mus-lemon?' Julie, returning, overheard their conversation.

'A tomb,' he replied.

'We don't live in a tomb.'

'It's a metaphor, Julie. That means comparing two things that aren't the same but have something in common,' he explained. 'It's symbolic.'

'Oh.' Her forehead wrinkled. 'Cordelia always says what's real and doesn't pretend it's something else so she's not a metaphor, is she?'

'No, she's a dummy, *Dummy*.' Isobel's belligerent tone broke the mood. Sophy knew she had overheard part of the conversation too and was probably wondering why her mother wasn't dancing with joy at Victor's proposal.

It made perfect sense to move into Mount Eagle but Jack's resistance to the proposal would be the biggest obstacle to overcome. The afternoon had affected her more than she had realised and Hyland Hall seemed even more dilapidated when she drove into the courtyard. What made Jack cling so tenaciously to its jaded shabbiness? She glanced into the rearview mirror. Her daughters' expressions mirrored her own discontent.

Charlie had been walking in the woods with Caesar. He entered the kitchen, the dog bounding ahead of him and almost knocking Sophy over. The girls fled to the den. Nothing would convince them that Caesar was as tame as Peeper and just as capable of being loved. Jack had been in fine form all afternoon, Charlie said. They had played chess and reminisced about their younger days.

When she entered his room, he was nodding sleepily in his armchair, a woollen hat covering his wrinkled scalp.

'Did you have a nice lunch?' he asked.

'Yes. Victor has a magnificent house.'

'I believe so.'

'You've never been in it?'

'I've better things to do with my time.'

She bit back a reply. Now was not the time to discuss Victor's offer.

The girls were still talking about their afternoon when she said goodnight to them. Charlie had organised twin beds for them and the old fourposter had been dismantled and moved into the annexe. Cordelia, propped against the pillows, was sitting in her usual place beside Julie.

Sophy sat on the edge of the bed and beckoned Isobel over to join them. 'I don't know if Mr Hyland will want to move into Victor's house.' It was best to be honest with them and not get their hopes up. 'Will it upset you very much if we're unable to move into Mount Eagle?'

'Ab-so-lute-ly.' Isobel smacked her lips with exaggerated determination. 'This place is a dump.'

'What about you, Julie?'

'It's a mus-lemon.' Julie looked as though she was stroking a silky moustache as she ran her finger over her upper lip and threw the words at Cordelia.

'I don't want to talk to Cordelia tonight.' Sophy snuggled her in her arms. 'Tell me what *you* think.'

'Well, it's okay here, *really*. You mustn't cry, Mammy, if Mr Hyland says no.'

'I'll cry,' said Isobel. 'And I'll scream as loudly as a banshee.'

'A banshee?' Julie's eyelashes fluttered.

'Stop it, Isobel. Banshees don't exist, Julie. They're just stories. I'm going to talk to Mr Hyland and I'll do my best to persuade him to move. I've no idea if he'll agree and I don't want any scenes if he says no. Understood?'

They nodded, Julie solemnly, Isobel with reluctance.

'Goodnight, girls,' she said. 'Sleep well—'

'And don't let the bugs bite,' Julie squeaked.

Her comment about Cordelia and metaphors before leaving Mount Eagle worried Sophy. Was Cordelia a channel for her younger daughter's thoughts, her only means to process the loss and events engulfing them? Looking at Julie's shining hair and the mannequin's artificial tresses, both almost identical shades of blonde, her uneasiness grew. Julie had loved dressing the mannequin and displaying her in the front window of Kid's Chic. She had changed her wigs regularly and had enjoyed the effects she could achieve with different hair shades. Lately, the blonde wig was the only one Cordelia wore.

They needed to move away from this foreboding house. Any change came with its own set of difficulties but Sophy had proved that a new beginning was always possible.

CHAPTER EIGHT

Isobel

The grandfather clock was striking midnight when Isobel left her bedroom. She hesitated in the hall and checked to see if there was a tell-tale strip of light shining under the door of the music room where her mum relaxed at night when The Recluse was in bed. It was in darkness, as was her mother's bedroom. Isobel waited until the twelve booms ended before moving across the hall.

A pool of darkness lay before her at the top of the stairs. She had decided to fight her fear and no longer cared that she was about to break the most important rule The Recluse had laid down. All that mattered was finding out what she could about this stranger who was controlling their lives.

Living with him was like sharing her life with a ghost. His existence was only made visible by the trays of food her mother carried up to him and his tablets in their bubble shapes that were kept in the first aid box. She had seen his clothes hanging on the line and heard his radio, his footsteps, his walking stick, but, otherwise, he was featureless, formless. Now, she could no longer ignore him. She used the flashlight app on her phone to light the way towards Fear Zone. She took one step, then two and three. After that it was easier to move upwards until she reached the curve of the stairs. The small alcove window framed a full moon. How close it looked as it rolled serenely above the trees.

The first room she entered was full of tall, pale figures with wide, sloping shoulders. She stifled a scream and was about to flee when she realised the shapes were just furniture covered in dust sheets. Feeling braver now, she adjusted the exposure on her camera phone and made horrified faces as she took selfies of herself standing in the midst of 'ghosts'. She wouldn't write any captions on her photographs when she posted them on Instagram. Let Sarah and Joanne think she had moved into a haunted house. That should worry them enough to respond to her posts.

The Recluse's bathroom door was open. A candle flickered inside a glass lantern and threw shadows over an old-fashioned bath on claw legs. Three steps led upwards towards a magnificent toilet. It reminded Isobel of a throne. She immediately felt the urge to use it. She climbed the steps and pulled down her pyjama bottoms. Peeing in Fear Zone was scary and at the same time exciting. She yanked the steel chain hanging from the cistern and straightaway realised her mistake. The water gushed and the pipes groaned loud enough to awaken the dead.

A door opened. Too late to run, she listened to his footsteps and the familiar thud of his walking stick. How could she have been so stupid? She grabbed her phone from the floor and searched desperately for somewhere to hide. She pulled open a door in the wall which revealed a set of rusty pipes and a boiler. This must have been a hot press once. Holding her breath, she squeezed in beside the boiler and crouched down. A broken pipe pressed against her ankle but there was no space to move her feet. She switched off the flashlight just in time before The Recluse entered the bathroom. The plumbing was quietening down but Hyland Hall was still full of night sounds. Just as well or he would hear her heart pounding. Caesar sniffed the hot press door. She scrunched even tighter into the small space and hid her face in her knees. Even when The Recluse called Caesar to heel and they left the bathroom, she stayed where she was, terrified to move in case they returned.

Just when she believed it was safe to emerge from hiding, she heard him speaking. 'Some music, Caesar? What do you think?' His voice appeared to rise from under her feet. Using her flashlight, she could see where the broken pipe was digging into her ankle. It had once been attached to the boiler and must be connected in some way to a pipe in his room. This was allowing his voice to travel. He turned on his radio. Music, haunting and lonely, like night trains whistling through dark tunnels, reached her. When the music stopped, she heard another sound, faint and rustling. He was either reading or writing. This time it was her ears, not her eyes, that were doing the work for her. He coughed a few times, a rasping, breathless gasp.

'My thoughts can wait for another night.' Again, his dis-embodied voice travelled along the pipe. 'Caesar, come here, boy. Time to rest.' A book was slammed closed. He shouldn't be playing music or wandering around Fear Zone at night but she'd never be able to tell her mother what he got up to when they were sleeping.

A door was opened, another closed. She moved silently across the bathroom floor. The landing was empty. She entered his living room. It was smaller than the den and would have been a bedroom in the olden days, according to Charlie. He said the rooms had been changed around before they arrived so that upstairs and downstairs could become two apartments. Apart from a fold-up table that served as a tray, everything else in the room – the two winged armchairs, his desk, an enormous trunk with a curved lid that matched the one in the hall, the bookcase filled with musty hardbacks, and the two chairs standing on either side of a table with a green leather top – belonged in a museum.

He must have been sitting at his writing desk. He had left its sliding top rolled open and a hardback journal lay closed on the surface, a pen still stuck between the pages.

Prying into someone's private diary was the worst thing anyone could do. She had kept a diary for three months when she was twelve then gave it up because all her entries had been the same. That was when she lived in the suburbs, of course, and her life was normal. Boring, she had thought at the time, nothing to report. Oh, how she wanted normal back again.

She opened his journal and the pen clattered to the floor. The noise it made sounded like the earth shaking but there was no answering sound, not even a bark from Caesar. His handwriting was wavery but the words were clear. She skimmed the opening page. It was all about dreams and being born a twin. She flicked the pages. Many were still blank and he had made notes at the back of the journal under the heading *May be Included*. She was about to close the journal when her mother's name seemed to jump from one of the notes. After that, it was impossible to stop reading.

Sophy is my salvation. Unlike the phoenix, I did not rise in glory from the ashes. I reached towards heaven and found myself in hell. She does not flinch from the reflection I avoid. No mirrors to haunt me and cast my true self back at me. I am alive yet, in truth, I am undead. A phantom. Insubstantial. A man in terror of his own face. A man who does not know if he is walking blindly through a dream or if there is life in him still. Surely that is a state of being undead. I have the blood of strangers in my veins and my grotesque body is the burden I must carry as a reward for life.

The children are unaware of how often I watch them. 'The Recluse,' they say. Beware... beware of The Recluse. But what does it matter? Names can't hurt me, not now. Imagination is gifted to the young. How can we blame them when adults turn it into a tinderbox?

The little one confides her fears into the ear of a statue and pretends they don't exist. She covers much with antics and laughter but the anger of the elder one is a potent force. If only I could channel it – show her another way – but she fears me too much. When their voices reach me, I am filled with contentment. It is an unfamiliar emotion but not unpleasant. If they are to accept my truth then I must move cautiously. But how can I get them to trust me when I am unable to gaze upon my own blemished features?

Caesar howled. How could she have forgotten what happened on the night of a full moon? She imagined Caesar throwing back his vicious head, saliva drooling between his fangs as he ran through the woods on his hind legs; his claws ripping the bark from trees and the flesh from the terrified night creatures that stood in his way. She closed the journal and ran from the room. Julie was still asleep and didn't stir when Isobel slipped back into her bed. She was never going back there again, never *ever*. She could hear him opening his bedroom door. Was he going to come downstairs and release his dog into the woods? She burrowed under the duvet and closed out every sound except the frightened rush of her own breathing.

CHAPTER NINE

Sophy

The accident occurred while she was driving the girls to Mount Eagle. Victor had given them permission to use the tennis court when he was at work and Sophy was relieved that they had found something enjoyable to do together. Jack had been left alone for only ten minutes but Caesar's barking alerted her when she opened the back door. Her alarm grew as she hurried up the stairs.

The door of the room next to Jack's bedroom was open. Part of the ceiling had collapsed and plaster now covered the carpet. Water was leaking in, soaking the dustsheets thrown over the room's long unused furniture. He had been asleep when she left but he was not in his bedroom or his living room. Caesar's barking drew her towards the end of the landing and around a corner to a door leading into the attic. Peering through the open door, she found Jack on the rickety stairs. The water tank was leaking, he insisted. Once she persuaded him to come down and return to his bed, he explained that the crash of falling plaster had awoken him and he had headed to the attic to turn off the water.

The water tank was ancient and rusted. Easy to see how it had sprung a leak. Once she had turned off the water, she rang Victor. His cheerful message on the answering machine asked for her name and number. She tried Charlie next, who picked up and said his nephew was a plumber. He promised they would come by as soon as possible.

Thinking about what could have happened if the ceiling in Jack's bedroom or living room had collapsed while she was absent from the house added to her distress. She needed a cup of tea to ease her nerves. But when she tried to turn on the kettle, she discovered the electricity was off. Was there anything in this house that worked? Anything that was not tarnished, broken or cracked? As if to prove her point, the kitchen chair wobbled when she sat down to ring Charlie again to let him know the electricity was also down.

Thankfully, he arrived shortly afterwards with his nephew, Billy, and two grandsons who would look after the electricity and plastering.

'Everything is under control,' she reassured Victor when he rang back later. 'Jack is fine. You don't have to worry about him.'

'I'll call in and see him on my way home from work,' he said.

'I'll see you then. Better rush. The house is full of workmen and I'm making lunch for them.'

When Victor arrived that evening, it was obvious from his worried expression that the accident was playing on his mind.

'This house is a death trap,' he said. 'Can you imagine what would have happened if that ceiling had come down on top of him?'

'Thankfully, it didn't. And Charlie has taken care of everything. It seems there isn't a skill his family don't have.' She tried to lighten the tone but she could tell he was still concerned when they went upstairs to check the repaired ceiling. Caesar growled from the bedroom next door then fell quiet with a suddenness that only Jack could command.

'Leave him alone for tonight.' Sophy touched Victor's arm as he prepared to enter his uncle's bedroom. 'I'm afraid he's in one of his moods and doesn't want to see anyone.'

'I'm not anyone, Sophia.'

'I'm sorry, Victor. I'm just relaying his wishes.'

'I hope he's not regressing. The mental strain—'

'It's nothing like that. He's just tired. If I noticed any signs of dementia, I'd contact his medical team immediately.'

'He's obviously quite shaken after what happened this morning. Have you spoken to him about moving?'

'Not yet. I'm waiting for the right time.'

'There is no right time, Sophia. Only lost time.'

Reluctantly, he walked away from the bedroom door and followed her down the stairs. 'You're doing amazing work with him,' he said when they entered the music room. 'Think how much easier it would be if he was willing to move into my house. The girls have turned it into their second home, as it is.'

'I hope you don't mind them using the tennis court when you're at work.'

'I told you it wasn't a problem. You should do the same.'

'I keep intending to but the day slides by and there never seems to be enough hours in it.'

'Make time,' he said. 'I know how demanding my uncle can be. I don't want you wearing yourself out in this wretched place when I can provide the perfect alternative.'

'*Stop* worrying about me.' She walked over to the grand piano and pointed to the framed photographs. 'You and Jack have had a very close relationship. I'm sure he still feels that same affection for you. I control his pain but medication can only do so much. With the burns he suffered, his moods are unpredictable, which is why he doesn't want to see anyone this evening.'

He glanced at the photographs and laughed abruptly. 'That's Laurence, not Jack.'

'Oh?' She bent closer to the photographs. 'I just assumed it was him. Obviously, I don't know what Jack looked like before his accident—'

'He looked exactly like that.' Victor lifted the photograph of the two men standing outside Hyland Hall. 'But looks were all my uncles had in common. Personality wise, they were poles apart.'

'Did he and Laurence live together at Hyland Hall?'

'No. Jack lived abroad for most of his life. He left here when he was twenty-three and stayed away for forty-three years. He never bothered coming back, not even for my mother's funeral.'

'That must have been very upsetting.'

'Water under the bridge now.' He shrugged and positioned the photograph back on the piano. 'You're right about the affection you see in those photographs. Laurence was like a second father to me. I was heartbroken when he died.'

The thudding sound of Jack's walking stick startled them both.

'I'd better check…' She shrugged as the thudding continued.

'Talk to Jack in your own time, Sophia,' Victor said. 'Like you, I want what's best for his continued comfort. I'll ring you tomorrow to see how he is.' The touch of his lips against her cheek was fleeting yet she could still feel the quivery impact on her skin as she walked with him to the front door.

'*Mum!* The Rec— Mr Hyland wants you.' Isobel, her arms folded, stood outside the den.

'I heard him.' Sophy waited until Victor had descended the steps before turning around to meet her daughter's challenging stare.

'Was he *kissing* you?' Isobel demanded.

'Don't be ridiculous, Isobel.' She hurried upstairs, her annoyance rising with each demanding summons.

'Has he left?' Jack asked when she entered his room. He was only sixty-six, she thought, yet he had the hunched appearance of a much older man. What a toll the fire had taken on him.

'Yes. He was disappointed he wasn't able to see you.'

'I'm sure he was.' His dismissive tone held a warning for her not to continue the conversation.

Caesar panted, eager for her to bring him outside for his nightly ramble. She had discovered a high wall dividing the two properties. It was covered in a thick blanket of ivy but she had been able to make out the shape of a gate. It was almost invisible and welded tight by clinging vines. She imagined Victor preparing his evening meal in his kitchen. Would he have a swim first? A solitary figure, poised on the edge of the pool. Or maybe he would relax in the hot tub. Such thoughts were unsettling, testament to the effect he was having on her. She was not ready to define this emotion. To do so would give it credence and she was too vulnerable to trust her heart to anyone.

Luke phoned as she was walking back to the house. He was ready to leave the Oasis of Hope and would travel to Clonmoore on Saturday to see the girls. Decision time was upon them. The sharing and caring, time slots and awkward handovers. She had known they would eventually have to make such arrangements but she was still unprepared for what would be involved.

CHAPTER TEN

Isobel

Her father had already arrived at The Coffee Bean and was waiting for them at a seat by the window. He stood up when they entered the café and gripped the edge of the table. Maybe he was frightened they were going to run away. Or maybe, Isobel thought, it was to stop himself from running away from them.

'Hello, Sophy,' he said. 'How are you?'

'I'm fine, Luke. And you?'

'Very well, thank you.'

Isobel couldn't believe her ears. Was that all her parents had to say to each other after being apart all these months? But she hadn't the slightest idea what she was going to say to him either. What had happened to their family was too enormous to be wrapped up in a few casual words.

He cleared his throat but he still sounded choked when he said, 'Thank you for bringing my girls to see me.'

'They've been looking forward to it,' her mum replied. 'I hope you have a nice day together. I'll collect them here at six o'clock.'

'Come with us, Mammy,' Julie pleaded. 'You'll have a nice day too.'

'I have to look after Mr Hyland, darling.' She turned away and hurried as fast as she could from the café.

It was weird being with her father again. Like meeting a stranger whom Isobel knew really well, which was a contradiction, but was exactly how she felt. He had lost weight. His face looked saggy, older. His brown hair was going grey; she'd never noticed that until today, and his eyes were swimming with tears. Julie threw her arms around him and he hugged her just as fiercely. When he held out his arms to Isobel, she hoped her anger would melt away. She wanted to remember everything she loved about him. But she was unable to move. He lowered his arms, as if he understood, and pulled out a chair for her.

The Coffee Bean was packed with lunchtime customers. The noise was deafening but Julie shouted above it, talking non-stop about her new friends and Golden Eye, and how she was able to jump him over hurdles. Isobel tried to think of interesting things to tell him but there was only one thing she wanted him to know. The kindest thing to do was to remain silent about Victor kissing her mother but the knowledge buzzed like bees inside her head. How she wished she was Julie with new friends and a pony to love.

He told them he had left the Oasis of Hope and was renting an apartment in Dublin. 'It's the size of a shoebox,' he admitted. 'If I move my big toe it hits the opposite wall.'

They laughed obligingly. It wasn't that funny but laughter seemed to fill the vast, empty space between them. He went back every day to the Oasis. Volunteering, he called it. He was building a fountain on the front lawn. Creating something beautiful for all the broken people with their broken lives who come to the Oasis to be cured. He squeezed Isobel's hand and refused to be upset with her when she said, 'And with all their broken promises.'

He attended meetings so that he could stay strong and learn to know himself. How ridiculous was that? He was in his forties. How come he didn't know himself by now? Wasn't that part of being grown-up? Being an adult? A father? But if he was only now beginning to know himself then how was Isobel supposed to make sense of anything?

'I want you to meet Golden Eye,' said Julie. 'You won't believe it when you see how well I can ride him.'

'Is it far?' he asked. 'I don't have a car with me.'

'*No* car.' They stared in amazement at him.

'How did you get here?' Julie asked.

'By train to Cork then a bus to Clonmoore,' he replied. 'Don't look so shocked. People travel by bus all the time. Now, I'm one of them.'

Isobel tried to imagine him sitting on a bus, staring into space with the same bored expression as all the other passengers. Impossible. But she could never have imagined them living with The Recluse in the middle of a deep, dark wood. Or her father gambling all their happiness away. Or Victor sitting like he belonged at the kitchen table and rolling that extra syllable around his tongue when he said, *So-phi-a.*

'Cordelia says—' Julie began and stopped when she saw him frown.

'*Cordelia*? Do you mean the mannequin?'

'Yes, Daddy. I'm training to be a ventril—'

'Don't tell me you brought it with you to Hyland Hall?'

'*Her*, Daddy.'

'She's singing now.' Isobel appealed to him. 'Tell her to stop. She wakes me in the morning with her stupid songs. First, it was "Ten Green Bottles", now it's "Yellow Submarine". It's wrecking my head.'

'It's Cordelia singing.' Julie stabbed at a chip.

'No, it's you driving me crazy. Cordelia's not real.'

'How do you know? Maybe *you're* the one who's not real.'

'Oh, yeah? Feel this.' Isobel shoved her arm forward. 'That's flesh, not *plastic*. And you can't remove my arms and legs.'

'No arguments,' he pleaded. 'Our time together is too short. Hurry up and finish your lunch. I want to see this amazing Golden Eye.'

At the riding school Julie trotted the pony in a circle and jumped him over a low railing.

'She seems so settled.' He leant on the rail surrounding the paddock and watched her. 'But I haven't seen you smile, *really* smile, all day, Isobel. Tell me what's on your mind.'

'Everything,' she replied.

'That's a heavy burden to carry.'

'You put it there.'

'I'm sorry I let you down. But I'll make things right again. You must believe me…' His voice trailed away.

'But how?' she asked. '*How?*'

'Trust me.' He rubbed his hand across his forehead and sighed. 'I'm taking one day at a time but—'

'Don't ask me to give it time,' she interrupted him angrily. Why couldn't he understand that their lives were changing while he was taking things one day at a time? One day led to two then three, and the days became months, years. 'I hate living here! I *hate* it! The Recluse is *so* weird. You've no idea how scary he is.'

'I'm sorry you're finding it so difficult,' he said. 'I want you to be happy more than anything in the world. But I can't make rash promises or make things right by willing them to happen. I can only fix what's fixable and you have to stay here for the time being. I'm glad Julie has settled—'

'That's what she'd like you to think. But that's all just for show.'

'In what way?'

'She's made Cordelia into the other side of her.'

'What other side? I've no idea what you mean?'

'Her whiney side. Julie never complains about *anything* anymore and she keeps going on about our exciting new adventure and how Hyland Hall is the most wonderful place in the world when I know she's really scared of The Rec— Mr Hyland. He has a hideous dog. Julie is convinced he's a werewolf and I'm terrified he's going to kill Peeper. And my friends no longer want to know me. They don't reply when I Snapchat them because they're so busy doing stuff that we used to do together.' She was no longer able to control her rage. It was like the night he told her about addiction all over again. 'Hyland Hall is just like being in prison.'

'Come on, Isobel, don't exaggerate.'

'It *is* like a prison. I don't know what we'd do if it wasn't for Victor.'

'Victor?' His Adam's apple bobbed when he swallowed. 'Who are you talking about, Isobel?'

'He's Mum's friend and he's got this *amazing* swimming pool. He lets us play tennis in his garden and he wants us to move in with him.'

'Move in—'

'The Recluse is his uncle. Victor wants to look after him. His house is *huge*. We'd all have our own bedrooms. Even Cordelia could have her own room if Julie could bear to be parted from her.'

'This Victor, how often does he call to Hyland Hall?'

'All the time. I saw him kissing Mum—'

'No, you *didn't*.' They hadn't heard Julie coming up behind them. 'You said it was only on her cheek. That's not a real kiss, is it, Daddy?' She slammed her fists against Isobel's chest. 'Liar… liar!'

'Easy now! Take it easy, Julie.' He pulled them apart and held Julie until she stopped struggling.

'Cordelia says Issy's a cruel, sneaky liar.' She was whispering to their father but Isobel could hear her. 'She hates Issy.'

The lines on his face deepened. 'That's hurtful talk, Julie.'

'It's not *me*, it's what Cordelia says.'

'Sounds to me like Cordelia talks too much. Why don't you put her away for a little while and concentrate on having fun with your real friends?'

'Cordelia understands me. And she tells me things.' Julie burst into tears. No warning, just sudden howls muffled only by their father pulling her close to his jacket.

'Dry your eyes, Julie.' He handed her his handkerchief. 'I want our day to end on a happy note. I'm sure Isobel does too.'

Isobel nodded. She felt mean and hurtful, yet she didn't know how to take her words back. 'Victor helps Mum with stuff in the house, that's all. He was just being nice to her when he kissed—'

'Let's forget this conversation ever took place.' He sounded stern and in control, as he did in the past, and she nodded. It was easier to pretend that hurtful words could be forgotten as easily as butterflies flitting through flowers.

They left the stables and stopped on the bridge that divided Upper and Lower Main Street. The river was running fast, curlicues of froth skimming the surface. He seemed mesmerised by the flow. Isobel dropped pebbles. She watched them plop and sink. Was this her life from now on? He was a Saturday Dad and they had nowhere to go except rivers and cafés and riding schools. They didn't speak again until they returned to The Coffee Bean where Sophy was waiting for them.

'Issy told Daddy you kissed Victor.' Julie was barely inside the car before she blurted out what had happened at the stables. 'He was as mad as a bear when he heard.'

'I did not!' Isobel yelled. 'I said it was Victor who kissed *Mum*. Big difference.'

'What on earth are you two talking about?' Her mother pressed her hand against her throat and took a deep breath.

'On your cheek,' Isobel explained. 'Julie says it's not a real kiss but it looked real enough to me. And he's here all the time making swoony faces at you—'

'Stop talking nonsense, Isobel. What you saw was nothing more than a friendly gesture. Like a handshake. Not that you'd notice the difference because you're too busy moping around the place.'

'I'm not moping. I'm adjusting to my life being ruined.'

'Ruined or not, you'll go to your bedroom and unpack your clothes as soon as we return to Hyland Hall. This is not a request, Isobel. It's an order. I've put up with this nonsense for long enough.'

Her mother's anger vibrated between them. Perhaps it wasn't anger. Isobel was unable to tell anymore. Where once there was certainty, she now felt only insecurity. If a hole opened in the ground in front of her, she wouldn't be surprised. If the moon plummeted to earth, she'd think, why not? What was holding it up there, anyway?

CHAPTER ELEVEN

Sophy

Lost. That was the only word that came to Sophy's mind as she drove back to Hyland Hall. She had read about the path to rehabilitation. The destruction of illusion and the rebuilding of a new, stronger self-awareness. She had imagined Luke emerging from the victory corner, arms aloft, exhilarated with the zeal of the reformed. Instead, he looked shrunken, hollowed out. His eyes shocked her the most. They reminded her of stones; pale, flat stones bleached by tides of tears and swept onto an unfamiliar shore. He was lost but had not been found again, either by himself or those who loved him. She had sensed Isobel's struggle to put the past behind her and rush into his arms. Unable to do so, she had glowered at both her parents and tugged at her sleeves. Julie's excitement had been mixed with nervousness as she asked Sophy to stay with them. Unable to bear her daughter's pleading expression, she had hurried from the café so that the girls would not notice her distress.

She drove back to Clonmoore at six to collect them. The afternoon had shaken Luke. He embraced Julie and shook Isobel's hand. No father–daughter forgiveness or bonding, then. Julie's eyes were swollen. The reason soon became clear. A kiss.

Isobel had told him some hare-brained story in an attempt to hurt him.

Later, when Jack was in bed and she had taken Caesar for his nightly walk, she entered the girls' bedroom. The first thing she noticed was Isobel's case, open and unpacked, on the floor. Julie was already asleep. Cordelia lay beside her, an eye mask hiding her bright blue stare. Isobel was reading when Sophy sat on the edge of her bed. 'Why did you tell your father I kissed Victor?' she whispered. 'Were you trying to make trouble between us?'

'How can I make trouble when it's already made?' Isobel retorted.

'Were you?'

'I was simply telling him what I saw.'

'What you *think* you saw.'

'Whatever.' She shrugged and turned a page on her book.

'You were deliberately trying to hurt him.'

'So what? It's not as if he never hurt us. Anyway, you hate him. I saw the way you looked at him.'

'Hate is a very strong word. It's not in my vocabulary and it should not be in yours.'

'But is… is *love*? With Dad?'

'I've loved him very much. But the feelings we had for each other got lost somewhere along the way to here.'

'Can't you love him again?'

'Love is not a tap that can be turned on and off at random.'

'I see.'

'I doubt you do. Someday when you're grown up, you'll understand about different kinds of loving.'

'I'm never going to fall in love. It sucks.'

'It certainly can,' Sophy replied. 'But that never stops people falling deeply into the heart of it.'

*

She had mistaken Luke's distressing silences after his mother's death for grief, which had been true at first. He had adored Maddie and was shattered by her loss, as were Sophy and her granddaughters. As the months passed and he found it difficult to look Sophy in the eye or to sit still in the evenings when they would normally have chatted easily to each other, she suspected he was having an affair.

His denials did nothing to ease her suspicions. She waited outside his studio one night and followed him as he walked towards the train station. Instead of entering it, he continued on towards a square of Georgian houses. She remained out of sight as she watched him disappear inside one of them. She mounted the steps and checked the sign on the wall. He had entered a casino.

When he returned home late that night, she waited for him to tell her where he had been. Instead, he claimed to have met with a client on the other side of the city and that their discussion on a new park project had gone on longer than expected. She searched his face for signs of the lie but was unable to read his expression. On their holidays abroad, he had never shown the remotest interest in visiting casinos whenever Sophy had suggested doing so. What had changed and led to this secrecy? This deceit?

The following evening before he returned from work, she searched the small room he used as a home office. She found the key to his filing cabinet and within it discovered the extent of his debts. They began to accrue during Maddie's illness and continued to mount up after her death. Her inheritance, which they had agreed to invest in his company and on home improvements, had been squandered in casinos and betting shops. He had tried to recoup his losses by borrowing from loan sharks, as

Sophy discovered when the intimidating phone calls began. Phone calls that threatened her and her daughters if the money was not forthcoming. Selling Kid's Chic had stopped the demands but by then her marriage was over. He had turned her into a wife who whimpered with fear every time the phone rang, knowing that an anonymous voice would warn her to have a care for her children's safety. Their house, now sold, had paid off his creditors but, as far as Sophy was concerned, the debt he owed to his family would be impossible to settle.

CHAPTER TWELVE

Isobel

Peeper was missing. Usually, he was snoozing on the outside kitchen window ledge in the evenings but he could also decide to take a wander through the bushes in the courtyard. Isobel wasn't panicked, not at first, but after he failed to turn up when she rattled his feeding tray to remind him it was dinner time, she began to fear for his safety. He had been used to roaming when they lived at Park View Villas but wandering through the back gardens of suburbia was not the same as exploring Hyland Estate and the countryside beyond it. Sometimes she heard gunshot. Someone was shooting rabbits. To think of their furry, little bodies being brought down by a gun was horrifying but this was the country, Charlie said. Life here was different from the city yet every time Isobel heard a gun going off, she stuck her fingers in her ears. What if Peeper was mistaken for a rabbit? Or if he'd ventured into Fear Zone? Cats didn't know the rules and Caesar— he'd devour her cat in two bites. She'd lost everything – she couldn't lose Peeper too.

She searched the courtyard, the annexe and the disgusting shower stalls, the outhouses in the backyard, the creepy old gate lodge that reminded her of the evil cottage in a fairy story.

'Peeper's an independent cat.' Her mother tried to reassure Isobel when she came downstairs after attending to The Recluse. 'He hasn't wandered upstairs. Try not to worry, love. I know he'll find his way back to you.'

Isobel hadn't cried since the night her father explained about addiction and she was determined not to start now. The tears come, regardless. It was comforting to be cuddled and soothed in her mother's arms, and for while it was possible to convince herself that Peeper was safe. She sat on the sofa with Julie and watched television but her eyes kept straying to the window for a glimpse of him. Soon, the sun would set. Unable to wait any longer she ran outside to the backyard and crossed to the paddock. She was constantly being reminded by her mother that the stables and barn were out of bounds but the possibility that Peeper could be trapped in the ruins could not be ignored.

The high barn behind the stables was still standing. The blackened steel walls and roof had survived the flames but everything inside had been destroyed. Victor said that that was where the fire originated. The Recluse had ignored the faulty wiring and a spark was all it took to set the racks of hay ablaze. She was sure the soot was settling on her skin when she entered the stable yard and called Peeper's name, but again there was no answer. Blackened hay racks, buckles and mouth pieces lay on the ground, also forks and shovels, their handles burned to ash. She walked across blistered planks of wood that cracked and crunched under her feet. Saddles and bridles hung from one of the walls, their tarnished hides split like gaping wounds. She could have been standing in a grotesque gallery where everything on display had been disfigured by a fire of such intensity that she was already recoiling from the smell that her intrusion seemed to have released from the scorched crevices.

Her foot hit against a charred stump of wood that must have fallen to the ground during the fire. The beam moved slightly when she pushed against it with her heel. A black puff of soot rose up then settled back in a thin film over her trainers. She started to cough. She was about to move away when she noticed something in the soot that must have been hidden under the beam. She picked it up and rubbed it on her sleeve. It was too solid and heavy to be a cinder. She spat on it a few times and rubbed harder. Gradually, the charred surface began to gleam. A line of red ran like a vein of blood through its tortured shape.

'What are you doing here?' The deep, gravelly voice froze her to the spot. The Recluse moved in front of her and spoke again. 'I asked you a question, Child. Don't you know the stables are out of bounds?'

'I- I- My cat, he's lost...' she stammered. Her mouth was dry, her heart thumping. She could see him clearly for the first time. She thought he was wearing a mask but, then, she realised that the shiny, red skin on his face was criss-crossed with pale scars. One eye was missing or perhaps it was hidden from view behind a black patch.

'I'm sorry to hear he's still missing,' he said in his raspy voice. 'Rest assured, Caesar does not like the taste of cats.'

Was he making a joke? His scarred mouth made it impossible to tell.

'What have you got in your hand?' he asked.

Her lips trembled as she held the object out to him. 'I found this in the soot. I wasn't going to keep it, *honestly*.'

He stiffened when he saw what she was holding. His body shook so much she was afraid he would fall as he swayed forward to snatch it from her. What would she do if he collapsed on the spot?

'Where did you find this?' He held the twisted object close to him. 'Answer me, Child. Where was it?'

She pointed at the beam. 'Under there. I'm sorry, I didn't mean to trespass…'

'Have you any idea of the danger you're in?' His growly voice was difficult to understand but she nodded, nonetheless. He put the object into his coat pocket and pointed towards the house. 'Don't let me see you near these stables again or I'll have to speak to your mother. Do you hear me?'

'Yes, Sir.' She took a step back from him, then another. He didn't move or speak again as she walked away. When she turned back, he was still standing in the same position, like a statue once carved from iron and now misshapen by flames.

She was still searching among the bushes in the courtyard when Victor arrived in his jeep.

'A clever cat like Peeper won't stay lost for long,' he said. 'Don't worry. He'll turn up soon.'

She wanted to believe him. He always said the right thing but that didn't mean he was *actually* right.

Bats appeared and skimmed through the air like scraps of charred paper. She pulled up the hood on her hoodie and held it tightly under her chin. They frightened her, the way they flew so silently above her. Like they were waiting to swoop and suck her blood.

She was about to give up searching the courtyard when she heard something that sounded like a meow. A thin, frightened cry, like wind whining through a gap in the door. Unsure whether or not it was her imagination she strained forward and traced the sound to the tree outside The Recluse's living room window. Peeper must have climbed too high and was afraid to move.

Isobel hoisted herself up onto the tree's lower branches. As she climbed higher, the light from The Recluse's window guided her towards Peeper. His frightened eyes gleamed in the dark and when she reached out to hold him against her shoulder, he meowed. They were both trembling but they were trembling together and that was all that mattered.

She could see into The Recluse's living room. He was sitting on an armchair with two fans on either side of him. Caesar was spread out like a furry, yellow rug at his feet. Sensing them at the window, the dog lifted his head and opened his yellow eyes. In that moment she held Peeper too tight and he let out a warning, yet soft meow, like he knew they were in imminent danger if she was discovered spying.

The Recluse stood. He had taken off his hat and he was completely bald; he didn't even have a few wispy hairs at the sides. Caesar also stood to attention as The Recluse's long fingers stroked his ears. They stayed in that position until the door opened.

Normally her mother carried up his evening meal but it was Victor who entered with a tray. He stopped when he saw Caesar. Even from that distance, Isobel could tell he was nervous. The Recluse waved his hand and Caesar sank down, his rubbery lips drawn back, his teeth bared. He must have been snarling yet he didn't move when Victor walked past and laid the tray on a small table beside The Recluse's armchair. He gestured, as if he was asking his uncle to sit down and eat but The Recluse ignored him.

It was frustrating not being able to hear what they were saying, like watching a silent film where Isobel had to concentrate on body language. But anger was easy to recognise and The Recluse was rigid with it. He raised his walking stick. She thought he was going to crack Victor 's skull wide open. She would be a witness to a murder. The urge to look away, to climb down and run to her mother, to bang on the window and yell at The Recluse to stop, all these instincts struggled together in her head. But before she could do anything, he lowered his stick. Caesar immediately stood and assumed his ready-to-attack position again. A werewolf preparing for action.

Victor moved backwards towards the door. He was still facing The Recluse and his werewolf when he reached behind him and turned the doorknob. Then he was gone. The power seemed to leave The Recluse's legs. Isobel didn't think his walking stick would support him as he came towards the window but, somehow, he managed to keep moving. She wriggled backwards until she was camouflaged by the sturdy boughs. It would be impossible for him to see her yet she imagined him stripping away the leaves and branches, stripping bark and sap and oxygen, until this tree was a dead, withered stump and she was exposed, trapped in his fierce blue glare. He drew the curtains and darkness fell over her.

Peeper was no longer afraid. He leaped from one branch to the other, waiting each time until she caught up with him. She wriggled to the ground and ran around to the back of the house. Her mother was sitting at the kitchen table with Victor, who tapped his fingers to his forehead as he spoke. He must be talking about his encounter in Fear Zone. She crouched under the window. It was slightly open and she wasn't surprised to hear Victor admit that his uncle was delusional and could even become dangerous. Their heads were close together as he spoke but they pulled away quickly when Isobel came into the kitchen.

Her mum rushed over to her and took Peeper in her arms. 'Where did you find him?' She nuzzled the cat against her neck.

'In the bushes,' Isobel replied.

'I told you he wouldn't go far,' Victor added. The fear Isobel saw on his face when he entered The Recluse's room had vanished. He smiled, his teeth so white and even and perfect.

The table in the kitchen had been set for five, so she knew he must be staying for dinner. He laughed a lot throughout the meal, especially when Julie did her ventriloquist act with Cordelia.

Unable to listen any longer, Isobel excused herself from the table and went into the den. She could hear the thud of The Recluse's stick upstairs as he walked up and down his room. Then, two sets of footsteps; her mother accompanying Victor to the front door. Would he kiss her on her cheek this time or on her mouth? Isobel stroked Peeper's silky coat and thought about the undead and the power they had over others. *In truth, I am undead. A phantom. Insubstantial.* His words haunted her. The roar of Victor's jeep faded into the distance as he drove away. Then all was silent. A silence only broken by Julie teaching Cordelia to sing, 'She'll Be Coming Round the Mountain.'

CHAPTER THIRTEEN

Isobel

Addiction. What was it like to be driven by a force you couldn't understand yet kept you under its control, Isobel wondered as she moved towards the bedroom door? To know you had to do something bad, something you didn't want to do, but were unable to stop? Was that how it was with her father? Had she inherited his addictive gene? She must have done so otherwise why on earth was she creeping back into Fear Zone in the middle of the night?

No matter how hard she tried to forget that Fear Zone existed, it seemed as if the old house was determined to remind her that only a flight of stairs separated her from a man who had returned from the dead. He could have killed Victor with his stick or ordered his werewolf to tear him apart. She was terrified of him yet unable to stop thinking about his journal where he had written the truth about his existence.

She tiptoed along the corridor, past the room with the dust sheets and the dodgy ceiling, past the bathroom with the night candle and noisy toilet. Caesar would not disturb her tonight. He was staying overnight with Charlie, who was bringing him to the vet in the morning for a booster injection.

After a short search through The Recluse's desk, Isobel found his journal. He kept going on about love. She skipped over that part. Reading about his love life would force her to think about vampire brides. She was only interested in finding anything he might have written about her family and it didn't take long to find her mother's name in his notes.

I watch Victor's eyes when Sophy enters with her potions and sage advice. She interrupts our angry exchanges and, later, when Victor has gone, she asks why I treat him so rudely when he only has my best interests at heart. Ha. His house is a magnet to someone who has lost everything, as she has done. I will not let him take her from me. I've told him many times that the only way I will leave here is in my coffin. When the time comes, Charlie will weave my final resting place from the reeds he gathers by the lake. I no longer fear death now that I know my essence will live on in another form.

Too horrified to continue reading, Isobel closed the journal. Until tonight, she had believed she was overreacting and allowing her imagination to be influenced by her surroundings. But this evidence proved she had barely scratched the surface of Hyland Hall and its terrifying owner.

She became aware of a noise, faint at first then growing louder – the low growl of an engine outside. Was Victor calling back again to see his uncle or, sneaking in the dead of night to see her mother? A week had passed since the 'love is not a tap' conversation and Victor had stayed for dinner *twice*.

This possibility faded as the noise became a heavier, straining rumble. A wavery glow swept across the ceiling and walls before plunging the living room into darkness again. The Recluse's bedroom door opened. She barely had time to shove his journal back into the desk and close the lid before she heard the thud,

thud, thud of his walking stick on the landing. He was coming towards his living room.

The noise from outside had stopped. It was a waiting silence that broke when a clunking, clanking clatter reached her? Steel on steel clashing, glass breaking and there was a lighter clang, as if tin cans were being flung to the ground. The fly tippers were back only this time they were dumping their rubbish onto the courtyard. Victor said it wasn't possible to prevent them trespassing unless The Recluse was prepared to hire a team of security men.

The door opened. She hunkered down behind the armchair opposite the one where he usually sat and pressed her face into her knees. This was as terrifying as the time in the stables, only now she had no excuse for breaking his rules. He switched on the light and came towards her.

His footsteps were silent; only the thud of his walking stick sounded his progress as he drew nearer. She could see his feet, his scaly toes and heels, the skin all scrunched and wrinkled. The noise grew louder when he opened the window. She thought of trains crashing together, banshees wailing, heavy metal music clashing.

She lifted her head above the rim of the armchair. He was wearing a long, red dressing gown with an image of a dragon embroidered on the back. His mouth was open but the noise from below made it impossible to hear what he was shouting. She imagined smoke churning; thick smoke filling his lungs. He raised his hands, as if he was striking the fly tippers with streaks of lighting from his fingertips. His hands were as raw as the skin on his face and she noticed for the first time that two fingers on one hand were missing. He stayed in that electrifying position for an instant longer then, as if the fury that had brought him to the window suddenly deserted him, his long, thin body crumpled to the floor.

What was she to do? The thought of touching him terrified her yet she was already moving from her hiding place. The smell rising from the rubbish was revolting. It stung her eyes, caught in her throat. Instinctively, she moved to the window and pulled it closed. The fly tippers were leaving, red rear lights on two trucks blinking as they turned onto the avenue. The moon, pale and clipped as a fingernail, rocked in an indigo sky. She retched, tears stinging her cheeks as she bent over his still form and reached for his pulse. His wheezy breath was the only indication that he was still alive.

CHAPTER FOURTEEN

Sophy

Making love to Luke in their bedroom in Parkview Villas; the pleasure building, familiar yet stronger than ever before, an almost painful intensity that awakened Sophy into a sensuous awareness that she had been dreaming. The old house seemed to be convulsed with noise and she wondered drowsily if she had drifted off into another dream, only this time it had become a nightmare. Another crash jolted her into full wakefulness. The noise was real, and growing louder. She switched on the bedside lamp and ran to the window. Nothing to see except her startled reflection and, beyond that, the cobbled backyard and outhouses. The noise was coming from the front of the house. No mistaking the clunk and clink of fly tipping. She had seen the site of the dumps, the plastic bags ballooning in the wind, the scraps of paper clinging like crushed butterflies to the branches of dead trees. Victor said Hyland Estate was in its death throes and was seen by notorious fly tippers as an easy target. She almost collided with Isobel when she opened her bedroom door.

'Mr Hyland's on the floor in his living room.' Isobel was breathing heavily, her eyes red-rimmed and watering. 'I think he's dying. The dumpers were in the courtyard. The smell is *terrible*. I closed the window but I don't think he can breathe properly.'

She was running towards the stairs while Isobel was still explaining what had occurred outside. 'Make sure all the windows are closed downstairs and check that Julie's okay,' she said when Isobel tried to follow her. 'Go out through the annexe and head towards the stables. I'll phone Victor and ask him to collect you.'

The faint odour on the landing grew stronger as Sophy entered the living room. Jack had hit his forehead when he fell. Blood streaked his face but he was still breathing. He gave a low moan when she bent over him to check his pulse and raised his hand before letting it fall limply to his side.

'Jack, can you hear me?' He groaned again and his good eyelid fluttered, as if in acknowledgement.

'I need to get you out of here. Can you lean on me?' She draped his arms around her shoulders and took his weight as he tried to rise. Somehow, he gathered enough strength to stand upright and she was able to support him to his bedroom. He was just a bundle of bones, she thought. A stick figure held together by stubbornness and determination. She stuffed towels along the door saddle and against the window frames. The air was still clear but it was only a matter of time before the stench permeated the house.

'You're going to be fine, Jack.' She applied a cannula to his nostrils and switched on an oxygen tank.

'They won't beat me. I'm not done yet.'

'Jack, stop… *stop*. You're wasting energy.'

When his breathing had steadied, she rang for an ambulance and was relieved to receive a clear signal. The emergency responder who took her call promised to send an ambulance immediately. Victor sounded sleepy when he answered his phone.

'I need your help,' she said. 'Jack has collapsed. Can you come over right now and take the girls to your house.'

'What's happened?' His voice sharpened.

'There's been another dumping. They used the courtyard this time and I think there are chemicals in the rubbish. Drive around to the side of the house. I told the girls to wait for you near the stables. Can they stay with you tonight?'

'They can, of course. Is my uncle all right?'

'He's okay for now. The ambulance is on its way. Hurry, Victor.'

Two trucks had arrived, Isobel said. The hulking mounds they left behind were steeped with a chemical substance that was already beginning to affect Sophy's eyes. She flung the clothes they would need for the next few days into a case. Cordelia was missing from Julie's bed. Julie must have grabbed her before the girls fled.

She was back in Jack's bedroom when Victor arrived a few minutes later. 'We've got to get my uncle out of here right now.' His forcefulness filled the room. 'I can drive him to the hospital while you take the girls to my house.'

'He's safe here until the ambulance arrives,' she reassured him. 'It'll be here shortly.' She gestured towards the case she had packed. 'Take that with you and collect the girls. They're afraid of the dark and frightened by what's happening.

'My uncle could die while we're waiting for the ambulance.' He clasped his throat and coughed. 'We're risking his life by waiting.' He knelt beside the bed and gently straightened the patch over his uncle's missing eye. 'I can't believe anyone would do something so appalling. I'm going to get to the bottom of this. There will be repercussions, I promise you—'

Jack's low moan interrupted him. He pulled at the cannula and gagged. Sophy helped him to sit up and held a bowl under his chin. Unable to watch his uncle's distress, Victor left the room. She could hear him on his phone demanding to know how much longer the ambulance would take to reach Hyland Hall.

'Stay with me…' Jack gasped. He pushed the unused bowl away and gripped her hand as he lay back. Each breath was a hard rasp against his throat. 'It can't be too late… it can't… it can't…'

'Don't talk, Jack.' She checked her watch. Maybe Victor was right. He needed to be removed as fast as possible from his surroundings but her fear that he would need treatment from the paramedics on his way to the hospital steadied her resolve.

'The ambulance will be another fifteen minutes at least,' Victor said when he returned to the room. 'I'm taking him in the jeep.'

'I'm his nurse, Victor.' She pushed the rolled towels back into position against the door saddle. 'He's protected from the fumes here and this is where I want to keep him until the paramedics arrive.'

'He could die…' His voice broke. 'He's my family—'

'I understand your anxiety but I have to do what I believe is best.'

Jack spoke again. His speech had deteriorated so much that she was only able to make out a few words. One of them was Isobel's name and something about the stables.

'Isobel is safe,' she said. 'She heard the dumpers and raised the alarm. I told her to wait with Julie near the stables where the fumes won't reach them.'

This information seemed to agitate him even further. His eye movement worried her yet his pulse was steady, as was his blood pressure when she checked. He was speaking again. She tried to decipher his garbled words; something about 'medallion' or 'Madelaine' and she could make out Charlie's name.

'Do you want me to ring Charlie?' she asked.

Coughing dryly, he nodded. Exhausted by his efforts to speak, he turned his head into the pillow.

She glanced across at Victor. '*Please* pick up the girls, Victor. I don't want them hanging around outside any longer than necessary. I'll ring you as soon as we reach the hospital.'

Without replying, he nodded and left the room. Jack remained uneasy until she rang Charlie.

'I'll be over right away,' he said when she contacted him. 'I'm used to dealing with hazardous materials. Tell Jack I'll take care of everything.'

The ambulance driver followed her instructions and drove around to the back of the house. The paramedics were wearing masks when they entered the bedroom. The taller of the two, a jocular woman with a buzz haircut, knew Jack. He was her 'Lazarus,' she said. They had met on the night of the fire, not that he would have any memory of that, she added. She handed a mask to Sophy and chatted cheerfully as he was lifted onto the stretcher. The second medic was about to phone an emergency number to report a spill of toxic waste when Charlie arrived to check what needed to be done.

Jack's condition remained stable throughout the hour-long journey to Cork. 'Don't bother driving here,' she said when she phoned Victor from St Philomena's Hospital. 'He's under observation in the intensive care unit and I've been told there's nothing more I can do for him tonight.'

'You were right to wait for the ambulance,' he said. 'I'm sorry if you thought I was taking over your responsibilities. Despite his contrariness, I care deeply about his welfare.'

'I know you do. How are the girls?'

'Sleeping soundly. My doctor came and checked them out. No ill effects, thank goodness. I made an appointment for you to see him in the morning.'

'Thanks, Victor, but that won't be necessary. I've been checked out here and all's well.' She yawned. Her skin felt itchy. She hoped she wasn't getting a reaction to the toxic waste. She would shower as soon as she reached Mount Eagle.

The journey back seemed to take forever. Suddenly, she swerved dangerously towards the grass verge, her eyes drooping closed momentarily. Stopping the car, she opened the window and drank from a water bottle. The night air was cold against her face. The tears came without warning. She allowed them to flow. No one to hear her except the wind and an owl hooting in the distance. The emptiness of the countryside, the impenetrable darkness.

Until tonight, she had not entered a hospital since Maddie's death. The atmosphere of sterile efficiency had instantly swept her back to those long, waiting days when she had sat by her mother-in-law's bedside. She and Luke had taken shifts, their lives on hold, anxious that Maddie would never be left alone during those final days as she drifted in and out of consciousness.

On one occasion, in the small hours of the morning, she had heard Maddie whispering her name. Her eyes were bright and her words coherent. She was due morphine relief and even though she was in pain she shook her head when Sophy offered to call the night nurse.

'Look after Luke,' Maddie said. 'He'll be in a bad way when I'm gone. I've tried to be both mother and father to him and he'll feel as if he has lost both his parents at the same time.'

'You're even more special than that to him.' Sophy pressed Maddie's hands reassuringly. 'You're also his best friend. I love Luke and I'll do everything I can to help him after... afterwards.' The time for pretence was over. Maddie knew she was only going in one direction and had asked Sophy and Luke to stop pretending otherwise. Even so, such conversations were difficult.

'His father...' Maddie sighed. 'I need to talk about him.'

Sophy hid her surprise. In all the years she had known Maddie, her mother-in-law had never once mentioned Luke's father. Nor did Luke ever want to discuss him. Shortly after they met, he told Sophy he had made a decision to airbrush this unknown entity from his consciousness. He made it sound so easy and Sophy had never allowed her curiosity to intrude on that decision.

'When Luke was young and asking questions, I told him his father was dead,' Maddie said. 'I invented a character who never existed. I even gave him a name. Darragh O'Malley. It had a nice roll to it, I thought. I told Luke he'd died in a South African gold mine and was buried over there. When children are young it's hard to imagine them as adults with minds of their own and that a day will come when they stop believing in the lies that we invent. Luke was eighteen when he told me he planned to visit South Africa and search for his father's grave. I was forced to tell him I'd lied. I tried to explain the reasons why. In truth, I had no excuse. I invented a lie to stop him tormenting me with questions I was unable to answer.'

Unable? Sophy had bitten down on the word. To be unable to name the father of her son, what did that imply? She had no wish to add to Maddie's distress yet she sensed her mother-in-law's determination to continue the conversation. Maddie, guessing her thoughts, had sighed. 'I know it'll sound strange to you but even still, after so many years, I find it hard to talk about him.'

'Maddie… were you…?' Sophy hesitated, the ugly word she wanted to use hardening on her lips. 'Did someone force you—'

'Luke was my love child,' Maddie's voice softened. 'Never think otherwise, Sophy. But my relationship with his father was a complicated one. I found it too painful to pass on that information to my son. I asked him to give me time to contact his father before I revealed his name. I found excuses to avoid doing so and gradually Luke stopped asking. When I realised how ill I was, I told him I was going to try to make that contact. He told me it no longer mattered to him. Whatever pain I'd endured should remain in the past, he said. I'm afraid I've left it too late to make amends, yet I keep hoping to hear word…'

The night nurse, hearing their whispered conversation, whisked the screens aside. 'Luke is outside,' she said. 'He's waiting to speak to Dr Moore. You should go home, Sophy, and take some rest. As for you,' she shook her head fondly at Maddie, 'what are you doing burning the midnight oil?'

Maddie's eyes were beginning to cloud. Her voice grew weaker as she held out her arm to have her blood pressure taken.

Outside the ward, Sophy had waited for Luke to finish talking to the doctor on duty. She debated discussing the strange conversation she had had with Maddie. Seeing his expression as he came towards her, she decided to leave it until later. That time never came. Maddie drifted in and out of consciousness over the next three days. Whatever she had planned to confide to Sophy remained unsaid as she gently drifted away from them.

Luke plunged into depression as soon as her funeral was over. Talking to him about his father drew a blank stare or a numbed shake of his head. Gradually, with the help of anti-depressants, his mood lifted then swung the other way into a continuation of the wild extravagance that would destroy their marriage. She had always taken the naturalness of loving him for granted, never questioning the course their love took as it ran freely through their relationship. Then it was gone. A light switched off so suddenly that it was difficult to find her way forward in the darkness that followed.

She was forced to become his furtive shadow, intent of tracking down the 'other woman'. That night she shadowed him through city streets had been her breaking point. She had watched him enter a hallway that blazed with welcome. When the door closed on him, she saw what she had become: suspicious, jealous, desperate, confused, fearful. And, finally, the truth revealed. Sophy could have endured a flesh and blood rival but his love affair had been with Lady Luck, and there was no coming back from that. All the emotions she had endured had blended together to create a fury that carried her through the months that followed as she forensically dismantled the life they had shared together.

After his visit to Clonmoore, Luke had phoned and demanded to know about her relationship with Victor. She reminded him that he had forfeited the right to ask her such questions. Now, how would he react when he heard they had moved into Victor's house? There was no chance of that information being kept from him. It didn't matter that the circumstances were beyond Sophy's control. The anger he had displayed after Isobel's harmless disclosure would be nothing compared to how he would react to this latest development.

Victor cooked an omelette for her while she was showering. She rummaged in her backpack for jogging pants and a loose top. The girls were sleeping in separate rooms. Sophy removed a book from under Isobel's chin and closed it. Another vampire mystery with a grotesque cover of fangs and dripping blood. The books she borrowed from Clonmoore library all had similar covers, haunted castles, skeletal zombies, vampires and black-winged birds. Shaking her head, she bent and kissed her daughter's cheek. She checked on Julie. Cordelia as always lay beside her.

The omelette, flavoured with herbs, was light and delicious.

'A drink,' he said when she finished eating. 'You look as though you need one.'

He poured brandy into two glasses and sat down beside her on a two-seater sofa.

'I can't thank you enough for helping us tonight,' she said.

'It was the least I could do. I hope what has happened to my uncle won't affect the progress he's made under your care?'

'Jack is stronger than he looks. The damage to his lungs is minimal. They're going to give him a blood transfusion. He was due to have one shortly, anyway. All told, he's lucky Isobel heard what was going on outside. It could have been a different story if he'd been exposed for longer.'

'All thanks to your quick thinking.' He lifted his glass in a toast to her. 'He's lucky to have someone as capable as you to look after him.'

'Capable?' She, too, lifted her glass. 'Is that what you think I am?'

'With him, yes. Capable and caring. You're a woman of many parts, Sophia.'

'Such as?' What was she thinking, making such a remark? He could take it the wrong way, yet she was enjoying the slow play of his eyes on her.

'Charm, passion, courage, devotion, need I go on?' He slid his arm across the back of the sofa. 'But, even with your help, we all know that if Jack survives this shock to his system, he can't go back to Hyland Hall. It's out of the question.'

'Let's see how well he recovers before we make decisions.' She swirled the amber liquid and raised the glass to her lips. 'Have you always lived alone here?'

'Since my parents died, yes.'

'That surprises me.'

'You think I should be married?'

'That's none of my business.'

'I was in a relationship for four years. We ended it mutually but it took a long time before either of us could move on.'

'What went wrong?'

'She demanded more than I was able to give.'

'Demanded?' What had been his breaking point, she wondered?

'She had problems with alcohol.' Victor had picked up on her thoughts. 'Addiction makes demands on those who love the addicted. Her problems became mine and I couldn't handle them anymore. It's hard to explain without sounding selfish, even pitiless.'

'I understand what you mean.' She filled in the silence that followed his admission. 'It's never easy to make such decisions but, sometimes, it's self-survival that drives us there.'

'Was that what brought you to Hyland Hall?'

'I guess.' She hesitated as she realised where the conversation was leading her and drained her glass. '*Wow,*' she gasped as the brandy flamed her throat. 'That's some after-burn.'

'Just take it easy, Sophia, and you'll get used to it,' he said. He was right. The second one went down as smooth as honey.

'My mother-in-law was an amazing person,' she said. 'She reared Luke on her own and built up a successful business.' She had no idea how the conversation turned to Luke and her marriage breakup but she was unable to stop charting each painful phase.

'The signs were there for me to see but there was always something else to distract me from looking,' she admitted. 'In the end, I was slapped in the face, so to speak, with the evidence and my marriage was over.' She faltered, remembering Luke's haunted expression, his bewilderment and shame that he had imposed such a burden on his family. 'I knew Luke was in hell but I was unable to relate to his distress. I should have recognised what was going on but,' she shrugged and laid down her empty glass, 'I didn't.'

'I often find that hindsight equates with guilt,' he said. 'And guilt will always hold us back when we need to move forward.'

'I hope I'm moving forward—'

'Does Luke still belong in your life?' His question startled her.

'He belongs to my past. All I need to do is make peace with it. It's as simple as that.'

'I hope it is.' His fingers gently stroked the back of her neck. 'Sometimes the simplest things are the most difficult to achieve.'

He was right. The fabric of her marriage had been ripped apart so suddenly and savagely that it was impossible to even find the frayed edges.

'Why do you think I want Jack to move into my house?' Victor asked.

'You believe it's more suitable than Hyland Hall.'

'Yes, I do. But there's another reason. You must be aware of it.' His eyes had depths that could sweep her into dangerous currents.

'If Jack agrees to move in here, and there's no guarantee he will, have you enough rooms for all of us?' she asked.

He nodded at the directness of her question. 'Let me put your mind at ease, Sophia. You will have your own room. There are no strings attached to my offer.'

'Why are you being so kind to us?'

'I could pretend it's my good nature but I doubt if you'll believe me.' He brought her hand to his lips. He kissed her palm, her wrist, the crook of her elbow. It seemed so easy, so natural to follow the path along her arm to her shoulder and linger there before moving to her throat. She moaned softly as he pressed his lips to her mouth.

She had discarded her wedding ring. Was she about to discard her wedding vows with the same pent-up passion? Passion of a different kind, driven by pleasure, not fury, and powerful enough for her to hungrily return his kiss. She held his hand when he offered it to her and walked with him towards the stairs.

A king-sized bed with a dark-grey headboard took up the centre of his bedroom. The walls were also grey and the black duvet cover matched the sheets. Wardrobes with mirrored doors covered one wall. It was a masculine room where the only flashes of colour came from a large minimalist painting above his bed. Dazed by the suddenness of her decision, she lay down with him. Amnesia, she could achieve it in his arms, even if only for some brief, overwhelming moments.

Julie's voice reached them from the bedroom next door. Her daughter's ventriloquism was improving yet Sophy knew she would never grow used to the high, artificial voice Julie projected.

'He's a vampire, Julie. Stop pretending you know best.'

'No, he's not, Cordelia,' Julie spoke normally. 'He just got burned in a big fire, that's all.'

'You stupid girl. No wonder Issy laughs at you all the time. Ask her. She'll tell you he's a vampire and his dog's a *real* werewolf with fangs.'

'No, he's *not*. You're stupid, stupid!'

'I need to go to Julie.' She eased from his bed and opened the door. Julie could be heard more clearly now. The bedside lamp was on when Sophy entered the room. Julie was sitting cross-legged on the bed facing Cordelia. She hunched her shoulders when she saw Sophy.

'I'm just telling Cordelia we're living in a new house,' she said. Her face was flushed, her eyes glistening.

'Do you think you could do something for me, Julie?' She was aware that Victor had followed her and was standing behind her, his hands lightly resting on her hips. She moved away from him and sat on Julie's bed. 'Will you let Cordelia sleep on the floor tonight and I'll sleep beside you instead.'

He stood for a moment longer watching them then nodded. 'I'll see you all at breakfast,' he said. 'Sleep well, Sophia.'

He had left for work when she awoke the following morning. She had fallen asleep with her clothes on. Easing from the bed so as not to awaken Julie, she left the room and entered the bathroom. Her lips should be bruised from his kisses, her cheeks suffused with the desire that had raged through her last night before they were interrupted by Julie. The face that reflected back at her was drained of emotion. She was missing an earring. Maddie had given the earrings to her shortly before her death. They had belonged to her own mother who had died when Maddie was a teenager. They were irreplaceable and Sophy treasured them.

Victor's bedroom door was open.

She found the earring on his dressing table. He must have noticed it on the floor and left it there for her. She opened a box on his dressing table. Made from jade, it looked like a present he would receive from a woman. Perhaps his ex-partner had bought it for him. Had she also purchased the elegant tie pins and cufflinks, the watches, the ornately engraved signet ring? She replaced the lid and, gripped by a sudden curiosity, she slid across the wardrobe doors. His suits hung on identical clothes hangers, all facing the same way. His shoes, also, and rows of shirts in different shades. He had used one section of the wardrobe for what must be his 'country' clothes, tweed jackets, casual trousers and check shirts, leather boots and a dark-green, wax jacket. They had the relaxed look of clothes that were well worn yet would never go out of fashion. The country squire, she imagined him striding across Hyland Estate, his gun half-cocked. She had not seen this side of his personality until now yet he fitted the mould perfectly. Town or country, he had the ability to blend into either.

She caught the faint whiff of stale cigarettes. Was he a secret smoker, she wondered? What did she really know about him? She heard footsteps, voices. The girls were awake. What would they think if they saw her in Victor's bedroom? She closed the wardrobe doors and left the room.

Luke phoned in the afternoon. Isobel had been in touch with him. Trust Isobel to embroider the story so elaborately that he was convinced his daughters had almost died from poisonous fumes before Victor rescued them and that they were now living permanently in Mount Eagle. He demanded to know why Sophy had not informed him immediately about their changed circumstances.

His accusatory tone sparked her own anger; an anger that had its roots in guilt as the scene from the previous night played over her mind.

'It's just a temporary arrangement,' she reassured him. 'We're only staying here until we're sure Hyland Hall is safe again.'

'How long will that take?'

'How do I know?'

'Why didn't you bring the girls to a hotel?'

'Don't be ridiculous. It was the middle of the night.'

'What's going on, Sophy? Isobel said she saw you kissing this... this *Victor*.'

'Isobel has a vivid imagination, as you well know. Victor helped us out of a very difficult situation. Living in Hyland Hall is difficult at the best of times and we'll be back there soon enough. I can't believe you'd begrudge your daughters some comfort.'

'Their comfort is all I care about, Sophy.'

'Then you should have thought about that before you made us homeless.' She had hoped that all the bitterness she held was easing but there it was, stark and inflexible. 'In case you've forgotten, you're the reason I was forced to move to Hyland Hall,' she continued. 'I chose to do so because it provided us with a roof over our heads.'

'So, what's Victor Coyne providing—'

She hung up before he finished the question.

He phoned to apologise the following day. He sounded subdued, worried. Was he jealous? Afraid that Victor would replace him in the girls' affections? As if she would allow another man to play a fatherly role in their lives. Since their separation, she had done everything she could not to pass on her anger to them. The number of times she wanted to vent, biting hard on her tongue to hold back a torrent of words that would endanger their bond with him.

They remained in Mount Eagle for a week. Victor made no attempt to rekindle the spark that had flamed briefly on that first night. He was at work during the day and retreated to his home office in the evenings. When Sophy was not at the hospital with Jack, she relaxed on the terrace and in the pool. In the evenings she cooked and when it was time to eat, she called the girls and Victor to the table. They ate in the conservatory. Garden lights glowed in the deepening twilight. The evenings were shortening and it seemed as if the earth had paused to take a breath before summer leached into autumn. As the days and nights passed, the shivering impulse that had led her upstairs and into his bedroom became more unreal, its choreography blurring into a dreamlike dance that had stumbled to a halt.

CHAPTER FIFTEEN

Sophy

Jack was ready to be discharged. He was sitting on the chair beside his bed when Sophy entered the ward, his walking stick clasped in both hands and planted firmly between his feet. No mistaking his determination. He was going home and nothing would stand in his way. He had made that perfectly clear when she spoke to him yesterday about Mount Eagle. No right time, as Victor had said, just lost time but she had waited until he was strong enough to listen to what his nephew had proposed.

'How would you consider moving in with Victor for the winter?' She had spoken carefully, her senses alert to his changing moods. 'He thinks you'd be more comfortable living with him, even if it's only for a few months. He has space for all of us and I think you'd be much safer there.'

'When it comes to my business, I'm not paying you to think,' he'd snapped in reply.

'But you are paying me to look after your welfare.' She had been taken aback by his abruptness. 'Look at everything that's happened. The dumps, the ceiling collapsing. The house is damp and needs to be insulated. Victor's house would be much more accessible for you and a much healthier, safer environment.'

'I appreciate that you'd like to improve your life, and that of your daughters, by moving into Mount Eagle but that's not going to happen if you want to continue working for me.'

'That's unfair, Jack.' She was stung by his comment. 'My concern for you is based purely on my professional opinion.'

'You're a good nurse but a hopeless liar,' he brusquely interrupted her. 'Have your feelings for Victor blinded you to the fact that you and I signed a contract in good faith?'

'Victor hasn't blinded me. That's a ridiculous comment to make.' Her voice rose defensively. 'His offer makes perfect sense. Why are you always so rude to him? He's your only nephew, your own flesh and blood—'

'Flesh and blood, indeed.' He had pushed up the sleeve of his pyjamas and held his withered arm towards her. 'Look at me. Not much flesh there, wouldn't you agree? As for blood, have you any idea how many transfusions I've had? I'm only alive because I carry the blood of strangers in my veins. The only way I'll move out of my home is in a box. I won't keep you in Hyland Hall against your will. If you decide to leave, I'll pay you the full terms we agreed on for the duration of your stay.'

'Are you firing me?'

'That's not my intention. I've come to rely on you but I need to know I can trust you.'

'Have I given you reason to doubt me?'

'That depends. How do I know you're not plotting with him against me?'

'There's no plotting going on.' She was alarmed at how agitated he had become. 'I'd never have suggested the move if I'd known how strongly you feel about Hyland Hall.'

'How strongly did you feel about losing your home?'

'I'd no choice but to sell it.'

'Thanks to your husband.'

'I'd rather not discuss my marriage if you don't mind.'

'I'm aware that you're hurt and angry with him. It makes you vulnerable—'

'Don't patronise me, Jack.'

'Was it a good marriage before his gambling took over?'

Had he any awareness of personal boundaries, she wondered? Did he appreciate the recurring tension that shivered through her whenever she thought about Luke? She was relieved when a nurse entered the ward to check his temperature. Taking this as her cue, Sophy had left before he could continue their conversation.

Later that night, Victor had accepted his uncle's decision with a resigned shrug. Isobel had protested loudly about having to move back to Hyland Hall and Julie had hidden her own feelings behind Cordelia's whiny complaints. It would be difficult to settle them back into the old house after their week of luxury but the sooner life settled back to normal, the better.

She had arrived to the hospital at the agreed time for Jack's discharge yet his impatience as he rose unsteadily to his feet seemed to suggest she had kept him waiting.

'It's a long walk to the elevator,' she said. 'I'll organise a wheelchair for you.'

'I'll manage.' He leant heavily on his stick as they made their way from the ward. He was silent on the journey home. She tuned the car radio to Southern Stream. As usual, Gavin Darcy was presenting Afternoon Stream with a mix of music and local information. Jack had an internet radio but the local radio station was the only one he ever wanted to hear.

Charlie was waiting at Hyland Hall with Caesar to greet him. Shortly afterwards, she collected the girls from Mount Eagle.

Only Cordelia was smiling as they entered the old house and slouched into the den. As Isobel said loudly enough for Sophy to hear, 'We journeyed to heaven but have returned to live in hell.'

The memory of Mount Eagle and its comforts faded quickly as they resumed their normal routine. School would begin in another week. Sophy collected Isobel's uniforms from Doretha's Drapery on Lower Main Street and hung it beside Julie's in the wardrobe.

Jack's latest brush with death appeared to have galvanised him into action. A team of workers came to Hyland Hall to insulate the house and repair the long-neglected central heating system. A new manager had been hired to look after the estate and would move into the gate lodge as soon as it was habitable. Benedict Hancock, Jack's solicitor, arrived one afternoon by appointment. She led him upstairs and into the living room.

Later, when she rapped on the door, the solicitor's voice reached her. 'It's a simple will yet watertight,' he said. 'There can be no arguments over your next of kin's inheritance and if—' He stopped when Jack called out to Sophy to enter.

They had been discussing Jack's last will and testament. His inflexible countenance gave nothing away yet she sensed that he was disconcerted by her appearance. He nodded at her to leave the tray of coffee and fresh scones Ellie had baked on the small table beside him. Billy, Charlie's nephew, who was overseeing the central heating, was sitting at the bureau with a pen in his hand. Charlie stood beside him and had probably already signed as a witness.

She apologised for disturbing them and hurried from the room. Victor would have to continue enduring his uncle's unpredictable moods but he would be well rewarded when Jack died.

He was in London on business and had sounded stressed when he rang her that previous evening. An unfamiliar edginess to his voice as he spoke about the demanding meetings he had to attend. He was working on an important property deal. She had seen his office on Upper Main Square. The sign *Victor Coyne, Property Analyst and Developer* was displayed in large lettering on the front of the building.

What does a property analyst do, she had asked him once? He had talked at length about property trends and financial forecasts that could be the deciding factor for property developers and investors.

The girls were in bed and she had settled Jack for the night when he called to Hyland Hall on his way home from the airport. He removed a bottle of wine from a carrier bag and filled two glasses.

'How is Jack?' he asked.

'Recovering well.'

'I'm glad to hear it. Have you settled back since your return?'

'It's difficult,' she admitted. 'You spoiled us.'

'It was my pleasure. The house seems much emptier now that you and the girls have left.'

'They loved living there.'

'And you?' He held a glass up to the light and studied the burgundy hue before handing it to her.

'Yes, of course I did. You have a fabulous house.'

'That's not what I'm asking you.'

'What are you asking me?'

'That first night… you remember?'

She nodded and waited for him to continue.

'I was afraid you might think I was taking advantage of you. That's why I didn't… well, you know?'

Unable to meet his gaze, she bent her head. Was she falling in love with him? The consequences, what would they be? But why must she always think ahead, plan, consider, endeavour to make the right decisions?

'I wanted you,' he said. 'Every time you brushed past me, I had to stop myself reaching out to you. At night, lying in the room next to yours was torture. You've no idea how often I stood outside the door willing you to open it and come to me. I've never felt like this before, Sophia…'

Spent passion, how easily it was forgotten. But passion still to be released was a dangerous lure. Uncaring of the consequences, she stopped his words with kisses. The girls were sleeping on the other side of the corridor. Jack was probably still awake but desire blasted such thoughts from her mind. He carried her to the sofa. Her tunic, unbuttoned, was flung to the floor, and, then, they were moving together, lips and fingers exploring, zips opening, hooks unhooked, elastic snapping and yielding. Her legs lifted to encircle him but their breathless, stifled gasps were not loud enough to silence the determined thud from above.

She stopped, aware that she was naked and exposed. Jack Hyland was demanding her attention and reminding her that she was his employee.

'Ignore him…' Victor pressed his hands to her ears but she was already struggling to be free, grabbing her discarded underwear, her hands shaking as she tried to fasten her bra. With her cheeks flaming and her lips swollen, how could she face him?

Somehow, she stumbled up the stairs and into his bedroom. The bed was empty. She found him at his desk in the living room, his dressing gown loosely tied around his gaunt frame. The gleam in his eye was fierce.

'Send my nephew away,' he said. 'I don't want him sneaking around my house behind my back.'

She resisted a wild desire to laugh out loud and pulled at the edges of her tunic, how she hated its crisp whiteness, now creased and buttoned askew. She pushed her hair back from her forehead. Pulled loose by Victor from the ties that that held it in place, it tumbled over her shoulders and veiled the colour on her cheeks. She tensed as the front door slammed. Victor was leaving without saying goodbye.

'You should be in bed, Jack,' she said. 'You're still very weak. Leave your writing until you're stronger.'

'Are you still in love with your husband?' His rasping voice was harder than ever to understand.

'What did you say?'

'Do you still love Luke?'

He enraged her with his blunt questions. 'I don't love anyone except my daughters.'

'Do you blame him for forcing you to put up with this cantankerous old fool?'

'I make my own decisions, Jack.'

'How is Luke?'

'Lost.' The word came unbidden to her and he nodded, as if he understood. 'It's a long journey back. My brother was a gambler. He carried his addiction with him to his grave.'

'I'm afraid Luke will do the same.'

'If you think that, you'll never be able to trust him again. Don't you believe in redemption?'

'He must look after his own redemption.'

'What about forgiveness?'

'No more questions tonight, Jack. You need to rest.'

He closed his journal and pulled down the lid on his bureau. He was stiff when he stood. She imagined his skin stretching, the pain it caused him. It was difficult to remain annoyed with him. His shoulders slumped as he crossed the floor to his armchair and lowered himself into it. A memory of Maddie came to mind, her grim resilience during her final months as she fought pain with her willpower and the same defiance Jack Hyland continued to display.

Victor had replaced the scattered cushions on the sofa and the music room had an unruffled appearance when she returned downstairs. Dizzy, reckless madness. Was she so hungry for attention that she would fall in love – no, not love, lust – with the first man to cross her path since Luke left? She needed to find her own way back from their break-up. Love on the rebound had no substance and could, like her marriage, be founded on quicksand.

Over the following days, Jack continued his struggle to regain his strength, placing one foot in front of the other as he crossed the courtyard and reached the avenue, celebrating each small triumph with a raised fist. He was determined to push his body to the limit of his endurance and on a sigh of pain he could still move Sophy from anger to tenderness and pity.

CHAPTER SIXTEEN

Isobel

'I see you have quite an interest in the Gothic,' Debbie Gibson, the librarian in Clonmoore Library, remarked when Isobel stopped at her desk. 'Vampires are very popular subject matter for authors at the moment.'

'Do you believe in them?' Isobel asked.

'There are a few bloodsuckers around here all right.' Debbie laughed as she stamped the books Isobel had borrowed. 'They come out at night but whiskey is their tipple, not blood.'

'So, you don't *really* believe they exist?'

'I was terrified by the thought of vampires when I was small,' Debbie admitted. 'I stopped believing in them when I was ten. To be honest, I still enjoy a good horror story. That's why the Horror and Fantasy section is so well stocked. But we also have a diverse selection of contemporary fiction for young adults if you'd like to try something different for a change.'

'Maybe next time,' Isobel promised. It would have been a relief to confide in Debbie but the librarian hadn't believed in vampires since she was ten and would think Isobel's suspicions were ridiculous.

'Don't you want to use the computer?' Debbie asked before Isobel left.

'Not today,' she replied. Or any other day, she thought as she placed her books in her bike pannier. She cycled past The Queen of Angels Secondary School. August was drawing to a close. Soon she would enter those gates as the new girl in town. Her uniform was hanging in the wardrobe. Grey, cream and maroon – the three colours she hated most.

A van with a sign on the side that read Bracken Plumbing passed her out on Marsh Road. She followed it to the Hyland Hall entrance gates. A second van was parked outside the gate lodge and two men in jeans, hi-vis jackets and hard hats waved as she cycled past. The gate lodge had a new red door. It still looked like it belonged in a fairy story filled with evil but the boards had been removed from the windows and latticed panes of glass installed. Her mother said The Recluse was going to hire security to stop the fly tippers returning. What about security for us, Isobel wondered? A silver bullet, a crucifix, holy water, garlic. A stake through his heart.

Two weeks had passed since that awful night when she and Julie had fled from the poisonous fumes to the shelter of Mount Eagle. The Recluse had been given more blood and had returned to Hyland Hall stronger and more powerful than ever. All thanks to her. By saving his life she had helped him to defy death for the *fourth* time.

She continued up the avenue until she reached a gap in the trees. On impulse, she cycled into the woods and followed a path through the trees. Some of them were leafless and bleached of colour, their skeletal branches reminding her of withered limbs. She emerged into a swaying sea of long grass. It needed mowing but it was clear from its length and breadth that she had reached Hyland Gallops. Charlie said the jockeys used to exercise the horses there and that Hyland Stables had once been famous for training champion racehorses. Even here, there was evidence that rubbish had been dumped and cleared away. The enormous ring of rotting, yellow grass reminded Isobel of entrails, not that she had ever seen any, but that must be what they looked like. Something that was hidden and then exposed in all its glistening ugliness. Seagulls dived towards the mulching circle and scavenged for worms. The smell was still there, like it had become part of the earth.

She stood on a lake shore and watched the swans. Moorhens stretched their necks as they sought shelter in the whispering reeds. A small island in the centre of the lake reminded her of a hulking, mottled-green tortoise. The shore was marshy and her trainers were soon covered in mud. Aware that she was sinking in the mire, she pulled free from its clutches and moved back onto firmer ground. In the distance she saw a building with a high domed roof. Drawing closer, she realised it was a derelict boathouse. An old, broken boat lay sideways by the edge of a wooden jetty. Slats were missing and the wood was covered in moss. A wide arch framed the entrance to the boathouse. Cobwebs swung like hammocks from the ceiling and bundles of reeds, tied with twine, were propped against the walls.

The gloomy interior matched her mood. She could no longer pretend that her friends missed her or cared that she was stuck in hell. No one had 'liked' her ghost pictures or sent laughing emoticons after they read what she wrote about growing roots and turning into a tree.

Joanne had advised her to 'stop obsessing about the past' in their last Snapchat. Only three months had passed since she was at the centre of her friends' lives but, now, she belonged to their past. She stood under the arch and shouted out their names – Joanne, Sarah, Lisa, Magda – and when the echo of their names had faded, she knew the time had come to let them go.

A rumbling sound reached her. A tractor or a lorry, she thought as she emerged from the gloom of the boathouse. Had the fly tippers returned? She eased around the side wall to check. Charlie was driving his hearse across the Gallops. She sheltered behind the boathouse until it came to a stop on the far side of the jetty. A door opened and a girl, who looked to be about her own age, jumped down. She was wearing dungarees with rips and her short, spiky hair was dyed purple. She strode into the boathouse and was followed shortly afterwards by Charlie. They emerged with bundles of reeds in their arms. Isobel remained hidden while they carried them from the boathouse and arranged them carefully in the back of the hearse where coffins usually rested. She could hear them talking. Charlie called the girl Kelly. She must be his granddaughter. Her parents had also split up and she had spent the summer in Australia with her father.

Charlie had many grandchildren but his voice was always extra loving when he spoke about Kelly. He seemed to believe that she had lots in common with Isobel and hoped they would become friends when she returned home. Having part-time dads was hardly a reason to exchange friendship bracelets, Isobel thought as she watched Kelly striding between the hearse and the boathouse. She looked so confident, like she was completely at ease in her surroundings and was not afraid of anything. Julie – who had become a purveyor of gossip from the pony club – had told her that Kelly Bracken was called 'Freak' behind her back because she touched dead people and wanted to be an undertaker when she left school.

A rat emerged from a tussock of sedge and ran past Isobel. Unable to hold back a shriek, she jumped into view just as Charlie was emerging from the boathouse with another armful of reeds.

'What are you doing here, Isobel?' he asked.

She was used to his smiles but, today, his expression was stern.

'Saying goodbye to my past,' she replied.

'Well, young lady, I suggest you find somewhere safer than this dangerous place to do so.'

'What are you doing here?'

'I'm collecting reeds. The best ones grow by the lake shore and make ideal coffins.' He said 'coffins' as casually as he would say 'basket' or 'cradle' and added that the reeds were perfect for weaving eco-friendly ones.

The meaning of the words she had read in The Recluse's journal came back to Isobel with shocking clarity. *When the time comes, Charlie will weave my final resting place from the reeds he gathers by the lake. I no longer fear death now that I know my essence will live on in another form.* What form would that take? A flapping cloak and fangs? Knowing she was being ridiculous did nothing to banish this appalling image. Unsuspectingly, she had performed her 'breaking away from her past' ritual while standing in a place of death.

Charlie's granddaughter, who had joined them, seemed amused by her horrified expression. When Charlie introduced then, she just nodded dismissively at Isobel and continued loading the hearse.

'Off you go now and stay away from here,' said Charlie.

Isobel didn't need a second warning. The wind shook the long grass and flurried the lake as she fled across the Gallops to the protection of the trees.

'It all starts here, girls.' Sophy parked beside the Hyland Estate signpost, where they would be picked up by the school bus. 'New school, new friends, new adventures.' Thankfully, the bus came into view and Isobel could escape her mother's dreaded platitudes.

'Morning, cubs,' the driver shouted when the doors slid open. 'First timers, eh?' His stomach strained against the buttons on his shirt and his flushed face split into a welcoming grin. 'Right then, no dilly-dallying. My name's Arthur and the sooner you come on board, the sooner you'll make friends with this gang of ruffians behind me.'

The 'gang of ruffians' were silent as she and Julie walked down the aisle of the bus. They had planned to sit together but only two single seats were free. Julie took the first one and sat beside her friend from the pony club. Isobel stopped midway down the aisle when she realised that the only available empty seat was beside Kelly Bracken.

'No standing allowed,' Arthur bellowed into his microphone when Isobel hesitated, her eyes darting right and left in the hope of finding another seat. 'You, Newbie! Sit down immediately.'

Kelly was dressed like everyone else in the Queen of Angels school uniform but that was where the resemblance ended. She had changed her hair from purple to tangerine and she was wearing a lip ring, black lipstick and eyeliner. Long, dangling earrings with skulls hung from her ears and an angel carrying a sword was tattooed on her cheek. Has she noticed Isobel's hesitation? Hopefully not. She was reading a book and paid no attention to Isobel when she eased in beside her. Isobel sneaked a look at the title. *A Thousand Splendid Suns* by Khaled Hosseini. She remembered her father reading it and recommending it to her mother. That was in the 'before' time when she believed all stories had happy endings. She opened her own book, *A Coffin Opens at Midnight,* and pretended to read.

'I read that when I was nine,' said Kelly. 'Even then, I knew it was unadulterated rubbish.' Her contemptuous tone made Isobel blush.

'I don't remember asking for your opinion,' she retorted.

'I'm just saying…' Kelly shrugged and returned to her own book.

She was right. *A Coffin Opens at Midnight* was rubbish but Isobel kept turning the pages in case Kelly was watching. They never spoke for the rest of the journey.

'Two minutes left!' Arthur announced into his microphone when he reached the outskirt of Clonmoore. 'Remove all chewing gum from your mouths but don't you dare, under pain of death, leave it stuck anywhere on my bus. Put away your comics, switch off your mobiles, ipads and Nintendos. And you, Kelly Bracken, get your act together if you don't want to start the new term with detention.'

Kelly removed her earrings. The lip ring also disappeared into her schoolbag and she peeled the tattoo from her cheek. A transfer, that's all it was. When the bus pulled up outside the two schools, the only sign left of Kelly's former image was her tangerine hair and her withering stare when Isobel snapped *A Coffin Opens at Midnight* closed. She strode ahead of Isobel towards the entrance to the Queen of Angels and was soon swallowed in a heaving tide of maroon, grey and cream.

Isobel's shoulders were stiff from holding them erect as the days passed. She was polite yet distant to the pupils who spoke to her and made excuses when they asked her to join their table during lunch break. She heard the words 'posh bitch' being muttered between two girls who sat close to her in Maths and knew they were referring to her. Let them think what they liked. Friendship sucked. She had been abandoned once by her friends and she had no intention of making new ones. At break and lunch, she sat alone in the school canteen. Kelly also sat by herself. She was a loner who didn't care what people thought about her; an outsider who delighted in being different. Isobel had always been a part of everything at her last school. Now, she didn't know where she belonged and it was the loneliest feeling in the world.

To add to her misery, she discovered that her mother was going on an actual *date* with Victor Coyne. He was taking her to the Silver Spoon, the poshest restaurant in Clonmoore.

CHAPTER SEVENTEEN

Sophy

Brendan Boyle, the owner of The Silver Spoon restaurant, escorted them to their table. He was one of Victor's closest friends and his greeting was effusive. Holding Sophy's hands in a warm clasp, he joked about the impact she was having on Victor. What had he said to Brendan about her? His expression gave nothing away yet every touch and glance reminded her of those wanton kisses in the music room, their entangled bodies, the swooning desire that had banished all rational thought from her mind.

'Compliments of the house.' Brendan presented them with a bottle of red wine and made a slight bow to Sophy. 'I'm delighted to welcome you to The Silver Spoon.'

The wine was expensive, she could tell by Victor's appreciative glance at the label. Brendan opened the bottle with an experienced flourish and asked her to sample the wine. She swirled the glass and sniffed the plumy aroma, aware that the two men were waiting for her reaction.

'It's perfect,' she said and the restaurateur nodded, as if any other reply was impossible, then left them to enjoy their meal.

Their faces glowed in the candlelight as they discussed films that they had both enjoyed, music they had loved as teenagers. They fell silent when the waiter arrived to clear away the dishes from their first course. The background music was unobtrusive yet it quivered through her when their knees touched under the table. Waiters nodded and smiled at Victor as they passed by. He knew them by name and it was obvious from their reaction that he was recognised as an important man in this close-knit community.

'Does Jack know you're out with me tonight?' he asked when their main course arrived, a fillet steak for him, pan-fried monkfish for her.

'Yes. Charlie agreed to stay with him and keep an eye on the girls.'

'Charlie is invaluable to him.'

'I don't know how Jack would cope without him.'

'They were boyhood friends,' Victor said. 'Not that Jack gave much thought to Charlie after he left here. Or to anyone in his family for that matter.'

'Not even Laurence?' She was surprised by his comment. 'Twins are usually so close.'

'No one gets close to Jack. You must be aware of that by now.'

'He's difficult, I admit but—'

'Do we have to discuss him tonight?'

'No, of course not,' she replied. 'Tell me more about Laurence. Jack said he was a gambler.'

'That's another one of his delusions.' His steak had been served rare and the tender meat quivered under his knife. 'Laurence liked an occasional flutter on the horses, nothing more than that.'

'He was obviously a very important person in your life.'

He nodded. 'My father was a workaholic who was either abroad on business or working late,' he said. 'My mother suffered with depression. Hyland Hall was my home-from-home. A place where I was always made welcome. Some change, eh?' He shrugged and laid down his cutlery. 'Forget about Jack. I'd much rather talk about us.'

'But why is he always so hostile towards you?' Better to steer the conversation back to his uncle than deal with a question she was not yet ready to address. She was still a married woman so, technically speaking, was she having an affair with him? And what defined an affair? Was it those few tumultuous moments on the sofa? Or the longing that would take hold of her, forcing her to a dazed standstill in the midst of the most mundane chores?

His fingers moved across the white tablecloth and came to rest above her hand. The light pressure of his skin against hers swept her again into the rawness of these new emotions.

'I'm not going to spoil our night by dragging up my family's past history,' he said. 'It's not a particularly edifying story.'

'If you want to talk about that history, I'm happy to listen, especially if it explains why you and Jack are always at such odds with each other.'

He turned his attention to his food. She thought he was going to ignore her offer until he swallowed and cleared his throat.

'Did you know that the twins were only twenty when their parents died in a car crash?' he asked.

'I'd no idea.' Shocked by his revelation, she shot back in her chair. 'What an appalling tragedy.'

'According to my mother, it brought Clonmoore to a standstill on the day of their funeral.'

'They were obviously important people in the community.'

'Yes, they were. And still in their prime of life. My mother's inheritance was the market garden. The twins inherited Hyland Stables and what was left of Hyland Estate.'

'Poor boys. They were so young to be landed with such responsibilities.'

'Jack had no interest in remaining there. He threatened to sell his share of the land if Laurence didn't buy him out. Laurence had to borrow heavily to do so and, once the deal was done, Jack left. No contact, nothing until he showed up out of the blue when Laurence was dying. That was my first time to meet him.'

'How sad to meet under such circumstances.'

'I'd moved into Hyland Hall to look after Laurence. His only wish was to die in his own home. Jack insisted on taking over his care as soon as he arrived and ordered me to leave. The next time I saw Laurence, he was in his coffin.'

'That's hard to believe,' she gasped. 'I'd no idea Jack could be so cruel.'

He lifted the wine bottle and refilled her glass. She was surprised to see how much the level had dropped. After one half glass of wine, Victor had ordered sparkling water with ice for himself, claiming drink driving regulations.

'From the time I was a boy, Laurence had told me Hyland Estate would be mine one day.' The ice clinked when he raised his glass to his lips. He winced, as if he had triggered a nerve in his tooth, then laid the glass carefully back on the table. 'Instead, Jack inherited everything.'

'You must have been absolutely devastated,' she said. The dense texture of the monkfish had been pleasantly flavoured with herbs and lemon yet she found it difficult to chew.

'I knew Laurence would only have changed his will under extreme coercion from Jack and, yes, I was devastated,' he admitted.

'Have you any proof that Jack put that kind of pressure on him?'

'Nothing that would stand up in court. I'm not sure how relevant all this is...' He paused, as if considering whether or not to continue. His steak must be growing cold but he made no further attempt to eat it. What tactics had Jack used to coerce his brother when he was on his deathbed? She imagined him as he was then, a strong and forceful personality who brooked no opposition.

'Laurence and I had planned a joint venture with a group of property investors,' said Victor. 'He was to sell Hyland Estate and I'd sell what was left of my grandmother's market garden. That's the waste land beyond the copse of trees.'

She nodded. 'I know where you mean.'

'Our lands were to be sold as a single parcel. Everything was organised to go ahead but, then, Laurence became seriously ill. He still insisted on continuing with the sale. We were about to sign the contract when Jack turned up.' He glanced worriedly at her. 'We're supposed to be enjoying ourselves, Sophia. Are you sure you want me to go on?'

'Yes.' She nodded. 'I want to hear what happened.'

The noise in the restaurant had increased after a group of men had been seated close to them. Golfers on an outing, they were winding down after eighteen holes and their loudness forced him to lean towards her.

'After the reading of the will, I had to swallow my anger and make an approach to Jack. I'd heard he was anxious to move on again and that he planned to sell the estate. He asked to see the documentation relating to the venture and agreed that we should proceed as planned. The only difference was that he insisted on taking full control of the negotiations.' He paused and pushed his plate to one side.

'Then the fire broke out. That changed everything. The man who came back from the dead, so to speak, was unrecognisable. It wasn't only his body that was damaged. Despite occasional flashes of lucidity, his mind had gone. Since then, he claims to have no memory of our agreement. All he wants to do is live in the past and revive Hyland Hall. Every time I visit him, he wants to discuss another crazy scheme that hasn't a chance of succeeding.' His face tautened and for an instant she glimpsed a different Victor than the suave personality she had come to know. 'I hoped that if he moved in with me, it would break his preoccupation with the past. But you saw his reaction when you suggested it. And this new manager he intends to hire worries me.'

'It's for security—' she began.

'No, that's not what it's about.' He dismissed her explanation with a shake of his head. 'This is something bigger than stopping a few fly tippers. Whatever he's planning, it's going to affect me.'

'How badly affected?' she asked.

'I'm hoping to become a partner in this venture. To make that investment, I need the money from the sale of my land to do so. However, the investors are only interested in the sale if Jack's land is included.'

'What about the documentation—'

'I searched for it when he was in hospital and couldn't find it. He'd left everything in a safe somewhere in Hyland Hall. Since then, I suspect he's shredded all the evidence that we'd ever agreed on a deal.'

'Does he have any other relatives who could inherit his estate?' she asked.

'No.' He shook his head vehemently. 'There's just the two of us but family means nothing to him.'

'I disagree,' she said. 'Hyland Estate will belong to you when he dies. If you can hold off your investors for a while, you'll be able to go ahead with your plans.'

'He'll probably live to be a hundred and leave everything to a cats' and dogs' home.'

'Not according to what I overheard from Jack's solicitor. The cats' and dogs' home will have to wait for another benefactor.' She tried to humour him but his expression didn't soften. The revelations about Jack and his callousness had spoiled the mood that had carried them through the earlier part of the night.

'What exactly did you hear?' he asked.

'I probably shouldn't have said anything about it.' She shook her head nervously. The wine was going to her head and she was already regretting her words. A watertight will that would effortlessly transfer Jack's estate to his next of kin, Benedict Hancock had said. Who else but Victor could inherit all his uncle possessed?

'Hyland Estate will pass directly to Jack's next of kin.'

'How can you be so sure?' Victor's intensity unnerved her, all his hopes hanging on a few words she had overheard.

Before she could reply, Brendan came to their table to enquire if there was anything wrong with their food.

'Our meals are delicious,' Victor said. 'But Sophia is proving to be too much of a distraction.' His smile embraced her as he poured the remains of the wine into her glass.

'I'd love to believe what you've told me is true,' he said when their plates had been cleared away. 'But I know how my uncle's mind works. I'd need to see the evidence with my own eyes before I could believe it.'

Surrounded by plush wall hangings, intimate lighting and attentive staff, Sophy had no reason to feel uneasy over the direction their conversation had taken yet it worried her.

'Are you asking me to search for it?' She put the question bluntly to him.

You'd do that for me?' He pursed his lips, his head tilted to one side.

'I'm not sure—'

'If I could prove for definite that my inheritance is secure, the start date can be stalled for a while longer. Hancock will have the will in his office but, knowing Jack, he'll have taken a copy of it. If I could get a photograph… He paused then shook his head. 'Forget it.' He spoke decisively. 'I won't let you do anything that would put your job in jeopardy.'

'How long can you stall the investors for?'

She knew the answer, of course. He was waiting for his uncle to die. He laid his hands flat on the table and pressed the tips of his fingers together.

'As his nurse, you're in a better position than I am to know the answer to that question, Sophia.'

The high wail of the violin and the deep pluck of the cello filled the silence as he waited for her reply.

'I can't predict how long Jack will live,' she said. 'I'm not even prepared to hazard a guess.'

He nodded. 'I shouldn't have expected any other answer from you. I apologise for putting you in an awkward position and spoiling our night.'

'It wasn't spoiled… I'm just sorry Jack has given you so much grief. What are your investors hoping to build on the land?'

'An out-of-town retail centre,' he replied. 'It promises to be a massive development.'

'Won't a retail centre have an impact on the town?'

'A positive impact. Think of the employment opportunities it will bring to Clonmoore. That was Laurence's dream for his community.'

'What will happen if this deal falls through?'

'My reputation will be ruined. I might as well close my company down right now.' His smile was forced. 'We've gone down quite a labyrinth tonight and it's all my fault. Will you come back to my house for a nightcap? I swear it will be a Jack-free Zone.'

'I'm anxious about the girls,' she said. 'They're not used to being left on their own. And I promised Charlie I wouldn't be late.'

'Another time?'

'I hope so.'

'I've been giving out all night about Jack yet we'd never have met if it wasn't for him. Do you remember that first time when I came to Hyland Hall?'

'When I was covered in soot and tears, do you mean?'

He nodded and laughed. 'You were still beautiful, Sophia. Do you believe in fate?'

'I'm not sure I do.'

'Nor did I, until that night.' He spoke softly, persuasively. 'I can't even begin to imagine what you went through before I met you. I'm not putting any pressure on you but once I have some hope that you're ready to move on, I'm content to wait on the side-lines for as long as it takes.

Jack was sleeping when she entered his bedroom. Caesar lifted his heavy head and gave a low growl of welcome. She bent and stroked his head, settled him back again into his basket before entering Jack's living room. The old-fashioned bureau with its roll-up lid was a beautiful piece of antique furniture but like everything else in Hyland Hall, it bore the brunt of neglect and woodworm. It was balanced on either side by two rows of drawers with brass handles. The writing desk with its green, leather surface slid out when a release button was pressed. A series of small, scalloped compartments ran across the upper section of the bureau. Underneath, files were stored in wooden partitions.

She searched the drawers and compartments for an envelope that could contain a copy of Jack's last will and testament. More than likely, he would have placed such an important document in a safe, as Victor had stated. She noticed a small, glittering object on one of the top sections. Lifting it out, she realised it was made from gold. Its shape was unrecognisable, twisted and bulging golden coils with faint veins of red radiating from the core. She couldn't tell what it was, perhaps a tiny sculpture. If it was sculptured, the mind that shaped it must have been tormented, she thought, as she reached forward to replace it.

'Sophy, what are you doing?' The question, sharp as the tip of an arrow, came from behind her.

Her hands stiffened as she turned her head, defenceless against his piercing one-eyed gaze.

'I'm sorry, Jack. I didn't mean to awaken you. I was just tidying your desk and I noticed this... this sculpture.' She stopped, knowing how absurd such an explanation sounded in the middle of the night.

He walked stiffly towards her and took the sculpture from her. 'Like humans, gold has many faces.' He displayed it on the palm of his hand. 'Even when it is distorted and melted by fire to a hideous form, it will always be gold. The beauty of ugliness, I call it.'

Was he talking about his own wracked features? Unable to understand him, she said, 'It's such an extraordinary shape. What is it?'

'A memory that was stolen from me on the night of the fire,' he replied.

'I don't understand.'

'In time, I hope you will,' he replied as he replaced it in the bureau. 'You had an enjoyable night with my nephew, I presume?'

'The food at The Silver Spoon was wonderful.'

'That's not what I asked? Are you in love with him?' His bluntness no longer surprised her.

'You've no right to ask that question, Jack. My personal life is my business.'

'But it's okay for you to invade mine at his behest.'

It was too late to pretend she was doing anything other than searching through his private correspondence. 'You're wrong. Victor has nothing to do with this. *Nothing*, do you understand?'

'Then, tell me truthfully, what were you looking for?'

Her eyes lit on his journal. 'I'm curious about what you're writing. I know so little about you.'

'Did you read it?'

'I was just about to open it when you came in.'

'You'll find nothing inside but the ramblings of an old man.'

'You're not old—'

'Don't try to flatter me. The fire wiped out those years that were to come.'

'The time you have left could be happier if you'd make peace with Victor.'

She had learnt to identify signs of pain on his countenance or from the way he held his body. He was suffused with it as he pulled down the lid of the bureau.

'Can I offer you a word of advice, Sophy? Don't interfere in issues that concern my nephew and me.'

'You treat him shamefully, Jack.'

'Mark my words, Sophy, all you will ever be to Victor Coyne is a conduit to me. I'm going to bed now. Don't come with me. I'm capable of looking after myself.'

Filled with rage and embarrassment, she was unable to reply. How much longer could she continue working for him? She followed him to his bedroom and made sure he was comfortable before going downstairs and tossing sleeplessly until the early hours.

The following morning, he was subdued when she brought him his breakfast.

'I apologise for last night,' he said. 'I overreacted. I'd like to explain my reasons—'

'You don't have to explain. I'd no right to check your journal.'

'This face…' He raised his hands to his cheeks with such ferocity she was afraid he would scratch his fragile skin. 'It's a mask I can't take off. Words form in my mind but they're not the ones I speak. Only when I write, do they make sense. The fire…' His voice shook. 'I lost so much that night. I need you here. Please tell me you'll stay.'

*

It was evident from Victor's flushed expression the following evening that his visit to Jack had not gone well.

'How long has he been behaving this way?' he asked when he entered the kitchen.

'What way?' Sophy stopped setting the table and pulled out a chair for him.

'His confusion is worse than ever.'

'Whatever he said to you, ignore it,' she advised. 'He insisted on going outside for a walk on his own tonight and he's exhausted.'

'I'm used to his behaviour. But it's different when he starts insulting you.' He paused and shook his head. 'I apologise on his behalf if he's offended you.'

'What did he say?'

'He thinks I'm brainwashing you. It's gibberish, nothing more, nothing less.'

'What else?'

'Honestly, Sophia, you don't want to know. He's losing the ability to control his thoughts. What comes into his mind comes out of his mouth. It doesn't make for pleasant listening.'

'It's important that I understand what's going on in his mind. What were his exact words?'

'He called you low-hanging fruit, easily plucked.'

'He *actually* said that?' She reached upwards towards the dresser and removed plates. So that was what Jack Hyland thought of her. An apple, plump and ripe, waiting to be plucked. 'Is there anything else I should know?'

'I've upset you, I'm sorry.' He sounded more embarrassed than angry. 'That's nothing compared to what he says about me. Crazy accusations that have no basis in reality. Let's not talk about him anymore tonight.'

'He claims that all I am to you is a conduit to him.' She was unable to drop the subject. 'In other words, he believes you're using me.'

'When did he make such a ludicrous remark?'

'When he found me searching for his will last night.'

'Did you find it?' He exhaled slowly as he waited for her reply.

'I only had time to check his bureau. He was furious when he discovered what I was doing—'

'Did he harm you? If he laid a hand on you—'

'Why should he harm me?'

'I know how aggressive he can become. I've had to deal with his violence in the past.'

'Jack has never shown any sign of being violent to me,' she said. 'He's rude, admittedly, and blunt. Was he telling the truth when he described me as your conduit?'

'Was he telling the truth when he called you a gold digger and accused you of whoring your way into my affections?'

'Those were his words?'

He nodded. 'Ignore what he says, Sophia. He'll need psychiatric help soon and we'll cope with that when the time comes. What are you cooking?' He sniffed the air. 'It smells delicious.'

'Lamb tagine.'

'Ah.'

'Would you like to eat with us?' Did he notice her lack of enthusiasm when he accepted her invitation? Instead of trying to make conversation across the table with him, she wanted to go into a quiet space and reflect on her future at Hyland Hall. Victor's excuse that his uncle was suffering from dementia had done nothing to soften the brutality of his insults. His phrases were seared on her brain. *Gold digger.* The term had a vicious sting, unlike 'low hanging fruit,' which was simply a pathetic insult. 'Whoring' her way into Mount Eagle was unforgivable.

She recalled the night with Victor in the music room when Jack Hyland had summonsed her and how she had felt lacerated by his half-blind stare. At a professional level, she had to rise above his insults – Victor's embarrassment convinced her that other equally offensive comments had been made – but this revelation had destroyed the fragile friendship she had formed with this damaged and complicated man, who still remained an enigma to her.

CHAPTER EIGHTEEN

Isobel

Julie travelled home from Clonmoore Primary on an earlier bus. Her mother collected her in the car and, if the weather was clear, she left Isobel's bike propped against the signpost. Empty seats were always available on the afternoon school bus run and it was a relief not to have to sit beside Kelly Bracken.

'See you tomorrow, Newbie,' Arthur shouted as she stepped off the bus. Kelly – who lived with her mother and Charlie further along Marsh Road – glanced coldly out the window at Isobel then stared straight ahead when Arthur accelerated. She was the unfriendliest girl Isobel had ever met and having to share a seat with her in the mornings was pure torture.

She picked up her bike and wheeled it across the road. A pickup truck was parked outside the gate lodge. The new estate manager must have arrived. She was half-way along the avenue when she heard the loud sound of an engine behind her. Looking over her shoulder, she saw the pickup truck. The driver was going so slowly he must have been afraid she would swerve out in front of him. She cycled onto the grass verge and waited for him to pass.

'Hey, Kid!' He lowered the window and leant his elbow on the frame. 'Do you want a lift to Hyland Hall?'

'Dad!' She couldn't believe her eyes. 'What are *you* doing here?'

He stepped down from the truck and removed his beanie, swept it in front of him and bowed. 'Luke Kingston at your service,' he said.

'Does Mum know you're visiting us?'

'I'm not visiting you,' he replied. 'I'm the new estate manager.' He lifted her bike onto the back of the truck. 'You said if I really cared about you, I'd sort everything out. Well, this is the best I can do for the time being.'

Still unable to believe what was happening, she climbed into the passenger seat. 'You don't look pleased to see me,' he said as he started the truck.

'I am, it's just—'

'Go on. Spit it out.'

'I don't want you working for *him.*'

'Why not?'

'Because he's crazy and evil and—'

'Give your imagination a rest, Isobel,' he said. 'My job is to look after the estate. Mr Hyland interviewed me when he was in hospital so I understand why he frightens you. But just because he hides away from people doesn't make him a monster. You must try and be more understanding.' He looked so relaxed in his beanie and padded anorak yet the strangeness of seeing him here was causing a swarm of butterflies to flutter in her stomach.

'Does Mum know you're the new manager?'

'She soon will.' His attempt to sound casual failed miserably. She could tell by the way he gripped the steering wheel that he was nervous.

'What about the Oasis of Hope, Dad?'

'What about it?'

'Did it work? Has it made you better?'

'I'd like to think it has, Isobel.' He drove around to the back of Hyland Hall and stared across at the charred remains of the stables. 'I can see why he needs someone to take charge.'

Julie had twined her pink feather boa around Cordelia's neck and was plaiting her wig when Isobel entered the den.

'The new manager is outside,' she said.

'So what?' Julie arranged the wig on Cordelia's head and stood back to admire the effect.

'He wants to meet you.'

'I don't want to meet him.' She sounded shy. 'Can't you see I'm busy?'

'Not that busy. Come on. Look out the back door and wave at him. You'll be sorry if you don't.' Isobel ignored her protests and coaxed her towards the kitchen.

'Daddy!' Julie shrieked when she saw him leaning against the side of the truck.

'Julie, my precious monkey!' He swung her up in his arms and covered her face with kisses.

Footsteps clattered on the stairs. Her mother was coming down from Fear Zone. Panic knotted Isobel's stomach as she ran to meet her.

'Dad's here!' she said. 'He's the new manager.'

'*What?*' The tray she was carrying tilted and a spoon clanged off the wooden floorboards.

'He's the new—'

'Where is he?' She stopped on the bottom step and bent to pick up the spoon.

'Outside with Julie. He's moved into the gate lodge.'

'Has he indeed?' Her frown deepened as she strode through the kitchen to the backyard.

'Isn't it brilliant, Mum? Julie shouted. 'We're all together again. I have to tell Cordelia. Wait 'til you hear her, Daddy. She sounds *amazing*.' Her hair bobbed against her shoulders as she dashed back to the den.

No one seemed capable of breaking the uncomfortable silence that followed.

'I'm sorry for springing this on you, Sophy.' He was the first to speak. 'I figured it would be easier if I told you face-to-face.' When he spread his palms upwards, Isobel was unable to tell if he was apologising or explaining why it was okay for him to be back with them again.

'I want to speak to your father in private, Isobel.' Walking back into the kitchen, her mother stacked the dishes she had brought from The Recluse's living room into the dishwasher. Isobel was surprised they didn't break from the force she used. Her father squeezed her hand and nodded at her to follow Julie.

'We've to leave them alone to talk,' she said to Julie, who was hurrying back to her father with Cordelia in her arms. 'Let's go into the den. You can show off with Cordelia later.'

Isobel wanted to eavesdrop so badly but her mother would guess what she was doing. It was possible to hear snatches of conversation if she pressed her ear close to the keyhole. She called it 'staying informed.' She had never felt that need when she lived in Park View Villas. Then, it had been easy to ignore sounds. Like the night she heard them arguing but decided they'd turned the television up too loudly. Or when she believed that chopping onions made her mother cry out loud. Also, silence, that too had had a sound, if she'd been willing to listen to the hum of high wire tension. Her parents were talking for a long time in the kitchen. Were they arguing or making up? She stared at Cordelia and had a sudden impulse to pull the long, blonde plaits from her smooth skull. The desire came and went. Thinking about Cordelia required too much energy. Peeper jumped up onto her lap when she sat down on the sofa. His purring always made everything seem a little less awful and frightening, and it was easier, then, to imagine good things happening again.

Later, when her parents had walked away from each other, Luke drove her and Julie to the gate lodge in his pickup truck to see his new home. The little rooms smelled of paint and plaster and had just enough furniture for him to manage.

'Another shoebox,' he said as they helped him to unpack his possessions. 'It's exactly right for me.'

Isobel positioned a family photograph on the mantlepiece. How happy they looked, everyone laughing at the camera. And there was her grandmother with her wide Maddie smile in the middle of them all.

He cooked dinner for the three of them when they'd finished helping. He had a stove like the one that had made their mother cry on the night they arrived at Hyland Hall but he lit it without any problem. When they said goodbye, he assured them that he had everything he needed; a bed to sleep on, a table to eat off, a hook to hang his jacket on, and, the most important thing in the world, his family reunited – almost.

CHAPTER NINETEEN

Sophy

The wood on the kitchen table was scored in places, as if the weight of the food being served and the conversations taking place over the decades had carved furrows on its broad face. When the girls left them, and Sophy had checked that Isobel was not eavesdropping, they had taken seats on opposite sides and negotiated their way forward.

'You obviously weren't expecting me,' Luke said. 'I assumed Jack would have discussed it with you.'

'Well, you assumed wrongly. Why would he hire you? I don't understand what's going on.'

'I refused the job initially when Charlie Bracken approached me,' he admitted. 'You've made no secret of the fact that our marriage is over.'

'So, why are you here?'

'To prevent a similar emergency like that chemical spill ever happening again.'

'Charlie has taken precautions to protect us.'

'It's not enough. And I'll have other responsibilities.'

'But it won't do. It *won't* do at all.' She sounded petulant and childish. All she was short of doing was stamping her foot. 'Our marriage breakup was tough on all of us but the girls have accepted the situation. As long as you're here, they'll keep hoping we'll get back together again.'

'I know there's no chance—'

'But *they* don't. You've undermined everything I've done to prepare them for the future.'

'I'm here to do a job, Sophy. I'll be able to see the girls every day. Are you going to deny me the opportunity to make amends to our daughters?'

'Mum, Mr Hyland's thumping on the ceiling again.' Isobel opened the door cautiously. 'He wants you.'

'This is not over, Luke,' she warned him before she left the kitchen. 'We'll talk later.'

Luke had been on the verge of a nervous breakdown when he finally admitted to his gambling debts. His revelations had torn their marriage apart with the ferocity of an earthquake. Now, he had landed another earthquake on her, but this time Jack Hyland was responsible.

He seemed unfazed when Sophy confronted him. His expression, as always, was frozen in the agonised rictus that had scared her so much in the early days at Hyland Hall.

'Your husband was an award-winning landscape artist before he decided to specialise in park installations,' he said. 'He's exactly what I need to protect my land. Is he not entitled to a second chance?'

'Yes, he is,' she replied. 'But he doesn't have to earn it here. I can't believe you never once considered my feelings when you hired him.'

'If I'd asked permission from you, Luke wouldn't be here,' he replied. 'Your children are happy to see him, are they not? Don't tell me your separation has not seriously impacted on them. The gate lodge where he lives will allow whatever degree of separation you need. Maybe, in time—'

'You're my employer, not my marriage counsellor. Time won't solve anything—'

'You're wrong. When time is limited, you realise how much it can solve. Will your children thank you for separating them again from their father if I send him away?'

He was incapable of expressing defiance, remorse or shame. Too angry to argue any further, Sophy went back downstairs. A text from Isobel informed her they were cooking dinner with their father in the gate lodge. The door of the den was open. She picked up the book Isobel had been reading. *Do Vampires Cast Shadows?* Her daughter's reading habits were continuing to regress. Cordelia, neglected for once, lay face down on the floor. Sophy seated her in her usual position on the chaise longue. Julie's unrestrained happiness when she saw her father had been so fervent. Isobel's true feelings had been more difficult to determine yet her fear of witnessing her parent's anger had been palpable. Jack Hyland was right. She could not separate them again.

The girls were still at the gate lodge when Victor arrived.

'What's going on?' He followed her into the music room. 'Lights are on in the gate lodge. Has the estate manager moved in already?'

'This afternoon.'

'Dumping rubbish on the Gallops has been going on for years.' He slapped his hand against his forehead in frustration. 'I don't know how many times I had to organise clearances for Laurence. What's the logic of throwing good money after bad and hiring some goon who won't make the slightest difference?'

'He's employed Luke to look after the estate.'

'Luke?' He swayed backwards, as if buffeted by the name. 'Luke, as in your *husband*?'

'My *ex*.' Was that, somehow, meant to make it sound better? 'I'd no idea what he'd planned until Luke arrived this afternoon.'

'Why on earth would my uncle do something so ridiculous?'

She sat down beside him on the sofa. 'It's outrageous but not ridiculous. Luke is qualified—'

'Qualified for what. You said he makes fountains.'

'He's also an award-winning landscape designer.'

'His qualifications have nothing to do with Jack's decision. He's brought Luke here for only one reason and that's to thwart me. He knows how I feel about you and he's determined to destroy our relationship.'

'Hiring Luke has nothing to do with us. Jack knows my marriage is over.'

'Then why on earth has he brought your husband here?'

'He believes the girls need their father. I'm furious with him for not consulting me but I agree with his decision.'

'Where does that leave us?'

'Exactly where we were before Luke arrived.'

'And where is that?'

'I won't be rushed, Victor,' she warned. 'We need to take things more slowly.' Unable to sit still, she walked to the window. Peeper, startled by her sudden appearance, leapt down from the outside ledge and scurried up the front steps. His movement triggered the outside light, which illuminated the desolate courtyard with its poisoned shrubs and shrivelled weeds.

'I can't keep coming back here,' Victor said. 'These walls are crushing me. If what we have between us is to have a chance, we should meet at my house in the future.'

CHAPTER TWENTY

Isobel

Every morning when they drove past their father on the way to school, he waved to them. Their mother lifted her index finger from the steering wheel to acknowledge him. It was a start, Isobel guessed. Adults! She lived on the edge of their lives, peering in but unable to understand the silent language they used to hurt each other.

Both her parents were working again yet Isobel still felt poor. It had nothing to do with money, more like a hole inside her that nothing except anxiety could fill.

It made no difference that her father was living so close to them. The Recluse was the only thing her parents had in common anymore and they were still getting divorced.

When her father had set to work on the estate, clearing away the withered bushes from the courtyard and organising workmen to knock down the blackened walls of the stables, a rusty gate was discovered in the dividing wall between Hyland Hall and Mount Eagle.

Once the ivy was removed it could be used to enter Victor's garden instead of driving the long way around. Twice Isobel had seen her mother going into Mount Eagle through the gate. Maybe she went more often without Isobel noticing. Would Victor end up becoming her stepfather? How would she ever get used to him calling her mother Sop-hi-a, like the sound of her name belonged only to him? He would be there at breakfast in the mornings and doing family things like holidays, birthday parties, school concerts and Christmas. She kept thinking of uncomfortable things like having to share the bathroom with him and seeing him in bed with her mother. How would he react if her report card was bad? There would be lots of E minuses if she came from a broken home. Most awful of all, she'd be related by marriage to The Recluse. She no longer wanted to read his journal. It was full of stuff she did not understand about coffins and how he felt about being undead.

This evening her mother and Victor had tickets to hear a Prince tribute band in The Clonmoore Grand Hotel. When she changed out of her white uniform, loosened her hair and kicked off her flat shoes to change into high heels, Isobel could once again see the glamorous woman who used to love dressing up and going to concerts. The Recluse thumped on the floor just as she was leaving. That delayed her so much that she almost bumped into Isobel's father on the stairs. He had promised to look after The Recluse until she returned from her date with Victor. His eyes opened wide when he saw her but he just nodded and said, 'Enjoy your night, Sophy.'

After he came downstairs from Fear Zone and into the kitchen, Isobel asked him why he was allowing Victor to steal her away from him.

'He's not stealing her from me,' he said. 'Your mother is not a possession. I never owned her and neither will Victor Coyne.'

'You should punch his nose,' Julie said in her Cordelia voice. 'He's a silly clown. She belongs to you, not him.'

'I've already discussed this with Isobel.' He stared crossly at Julie who ducked her head and pretended she was fixing Cordelia's shoes. 'Your mother belongs to herself. I don't want to hear any more of this puerile nonsense.'

'What's pure isle, Daddy?'

'Puerile means silly,' Isobel explained. 'It's what Cordelia talks all the time.'

'How dare you?' squeaked Cordelia. 'You're a pure isle cow.'

'Enough! I'm going to make dinner. I don't want to hear any more nonsense from either of you.'

'Three of you,' squeaked Cordelia, but even she stopped being annoying when he clattered the cutlery onto the kitchen table.

He cooked chicken nuggets and chips. The chicken nuggets looked overdone when he removed them from the oven.

'Victor cooks Thai red curry shrimp,' said Julie. 'Will you make that for us the next time?'

'He buys them at The Silver Spoon.' Isobel had seen the containers in the bin. 'That's not real cooking.'

'Does he buy those meatballs, too?' asked Julie. 'They're *delicious*.'

'Enough!' Luke slammed the oven door so hard he set off the smoke alarm.

After dinner they watched television with him in the den, the three of them sprawled on the sofa. Apart from the prowling sounds upstairs and the prowling thoughts in Isobel's mind, it was almost like old times.

'Mammy looks just like she used to,' said Julie when they were in bed. 'Do you think Victor will kiss her on the mouth this time?'

'How should I know?'

'I think it'll still just be on her cheek.' She buttoned Cordelia's pyjama top and put her feet into a pair of panda slippers. Propping the mannequin against the headboard, she searched the dressing table for the eye mask she placed over Cordelia's eyes at night but was unable to find it.

'Victor's going to be your new daddy.' The squeaky voice grated against Isobel's ears.

'Shut up, *you*,' Julie hissed.

'Well, he is,' Cordelia hissed back at her. 'Your daddy can't stop it.'

Isobel couldn't believe it. For the first time ever, Julie was angry with Cordelia and was on the verge of tears as she glared at the mannequin.

'What does Cordelia say about Dad?' Isobel asked her.

'She calls him an addict...' A sigh shuddered through Julie as she climbed into bed. 'She says addicts never change but I love him all the time. Don't you?'

'Yes. But he makes me so angry I think my heart will explode,' Isobel admitted.

'That's how Cordelia feels too.'

'No, Julie. It's how *you* feel.'

'It's not... it's not...' She hugged her knees, her hair shielding her face.

The sight of their two blonde heads together, the long fringes shading their eyes, was unbearable. What if a day came when Isobel could no longer distinguish one from the other? If Julie's voice grew so faint that Cordelia was the only one speaking?

Unable to hold back any longer, Isobel grabbed the mannequin from the bed and flung her on the floor. Cordelia's wig fell off and Peeper pounced, his paws tangling in the shiny strands.

'You mean cow, you've hurt her!' Julie cried as she clambered from the bed and gathered Cordelia in her arms. 'I hate you, Issy Kingston. I hope you run away and never come back.'

'I hate you, too. All you ever think about is that horrible dummy. You're not real any more, just a squeaky voice saying the same *stupid* things over and over again.'

'You're the one who's *stupid*. You don't have any friends, not like me. I've loads of new friends and I've Golden Eye and Cordelia.

Mammy's right. This is an exciting new adventure even if you keep pretending it isn't.'

One insult followed another. Cordelia, silent for once, lay on her back, her blank, blue eyes staring at the ceiling. It felt good to shout at each other without a third voice joining in. A voice that conjured up all those fears they struggled so hard to control.

Her mother had changed out of her skimpy dress and high heels when she called into their bedroom to say goodnight. Her hair was in a topknot and she was wearing her dressing gown. Isobel wasn't fooled. The grandfather clock had boomed out the hours. Seven o'clock when she went out and it was after midnight when she returned. That, as far as Isobel was concerned, was a marathon, not a date, and she was suspiciously vague when Isobel asked questions about the tribute band.

'I'm surprised you're both awake,' she said. 'You'll be exhausted in the morning.'

'Julie's upset because you and Victor went out together again,' said Isobel.

'I didn't mind,' whispered Julie. 'It was Cordelia who was as mad as a bear. Can we sleep in your bed?'

'You can, of course. And Isobel, too. But I want you to leave Cordelia here.'

'I'm staying in my own bed,' said Isobel.

'Are you sure?' her mum asked. 'We could—'

'Absolutely, thank you very *much*.'

Unable to sleep after they left, she tried to read *The Vampire's Stepdaughter*. The words scrambled before her eyes. She looked out the window. The wind was rising. Clouds hurtled past the moon and down below in the courtyard, she noticed her father's pickup truck. Why was he still here? She needed to talk to him. To say, *Fight for her. Fight! Fight! Fight!*

His jacket was hanging from the coat rack in the hall but he was not in the kitchen or any of the other rooms downstairs. She looked up towards Fear Zone. Where else could he be? She jumped when The Recluse's stick clattered on the floor. Before she could change her mind, she tiptoed up the stairs and along the corridor. A light shone beneath his door. She pressed her ear to the keyhole. Two people were inside but she was unable to hear what they were saying. But there was one place she could go to find out.

She tiptoed into the bathroom and hid inside the hot press. As she crouched deeper in the darkness, the broken pipe stuck into her ankle again. She had forgotten just how loudly sound echoed in the cramped space and she could hear her father clearly.

'You know you can rely on me,' he said.

'The way she relied on you?' The Recluse's voice was as harsh as Isobel remembered.

'My marriage is not your business—' Her father tried to reply but was rudely interrupted.

'I'm an old man with little time left to say the things that matter. This woman you claim to love, what did she ask of you?'

Her father cleared his throat but didn't reply.

'Did she demand fancy words of love? Fine promises? Grand gestures? Answer me, Luke. It's not a difficult question.'

'She asked me to keep my word,' he finally spoke. 'To give her and our girls the security they needed.'

'She trusted you to keep your promise, not once but many times. And you failed her. You gambled your family's love on the toss of a coin.'

'I was a fool…'

'You are an addict. Don't look away from me, Luke Kingston. It's still in your blood. You'll always want to take that last gamble.'

'That is my curse. I'm never—'

'Do you know what I was called in my youth?' Once again, The Recluse interrupted him. 'Midas. I had the golden touch, you see. All my investments turned to gold. You could call that a gamble but what had I to lose when I'd already lost everything that was precious to me? So, I gambled and won. You gambled and here you are, trying to win back your wife and children. You're too late. Victor Coyne will give your family the security they need.'

'Why are you tormenting me?'

'To make you face the truth. You say you're cured. Changed. Reformed. Fine words, indeed. Prove it to me.'

'How am I supposed to do that?'

'With this coin you see in my hand. Feel its weight. Solid gold, Luke. Call heads or tails. If you win you will have the wealth you need to provide for your family.'

'And if I lose?'

'You remain as you are. A man with nothing. But if you win? What then? Think of the glittering prize. Are you ready to challenge Lady Luck tonight?'

Isobel wanted to tear open the door into that room and drag him away from The Recluse's evil presence.

'I'm not going to gamble with you,' her father said.

She wanted to cover her ears so that she wouldn't hear the wobble in his voice but she was too petrified to move.

'Even when the stakes are in your favour?' The Recluse wheedling promises would destroy him. 'Come, let your curse humour me tonight. On the toss of this coin you can regain all you have lost through your recklessness. I have the power to make it happen.'

'*No!*'

'Heads or tails?' He ignored her father's cry. 'How will she flip? Dice with me and make it happen. Heads or tails, Sir? There, I've tossed it for you. Call quickly before she falls.'

Isobel imagined her father looking into the distance at something mysterious and wonderful. More important than her and Julie and their mother. More important than their house in Park View Villas and all the things they used to do together. The coin would be spinning across the table, tempting him, tormenting him.

'Heads or tails, Kingston. This is your last chance.'

'Why are you trying to steal my soul?' He sounded as if glass was stuck in his throat.

'I call tails.' The Recluse's voice was like a silken thread drawing him towards the coin. 'Speak before I raise my hand. Call heads and your fortune will change tonight.'

Outside, the wind moaned. Branches lashed against the bathroom window. A storm had been forecast on the news. She would suffocate if she didn't escape from the closet. They were trapped, all of them trapped in The Recluse's power. The power of the undead.

She ran down the stairs and into her bedroom. Cordelia was still stretched on Julie's bed. Her blank stare was unbearable. So were her lips, always curving upwards in that red, tempting smile. She represented everything that was bad about living in Hyland Hall.

Isobel shoved her into a chair in front of the dressing table. She remembered a story her father used to read to her when she was small and snuggled in bed, safe. A story about a princess who whispered her secret into a deep, dark well. Everyone needed somewhere to spill their secrets.

She told Cordelia they were living with an undead. A vampire filled with a stranger's blood who lay in a coffin in the boathouse by the lake. All the fears she had tried to keep at bay since they arrived at Hyland Hall tumbled over each other and demanded to be released. She stared at the mannequin's reflection in the mirror, at the multiple reflections beyond that, and imagined those fears passing from one Cordelia to the next Cordelia – another and another Cordelia, the reflections shrinking and shrinking until, finally, there was nothing left to frighten her.

'Liar!' hissed Cordelia.

Her accusation whipped towards Isobel. Cordelia spoke again but her words trembled on a sob, and the face staring back at Isobel remained blank, smiling.

'Big, ugly, stupid liar. There's no such thing as a vampire.' Julie was standing at the bedroom door, her face stricken with fear. She walked towards the mirror and stood beside Cordelia, her body also multiplying and reducing into never-ending reflections of terror.

'Is it true?' She spoke to Isobel in her normal voice. 'Are we really living with a vampire?'

'It's only a joke.' Isobel tried to remember the torrent of words she had spewed out. 'I was playing a trick on Cordelia and I made it all up. Don't tell Mum or Dad. Promise you won't tell them or they'll blame me for scaring you.' She kept talking, desperately trying to banish the fear from her sister's face.

'Is Issy telling me the truth, Cordelia?' Julie eyelids flickered as she tried to blink her tears away. Her mouth skidded sideways as she brushed her fingers over her lips.

'She was only pretending,' Cordelia replied. 'It was all a story. A brilliant made-up story.'

CHAPTER TWENTY-ONE

Sophy

The day when everything changed began like any other and continued that way until the afternoon. Sophy collected Julie from the school bus and left Isobel's bike at the signpost. She brought Jack up a cup of tea which he always drank before he took a nap. His hand dangled over the armchair and fondled Caesar's ears. He seemed incapable of affection yet the love he lavished on his dog could not be doubted.

Julie's voice floated upwards from the den. Her words were muffled but when she spoke as Cordelia, the high-pitched, squeaky pitch was audible.

'I'll tell her to quieten down,' Sophy tried and failed to hide the terseness in her voice. He showed no signs of noticing her barely controlled anger but how could she tell?

'Leave her be,' he replied. 'I enjoy listening to her.'

Back downstairs, she stood outside the den. Julie was arguing with Cordelia about vampires and whether or not they existed. A fixation, Luke had called Julie's need to speak through Cordelia. Sophy had dismissed his concerns as an overreaction. Julie had always been a fanciful child who had had a succession of imaginary 'friends' when she was younger. This phase ended when she started school and had not resurfaced until Kid's Chic was sold. As the two voices batted the question back and forth with Cordelia's voice dominating, Sophy was forced to accept that Luke was right. This hobby, which she had perceived as harmless in the beginning, was consuming Julie and it had to end.

'Go outside and play on the swing,' she said. Luke had hung an old tyre from a rope and tied it to one of the trees on the avenue for the girls to swing on. 'The rain has stopped and it's a lovely day now.'

'I don't want to leave Cordelia. She's scared.'

'Scared of what?'

'Vampires.'

'Do you have any fears like that?'

'Isobel says vampires don't exist.'

'She's quite right. I promise to look after Cordelia until you get back.'

'Okay.' She shrugged and reluctantly left the den.

'Don't go into the woods,' Sophy warned her when she reappeared in her anorak and wellingtons a few minutes later. 'I don't want to send out a search party for you.'

'I promise.' Julie waved both hands in the air before skipping across the courtyard.

Isobel arrived home from school shortly afterwards. 'Where's Julie?' She was frowning when she emerged from the den. 'I can't find her anywhere.'

'Playing on the swing.'

'Okay, I'll go and give her a push.'

'Aren't you going to change your clothes first?' Usually, Isobel tore off her hated school uniform as soon as she arrived in from school.

'I'll do it later,' she shouted as she ran from the house.

'Don't be too long,' Sophy shouted after her. 'It's time for Julie to start her homework.'

She went upstairs to check on Jack. He was sleeping soundly. She stared down at his ravaged body. A pillow over his face. If she sedated him first, it would be so easy to break the frail thread that held him to life. This thought, coming to her with such clarity, shocked her. A band of pain tightened around her forehead. The feeling of being on a battlefield without any understanding of the rules of engagement kept intensifying. She settled the duvet that had slipped from his bony shoulder and left the room to continue her search for his safe.

She had checked for it behind every painting, bookcase and cabinet. She had entered rooms filled with old furniture and an attic groaning under the weight of memories. Nothing. The only place she hadn't searched yet was the basement. It was located past the kitchen and entered through a narrow corridor at the back of the house.

She pushed open the basement door and descended wooden steps. Looking at empty shelves and long trestle tables, she figured it must once have served as a storehouse for the wine and home-made preserves Jack's mother had made from the fruits she harvested. The possibility that Jack had hidden his safe anywhere in this mouldy basement was soon discarded. She was about to abandon her search when she discovered a single track leading into a tunnel at the far end of the basement. A truck would have been used to transport the fruit and vegetables from the market garden to the basement. The tunnel was sealed by a door that had been wedged tight by damp. Eventually, the door gave way under her shoulder. The passage beyond it led her into the open air. The track continued on a slight upward trajectory then disappeared under an overgrowth of bush.

The wall that marked the demarcation line between Mount Eagle and Hyland Hall ended before it reached this area and a barbed wire fence was all that divided the two properties. The earth was damp under her feet from the earlier rain. She was standing in the abandoned orchard at the end of Victor's land. The trees were laden with apples and pears. Most of the fruit had rotted on the branches or was mulched on the ground. She was able to see faint semblances of what would once have been the market garden; wooden frames that would have enclosed herbs, raised beds where vegetables had grown, a back wall covered in ivy. Victor's house lay beyond the copse of trees.

Last night, Victor had torn up the tickets he had bought for the concert. She lay on his bed and freed herself from the binds of her marriage. In the end, it was such a simple thing to do. He had pleaded with her to stay with him until morning but her blood had cooled by then and she slipped away while he was sleeping.

She had showered when she returned to the house but how could such a memory be erased? Luke was still with Jack when she checked the living room. He would stay for a while longer, he told her, and make sure Jack was settled for the night before he left. How was it possible to speak so calmly to her husband when the taste of another man was still on her lips? Unable to meet his gaze, she had hurried back downstairs. Did the girls suspect where she had been with Victor when she called into their bedroom? She longed to fold her arms around them as she had done when they were small and convince them that their mother could do no wrong. Isobel's accusatory stare had told her otherwise. Sophy had taken her younger daughter into her bed but even Julie had left her side and sought the plastic comfort of Cordelia.

Afterwards, unable to sleep, Sophy had heard the stairs creak. Afraid that Jack was wandering or sleepwalking, she had hurried to the hall just as Luke reached the last step. His face was blotchy, as if he had been weeping.

'I thought you'd left hours ago?' she said.

'As you can see, I'm still here.'

'Doing what?' she asked.

'Finding myself.' He had walked across the hall and closed the front door behind him.

She was wasting time standing in this lost garden. The girls would be back by now and wondering where she was.

To her surprise, they had not returned from the woods. The soups and sandwiches she had prepared for them were still untouched. She rang Isobel's phone but heard it ringing from the den. She walked up the hall and stopped when she noticed that Jack's coat and hat were missing from the coat rack. Panicking, she dashed up the stairs. His living room was empty, as was his bedroom. A quick search confirmed her worst fears. He had ventured out alone while she had been exploring the basement.

CHAPTER TWENTY-TWO

Isobel

Isobel collected her bike at the signpost and cycled towards the gate lodge. Her father had left his muddy boots on the doorstep and the front door was open, like he was expecting her to call in and say hello. He was moving about inside the gate lodge but she was unable to face him after last night. Did the coin land on heads or tails? Isobel longed to ask him if The Recluse had succeeded in stealing his soul but she would be unable to bear it if he looked away from her and uttered some hollow lie in reply.

He came to the door when he saw her and shouted, 'The kettle is on the boil, kiddo. Fancy a sandwich?'

'No thanks. Mum's expecting me.'

She bent her head and continued up the avenue. It had rained earlier. The branches gleamed and the turning leaves fluttered before her. A squirrel scurried across the avenue then stopped to eat the nuts Julie left each morning on the stump of a tree.

Cordelia was sitting on her own in the den. She had been wearing red satin pyjamas and her panda slippers when they left for school this morning. Julie had changed her clothes since then and replaced the pyjamas with a black, glittery top that once belonged to her mother. She had turned it into a dress and the wide belt that gathered it at the waist had metal studs. She had chosen the black wig with the Cleopatra fringe and the sleek, straight hair fell to Cordelia's shoulders. Her nails were painted in blood-red polish, her eyes were ringed with black eyebrow pencil and Julie had smeared her mouth with scarlet lipstick. Cordelia looked exactly like the girl on the cover of *The Vampire's Stepdaughter*.

'Where's Julie?' she asked her mother.

'She's playing on the swing,' Sophy replied.

But Julie wasn't on the swing. Rain had gathered inside the tyre. Droplets glistened on the rim where Julie normally sat and it was clear that she hadn't been on it today. She must have gone deeper into the woods, even though that was strictly forbidden.

The leaves flaunted their autumn pallet, boldly red and burnt orange, a searing yellow-gold that clung to the branches until they fluttered to the ground on a passing breeze. They squelched and rustled beneath her feet as she ran along the shadowy trails. Mushrooms with mottled faces festered in the brown bracken. Birds darted from the hedges when she called Julie's name. Her heart pounded as she sprinted from the shelter of trees towards Hyland Gallops.

The air was clammy on her cheeks. A mist was creeping over the Gallops and it was difficult to see the lake. She called Julie's name over and over again. No answering cry came back to her.

Last night, what had she said to Cordelia? Had she mentioned the coffin? Words came back to her in snatches and horrified her. She moved parallel to the shore and tried to keep her bearings. Bubbles burst and splattered as mud slid over her shoes. She felt her feet sinking into the swampy earth. She lost her balance and almost fell backwards as she struggled free. She staggered back to the edge of the lake where the ground was firmer. A faint noise reached her. Was it a bird lost in the mist? A hare searching for its form? An echo of her own voice? Isobel didn't want it to be her sister because it was a frightened wail, disembodied, lost, and appeared to rise from the lake.

'Julie, Julie! I'm here!' She thrashed the reeds and forced them apart. When she screamed, tendrils of mist shifted, as if shocked by her terror. Julie's arms lifted, as if she was reaching for the light but she was in the water and beyond Isobel's reach. Slithery stalks twined around Isobel's ankles and she knew she was unable to go any further. She yelled at Julie to stay still. Struggling was the worst thing she could do. But it was no use. Mud was gurgling and oozing under her and she could see, as Isobel could, the grey swell of the lake waiting beyond the reeds to claim her.

Something or someone moved. Black and gaunt, a hat brim pulled low over his forehead, the hulking figure of The Recluse emerged from the mist. He grabbed Isobel's arm and pulled her back from the edge. She struggled but his grip was surprisingly strong. He held both her arms and ordered her to look at him. His eye was a cold, blue glitter. Its power forced her to a standstill.

'Go to the boat and take out the widest plank,' he said. 'Now is not the time to be scared of me.' He pointed to the right of him. 'Run, run! It's that direction.'

Only one thing mattered now. All her fears, her imaginings, every thought, every nightmare was nothing compared to the real danger that had trapped Julie. The boat planks were loose as he had said and she was able to pull the widest one free. When she returned, Julie was no longer flailing. She was a statue, motionless.

The Recluse was telling her a story about how he almost drowned in the lake when he was a boy. He demanded that she look at him, an old man, battered and bruised – but alive and ready to come to her aid. Caesar waited, quivering. Isobel had never seen him so still. The Recluse told her to lay the plank like a surfboard between the reeds.

'Don't be afraid, child,' he soothed her. 'Nothing will happen to you. I won't allow it.'

He knelt with great difficulty and eased his body along the length of the plank. Isobel was convinced it would sink but apart from the water lapping the edges it remained afloat. The reeds bent before the plank and Julie, slowly moving one arm, reached forward to grab his walking stick.

'Isobel, your father is in the woods.' His voice demanded that Isobel concentrate. 'Listen for the sound of the chainsaw. Go quickly and fetch him.'

She ran through the woods, calling and calling, until, finally, she heard the chainsaw. Her breath heaved and she could hardly get the words out before her father was running ahead of her towards the Gallops.

When Isobel reached the lake again, Julie was lying like a rag doll in their father's arms. Mud dripped in splodges from her feet and her drenched clothes clung to her skinny body. A whooping sob gathered in her chest but it was silenced when he covered her mucky face with kisses.

The Recluse's hands were stiff with mud. His clothes smelled of the festering mire. He staggered and would have fallen if Isobel hadn't grabbed his arm and steadied him. He leant on her for support and it was that gesture that gave her the courage to help him walk back to Hyland Hall. She realised then that he was just a frail, elderly man; not undead, not a vampire.

Her mother came towards them. Leaves clung to her hair and there was a long scratch across her nose. She stared at Julie, lying limp and waxen in her father's arms. Her cries ricocheted across the Gallops as she sank to her knees and covered her eyes. The rooks shot from the trees and swirled above them, black streamers dancing in the sky.

PART TWO

CHAPTER TWENTY-THREE

Wildfires
A Memoir by Jack Hyland

The fire took so much from me yet it left the bliss of my dreams untouched. Last night I returned to Withers Island with Madelaine. My second chance to hold her in my arms and tell her how much I love her. When I awoke to the sound of Caesar's bark, I felt my soul shudder and leave my body. That, too, was imagination. My soul, if it exists, is still a living force, as is this wasted body that tethers me to this world.

I need to write my story. Words lend solidity when thoughts and dreams are in disarray. Is it one of love or betrayal? Loss or gain? Loss is easy to define but what of gain? How must that be measured?

Eighteen minutes, that was how long it took me to follow Laurence into my mother's arms. Until then, no one knew of my existence. I was the 'hidden' twin, and while the midwife was admiring Laurence's lusty wails my mother cried out that something was happening to her. That 'something' was me announcing my arrival. When I think about those eighteen minutes of aloneness, I imagine myself expanding, taking over the space occupied by Laurence, flexing my tiny body as I prepared to leave that warm cocoon. But in those crucial moments my brother had already conquered the world we would occupy. Once I was born, I became a pea in a pod, an almost invisible one.

When does a child's memory begin? Is it in the pram where most of the space is occupied by a twin brother? Do I remember that or have I just transposed my later experiences onto those early years? It must have been the same in our mother's womb. If sound existed in that watery sphere, he would certainly have shouted me down. Laurence did not laugh, he guffawed, and everyone laughed with him. He rattled the bars of our playpen, demanding to walk and talk and be loved the most. I was his pale shadow and if a question was asked, or a comment made, it was usually directed to him or, perhaps, it was he who always answered the quickest.

Despite our differences, I adored him. I'd never have dreamt of snitching, even when my nose bled or my eye ballooned from one of his punches. I fought back. I was not a coward or a pushover but, whatever battle we were fighting, I always accepted that Laurence would win. Until the day I met Madelaine Boylan and fell headlong in love with her.

But I digress from the chronology of my story. Hyland Stables was renowned for training champion racehorses and our world consisted of people who worked on the estate, the stable hands and grooms, the trainers and jockeys, the gardeners, the office staff, the farriers and vets who called regularly. My mother's market garden ran in tandem with the stables and staff often overflowed from one to the other when necessary. When he was old enough to handle the horses, Charlie Bracken spent his school holidays and all his spare time working with me in the stables. His father had other plans for him but Charlie was determined to forge his own *path and become a jockey. I was closer to him than to my twin brother, who constantly challenged me to compete with him.*

Everything with Laurence was a bet. 'Bet you all your marbles you won't jump from that wall.' He would point to the highest wall on the estate and prove his own courage by jumping first. 'Bet you all your comics I can reach the top of that tree faster than you.' He would point towards the tallest trees and count, 'One, two, three. Go!' My possessions disappeared bit by bit. Not that they really disappeared. They were still in our bedroom and Laurence showed no further interest in them once they belonged to him. A week could pass, sometimes more, before he issued another bet. They became more daring as we grew older. Sometimes, I refused the bet, frightened as much for his safety as for my own.

He was thirteen the first time he was caught leaving the house at night to play poker with a gang of older boys from the town. He knew the ways of our house. He found the hidden chinks and unguarded openings that gave him the freedom to leave and return at will. His favourite was the skylight in the annexe shower room. We were sleeping in separate rooms by then yet I always knew what was happening and could judge by his mood the following day whether he had won or lost.

We were separated for the first time when we were fifteen. My father, concerned about Laurence's gambling, sent him to boarding school. Freed from his shadow, I could feel myself expanding, just as I must have expended when I was alone in my mother's womb. He wrote regularly, always complaining about the conditions in the school. Food was top of the list. He called the meals 'starvation rations.' He also caught the childhood illnesses he had avoided until then. German measles, mumps, sore throats and chilblains earned the school the nickname, 'The Pox'.

Eventually, he was expelled for running a poker school. Life at Hyland Hall settled back to the old routine when he returned and soon enough he threw down a new challenge: to swim to Withers Island.

Withers Island was our nickname for the island in the middle of Marsh Lake. When we were smaller, our father told us the lake was bottomless and forbade us to swim there. As we grew older, and knew this to be impossible, he told us that the lake was fed by an underground river. It created dangerous currents that could sweep us to our death. The ban stayed, even when we were older and strong swimmers.

While I hesitated on the lake shore, Laurence stripped off his clothes and waded naked into the reeds. His feet sank into the soft mud before he dived headfirst into the freezing water. He was a strong swimmer and was soon within reach of the island. I tried to pluck up the courage to follow him. I could see him in the distance, slapping his hands against his chest and jumping up and down to warm himself. Soon he would dive back into the lake and return to shore, triumphant, demanding his prize. This was the first time he'd ever demanded my pocket money and he always collected on a bet.

I pulled off my clothes and dived into the water. The cold sucked the breath from my body but I swam strongly, ignoring the swans who kept a safe distance from me. Laurence looked angry, as he always did when he lost a bet. He was chilled, his mouth clenched, his lips turning blue.

'I won,' he growled. 'You waited too long.'

'No, I didn't.' I was still breathless from the swim. 'You didn't set a time limit.'

'There's always a time limit on a bet.' He spoke with his usual force. 'You lost. Pay up or else.'

'Or else what?' I demanded.

'Or else there'll be trouble.' He shoved his shoulder forward and held up his clenched fist.

'You and what army?' I said. The chill from the water was replaced by a hot anger, a new emotion and one that I found to be curiously exciting. 'You're not getting a penny from me.'

'You have to pay your bet.' He swung his fist at me. I ducked and lost my footing. My head hit against a rock as I tumbled into the lake. Water flooded my mouth and blinded my eyes. I surfaced into a hazy, silvery world. The sky wavered above me before I went under again. I knew the lake was not bottomless. Even the deepest ocean has a floor yet, still, I believed I'd sink forever into a black, eerie underworld of bubbles and dangling roots.

Laurence rescued me. He dragged me back to Withers Island and hauled me to safety. I was vomiting water when we became aware of another sound. The clunk of oars against the side of the wooden rowing boat that was usually moored by the jetty. My father and Charlie were rowing towards us.

Ten lashes on our bare backsides with a cane. My father administered the punishment. When it was over, Laurence demanded his bet. How could I refuse? I owed my life to him. No price was too high to pay.

We had turned twenty when Madelaine came to work in the market garden for the summer. I can see her still. As clearly as if she's standing before me now, I watch the sway of her long, chestnut hair. Sometimes, it hangs loose to her shoulders, at other times it swings in a ponytail. I see her bending over rows of carrots, the fronds cascading over her hands as she shakes clay loose from the stems. Or reaching upwards on a ladder to pick ripe plums, her sweater taut *against her breasts. When these images come to me, I think my breath will finally leave my body.*

Last night I returned with her to Withers Island where we once lay together on that wind-blown atoll. The aching cruelty of dreams. They promise bliss but deliver nothing more than the dawning of another pain-filled day.

CHAPTER TWENTY-FOUR

Madelaine was eighteen when she came to work in the market garden. Our two mothers had been school friends and, as she was the same age as my sister, Olive, my mother hoped the two girls would become friends. She was wrong. Olive had her own circle of friends and had no interest in sharing her summer with a stranger.

Madelaine seemed unperturbed by Olive's chilly reaction and soon became part of our team. She helped out in the stables when my mother could spare her. I loved to listen to her laughter. Infectious as it was, there was a deeper resonance beneath it, and I was the only one to hear it.

I found her crying in the barn one day. She was huddled against a bale of hay, hidden from view, or so she thought, until I sat beside her. She nodded when I asked if she was missing her mother and leant into me when I put my arm around her shoulders. Anna Boylan had died the previous year and Madelaine's father was drowning his sorrows in a bottle. He'd been a functioning alcoholic while his wife was alive but since her death his drinking was out of control. She had taken the summer job with us to get away from him and earn enough money to finance her first year in college. I stayed with her until she stopped crying and held her hand as we walked back to the stables. Her scent was – citrus, lemon or lime, I wasn't sure – intoxicating. And I, at twenty years old, was intoxicated with love.

Laurence was leading one of the horses towards the paddock when we entered the yard. I know from the set of his mouth that he'd seen us coming from the barn.

'You like her, don't you?' he asked when we were alone in the kitchen that night.

It was a rhetorical question and one I'd no desire to answer.

'Go on, admit it.' He nudged me with his elbow. 'You follow her around like a dog with your tongue hanging out.'

I stayed silent. I'd learnt to use silence as a weapon, knowing how much he hated to be ignored. Noise, arguments and action, that was how Laurence drew his energy. Silence challenged his authority and I held on to it as he continued to goad me about my feelings for Madelaine.

'Bet you fifty pounds that I'll be the first to get into her knickers,' he said.

I smashed my fist into his face. He laughed, even as he wiped the blood from his nose with the back of his hand.

'Don't you even dare think about it,' I roared. I waited for him to retaliate. Instead, he walked away, his laughter trailing behind him.

Madelaine was the first person to see me, really see me as an individual and not as a shadowy copy of Laurence. She never fumbled our identities, as others often did, searching our faces for clues, an identifiable mole or a cowlick, a smattering of freckles, before they spoke our names.

We shared our life stories. Her story had an edge, a father given to outbursts of violence and abject repentance, her mother determined to keep their secrets behind closed doors until her quiet death. She saw my childhood as an idyllic adventure until I told her about the bets and the fights, and the constant struggle to define my own identity.

'Peas in a pod is a lazy way to describe you and Laurence,' she said. 'Don't ever let him eclipse you, Jack.'

I agonised over her remark. Was there a hidden meaning behind it? Did she know that Laurence was also in love with her? I watched him watching her. I saw the heat in his eyes, the slope of his bottom lip, as if he was already crushing her mouth with his kisses.

Did the sun shine every day that summer? There must have been dank days when the mist swallowed Hyland Gallops and the rain splattered from the trees. All I remember is the red dawn and the steaming breath of horses as we rode across the Gallops and, later, hidden from Laurence's watchful gaze, how we kissed for the first time in the shadows of the old barn. And the kisses that followed in those secret nooks we found where we could be alone.

Oh, those days… the plans I made… if broken dreams had a path it would glisten with shattered glass.

CHAPTER TWENTY-FIVE

In years to come, I would be known in financial circles as Midas. A metaphorical nickname for it seemed that everything I touched had the potential to turn to gold. Back then, my only interest in gold was the medallion displayed on the front window of Fine's Jewellery on Lower Main Street. A circle of gold with a ruby set into the centre.

'Ah, gold for endurance and ruby for love,' said Mr Fine when he packaged it for me. 'Is there a lovely woman in your life now, Jack?'

'I hope so,' I replied and knew with absolute certainty that it was true.

On the afternoon of Madelaine's nineteenth birthday, we took the boat to Withers Island. Madelaine packed fruit from my mother's garden, cheese from the dairy, bread freshly baked by Pinkie, our housekeeper. It was a hot August Sunday afternoon and the sky was clear. No bobtail clouds to dapple its peerless blue breadth. No breeze to disturb its distant solitude. The sun flung a million glittering spangles on Marsh Lake as I rowed us across to the island where I once believed I was going to die. It was Madelaine's idea that I should imprint it with a happier memory. I know now that she, like me, was anxious to escape Laurence's watchful gaze. Olive, also, found it hard to hide her jealousy over the affection my parents had shown to Madelaine since she came to live with us. My mother would have organised a party had she known it was her birthday and Madelaine was anxious to avoid increasing the tension between her and my sister. We moored the boat and walked upwards on slabs that nature had shaped into weather-beaten footholds. I'd no memory of trees from my previous time there, only rocks with bowed shoulders and melancholy faces, yet they must have been there, a stunted forest of wind-tossed branches that led us deep into the island, away from the honk, croak and quack of life on the lake, away from Laurence's unspoken desires, or his threats – I was unable to distinguish between the two.

We found shelter from the sun under a canopy of green. The loamy floor was our table. Juice ran down her chin when she bit into a plum. I longed to taste this ripeness, to bring my tongue to her skin, to the sweetened curve of her lips. As if guessing my thoughts, she held out the plum, the indent of her mouth on the amber flesh, and I bit deeply into it.

Did I make the first move? Did she? Was our coming together so preordained that it did not need to be defined by decisions? I took off her sunhat and opened the buttons on her dress. I was afraid I would fumble as I unhooked her bra but it was a flimsy thing that yielded easily under my eager fingers. It was the first time I had touched a woman in this way and she, too, whispered about the newness of it all.

No nervousness between us, no shyness. I tried to pull away from her before I lost all reason but she was caught in that same shuddering paroxysm of pleasure and then it was too late to stop.

'I'm sorry… sorry,' I gasped as our heads cleared and our bodies cooled. The sun was warm on our bare skin, the remains of our picnic scattered around us.

When the wind gusted and the clouds began to gather, I wrapped the rug around us. We were reluctant to leave and, in that warm cocoon we created, it seemed as if nothing bad could ever penetrate our dazed happiness. Before we left the island, I fastened the chain of the medallion around her neck. I promised her that when I bought gold for her again, it would be a ring.

How did I let all that loving slip through my fingers? Sometimes we make decisions and fate flings dust in our faces. Sometimes, things just happen and reasons can never be found for the twists that steer us in a new direction. Heartache brings its own confusions. Did she leave me or did I let her go? Our reasoning at such times is not to be trusted but I believe that the pattern established during my earlier, formative years was responsible for her sudden departure. In other words, and to put more simply, I allowed Laurence to overshadow me again.

The following night I awoke when my bedroom door was opened. Olive was just about to close it again when I switched on the bedside lamp.

'What do you want?' I asked. 'Is something wrong?'

'Wrong or right depends on which position you take.' She giggled and splayed her fingers across her lips. She was returning from a dance at the Clonmoore rugby club and it was obvious she had been drinking. 'I was just checking to see who won the bet on her.' Olive never referred to Madelaine by name. 'I wasn't sure whether it was you or Laurence I saw coming from the barn just now.' She came to the edge of my bed and bent over me. 'That's where she is right now. I checked her room. It's empty. She's been dangling you on a string all summer but, in the end, it's Laurence who's won the bet. It's time you stopped making a fool of yourself.'

In that instant, her pouting mouth seemed to personify the ugliness of her lies, for that was what I believed they were. I pushed her from the bed and ordered her to spread her poison elsewhere.

'There's one way to prove who's the liar,' she said. 'Check her room yourself.'

After she left, I listened for footsteps. Hyland Hall has its own language, the squeak on the third step of the staircase, the louder one on the bend. The wooden floorboards give off a faint vibration when footsteps are heavy or rapid. Attuned as I was to every sound and movement, I'd already heard Laurence return but had believed he'd been playing poker in the boathouse.

Unable to bear my suspicions, I made my way to Madelaine's bedroom. Her bed was empty. I was unable to find her in the kitchen or anywhere else in the house. The light wasn't working in the barn. I'd brought a torch with me but was unable to see her among the sheaves of hay. Some years previously, my father had replaced the old wooden barn with a modern one made from corrugated steel sheets. Even the bales of hay, tightly stacked, could not soften the clang and clink that reverberated from the walls. She was on her knees when I found her. Her hair was wild, free from clips and combs, and there was hay among the dark strands. Her brown eyes, I can see them still, fathomless as she rose to her feet and stared into the beam of light. She knocked the torch from my hand then struck my face with such force that I staggered back and tripped over a rake. I hit my head off the stone floor but she had already reached the open entrance and didn't look back.

By the time I reached the house she was in her bedroom, the door locked. I begged her to let me in. Laurence and

Olive stayed in their rooms when my parents came from their bedroom, and demanded to know what was going on. Eventually, they persuaded me to go back to bed. My mind raged. Tomorrow I would demand the truth from both her and Laurence. I couldn't sleep that night and yet I must have drifted off. I never heard her leaving in the early morning.

She left a note for my mother stating that her father was ill and needed her. I knew enough about his drinking to understand why that seemed like a reasonable excuse for her sudden departure. Not that I believed it and Olive's knowing glances from Laurence to me proved she didn't believe it either.

Laurence claimed he had been playing poker all night. If Madelaine had been with someone, it must have been one of the grooms or the gardeners. All my life I'd been jealous of him. I'm not sure if I repressed it or simply accepted it as a natural feeling but when it was released, it became a fever that broke sweat on my forehead, quickened my pulse.

I returned to the spot where I'd seen her kneeling and found the medallion in the hay. The chain had been snapped in two. I took it with me back to my room and it remained in a drawer until I sought her out. It took a fortnight for my anger to ebb and reason to return. Only one person could tell me the truth.

I drove to Douglas where she lived and knocked three times before the door was answered by her father. It's always a shock, but seldom a surprise, when people fit the exaggerated caricatures that we've created of them in our imagination. Seamus Boylan looked as though he'd slept in his clothes. His flushed face and bloodshot eyes revealed a man in crisis. Madelaine had arrived home unexpectedly and left just as quickly, he said. He shook his head when I asked where I could find her. She'd deserted him, left him bereft and grieving for *his dead wife. His self-pitying whine disgusted me yet I was hungry for information and he was hungry for company. I went with him to his local pub. We sat on stools in a snug. He cradled a whiskey then drank it neat before he called for another and waited for me to pay for it.*

He thought she might be staying with friends or with an aunt who lived north of the border. Fermanagh, he thought, or maybe it was Armagh. His arm trembled when he lifted it to check his watch. Time seemed meaningless to him and the constant checking was as habitual as a tic. Unable to bear his company any longer, I bought him another whiskey and left him staring at the smoke-stained partition. I also left an envelope containing the medallion with him and asked him to return it to her. No note. Let her form her own conclusions.

Why did I give up so easily? There had to be another truth than the one Olive had set before me. I should have scoured the countryside and the cities to find her but a week after that meeting with her father, I was sunk too deeply in my own hell to think beyond it.

A learner driver broke the red lights on the bridge at Lower Main Street. Now, that once-narrow stretch has been widened and is controlled by traffic lights but back then, drivers depended on common sense and caution when deciding which car would stop to allow the approaching driver to go forward. One night, as my father was mounting the arch on the half-way point, a young learner driver, impetuous and reckless, killed him, my mother and himself when he crashed headfirst at speed into their car.

That's it. I'm unable to write anymore tonight. I cannot describe love, nor can I describe grief. Both render me wordless.

CHAPTER TWENTY-SIX

Time has passed since I last opened my journal. Foul air surrounded me. Right to my doorstep they came with their poisonous load. My body, once so strong, is a feeble joke and I forgot its limitations when I heard them trundling up the avenue. Fury left me senseless and lost to caution. It was like the night of the fire. Pandemonium let loose. What would have happened if Isobel had not found me? Dead, no doubt, and my secret buried with me.

Caesar is restless tonight. Is it the moon that draws him to the door? How full and bountiful it looks. My heart races with longing to be out there in that moonlight, running fleet of foot through the woods as I did when I was young and my future seemed set in stone.

But stone can crack under duress and turn to sand. There we were, Laurence and I, owners of Hyland Stables when we were yet to reach our twenty-first birthdays. Equal shares, declared the solicitor, who read our parent's will to us. Olive inherited one third of the land and the market garden. She disliked horses and had never shown any interest in the stables. Three years after the death of our parents, she married Maurice Coyne, an auctioneer from Clonmoore. They built their house where vegetables once grew. The strawberry beds became a tennis court and a sun terrace. A wall was erected between Hyland Hall and Mount Eagle with a gate to allow easy access. Not that we called often to see each other. I was too busy struggling to keep the stables going. Laurence no longer pretended to have any interest in the training programme my grandfather and father had perfected. He bought a dark green Aston Martin and drove through Clonmoore with the roof down. He no longer gambled with the men from the town. When he was not at the racetrack, he spent most of his time in Cork or Dublin. Initially, I'd no idea what he did there. All I knew was that the decisions he made were affecting the reputation of Hyland Stables.

He believed we should close down the stables. We could sell the land or lease it to farmers. Anything was better than the endless, back-breaking work of training horses that might, or might not, become champions. I violently disagreed but I was adrift without my father's wise voice to guide me.

We fought one night in the stable yard. We'd had to lay off staff and others had left. As Charlie said, they knew which way the wind was blowing. Only the horses watched as we wrestled each other to the ground. I was so angry I could have killed him. My hand closed around an iron bar that one of the grooms had left lying against the stable wall. Lifting it, I knew I'd be prepared to bring it down on my brother's head. One of the horses whinnied. Thunderbolt, a troubled stallion that my father had turned into a champion. Sensitive to violence or just bored by the antics of humans, I'll never know why he chose to whinny at that instant but the high-pitched call brought me to my senses. I dropped the bar and staggered away from Laurence.

'You can't handle it.' He wiped blood from his forehead with the back of his hand. 'I told you I'd have Madelaine

Boylan first and she was all for it. How about ponying up that money you owe me.'

They say the truth is better out than in. Balderdash.

'We have to choose.' My lips were bleeding, my heart broken. 'Only one of us can remain here.'

'We'll toss for it,' he said. 'It's the only way to settle this.'

Why did I agree to such madness? I guess because I was maddened by grief and loss.

'I call heads,' Laurence said.

The coin spun, a piece of glinting gold that would decide our future. It landed on heads.

'You lost the bet,' said Laurence, as he had said so many times in the past. 'Hyland Estate belongs to me.'

At daybreak the following morning I rode Thunderbolt across the Gallops. The sun was rising in the east. It touched the leaves of the great chestnut tree, dropped into the stillness of the lake. On and on it flowed, that golden dawn, stirring the birds to song, the horses to stir restlessly in their stables. I captured that moment in the retina of my eyes and knew I could move on physically, but no matter where I travelled in the world, this was what I would see when I closed my eyes.

PART THREE

CHAPTER TWENTY-SEVEN

Southern Stream FM

News had just reached us that the emergency call from a young teenager, who claimed she was being held at gunpoint is genuine. Gardai are not releasing details of the incident and the only information I can bring you with any certainty is that the location where this incident is taking place has been traced. We have also been told that the unnamed teenager is not the only hostage. Her mother, who is believed to be a lone parent, is also with her. She has one other daughter whose whereabouts are yet to be established.

The names of the hostages have still not been released, nor has the location. Morning Stream will bring further information to you as soon as this news embargo is lifted. Online speculation as to where the siege is taking place is rife. Once again, journalists and broadcasters must cope with outdated regulations that prevent vital information being shared on mainstream media while it's widely disseminated online. But that is an issue for another day and, presently, our thoughts and prayers are with the besieged teenager and her mother.

Stay tuned to Morning Stream for continuous coverage of this unfolding siege.

CHAPTER TWENTY-EIGHT

Sophy

The gate in the wall had been oiled and opened easily. No shrieking hinges to startle the rooks and scatter them from their roost. Sophy had been able to step without hindrance from one world into another, or so it had seemed, each time she entered Victor's domain. For those few hours in his company she could forget that she was an angry wife, an anxious mother, a troubled nurse. Victor loved her, desired her, devoured her with his bold, blue stare. Her only responsibility was to love him back. That should not have been difficult but each time she went to him she left a little bit more of herself behind in Hyland Hall.

She was haunted by flashbacks. The image of Julie's limp body in Luke's arms. Would it ever fade? She had been doing Victor's bidding while her daughter almost drowned. The horror of what could have happened clogged her chest. Being loved by him, no matter how passionately and how often he declared it, could not wipe away her guilt. Since that terrifying afternoon, there was no going back into the other world he had created for her. Jack's delusions about her, however insulting and unjustified, no longer mattered. He had sacrificed his health to rescue Julie and that was where her loyalty lay.

She made excuses when Victor rang. Julie was still recovering from her ordeal. Isobel had a cold that kept her out of school for a week. Jack needed more physio, more attention. Was Luke the reason she was avoiding him, Victor demanded? No matter how often she explained to him that she seldom saw Luke, he still believed that the return of her husband was driving a wedge between them.

She was not lying when she told Victor she was busy. Jack was growing weaker and needed more attention. Workmen came and went from the house. Each job they undertook revealed another one that needed to be tackled. Luke and Charlie were spending a lot of time with Jack in his living room. Whatever they were planning energised him for brief periods but he quickly tired as the day wore on.

She watched in wonder the gentle unfolding of a new friendship between her daughters and the man who had terrified them. As their fears faded away, so, too, did Jack's reticence. He came downstairs in the evenings to eat with them. Later, he would sit in the music room and watch the sun setting the sky ablaze. Then, like a sudden extinguishing, the darkness of winter would descend and close out the light.

Victor rang one afternoon from his office. This time, he cut her excuses short and demanded to know why she hadn't told him his uncle planned on turning Hyland Estate into a refuge for clapped out horses?

'A refuge?' Sophy was unable to hide her surprise. 'Where did you get that information?'

'He's applied to the council for planning permission to extend Hyland Hall and turn it into a residential facility for junkies and ex-cons.' A second phone rang in the background and a printer that must have been close to him clattered loudly yet nothing could overlie the panic she heard in his voice.

'That can't possibly be true.' But even as she denied such a possibility, it explained Jack's animation and his constant meetings with Luke and Charlie.

'Brendan Boyle has all the details,' said Victor. 'He hears everything that's going on in Clonmoore.'

'There has to be some mistake,' she argued. 'I'll check with Jack and find out exactly what's going on.'

'Abandoned race horses,' Jack explained as he unrolled his plans from a cylinder and spread the sheets of paper before her on the card table. She recognised Luke's precise drawings and his handwriting. On the top of the sheet he had written *The Hyland Equine Foundation*.

'It happens when these racehorses don't prove their worth on the track and their owners are no longer willing to invest in them,' he said. 'I'd stabled the first one here when the fire broke out. Charlie is looking after him for now but I'll take him back when the stables are rebuilt.'

Rebuilding the stables would be his first priority. Refurbishing the house and the outhouses would provide accommodation for young people with addiction problems. He planned to bring them to Hyland Hall when they were in the final stages of their recovery. Caring for the horses would be their responsibility. The Hyland Equine Foundation was wonderfully idealistic yet destructive of everything Victor hoped to do.

'What about the retail centre?' she asked when she finished examining the plans. 'Victor told me you'd planned to sell your land to a group of property investors.'

'My nephew has been whispering in your ear for far too long, Sophy. It's my land and this is what I intend doing with it.' He tapped his hand off the plans. 'Charlie and Luke will see that my foundation comes to pass.'

'This horse refuge – equine foundation – whatever it's called, will ruin Victor.'

'Then, let him be ruined. I'm no longer interested in his schemes.'

'So, you do remember discussing the retail centre with him?'

'We discussed it many times. Laurence had also spoken to me about it and I was—'

He broke off when the door opened and Charlie entered the room with a basket of logs. He handed Jack a copy of the Clonmoore Weekly and the two men began to discuss the front page headline about a proposal to turn Lower Main Street into a one way traffic flow.

That night, when Jack was sleeping, she asked Charlie to stay with him until she returned from Mount Eagle. She opened the gate and stepped onto Victor's garden. Outside lights illuminated the terrace where sun loungers were stacked together. She walked past the swimming pool, drained for the winter, its cover splattered with dead leaves. Victor brought her into the conservatory and gestured towards the two-seater sofa.

'I've missed you,' he said when they were seated together. 'After our last time together, how could you stay away for so long?'

She shied away from the intimacy of shared memories. All that passion released while her daughters were fantasising about shadows. When they had returned from the lake, Julie had explained her reason for going there. Cordelia had dared her to find out if there were vampire coffins in the boathouse. Only for Jack's keen hearing – he claimed it had been sharpened, rather than damaged by the fire –she could have lost her child. Her spine tingled as the flashback came again. The haunting pieta image of her husband coming towards her with Julie in his arms.

'I've spoken to Jack,' she said. 'What you've heard is true. However, his vision of how his foundation will operate is quite different to yours.'

'I'm not concerned about the finer details,' he said. 'Only on how it can be stopped.'

'How would you envisage doing that?' she asked.

'By acquiring power of attorney over his affairs.' There it was, a blunt declaration. No frills or drumroll to moderate his intention. His features seemed sharper than she remembered, the jut of his jaw more defined. 'I can't tolerate his craziness any longer. Not only has he stolen my inheritance, he's now determined to squander it on this hare-brained scheme. I won't allow it, Sophia. I *can't*. This has to stop now.'

'Jack will never agree to signing power of attorney over to you. What makes you think that would be even possible?'

'The care he's received from you can't be faulted but his mental health is a different matter. His delusions are not only alarming, they're dangerous. You must be anxious, as I am, that he receives the attention he needs.'

They were sitting too closely together. She felt squashed between the side of the sofa and pressure from his shoulder, yet to move away from him would emphasise an awkwardness she had never felt in his company until now.

'I want only what's best for Jack,' she said.

'Then, as his nurse, your best course of action would be to write a detailed report on all that's occurred since you started looking after him,' he said. 'Describe the verbal abuse you've suffered. His illusions about you. His obsessive reclusiveness and night wanderings. Did you know that he's been phoning me in the small hours ever since I stopped visiting him?'

'I wasn't aware of that.'

'I won't repeat his vile comments but they're truly disturbing. I worry about you and the girls being alone with him.'

'If I write this report, what will happen then?' she asked.

'Combined with mine, we can present it to his medical team and make a case for him to receive the psychiatric care he needs.'

'You think he should be committed?'

'He's lost his mind, Sophia. Do you honestly believe he'd go voluntarily into a psychiatric hospital?'

'No, I don't see that happening,' she agreed. 'What will happen to me if I'm no longer employed to look after him?'

'What a question to ask.' He cupped her chin in his hand and drew her face towards him. 'You and the girls will move into Mount Eagle. It's what we've planned all along.'

'Your uncle's health is failing,' she said. 'And this foundation is his dream. After he's gone, the land will be yours. You can do what you want with it then.'

'That'll be too late. I've made promises to certain investors that must be honoured. They're hard businessmen, like Jack was in his day, and they're not going to tolerate any more delays.' His grip on her chin tightened. 'Just tell the truth in your report. That's all I'm asking you to do.'

She had the means to write such a report. How easy it would be to frame a narrative through Victor's one-dimensional gaze. And afterwards, the reward; a home for her daughters, security, new beginnings, all of it dependent on her cooperation.

She pulled away from him and hugged her arms to her chest. 'I was hired to nurse your uncle back to health and you're asking me to kill him... yes, *kill* him,' she stressed when he tried to interrupt her. 'That's what will happen to Jack if he's committed to a psychiatric hospital.'

'Don't over-dramatize what I've asked you to do,' he said. 'Jack Hyland disinherited me without a second thought and now he wants to ruin the most important property deal I've ever organised.'

'It was Laurence who disinherited you,' she said. 'Why would the man you considered to be your second father do something so cruel to you?'

'What kind of question is that? You know the reason. He was forced to change his will when he was on his deathbed.'

'All I've ever heard is your side of the story, Victor.'

'Are you calling me a liar?'

'If you insist that Jack is crazy, then you undoubtably are a liar,' she said. 'I've no intention of writing that report. I'll vouch for his sanity before any medical panel. I'll tell them how he risked his health to save my daughter from drowning. I should have been looking after my children but, instead, I was in the basement searching for information you needed.'

'Don't offload your guilt onto me. I told you not to do anything that would jeopardise your job.'

'That's true,' she admitted. 'You're more subtle than that.' Her chest expanded when she eased out of the chair and stood before him. Determination had chiselled his face into harsh, unfamiliar lines. No, she thought, not so unfamiliar. She had glimpsed that same expression when he entered Hyland Hall on the night of her arrival and realised that his plan to control his uncle had failed.

'Did you ever have any feelings for me?' she asked. 'Or have I always been simply a means to manipulate Jack—'

'Sophia, can you hear yourself?' He sounded bemused. 'If I wanted you to manipulate my uncle, I'd have been sadly disappointed. He's still living in that mausoleum. You couldn't even persuade him to have Sunday lunch with me.'

'He's capable of making his own decisions.'

'As are you. Have you given a thought to your future? What will happen to you and your daughters when he dies and Hyland Hall is rubble? I've offered you my home and my love. Will you destroy all that to protect a man who calls you a gold-digging whore?'

Three weeks ago, she lay on his bed and took him into her, not once, but twice, with hardly a pause into between. Such heat, electrifying, tumbling her through waves of pleasure, every nerve pulsating. Now, she was chilled. The cold wind of reality blowing away every sensation she had experienced in his arms.

'You're the only person to use that word, Victor,' she said. 'And if you want me to be your whore, Mount Eagle would be a poor reward for my services.'

She had stood by Jack's bedside and considered how easily he would die if she held a pillow over his face. How had she allowed her mind to become so unhinged? Low hanging fruit, easily plucked. Strings, invisible and controlling, how deftly Victor had operated them, pulling her this way and that. She had been his marionette but the strings he'd held were now severed and she had only one thing more to say to him before she left.

'My name is Sophy,' she said. 'It's *Sophy*.'

CHAPTER TWENTY-NINE

Isobel

Fear Zone turned out to be such an ordinary place. The name sounded silly now. So, also, did the name she had given to Jack. He had risked the treacherous mud to rescue her sister and the word 'recluse' had an alien sound. Isobel would never use it again. She started to call him 'Mr Hyland' at first but he said 'Jack' would do just as well. His face with its scars and puckers still upset Isobel but only because of the pain it caused him. Each time he told her a little bit more about his youth, she imagined the ghost of his family moving past. Not in a scary way but as if they were gently stirring the air around them when he spoke their names.

The shock of what had happened to Julie had not brought her parents any closer. Happy endings only happened in books. In real life, hurt feelings and broken promises were not easily forgiven or forgotten. Admittedly, they were talking to each other and her father sometimes came into the kitchen with Charlie for tea and sandwiches. Mostly, he ate at the gate lodge and was happy to be close to them again.

Isobel was afraid to ask him about the gold coin and his head or tails decision. Every time they were together, the question bubbled up inside her yet it was easier not to know. He had changed since that night. He seemed to be standing straighter yet she didn't remember him being stooped. Sometimes, she found him sitting on the stump of a tree, just gazing ahead. She trusted his silence and knew that when he was ready, his thoughts would come back to them.

He was working in the woods one afternoon when she brought him sandwiches and a flask of tea. He looked burly and flushed in his padded anorak. Sweat had darkened the navy bandana he had tied around his forehead. He tore off the wrapping on the sandwiches and took a huge bite. 'Mmmm! Chicken and stuffing, my favourite.'

'Is Jack going to die?' Isobel wiped a smudge of muck from his cheek.

'We're all going to die someday,' he replied and chewed faster.

'That's not an answer. Is he?'

'I don't know. And neither does he.' He shrugged, as if he was not particularly worried but the line between his eyebrows deepened. 'Why all the questions?' He poured tea from the flask into a mug and took a sip. 'Just the way I like it. Strong enough to trot a mouse on top.'

'*Gross*. If Jack dies you won't have a job,' she said. 'If Mum can't look after Jack any more, then she won't have a job either.' Isobel waited for him to say something. When he remained silent, she added, 'That means you'll be separated from us again.'

'We're still separated, Isobel. Distance is not the only thing that makes a separation. But Jack won't die until his work here is done.'

'He can't cheat death a *fifth* time.'

'Everyone's luck runs out sooner or later.'

'Like yours did?'

'I allowed my luck to run out. I had a fortune right in front of my eyes and I squandered it all.'

'Do you mean us?'

'Who else could I mean?' He pinched her cheek and smiled. 'Who needs Lady Luck when I have my two wonderful girls to love. How do you feel about Hyland Hall now that you've become acquainted with Jack?'

'I hated it so much but …' She tried to explain her confusion. 'I guess it's okay in ways and Jack doesn't frighten me anymore but I just wish… You know what I wish…'

'I know, I know.' No explanations were necessary. 'I'm sorry your mother and I can't grant it. But, hear this, no matter what the future holds…' He paused for emphasis. 'I'm only *ever* going to be a hand's reach away from you and Julie.'

Soon it would be Christmas. Frost glistened on the trees but with the central heating repaired, Hyland Hall was as warm as toast. Her father cut down two fir trees. They would decorate the dining room and music room. Isobel and Julie decorated them with fairy lights, and made garlands of laurel for the mantelpiece and bannisters. Holly wreaths hung from the front door and were draped around the necks of the stone lions. But the mistletoe was the most important Christmas decoration of all.

Isobel went to the woods with Charlie, who pointed to what looked like a deserted bird's nest high up on a sycamore tree. She climbed into the branches and gathered handfuls of waxy green stems with white berries. When she returned to Hyland Hall, she decorated the house with it. As an extra precaution, she hung sprays of berries over the front and back doors. She didn't believe in vampires but she had never stopped believing in the magic of Christmas.

On Christmas Day, Hyland Hall smelled of spices, herbs, plum pudding and a roasting turkey. Her mother was basting the turkey when her father entered by the back door. A sprig of mistletoe hung directly above them but they didn't notice it. He put his presents down on the kitchen table and opened his arms to Isobel. Instead of his usual muddy jeans and anorak, he was wearing a casual jacket and black cords. His black shirt was open at the neck. He looked smart and handsome, just like he used to do. She wanted her mother to turn around and look at him, really see him. But the roasting tray almost overbalanced and she said, 'It's okay, I can manage,' in a breathless voice when he tried to help.

'What's with the mistletoe, Isobel?' He finally noticed the sprigs on the ceiling. 'You've hung it everywhere.'

'I picked too much and didn't want to throw it away,' she replied.

'You have to kiss me under the mistletoe, Daddy.' Julie rushed into the kitchen and hugged him. He kissed her forehead, then added his presents to the growing pile under the tree in the music room.

Jack glided downstairs on the stairlift with his presents in his arms. Isobel had learnt to tell his moods by his gestures and she could see his happiness as they gathered around the table. Julie and Cordelia were wearing Santa hats and flashing earrings. Everyone clapped and laughed when they pretended to really believe Cordelia was singing 'Jingle Bells'. They put on the funny hats from the Christmas crackers and laughed at the awful jokes – and groaned at the riddles, which were even worse. They fed Caesar and Peeper from the table, even though that was forbidden, and, for once, their mother looked the other way.

After dinner, they went into the music room to exchange presents. As far as Isobel was concerned, the presents her parents bought for each other were disgraceful. Sophy gave him a bottle of wine in a glitzy bag with The Silver Spoon printed on it. Luke bought her a scarf. It didn't matter that it was made from silk and had a hand-printed design, and that the wine was very expensive. They were still the kind of presents parents gave to teachers.

Her mother had found a box of old photographs in the attic. She'd had them restored and had arranged them in an album for Jack. His parents were standing in the stable yard and a horse, peering over the half-door, was nuzzling his mother's shoulder. His twin brother looked like him when they were young yet Isobel could tell the difference from the way Laurence jutted his chin. His sister Olive had a haughty expression and looked like she was doing the camera a favour when she put on her pouty smile. In another photograph, Jack was riding with Charlie over the Gallops. They both planned to be jockeys, only Jack grew too tall and Charlie's father insisted that his son join the family business and become an undertaker. To groom the dead instead of horses, Isobel shied away from such a thought on Christmas Day.

Jack's voice was even hoarser than usual when he thanked Sophy for the album. His gift to their father was a painting that used to hang in the den. Isobel had never paid attention to it until that moment. The artist had painted a ploughed field with rough furrows and clusters of stones. The fields seemed empty of life except for a green stem, so fine it was almost invisible, yet it had forced its way through the lumpy clods. Her father kept staring at it and biting his lip, which Isobel did when she was battling tears.

More presents came. Books and diaries and fluffy slippers from Jack, even a pair for Cordelia in her correct size.

'I've something for my girls.' Their father gave them heart-shaped lockets with a photo of him on one side and their mother on the other. 'Just to let you know we'll always be together inside your hearts,' he said when he fastened the chains around their necks.

Their mother muttered something about checking mince pies and almost ran from the room.

'Go and speak to her,' Jack said in his growly voice that always sounded cross, even when he was telling stories and yearning to be young again.

'She won't listen to me,' her father replied.

'Words of love may not be heeded but they are never wasted.' Jack turned his fierce gaze on Isobel. 'Don't you agree, child?'

'I guess…' she began.

'I've something to say and I need you all to hear it together.' He was speaking to her father again. 'I need Sophy here beside me.'

Her parents were missing for so long that he asked Isobel to tell them to hurry up. They had just returned from the kitchen when the front door opened.

'Ho! Ho! Ho! Merry Christmas one and all.' Victor's face was flushed, his eyes bloodshot as he swayed on the threshold of the music room. 'I couldn't let the season pass without paying my respects to my beloved uncle.' He almost fell over when he made a mock bow to Jack.

Isobel was afraid to look at Julie, knowing that if they started giggling together, they'd go into convulsions.

'I came bearing gifts,' he said and handed Jack a small box with a watch inside it. Not only could it tell the time, it could also monitor his blood pressure and heart rate, and count all the steps he would take every day. Everyone except Victor could tell that Jack hated it. Her mother was holding her shoulders high, as if she was mortified by his arrival, especially when he lifted up the painting and insisted it was part of his inheritance. He was so drunk that he kept going on about cuckoos invading his nest or, maybe, it was about Jack living in cloud cuckoo land. He was speaking so fast it was hard to make out what he was saying. He pushed her father away when he was asked to leave and almost fell on top of Cordelia when he plonked himself down beside her on the sofa.

'Anyone care to join me?' he said and laughed when he saw the mistletoe on the ceiling. 'Sophia, how about a kiss for Christmas? I've missed our—'

'You're not welcome here.' Jack spoke so suddenly that Victor stopped in mid-sentence. 'I've tolerated your presence for long enough. I may be half-blind but I can see through smoke and mirrors. And when the smoke is dense enough, I see even more clearly.'

Jack was always speaking in riddles but Victor was no longer laughing as he heaved himself up from the sofa.

'It's a sad day when my uncle refuses to welcome me into his home at Christmas,' he said. 'Oh, well, I guess I'll be in my way then.' He shrugged when no one answered him and closed the front door with such force that it rattled the horseshoe knocker.

'What did you want to tell us, Jack?' Her father turned from the window where he and Isobel had been watching Victor walking unsteadily towards the gate in the wall.

'The moment has passed but it will come again.' Jack shook his head and the happiness that had carried him through the day left him.

Sophy was by his side instantly. 'I think you've had enough excitement for one day,' she said. 'It's time to rest.'

'It's the first time since the fire that I've been able to forget this body.' He touched the wrinkled skin on his cheek. Isobel guessed it was his way of saying he'd enjoyed himself, apart from Victor's unexpected arrival.

Her father said it was also time for him to leave. He hugged her and Julie really hard and shook Jack's hand.

'Goodnight, Sophy,' he said. He hesitated, as if he was going to hug her, too.

'Goodnight, Luke,' she replied then bent to help Jack to his feet.

Above them, the white berries on the mistletoe glistened like tears that could not be kissed away. No magic this year.

CHAPTER THIRTY

Sophy

Victor's visit had taken a severe toll on Jack's energy yet he was reluctant to go to bed. Sophy helped him into his armchair and Caesar, overfed on turkey scraps, sprawled drowsily on the living room rug.

'This is my last Christmas,' he said. 'But, of course, you're as aware of that as I am. Thank you for making it a very happy one.'

'I'm not God, Jack,' she replied. 'Neither are you. You've a strong heart and a will of iron. Hopefully, we'll all be together again this time next year.'

'She's calling me,' he said. 'I hear her voice more clearly every day.'

'Who is?' she asked.

'The love of my life. I planned to tell you about her today but Victor wearied my heart.'

'I'm sorry he upset you.'

'What about his heart? Have you broken it, Sophy?'

'His heart is hard to find and even harder to break.' She smiled ruefully. 'You did warn me.'

Victor's arrival had ruined the cheerful atmosphere Sophy had tried to maintain throughout the day. She had been awash with memories of other Christmases she had shared with Luke, the anticipation and excitement, the sheer joy of making it a special occasion for their family. The longing to forget the hurt and bitterness had swept over her when he followed her to the kitchen. He told her he loved her. He spoke clumsily where once he would have uttered such endearments with passion and confidence, yet his words had touched her. The moment passed when Isobel opened the door and demanded to know what was keeping them. Jack was waiting to make his important announcement.

Victor had arrived at the same time. The provocative slope of his bottom lip flaunted their shared memories and Luke had turned away, as if sickened by the knowledge he saw there. Jack's mood had also changed and whatever he had planned to tell them still remained unsaid.

He exhaled loudly and tapped the watch Victor had insisted on strapping to his wrist. 'This is his reminder that I'm marking time. Take it off and leave it in the bureau. Charlie can give it to one of his grandchildren.'

When she opened the bureau, she noticed the tiny gold sculpture in its customary compartment.

'This intrigues me.' She lifted it out and carried it over to him. 'The beauty of ugliness. What did you mean by that remark?'

'Isobel found it in the stables when she was searching for her cat. She thought it was a cinder.'

'A *cinder*?'

He nodded. 'It was originally a medallion but it melted in the fire. Charlie was able to remove the soot and allow its beauty to shine through.'

'Isobel never told me she met you in the stables. What were you doing there?'

'I was searching for anything that could reveal how the fire started. I refused to believe it was caused by faulty wiring, despite what the surveyor stated in his report. Isobel stumbled on the truth, not that she was aware of it. The child was terrified when she saw me.'

She could imagine Isobel's reaction when she was forced to confront the subject of her exaggerated fears, yet she had never mentioned this encounter to Sophy. The secrets of children, how could she have forgotten the terrifying depths of their private world?

'How could you even tell that this was a medallion?' she asked.

'It spoke to me.'

'*Jack…*'

'Sometimes, words don't have to be audible to be understood.' Despite his tiredness, he was speaking clearly. 'I was robbed on the night of the fire. Cufflinks, tie pins, watches, some rings were taken. I don't believe I'd have noticed the jewellery was missing if the thief hadn't also stolen this medallion. It was by far the cheapest item taken yet its value to me was priceless. The fire broke out shortly afterwards and the robbery was wiped from my mind until Isobel found the medallion.'

The tiny statuette gleamed even brighter when he took it from her and balanced it on the palm of his hand.

'How did it end up in the stables?'

'That is a question that haunts me.'

'Was the thief… are you saying that someone was there when the fire broke out?'

'I believe so.' He ran his hand with the missing fingers over the raddled surface of the medallion.

'Who do you think that was, Jack?'

His sunken cheeks and scarred features were immobile as he considered her question.

'Ever since the fire, my thoughts are scrambled,' he admitted. 'It's only when I write them down that they begin to make sense, and I still have much writing to do.'

What secrets did it carry in its warped crevices Sophy wondered as she replaced the medallion in the bureau?

He awoke from sleep that night. His chest was wheezy, his breathing more laboured. Victor's wait would soon be over, she thought as she settled him down and returned to her bed.

Twelve days since Christmas and the glitz had faded. Sophy climbed the stepladder and took down the first sprig of mistletoe from the ceiling. Tinsel and fairy lights had added a festive air to the rooms and the house looked even more dilapidated than usual when they were removed. Luke had left for Dublin early in the morning. He volunteered once a week at the Oasis of Hope and returned late to the gate lodge on the same day.

Pale wintery sunlight streamed into Jack's living room when she opened the curtains. The woods were stark against the skyline, the bare branches softened by the tall evergreens. Something moved within the stillness then disappeared so quickly she could have imagined it. The fly tippers had not returned since Luke's arrival. The erection of notices warning that CCTV equipment was installed on Hyland Estate was obviously acting as a deterrent. She waited at the window to see if it reappeared. The flash of silver was all she needed to confirm her suspicions. Victor was driving his jeep along the lane once taken by the fly tippers. She had discovered this lane when the council cut back the hedgerows. A wooden barricade that had once guarded the entrance had been snapped apart, the broken poles wedged into the earth. The rutted imprint of tyre tracks revealed the routes the drivers had taken on their journey to the Gallops. Luke had replaced the barricade and erected a surveillance camera. He would probably not arrive back until midnight and Victor was taking advantage of his absence.

A second car came into view behind the jeep. She pulled on her coat and called Caesar to her side. He ambled slowly behind her, snuffling into the bushes and enjoying the crisp, frosty air. His mood changed as they approached Hyland Gallops. Hackles raised, he began to snarl and run ahead of her. In the distance she could see Victor and a second man standing by the lake shore. Victor was wearing his waxed jacket, a check shirt and peaked cap, his trousers tucked into wellingtons. The second man, dressed more casually in jeans and an anorak, was staring through a theodolite mounted on a tripod. She was familiar with the instrument. Luke used one for measuring angles and distances. The use of it on Hyland Gallops could mean only one thing. Victor was surveying the land he would inherit when Jack died.

He had not been back to Hyland Hall since his unexpected and unwelcome visit at Christmas. The two men were standing still as they waited for her to approach them. She had to call Caesar to heel twice before he came to a halt.

'What are you doing here?' She spoke with an authority she was far from feeling.

'Well, good day to you too.' Victor doffed his cap and inclined his head towards her. 'To answer your question, I'm just doing as you asked and being patient.' He took a step closer to her and gestured towards the Gallops. 'This is just an initial reconnaissance.'

'Both of you are trespassing on land that doesn't belong to you.'

'You mean land that doesn't belong to me *yet*,' he said. 'How is my uncle, by the way?'

'If you don't leave immediately, I'm contacting the police.' She held up her phone as a warning.

'By all means, do so.' Victor waved a dismissive hand towards Caesar, whose lips were drawn back from his fangs, the yellow and black hairs bristling on his face. 'That beast needs to be kept under control. I'm amazed you allow him near your children. Don't you care about their safety?'

His bluster didn't fool her. He was just as unnerved as his companion by the dog's nearness. She kept her hand on Caesar's collar but the second man was already dismantling the tripod.

Ignoring Sophy, he spoke directly to Victor. 'I don't trust the look in that dog's eyes. We can do this another day.'

'There won't be another day,' she warned them. 'Otherwise, I might not be able to control Caesar if he decides to protect his master's property. Enough damage has been done to it already. Fly tippers, poisoned trees, no wonder Jack's estate is dying… but you wouldn't know anything about that, of course.'

The air between them seemed denser. The jut of his cheekbones and his eyes, blue ice, warned her that her thoughts, if spoken aloud, would gather their own momentum.

'You're quite right, I don't,' he replied. 'What I *do* know is that under your care, my uncle wanders at night and has collapsed on more than one occasion. He was alone in the house when that ceiling fell. He also strayed from the house when you were missing and could have drowned in Marsh Lake. I'm compiling quite a detailed report on your negligence for his medical team.'

Caesar growled low in his throat, his tension rippling through her arm.

'Good day to you, *Sop-hi-a*.' He turned and sauntered towards his companion.

She ignored the gritted emphasis on her name and waited until the men had disappeared before returning to Hyland Hall.

'Victor was on the Gallops with another man,' she said when she brought Jack's breakfast up to him. 'I think he's a surveyor.'

'That'll be Jason Woods,' said Jack. 'Small man with a moustache, thinning hair?'

Sophy nodded and sat down beside his bed. 'Has Victor been ringing you, Jack?'

'I get the occasional call to check that I'm still alive. His calls don't bother me.'

'Tell me if they do. We can easily block his number.'

'That won't be necessary. I can handle my nephew.'

Returning to the kitchen, she stared at the kitchen wall where Victor had cracked the plaster with his fist on the night she arrived. His venom escaping before he reined it back and set about moulding her to his will.

It was after midnight when Luke returned from the Oasis. The journey from Cork to Dublin and back again would have taken all his energy and she was surprised when he rang to see if she was free to talk.

'Do you mind if I come up to the house now?' he asked.

Was this going to be a repeat of Christmas Day, she wondered, and, if so, how would she respond? Her feelings were no longer a barometer she could trust.

'I know it's late, Sophy,' he said when she didn't reply. 'But this is important.'

She was startled by the urgency in his voice. This was not going to be a conversation about love and forgiveness, she thought, as she waited for him to arrive.

'How did it go at the Oasis?' she asked when he sat down at the table. He would not have stopped for food on his return journey and she had heated up some leftover lasagne for him.

'All good,' he said. 'The fountain is working perfectly. The group session also went well.'

'I'm glad to hear it.'

'I'm not here to discuss my therapy,' he said.

'Then why are you here, Luke?'

'I could ask you the same question,' he replied. 'Why are you here?'

'Surely that's obvious. I'm looking after Jack—'

'But *why*? How did it happen that you ended up here at Hyland Hall?'

'I was told there was a job going with accommodation and I applied for it. At the time, it seemed like the answer to our problems.'

'Did it strike you as convenient that the perfect solution could come along so easily?'

'Perfect solution? Is *that* what you think this is?' How easily he could still rouse her to anger. 'I'm sorry, Luke. I don't want to start an argument. Why don't you eat and we'll talk afterwards?' She took beer from the fridge and uncapped the bottles, passed one to him. Her chair wobbled when she sat opposite him. She must remind Charlie to fix the leg.

'Does the name Vivian Ford mean anything to you?' he asked when he finished eating.

How could he know that name? Vivian Ford, her ship in the night. A slight, grey-haired woman who came to view Park View Villas and suggested – no, not suggested, *persuaded* – Sophy to grab a lifeline that would give her and her daughters shelter.

'Vivian Ford viewed our house but she had no interest in buying it.' Luke had her full attention now. 'It was through her that I heard about Jack. Do you know her?'

'Not personally. But I believe she organised my stay at the Oasis.' He paused, as if trying to frame what he was going to say next. 'I'd been attending meetings at Gamblers Anonymous when I received a phone call from a woman who told me about her charity. She said they chose people with addiction problems whom they believed could respond to treatment at the Oasis of Hope. I was in the horrors at the time and grabbed the lifeline I was offered with both hands. Until recently, I never questioned how my stay there was funded. I wanted to thank this woman for saving my life, for that was what she did, but none of the groups I've contacted have heard of her charitable organisation.'

'There're so many charities out there—' The chair wobbled again but that could have been Sophy's grasp on reality slipping away from her.

'I don't believe it exists. I've checked the Register of Charities but I haven't seen the name she gave me listed anywhere.'

A receptionist at the Oasis of Hope had helped him in his search. Kathy was her name. She must have broken company protocol by checking the records to find that evidence for him. She had been able to tell Luke that Vivian had signed the correspondence relating to his stay at the Oasis. If enquiries were made, the identity of the benefactor who had paid his fees was to remain anonymous. Kathy, searching even more thoroughly, had discovered a photocopy of a cheque paid to the Oasis. It had been signed by Jack Hyland.

'Why?' Sophy's bewilderment grew as she realised the full extent of Jack's reach into their lives. 'What does he want with us – or *from* us?'

'I've no idea.' Luke seemed equally baffled.

'He has to explain what's going on.'

'I agree,' he said. 'We should talk to him in the morning?'

'No. He has a hospital appointment and he's always exhausted afterwards. The following day, definitely.'

Only one thing was certain, she thought as she undressed for bed after Luke left. The decisions they had taken as their relationship fell apart has been orchestrated by others. Jack Hyland was the key to the mystery and they would demand the truth from him.

CHAPTER THIRTY-ONE

Isobel

How could Isobel ever have believed Caesar was a werewolf? He was just a big, old, lumbering dog who loved chasing birds. Not that he had any hope of catching them. So many birds, Isobel had never seen anything like it. Charlie called it a 'murmuration'. He claimed the best view was from Hyland Gallops and there they were, hundreds and hundreds of starlings forming a filigree of black lace as they swerved and swirled above the lake. How did they do it, she wondered? All of them waltzing to the same inaudible tune. Caesar seemed defeated by their number as he ambled off into the woods.

The bundles of reeds stacked against the walls of the boathouse no longer frightened her. They had a purpose. Kelly Bracken's mother would weave them into a coffin for Jack when the time came for him to die. He spoke about death as if it was the most normal thing in the world which, thinking about it, was true. He had told her about his near-death experience after the fire. It sounded like a flying dream. Isobel had them occasionally. She loved the sensation of floating through air but always jerked with shock when she landed with a bump and woke up.

He had been lying on his hospital bed when it happened. The doctors and nurses were trying to bring him back to life but, then, suddenly he was looking down on them from the ceiling.

'Every earthly sound fell away,' he said. 'I was floating through a vast silent plain and travelling so fast that everything blurred until I came to the lake.'

'Marsh Lake?'

'Yes.' He nodded. 'It was on fire, or so it seemed, and I was flying into the middle of it. I was convinced the flames would take me again. I was wrong. There was no heat, no pain. Just a kaleidoscope of colours. Such colours, you can't imagine them, Isobel. The luminosity of spring and the blue swathe of summer. Autumn, too, that golden tumble, and winter's silvery stare.'

'Do you think you were hallucinating?' Isobel tried to imagine all the seasons becoming one. 'Or did that really happen?'

'Who knows, Isobel?' He sounded sad yet uplifted. 'A woman came towards me. Her arms reached out to hold me and I knew my waiting days were over. But my vision suddenly changed. I saw bulldozers on my land. The roots of trees shrivelled as they were wrenched from the ground. The woods were buried under cement, the lake drained. My home disappeared, a mushroom cloud rising then collapsing into a new shape. The only thing I knew for certain was that my journey through this life was not yet over. My heart began to beat again and the pain came back to claim me.'

'Do you think that woman is still waiting for you?'

'With all my heart I hope she is.'

'Was she someone special from your past?'

'She was only a small part of my life story,' he said. 'Yet she has been with me every step of the way.'

Being 'undead' was so different to what she had feared. Her imagination had driven Julie to the lake. A fist seemed to tighten around Isobel's heart every time she thought about what could have happened on that misty afternoon.

The starlings' murmuration wavered when a shot rang out then gracefully reformed. Someone nearby was shooting rabbits or hares. This gun only sounded once. Even still, it unsettled her as she hurried towards the woods.

There was no sign of Caesar anywhere. No bark to alert her when she called his name. She knew the exact path to take between the trees but she veered away from it as she searched for him. She was surrounded by minor trails that criss-crossed each other and led her into tangled bushes and briars. Some of the trees were dead, the bark flaked and bulging like tendons of old skin. Others were covered in massive fungi warts. Still no sight or sound from Caesar. A rabbit darted from the undergrowth, almost colliding with her before it veered sharply away. Her anxiety grew as the sun began to sink and the woods darkened. Soon it would be impossible to see in front of her. She was just about to give up searching and call her father for help when she found Caesar lying between the trees on a bed of leaves. His fur was still so warm that it was impossible to believe he would not breathe for her.

She was crying so hard she was unable to speak to her father when she finally managed to ring him.

'Where are you?' he kept shouting. 'Tell me where you are, Isobel.'

How could she describe bare boughs that bulged like skulls and crooked, bare branches, all of them identical?

'Stay where you are,' he said. 'I'll call Charlie. We'll find you in no time at all.'

She heard something behind her but she could not be certain if it was her imagination playing tricks again. The rustle of leaves being kicked aside, the snap of dead wood underfoot. An animal could make such sounds, a fox or a badger. Was that a shoulder she saw? It was almost indistinguishable from the wood-green spruce and her terror grew as she waited for the form to become real but there was nothing more to hear or see until she was dazzled by flashlights. Her father lifted her as effortlessly as he had carried Julie from the lake. He dried her tears and told her that Caesar would have died instantly. Charlie would take care of his body. They would bury him on the Gallops tomorrow.

'I was supposed to mind him,' she sobbed into his jacket, 'Jack will be furious with me when he comes back from the hospital.'

'No, Isobel. Caesar ran freely through the woods as he always did. Accidents happen. You can't be responsible for the mistakes foolish people make with guns.'

The grandfather clock was striking six when she returned to Hyland Hall and ran straight into her mother's arms. Julie was sobbing about Caesar, really sobbing, and not doing it through Cordelia. A thought flickered at the edge of Isobel's mind but it was gone and forgotten just as quickly as she left the draughty hall and entered the kitchen.

'Do you think Jack will cry twice as many tears from his good eye?' Julie asked when her parents went up the stairs to break the news to him.

'I don't know how that works,' Isobel replied. 'I think he'll cry even more than a waterfall.' She remembered her fears when she saw Caesar for the first time. The werewolf stories she had created when all the time he was just a dog, unable to survive a shot through his heart.

She was in bed and sleepless when the thought came back to her. The glass cabinet where the gun was kept had been empty when she returned from the woods. She switched on the hall light and walked past the grandfather clock and the old trunk with the domed lid. Spiders still spun their webs from the cabinet and the gun was in place, as it always was. Imagination, once again, always playing tricks with her mind.

CHAPTER THIRTY-TWO

Sophy

Smoke and mirrors, said Jack. Muddying or embellishing the truth. Sophy could understand why Jack would use that expression when speaking about a nephew who feigned affection while he waited impatiently for him to die, yet Sophy had sensed that something deeper lay behind those words. They had nagged at her ever since Christmas Day and Caesar's shooting had brought them even more forcibly to mind.

The rug where Caesar used to sleep was still in its customary place on the bedroom floor. Jack had refused to allow it to be removed and the smell of the old dog was still strong. Funny how Sophy barely noticed it when Caesar was alive yet, now, its pungency was a constant reminder that he was gone. Charlie had made enquiries throughout Clonmoore and the surrounding townlands but no one, it seemed, had been hunting in the vicinity of Hyland Estate that day. Sophy was not surprised. The person who shot Caesar did so at close range. She had kept that information from Jack and had talked him out of inspecting his dog's body, fearful that the shock would weaken him even further. He took her advice reluctantly and the fact that he agreed to do so confirmed her belief that he had been seriously debilitated by the shooting.

The atmosphere in the house was oppressive. Even Charlie's cheerful presence and Ellie's quiet determination to make it shine failed to lift the mood. Isobel's recollections of the shooting were unclear. Her story kept changing. She thought she had heard footsteps close to the scene but that could have been a fox. She thought she glimpsed a figure in the shadows but claimed it could also have been the movement of trees. Unable to stop crying every time she spoke about Caesar, Sophy had stopped pressing her for a clearer description.

Was this heaviness she felt as she climbed the stairs to tend to Jack due to the weight of secrets? As yet, she and Luke had not asked him about Vivian Ford. The shooting had affected everyone and so they had decided to hold off questioning him until he was more stable.

Smoke and mirrors… smoke and mirrors. Her mind had stalled on those words. Unable to bear their repetition, she drove to Mount Eagle one morning after the girls had boarded the school bus. Victor's jeep was missing from the driveway. She drove back to the courtyard and, knowing that she would change her mind if she hesitated, she hurried through the gate in the wall.

Victor had never offered her a key to his house and she had no idea if he kept a spare one outside. She searched beneath the terracotta plant holders and checked his garden shed where everything had a place and a purpose, and found a key to the back door under a can of weed killer.

Once inside, she moved quickly up the stairs and into his bedroom. It was as tidy as she remembered. She opened the box of jewellery on the dressing table and removed the pieces one by one. Many of the pieces would have been presents to Victor from women. This was confirmed when she saw an inscription on the back of a watch, the initials *VC* intertwined with *BM* inside a heart shape. A similar intertwining was carved on a bracelet, only the second initials were *DR*. She continued searching until she picked up an ornate signet ring. She could tell by the uneven depth of the block initials that they were hand-carved. She had admired the design on the morning she rummaged through his jewellery but had not been aware of the initials, not consciously, at least, yet the memory of that ring had drawn her back here. The initials had an intricate flourish but there was no mistaking the letters *JH*.

She laid it back in the box and crossed to the wardrobe. The mirrored door slid noiselessly across. She pulled out his wax jacket. Holding it to her face, she breathed deeply. It was still there, faint enough to be ignored, a smoky smell that lingered on the fabric like a thumbprint from the past. She carried the jacket to the window. One of the pockets was torn and had been repaired. The different shading in the stitching was slight and would not have been noticed under normal circumstances. But there was nothing normal about her thoughts as she replaced the key in its hiding place and hurried back to Hyland Hall.

Why would Victor rob his uncle? Or set fire to his property? She shuddered. If she allowed herself to think the unthinkable, what then? Was Victor a thief? An arsonist? A potential murderer? It made no sense. He and Jack had been intent on a land deal that would have enriched them both and were on the verge of concluding it when the fire broke out.

Should she reveal her suspicions to Jack? Would he believe her. Blood was thicker than water and what evidence could she place before him? A ring that he might have given to Victor. A jacket that held a faint whiff of smoke… from a cigar or two, perhaps, or a pipe. He might once have been a smoker. What did she know about his past? Would Jack reject her findings out of hand or was he already haunted – that was the term he'd used on Christmas night – by the same suspicions?

Tonight, he was back to his old habit of wandering from room to room in the small hours. She heard him on the monitor and awoke instantly. The bedroom window was open when she entered his room and found him poking a flashlight into the night.

'What are you doing, Jack?' She stood beside him as he swept a circle of light across the backyard.

'There's someone out there,' he said.

'Where are they?' She took the flashlight from him and directed it towards the disused storerooms and tool sheds. 'I can't see anything.'

'The fly tippers are back,' he said. 'They're over by the barn. I heard them.'

The gusting wind flailed her hair when she stretched out to close the window. He was shivering, his pyjamas clinging to his thin frame. 'Are you trying to kill yourself?' she demanded.

'I trust my ears,' he said with his usual certainty. 'I've nothing else to depend on since Caesar went. There's trouble about tonight.'

'Then I'll sort it out,' she said. 'I'll go over there right now and check if anyone's hanging around.'

'It's not safe,' he protested as she guided him back to his bed. 'Ring Luke—'

'He's not back from Dublin yet. Promise me you'll stay in bed until I get back?'

He nodded, reluctantly. She had to trust him to keep his word. She dressed quickly and buttoned her coat against the biting wind. Frost would lie on the ground in the morning.

The flashlight was heavy duty and lit the way for her when she checked the old storehouses and tool sheds. As she suspected, they were empty. She left the backyard and crossed to the paddock. The wind stung her cheeks as she approached the ruins. Some of the rubble from the stables had yet to be removed and work had started on dismantling the charred remains of the barn.

The domed roof had already been removed and lay beside the rubble. The crane Luke had hired to dismantle the rest of the barn was a gaunt silhouette in a slant of moonlight. Her ears strained for a sound that would confirm Jack's suspicions but the faint hoot from an owl deep in the woods was all she could hear. She walked around the barn but was unable to see anything untoward. The wind could have caused it to clang and awaken Jack but it was difficult to see how that could have happened. A more probable reason was that he had been dreaming. A nightmare filled with flames, more likely. She tried to imagine the combustion when the bales of smouldering hay caught fire. The flames would have leapt quickly to the stables and started a second conflagration. She was unable to stop thinking about Victor as she hurried back towards the house. On an impulse, she walked around the side and entered the courtyard. The gate leading into the back of Mount Eagle was closed. All was quiet. The automatic courtyard light switched off and she was plunged into darkness. She tensed when she heard a faint grinding sound that stopped and was not repeated. She switched on her flashlight and gave her surroundings another wide sweep before returning to Jack and assuring him that all was well.

The rest of the night passed without interruption. He was still adamant in the morning that he was right.

'When you became a shadow of your former self, you rely on what you have left,' he said. 'In my case, it's my hearing.'

'I'll get Luke and Charlie to check everywhere,' she promised. 'If any rubbish has been dumped, they'll find it.'

'I'll do a thorough check before I start work on the barn,' Charlie promised when he arrived. 'Luke was wondering if you'd drop into the gate lodge. He wants a word. I'll stay with Jack until you get back.'

He must be curious about their marriage but he never asked her about it. The ability to avoid awkward questions had to be the hallmarks of a successful undertaker, she thought as she drove down the avenue. Luke must have news for her about Vivian Ford. Her anticipation grew as she parked outside the gate lodge.

Isobel called it the Hobbit Hut. Easy to understand why. Perhaps it was the spaciousness of Hyland Hall that made it seem so cramped. Luke seemed indifferent to his surroundings as he fussed over a coffee machine. He had bought it in Dublin and was still getting used the mechanics of it, he said, when he presented her with a frothing cappuccino and a photocopy of a newspaper clipping.

'I've checked Vivian Ford online. Plenty of entries under that name but none of them seemed right. I was about to give up when I found an old newspaper feature about a mother and daughter reunion. The daughter had run away from home when she was sixteen. To all intents and purposes, she had fallen off the edge of the world but she was traced by a private detective. According to the report, this detective had a reputation for finding people who, for whatever reasons, had been separated from their families. Here it is.'

He spread a photocopy of the article over the table. Vivian Ford was twenty years younger, according to the date on the paper. Her hair was brown then, her skin smoother but Sophy recognised her straightforward gaze. If her age was any indication, she should be retired by now, but she was obviously still active and working for Jack Hyland.

'Let's talk to him this afternoon,' Sophy said. 'He looks exhausted this morning. I want him rested and coherent when he answers our questions.'

'That's okay with me.' He bent down to knot a bootlace that had come undone. 'I'll head off now and check for a dump, though I doubt if I'll find one.'

He was dressed for work: jeans, jumper and an anorak she had bought for him some years previously. Everything about him was familiar yet strange, as if his time spent in the Oasis and the time before, when he was lost to them, had changed him in ways she would never be able to fathom.

The last time they spoke he told her something she had never known about him. His gambling began when he was eighteen and had been triggered by the discovery that his father had not died in a mining accident. His mother, the woman he trusted more that anyone, had lied to him. Nor could she tell him who had fathered him. How many hours of therapy and soul-searching had it taken to link his addiction to trauma, disappointment, disillusionment, grief, loss? Was that to be the pattern of his life? He wrestled with that question every day.

Their marriage might have stood a chance had she agreed to share in his rehabilitation. Anger had blinded her to the possibility of a future with him and exploring the complexities of his gambling addiction had not interested her. Would it have healed them? It was too late now, she thought, as she drove back to Hyland Hall. She had forged a new path for herself. It was strewn with obstacles but they were of her own making and she would walk its craggy surface alone.

When she brought Jack up his morning medication, his breakfast was untouched, apart from a few sips of tea. The rug looked bare without the sprawl of the old dog across it. His bedside radio was tuned to Southern Stream FM as usual. The familiar voice of Gavin Darcy, his favourite presenter, was reporting on an event that had taken place at the Clonmoore community centre. Jack had no interest in tuning into national or global news stations.

'I lived my working life on a rolling news cycle,' he told her once. 'Economics and politics turn the wheels of finance and I always needed to be ahead of the next surge. Now, I've discovered

I don't have to turn the dial. Just listen local and the same wars are played out across the airwaves.'

Luke texted to say the estate had been searched and they had found nothing to foul the crisp morning air. She stood by Jack's bedroom window and watched him enter the cab of the crane. The frost was beginning to melt. Droplets glistened on the black branches and the sheen of silver still covered the backyard.

'It's a beautiful day,' she said but Jack had closed his eyes and appeared not to hear her. The clanking reverberations of the crane reached her as Charlie came into view from behind the barn. He looked upwards as the yellow arm of the crane clutched a section of metal and lifted it from the frame. What followed seemed to happen in slow motion yet Sophy was conscious of how it would end when she saw a section from one of the blackened walls sway. For an instant the wall remained poised then with a sudden force that tore a cry from her, it fell. The shriek it made as it hit the ground where Charlie had been standing could be clearly heard. She was unaware that she had cried out or that Jack had left his bed until he stumbled to her side. His bony fingers gripped the window ledge as he watched Luke jump down from the cab.

Instantly, she was on her phone to the emergency services while trying to move Jack away from the window at the same time.

'Go back to bed. Everything's okay… I'm going down to check. *Stay* in bed,' she pleaded. Her mind was already racing across the paddock but she could not leave him until he was safe.

'Save my friend.' His voice trembled as he lay down and pressed his face into the pillow.

Luke was struggling to lift the section of wall from Charlie when she reached him. Unable to budge it, he yelled at her to move away. He returned to the cab of the crane. He began to work the joysticks and slowly, agonisingly, the wall moved upwards and was laid to one side. She knelt beside Charlie and forced back a sob. No need to search for his pulse or harbour any false hope. Luke had jumped from the cab and was on his knees beside her. Charlie had died instantly and Luke, knowing this, removed his anorak and laid it over his face.

An ambulance was on its way, she told him. So were the gardai and the fire brigade. He nodded, too stunned to respond. She took him in her arms and was washed in his tears.

'Jack saw everything,' she whispered. 'I have to go back to him.'

She left him weeping over Charlie's body and ran towards the house. Thankfully, Jack was not standing at the window but her relief was short-lived when she was unable to enter the bedroom. He must have collapsed – she refused to think of a worse scenario – and his body was on the floor.

When she thumped on the door and called his name, he gave a low moan. 'Jack, can you hear me?' she shouted.

He moaned again and the door gave way slightly.

'Are you able to move even a little bit more?' she asked.

She heard a dragging noise, accompanied by more moans. At least he had some mobility and enough consciousness to understand her. She squeezed through the narrow space that opened up and found him breathing heavily as he continued to drag himself across the floor. He must have been trying to leave his bedroom when he collapsed. No bones had been broken in his fall but his breathing alarmed her, as did his low blood pressure. To her relief, he was able to stand unsteadily and rest on his bed until the second ambulance arrived.

'I heard him… I always hear him…' She managed to decipher his croaking words.

'Hush, hush,' she said. 'Save your energy. The ambulance is here. You're going to be all right, Jack.'

He was still muttering to himself when she ran downstairs to open the front door. He quietened down when the paramedics entered his bedroom. They were grim and efficient, no joking this time, though it was the same team as before. The reality of Charlie's death lay heavily on everyone. Jack's phone lay on the floor. She checked the last phone call he had received then shoved it into her pocket.

Victor had already arrived in his jeep. He must have heard the crash from his house and was insisting on accompanying his uncle to hospital. Emma, the paramedic with the buzz haircut, was arguing with him. She understood his distress but the only person who could accompany Jack in the ambulance was his nurse. Her formidable tone silenced his protests but his distress was apparent as Emma stood aside for Sophy to mount the steps.

She held Jack's hands as the ambulance hurtled along the country road. Victor followed closely behind. The second ambulance with Charlie's body, watched over by Luke, had no need to rush.

CHAPTER THIRTY-THREE

Isobel

A piper walked slowly along Upper Main Street at the head of the funeral procession. The swirling, lonely wail of his pipes reminded Isobel of her grandmother's funeral. Those walking behind the piper carried Charlie's coffin on their shoulders. It was comforting to know that it had been woven by those who loved him from the reeds she had discovered in the boathouse. One of the bearers was Tina Bracken, Kelly's mother. Today, she was a mourner, not an undertaker. Kelly, walking behind the wicker coffin, kept her hand on it the whole time. She had shaved off her hair. Her eyes looked enormous and her ears reminded Isobel of pixies.

Maddie had had a shaving-off-her-hair party before she started chemo. Isobel remembered how her father had gently run the clippers across her scalp.

The urge to cry swept over her. She should be used to those sudden waves by now yet they always took her by surprise. Was her father also remembering? He stared straight ahead and his bleak expression reminded her of the first time he came to Clonmoore. A Saturday Dad who wanted to make everything all right again.

Kelly Bracken had not been on the school bus for the last three mornings. Isobel took no pleasure at having the seat to herself. She knew what the pupils were whispering. It was the same accusation that Victor made when he came to Hyland Hall after Charlie died. He called her father a murderer. It was all his fault that the wall collapsed. He said that Charlie's blood was on her father's hands because he had not followed health and safety regulations. Isobel had listened outside the music room to him shouting at her mother and accusing her of negligence. She had left Jack alone so often that it was a miracle he had survived this latest fall. It was her fault for not listening to Victor's advice. Her mother called him a vulture and Victor left in such a temper that he hit one of the stone lions with his jeep and broke it into pieces.

Now, as Isobel walked in the funeral procession with Julie and her parents, she was aware that people were looking at them. She never caught them staring, just hurriedly looking away or pretending they had seen something interesting over her father's shoulders. They were thinking the same things about the accident as Victor had said. Isobel hated him now. How could she ever have imagined him as a stepfather?

Traffic through Clonmoore had been diverted and cars were not allowed across the bridge until after Charlie was buried. It was Saturday and the town had come to a standstill on this usually busy day. The procession reached the cemetery. Everyone gathered in a circle around the grave. Kelly was standing opposite her. A hesitant smile crossed her face when Isobel made a heart shape with her hands.

After Charlie was buried, her parents dropped Julie off at her pony club and drove to the hospital to visit Jack. Isobel remained behind in the old graveyard. The tombstones sloped at odd angles, as if they were tired standing upright after so many years. The inscriptions were almost illegible but she was able to read the names on Victor's parents' grave; Olive and Maurice Coyne, buried together. She saw Jack's parent's names, Bernard and Stephanie, on another tombstone and a newer grave where Laurence, Jack's twin brother, was buried.

Two yew trees stood like bookends at either side of a stone bench. It was peaceful sitting there. Even the birdsong sounded softer, as if the birds were in tune with the ancient memories that lay around her. The clouds billowed like sails on a ship before the wind sculptured them into other, new shapes for her to decipher. Her life, also, was constantly changing. She thought about Jack's vision and how he had made a choice to come back to this world again. Did Charlie have that same experience? Was he able to decide to go or stay as the barn wall fell on him? Did Maddie? Her grandmother seemed very close to Isobel, even though her ashes were far away at sea and floating with the tides.

'Thanks for coming to Gramp's funeral.' Isobel had not heard Kelly Bracken approaching the bench. She stood awkwardly in front of Isobel, a rose from one of the wreathes clasped in her hand.

'I liked Charlie very much,' Isobel said. 'I'm *really* sorry he's dead.'

'Yeah, Gramps was kinda special.' Kelly sat down on the bench and laid the rose between them.

'Is he the reason you've shaved off your hair?'

'I did it to help him transition into the next life.' Kelly made it sound like transitioning was the most natural thing in the world. 'Gramps taught me a lot about different death rituals from around the world. I liked this one best.' She ran her hand over her scalp. 'It also makes life easier. I don't have to stress over which hair colour will freak everyone out most on the bus.'

'I liked tangerine best,' Isobel said.

Kelly's doe eyes lit for an instant then dulled again. 'Gramps liked your dad. He'd be furious if he knew the stories that are going around the town about his accident.'

'Victor Coyne started them.'

'I know. Mum called him a liar to his face when she heard. Are you glad your dad's living with you again?'

'He's not really *living* with us. Him and Mum are separated.'

'Like my parents. My dad's in Australia. Where did your dad live before he moved here?'

'He was in rehab.'

'Drugs?' Kelly didn't bat an eyelid.

'No. Gambling.'

'Is that an addiction?' She sounded surprised.

'He says it's an addiction when the money you win is never enough to satisfy you. That's why he gambled all our money.'

'Is he the reason you're so angry all the time?'

'I'm not angry... well, not *all* the time. That first morning on the bus...' Isobel hesitated, swallowed hard. 'I wanted to sit beside you.'

'No, you didn't,' Kelly replied, matter-of-factly.

'Well... you were so intimidating. And you'd blanked me at the lake.'

'You thought I was a freak when all I was doing was helping Gramps.'

'I had this thing in my head about Mr Hyland... Jack. I was so scared of him.'

Kelly nodded, as if she understood. 'Before his accident I was always in his house with Gramps. I visited him in hospital after the fire and nearly fainted when I saw his face. After that, I wasn't allowed to see him anymore.'

'We weren't allowed to see him either.' It seemed such a natural thing to tell Kelly about the fears that had taken over her imagination. She waited for Kelly to laugh or sneer but she listened without interrupting her and only widened her eyes when she heard about Julie's accident.

'Are you still frightened of him?' she asked.

'No. He's just sad and in pain all the time.'

'He'll be lost without Gramps. We all will.'

She blew her nose and shoved the tissue back up her sleeve. 'He had this bench erected after his twin brother died. I wrote that poem for him.' She pointed towards a plaque on the back of the bench.

Let all who rest upon this seat
Remember loved ones we shall greet
Beyond the bounds of worldly woes
In blissful, heavenly repose.

'You're a poet, not an undertaker.' Isobel was impressed.

Kelly laughed. 'Actually, I've changed my mind. I'm going to become a pathologist and look after the dead before they reach the undertaker.'

'Isn't it scary being with dead people?'

'It's alive people who're the scariest, that's what I think.'

'Do you mind what the others say about you?'

'Kelly shrugged. 'Let them talk. I honestly couldn't care less.'

People had so many different voices, Isobel decided, as they walked between the tombstones. Exciting new adventures voices, whiny voices, squeaky voices, pleading voices, angry voices, and the one that hid any sign of hurt most of all. The 'I couldn't-care-less' voice that Kelly Bracken used to dismiss those who called her a freak.

CHAPTER THIRTY-FOUR

Sophy

That terrible day when Charlie died had finally come to an end but the rumours had already started by then. Victor's lies, always plausible, always convincing, carried weight in this close-knit community. The confidences Sophy had shared with him were being regurgitated for public consumption. Details of Luke's gambling addiction had been released with deliberate precision. Gavin Darcy from Southern Stream FM had asked him for an interview. He declined and sought advice from Jack's solicitor, who told him the only comment he should make was 'No comment'. He had been questioned by the police. Nothing had been found to explain the instability of one section of the barn but that made no difference to the speculation surrounding the accident.

The solitary lion looked lonely without its companion. The remains of the second one, too damaged to be repaired when Victor's jeep overbalanced it, had been swept up and thrown away. Sophy patted the stone head when she reached the bottom step then hurried across the courtyard towards the gate in the wall.

On the day the accident occurred, she had been too distraught to notice if the bull bars were missing from Victor's jeep. Yet, somehow, in the midst of the pandemonium, an impression must have registered with her. They had not been replaced when he parked his jeep outside the cemetery yesterday morning.

She walked through the copse of tress into the land he hoped to sell. The derelict market garden was even wilder than she remembered. Knee-high grass and brambles made it difficult to penetrate some areas but she forced her way through the undergrowth. Anger helped. It gave her the strength she needed to continue searching when briars tangled in her hair and nettles stung her hands.

She was about to give up the search when she came across the rusting frame of an old greenhouse. Some of the glass panes were still intact but most were cracked or broken. Glass crunched under her feet as she drew nearer. The door hung open on one hinge. She stopped, alert and cautious. Weeds and creepers had been flattened and crushed. A crumpled tarpaulin was bunched on the floor. She pulled up one side of it and saw what she had suspected. The bull bars were badly dented and bent in places. Jack had been right. His hearing had not deceived him. Victor had used his jeep as a weapon to destabilise the barn and end Charlie Bracken's life. Had Luke been the intended victim? Or had Victor chosen Charlie, just as he had chosen Caesar, to take all that was precious from Jack and speed him towards his death.

She returned to Hyland Hall and rang the hospital to check on Jack's condition. She and Luke were taking turns to stay with him. He was stable, the nurse told her, no change. He was weak but was willing to allow Luke to feed him small morsels of food. They both knew he was dying. This time there would be no pulling back, no miracle.

She collapsed on her bed and lay there. Her hands were covered in nettle rash and scratches but they were insignificant injuries compared to her tormented thoughts. Who would listen to her if she voiced such suspicions aloud? Victor would demolish them with oily words of sincerity. A battered set of bull bars, what did that prove? He would argue to the gardai that the damage had been caused by a stray deer or a sheep. Roadkill, he had told her once, it happened.

Luke returned from the hospital and called in to see her. 'Jack keeps asking about a journal,' he said. 'Have you any idea what he's talking about?'

'I do. I'll bring it with me.' She longed to tell him about her discovery in the greenhouse and what she had found in Victor's bedroom. The words refused to come to her. Her mind was not yet ready to admit that the man she had loved briefly, yet passionately, was capable of such evil. Could evil lie so deeply under the skin that it obscured all signs and signals or had she been so blinded by his attentions that she had refused to heed them?

She was relieved that Luke had returned to the gate lodge when she came downstairs with the journal. Later, they would talk. She would watch his disgust grow as he realised that it was her familiarity with Victor's bedroom that first triggered the suspicions that had led her to a dangerous and horrifying deduction.

When she reached the hospital, she could tell by Jack's breathing that he was heavily sedated.

'I need to speak to Luke,' he said. 'Where is he?' His dependence on Luke had increased since he was admitted to hospital.

'He's at the gate lodge but he'll be in to see you later.'

'Tell him to come *now*.'

'He was here most of the night, Jack. Can you wait a few more hours until he's had a sleep?'

He pulled himself upright, his bony shoulders rising as he tried to support himself. His fingers clutched the sheet, his hands opening and closing. 'Fear is the worst disease of all. I've waited far too long already. I need to see him immediately.' His agitation warned her that he was being driven by something other than dependence.

'Is this anything to do with Vivian Ford?' she asked.

He fixed his one-eyed gaze on her and nodded.

Outside the ward, she rang Luke. He was sleepy when he answered. 'It's important,' she said. 'He wants to tell us something about Vivian Ford.'

'I'll be there as quick as I can.' His tone sharpened. 'Traffic allowing, I should be with you in an hour.'

'Luke's leaving now,' she said when she returned to the ward. 'He's coming as fast as he can.'

'Do you have my journal?' he asked.

'Yes, here it is.'

'Read it,' he said. 'That will help you to understand the conversation I must have with Luke. I need to rest before he arrives so take it with you to the café.'

Mystified, she left his bedside and took the elevator to the cafeteria. The afternoon rush was over and she was able to find a free table that offered her some privacy. She ordered coffee and opened his journal. She had come upon him so often when he was lost in a reverie, the pages open, his pen lying idle along the spine.

He had been writing his memoir. She read about a bullying sibling, the struggle for identity, a love won then lost, the slow erosion of dreams, a life lived to the full yet devoid of affection, of belonging. Her coffee grew cold as she turned the pages. Sometimes, the writing blurred when her tears came. She read the notes he had written at the back of the journal. His troubled thoughts so vividly expressed. Not only had the fire destroyed his future, it had also stolen his sense of his own identity. Luke would be here soon. She checked her watch. Five minutes more should bring Jack's story to a close.

CHAPTER THIRTY-FIVE

Wildfires
A Memoir by Jack Hyland

Heads or tails. How will she spin? I left Hyland Hall with nothing. No love, no home. I moved to New York. Computers, those massive pulses of energy that we have now encapsulated into a phone that fits in my hand, made my fortune. I started companies and sold them on, to begin all over again. I loved women but I'd no desire to settle and our relationships ended quietly or, sometimes, stormily. I believed I'd found perfection with Madelaine but then discovered it was a mirage. Marked for life by her deceit.

Charlie was my link with Hyland Hall. His business prospered. The dead do not trend or buck the market. Their state is consistent, reliable. He did as his father demanded and became an undertaker but he left his heart on Hyland Gallops, as I did.

In the beginning, his letters reached me. I knew that Olive had a son but I was too bitter to make contact with her. Laurence married and separated some years later. Hyland Hall was falling into disrepair. The stables closed down and it seemed as if Laurence had become an island, isolated in a grand house that had no function. He was an experienced gambler and survived on skill and lucky breaks.

Some letters from Charlie were lost in transit as I moved from one continent to another. Olive was buried six months before news of her death reached me. I contacted Victor, the nephew I'd never seen, to express my sorrow. We began to exchange emails. His were filled with plans and ambition. He reminded me of myself in those early days when I arrived in New York. I was rediscovering a sense of kinship. Until then, I hadn't realised how tough my skin had become, a barnacled hide that had forgotten the softness of belonging to something greater than myself. Family. With every day that passed its pull was drawing me back to Hyland Hall.

In time, I grew weary of Victor's charming words. His declarations of affection inevitably became a request for money. I only realised the extent of his duplicity when Charlie phoned to tell me Laurence was dying. Victor had moved into Hyland Hall and was refusing permission to anyone to visit his uncle. Somehow, Laurence had managed to phone Charlie and begged him to make contact with me.

I returned home. When Victor answered the door, his expression told me all I needed to know. Laurence was weak and emaciated. He was terrified of Victor, who kept demanding to see his will. I threw him out of the house.

I called a doctor but it was too late for hospitalisation. Laurence was made comfortable by the hospice medical team and had enough strength before he died to press a coin into my hand. Pure gold and two-headed, he'd won it in a wager and used it to disinherit me.

I'm no stranger to savage urges and I feared my rage would be impossible to control. Somehow, I found the strength in those final days to forgive him.

Madelaine's name was the last word he uttered. His lips quivered, as if he wanted to spill out his secrets yet knew they would go with him to his grave. Then, he sighed and closed his eyes.

In his will, he gave me back what he had taken from me. Hyland Estate was mine again.

Victor was unable to hide his shock and fury when the will was read. It didn't take long to unravel that he'd planned to sell the land in a deal with a property syndicate. He'd borrowed heavily on the strength of the deal and was living way beyond his means. He'd built Mount Eagle on the site of his family home, which was demolished as soon as his mother died. He was Olive's son and I couldn't bring myself to take him down. I paid off his debts but I kept uncovering other schemes, all based around his belief that Hyland Estate would have belonged to him.

I intended to rebuild the stables. I would buy and train the finest race horses. But a greater dream came – with a letter from Madelaine. It tore away the barnacles that had protected me from pain, and left me raw and gasping. It came to me by such a circuitous route and had crossed continents to reach me. A year lost in transit. All those delays had stolen time we could have spent together. The fire broke out before I could act on the information she sent me. Even now, it is difficult to separate the two events.

Caesar's barking awakened me on that dreadful night. I could see the fire from the window. It had started in the barn and spread to the stables. A horse was stabled in one of the stalls. As I ran across the paddock, I could hear Caballero's panic, his hooves plunging against the door. I saw movement beyond the smoke. A figure so distorted and yet, how could that be? My tongue seemed swollen when I tried to call out.

No saliva in my mouth, just an acrid taste, as if the smoke had taken possession of my lungs. The latch on the door was hot to touch but with the help of a towel I managed to open it and Caballero plunged free.

Above me, a stable beam cracked. I heard it splitting but I was unable to move aside in time. Churning dust swept over me and the figure disappeared. Was it my imagination playing tricks? A phantom, created from smoke and flame. That is my last memory of that night. I would have died if Charlie had not phoned the fire brigade. He saw the smoke rising above the trees and Caesar, my faithful hound, led them to me.

I believed the fire was accidental until Isobel found Madelaine's medallion among the ash. Melted and misshapen, it still spoke to me. The medallion had been stolen in a robbery that had taken place shortly before the fire started but forgotten in the cloudiness of my thoughts as I struggled to recover. I knew then for certain that I had not imagined that figure beyond the smoke.

After the fire, I wanted to forget about the letter. Madelaine was dead. I did not need proof. I saw her in that hovering instant when I was poised between two worlds. In that vision I was whole but, when I was conscious again, I believed that my vision of myself was too degraded to be of value to anyone.

I would have passed my days in the isolation of a nursing home if Charlie had not intervened. He went behind my back and contacted his cousin, Vivian. She was retired but he persuaded her to find the truth that Madelaine had revealed in her letter. The story she brought back was a sad one. When Charlie revealed it to me, I told him to go away. I was all but dead to the world. He said my anger was a good sign. In all his years as an undertaker, none of his 'clients' had ever argued back with him. He made me laugh and, though it was a grim cackle, that laughter gave me hope.

Will Luke understand? I tossed a two-headed coin. He could not have lost the toss but in winning he would once again have lost everything. He says I lifted a curse from him that night. He's wrong. He lifted it through his own free will. In the end, that's what it comes down to: our own free will. I could confide my dark suspicions about Victor to him but what proof have I got, except for that piece of molten gold, the ruby red.

CHAPTER THIRTY-SIX

Sophy

She was weeping freely when she reached the last page. Nurse Dwyer texted to say that Jack was awake again and asking for her. He was in an armchair beside his bed when she returned to the ward. He had lost even more of his sparse weight since Charlie's death. His dressing gown with the dramatic dragon on the back, a memento of his time spent in Hong Kong, clung to his wasted body. Wordlessly, she left the journal on the bedside locker.

'Were you going to tell us on Christmas Day?' She pulled over a spare chair and sat beside him.

'That was my intention.'

'Until Victor intervened?'

'Yes. After he left, my words were mangled. When I write they flow from me but speech is torture. He has brought me to the brink of death many times. This time he has succeeded. Charlie...' He held his head upright with difficulty.

'I know... I know that now, Jack. I wish—'

'Listen carefully to me.' His hands began to tremble. 'You and Luke have to be careful. I saw the way he looked at Luke when he discovered I'd gifted him the painting. Such a small gift yet he resented losing what he believes should belong to him when I die. Until Isobel found the medallion in the soot, I'd planned to make generous provision for him in my will. But now my will is watertight and he will not inherit a red cent from me. Be careful, Sophy. My nephew is as dangerous as he is avaricious. My fears grow as my time to leave you all draws nearer.'

He fell silent when the door opened and Luke entered. He sat on the edge of the bed and leant his hands on his knees. 'I came as quick as I could, Jack,' he said. 'How are you doing?'

'I've known better days.'

'And you'll have them again.' Luke's voice was too hearty. Aware that no one believed him, he cleared his throat apologetically.

'Do you wonder about me?' Jack asked.

'I'm confused,' Luke admitted. 'I know you've financed my time at the Oasis. I'll be forever grateful to you but I need to understand why you chose to help me.'

'I'd hoped to have this conversation under different circumstances but events have foreshadowed this moment from the beginning.' He beckoned to Sophy. 'Pass the journal to me.' His voice was even more gravelly than usual, a sure sign of his nervousness.

'I want you to read a letter, Luke.' His hands trembled when he opened the journal. The envelope he removed from an inside flap in the back cover fluttered as he passed it to him.

'This is a letter from your mother,' he said. 'It's the most precious gift I've ever received.'

Sophy knew what was coming. Maddie… Madelaine… the possibility had simmered within her from the moment she came across the name in this story of unfulfilled love. She would not have hesitated to join two and two together if he was writing about Madelaine Kingston but the surname Boylan made no sense. Anyone who had loved as deeply as Jack would not make such a mistake. Watching the colour drain from Luke's cheeks as he read the letter, she could feel the certainty hardening inside her. Boylan or Kingston, it made no difference. Maddie was the young woman he had loved and lost.

Minutes ticked by without anyone speaking. When Luke cried out, she was about to go to him when Jack grabbed her wrist.

'Leave him be.' Despite his trembling, his grip was still strong. 'He needs to read to the end of it.' His gaze remained on Luke. It seemed as if all the emotions his petrified features could not convey were concentrated in his undamaged eye. Protectiveness, she thought. That was what she could see there. And something else… a yearning; such a powerful yearning that embraced Luke as he reached the end of the letter. He exhaled loudly before handing it to Sophy and burying his face in his hands.

She recognised the paper, a pale shade of pink with delicate sprays of roses decorating the sides. Isobel had bought it for her grandmother as a present on the final Christmas they spent with her. The handwriting was also familiar, though slightly shakier than Maddie's usual, sweeping script.

Dear Jack,

I'm sure you'll be surprised to hear from me after such a long time. Decades have passed since I left Hyland Hall yet I still recall that summer as if it were yesterday. In the beginning, I wrote many letters to you. I never posted them. They seemed so trite when I read them back. They were unable to convey the anger and heartache I carried inside me. As time passed, I no longer felt the urge to contact you. To continuing holding onto my anger would only have dragged me down.

I will die soon, Jack. I've battled cancer but it has had its way with me. I leave behind a son who will grieve sorely when I'm gone. He has been my light since he was born and that light grew brighter when he married a wonderful woman, who gave birth to my two adorable grandchildren. So, you see, Jack, my life was happy and fulfilled. However, that happiness meant that I could never eradicate from my memory the summer I spent with you and your family.

My son's name is Luke. Through no fault of my own, I did not know the identity of his father until some years ago. That is why I'm writing to you. You have many years left to live and I cannot any longer deprive you of this knowledge. I leave it in your hands to decide what to do with it.

That summer, I used to wonder how I could love you so much yet despise Laurence. He pursued me, as you did, but for difference reasons. To him I was a challenge. The more I rejected his advances the more he wanted me. I was able to ignore him until you and I went to Withers Island. Do you remember that afternoon or has life wiped it from your memory? You wanted to keep our love a secret. I didn't understand why and was unaware of the bet Laurence had proposed.

I'd no reason to believe that a note slipped under my bedroom door the following day was anything but genuine. I was to meet you in the barn at midnight. The light in the barn was broken and whispers are deceptive. They lack clarity, nuance, an identity. In the darkness, they are sensuous and devious. I was too naïve to know the difference between love that is stolen and that which is freely given. How could I not have known it was Laurence who held me in his arms and put his lips to mine? For years this question tormented me. Innocence, ignorance? I don't know. His kisses were sweet and it was only when he cried out at the end that I heard his true voice. No words of love, just expletives that expressed his satisfaction, and then he was gone. I tried to convince myself I'd been mistaken but I knew that you would never have left me so abruptly and in such distress.

The horses were sleeping in their stalls when I passed the stables. The air was filled with their breath, their smell, their honesty. I met Olive by the back door when I returned to the house. She was coming home from a dance but I now know she had been waiting for me. The outside light was on. She was smiling. I've never been able to forget her words.

'Who won the bet? Laurence or Jack?' she said. 'Didn't you know? They made a bet as to who would be the first to bed you.'

The betting game you'd played as children had changed into a cruel game for adults.

I ran back to the barn. I felt I would go mad as I wrenched the medallion from my neck. That was where you found me and where I rejected you. I'm sorry, Jack. I should have believed in you. Instead, I ran away.

When my father discovered I was pregnant, he beat me. He was drunk and furious that I was going to shame his family name. So, I changed my name. I moved to Dublin and began a new life.

Many years later, I met Olive again. A chance encounter in the Shelbourne Hotel where I had a business meeting. I was unaware that she was sitting at a table nearby and I was leaving the hotel when she called me. It was so long since I'd heard the name Boylan. I didn't recognise her at first. When I did, I wanted to walk away. She asked me to have coffee with her. I could have refused but she was much changed from the svelte and spoiled girl I'd known. It was obvious she was ill. She'd come to Dublin to consult with a heart specialist and the prognosis was not good. Perhaps that was the reason she decided to apologise to me for the remarks she'd made that night. She also told me that you had had no hand, act or part in Laurence's bet.

I didn't tell her about Luke. Olive was never interested in the lives of other people and that hadn't changed in the intervening years. Instead, she talked about her own family. That was how I heard you were uncontactable but 'fabulously' wealthy and that Laurence's marriage had broken up because of what she called his 'fertility issues.' Apparently, he'd caught mumps when he was at boarding school. It had impacted on him in the cruellest way possible yet I felt as if a black crow that had sat on my shoulders since that night in the barn had lifted and taken flight.

Jack, we made a son that afternoon on Withers Island. Luke is talented, a wonderful designer of beautiful objects. He does not know his father's identity. How could I tell him when I did not know myself? After my meeting with Olive I made a decision to keep the truth from him. Years earlier, when he eighteen, he began to gamble. He was stressed over the identity of his father and when his gambling became compulsive, I feared it was genetic. He managed to overcome his addiction and I was afraid that a further disappointment could trigger it again. Forgive me, Jack. I did what I believed was best. Why stir old memories when Luke no longer wanted that information.

But illness sharpens the mind, reduces uncertainty and indecision. I knew I had to make contact. Olive had mentioned that Charlie wrote to you occasionally. I've contacted him and asked him to pass this letter on to you. You might not remember me so I'm enclosing the medallion you gave to my father. I found it among his possessions after he died.

You are so far from home, Jack. I know your heart was broken when you left Hyland Hall. Charlie says you're a rolling stone and you've never settled. No wife, no family. If you decide to meet our son, show this letter to him. I will be gone by then. Love my family as I loved them. Enjoy them as I did.

I leave you with our son's name and address:
Luke Kingston
5 Park View Villas,
Reedstown,
Co. Dublin

Goodbye my dear, lost love,
Madelaine

Sophy folded the letter and handed it back to her husband. 'You came from love, Luke.' She spoke softly, aware that his father was listening. 'It flows through Madelaine's letter.'

'Yes, it does.' Luke stirred himself. His shoulders straightened as he gazed at Jack. 'After she died and we cleared out her house, I searched for a name. Anything that would lead me to you. Something other than a birth certificate with *Father Unknown* written on it.' He swallowed, his throat working, and his voice, when he spoke again, had hoarsened. 'I found nothing. No hidden love letters or photographs. I thought there might be something in her financial records about child allowance payments with an unknown signature. In the end, I had to believe what she'd told me was true. You were a shadow who passed through Maddie's life one night then disappeared.'

'*Madelaine* shadowed my entire life.' Her name was precious to Jack and would not be truncated. Sophy understood the possessive nature of a name. 'Take this with you.' Jack was in pain when he handed his journal to Luke yet nothing could disguise his happiness. He was enclosed in an aura of bliss. One that was only visible to those who understood the tortured path that had brought him to this moment.

'Tomorrow I'll answer all your questions,' he said when Luke helped him from his chair to his bed. He rested his head against the pillows and held on to his son's hand. 'Go back to Hyland Hall and read my journal. Then share our story with my granddaughters.'

CHAPTER THIRTY-SEVEN

Isobel

Clouds were gathering, charcoal-grey and heavy with rain, when Isobel stepped down from the school bus and collected her bike. Kelly, whose stop was further along Marsh Road, drew a heart on the steamy bus window as Arthur drove off.

No chance of a lift up the avenue today. Her parents were at the hospital with Jack and Julie was spending the afternoon with her friend, Siobhan. Isobel still found it impossible to get her head around it. The man who had caused her so much terror, and then became her friend, was her grandfather. It was like an incredible epic, sweeping story. Far better than any book she had ever read. She had longed to confide in Kelly but her parents had warned her it was a secret.

'It's very important that we keep this information to ourselves.' Sophy kept stressing this point. Her anxiety reminded Isobel of the early days when they first came to Hyland Hall. 'Jack wants you to know that he's your grandfather. It means so much to him to have his family around him at this special time. But our secret must not be shared with anyone else.'

Isobel had never really thought about her father's father. She believed he'd died on some faraway continent and Maddie never spoke about him. It had been an unwritten rule to never ask questions. And all the time Jack had loved Maddie whose loud, contagious laughter and embracing arms had been such a huge part of Isobel's childhood.

This evening, she and Julie were going to visit him. Would it feel different, knowing he had once loved Maddie? Why had he taken so long to tell them? Fear, she thought. It was at the centre of everything. And it was still there, along with the excitement of knowing Jack had a family. He had known who they were from the beginning but he had feared her and Julie every bit as much as they feared him, only his reasons were different. Their mockery and terror when they saw him, their footsteps running from him in disgust… he would have been unable to bear it. She was so glad she had come to know the kindness and love that was hidden behind the scars on his wounded face.

The rain began to fall before she reached the entrance gates. She was drenched in minutes. Her father had given her and Julie keys to the Hobbit Hut. Better to shelter there until the rain stopped.

Victor's jeep was parked in the space where her father usually left his pickup truck. The light in the little parlour had been switched on and the front door was open. She edged closer to the window and watched as he took the painting of the ploughed field down from the wall.

'What are you doing with my father's painting?' she demanded.

He turned and saw her standing in the doorway.

'For goodness sake, Isobel, why are you always creeping around the place?' He tightened his hands on either side of the painting.

'I don't *creep*. This is my father's house.'

'It certainly is not your father's house.' A roll of bubble wrap was on the table, with scissors and a reel of sticky tape beside it. His movements were quick and efficient as he wrapped the painting. 'This valuable painting is part of the Hyland art collection,' he said. 'It should never have been removed from the house.'

That fragile green stem pushing upwards through the ploughed earth was her father. He'd pointed to it and said it symbolised him making his way back to his family. That was the moment Isobel had known for definite that he had not called heads or tails. Jack had challenged him to choose and he had chosen them instead of Lady Luck.

'I'm visiting Jack tonight,' she said. 'And I'm going to tell him what you've done.'

"Giving this painting away is not the first foolish decision he's made and it won't be his last.' His impatience was obvious as he carried it towards the door.

'You're lying!' The words were out before she could stop herself. 'You're stealing my dad's painting. It's not yours to take.'

'Are you calling me a thief?'

'I'm just saying—'

'My uncle is delusional but still sane enough to want his valuables guarded. What if this painting disappears? If your father uses it as a wager? Unfortunately, a leopard doesn't change his spots.'

'My father is not a leopard. He's Jack's—' Her mouth was dry with knowledge she must not share.

'Jack's what?' A nerve twitched in his cheek.

'He's... he's...' She wanted to shout the truth into his arrogant face. 'He's Jack's estate manager.'

He studied her for an instant, as if weighing up her reply. It was more than that, though. Like she was an insect he was inspecting under a microscope.

'Move aside immediately,' he shouted so loudly that she instinctively stepped aside to let him pass. He put the painting on the back seat of his jeep. The small house where her father lived seemed violated. The engine roared and he was gone.

*

She didn't tell Jack about the painting. It would have spoiled his special time. His body hardly dented the bedclothes and his face seemed to have fallen in over his bones. All his energy seemed to be contained in his eye. That steely gaze was soft and teary when he told them how much joy they had brought to the last few months of his life. He said Isobel was the image of Madelaine and that Julie reminded him of his mother, Stephanie. He was sorry he had waited so long to tell them who he really was. All those missed opportunities. When he sighed, and his chest rattled, Isobel noticed the glance her parents exchanged. It brought her right back to the time Maddie died. She had been heartbroken that night when she waved goodbye to her grandmother. Tonight, when she and Julie left the hospital, all she could think about was his vision and the woman who waited beyond it to welcome him. That woman had a face now. She was as clear and as dear to Isobel as when she had lived among them.

CHAPTER THIRTY-EIGHT

Sophy

When Maddie died, Sophy had imagined a ship advancing through calm, dark waters to carry her into lightness. Not so with Jack. He used his fists to fend death off and gasped words she tried to unscramble. She soothed him and gently lowered his hands until they rested on the sheet. He kept repeating his son's name and only calmed down each time Luke reminded him he was there at his bedside.

She felt the same agitation. The initial joy that had followed Jack and Maddie's revelations had passed quickly. A new reality existed and Jack was struggling to explain what it meant to them. He held both their hands but was too weak to bring them together. To unite them, as he had always longed to do. He was ready to die but fear of Victor kept his heart beating. He repeated Charlie's name, sometimes feverishly, sometimes with cold lucidity. He wanted justice for his friend's death. Sophy assured him that would be done and tried to ease his passing with comforting words. His greatest worry, which she shared, was how Victor would react when he discovered the truth about Luke.

Did he know that his uncle's life was drawing to a close? Jack refused to see him and had insisted that Luke be recorded on his medical records as his next of kin. He had also issued instructions to the medical staff that Victor was not to be present at his death bed.

Life was condensed into hospital shifts, long drives there and back, snatched meals and snatched time with the girls. Four days passed in a limbo state between consciousness and coma until the call from Luke came at midnight. Jack was sinking fast and asking for her.

Isobel awoke, her face scrunching with awareness, when Sophy entered their bedroom.

'Is Jack dead?' she whispered.

'Not yet, darling. But he will die soon. I need to go to him.'

'Where are you going, Mammy?' Julie pushed the duvet down from her face and sat up.

'To the hospital to see Jack.'

'But it's dark.'

'I know it is, Julie. But Jack needs me now. He's going away from us and—'

'Like Maddie did?'

'He's going to Maddie.' Isobel spoke with conviction. 'He's wanted to be with her for a long time.'

'Is that true, Mammy?'

'Yes, my love. It's perfectly true. I'll be home as soon as I can. Will you be okay on your own?'

Isobel stretched out her hands to her sister. 'You can sleep with me, Julie.'

'And Cor—'

'Yes.' Isobel sighed. 'You can bring Cordelia with you.'

The traffic was light as Sophy drove towards St Philomena's Hospital. Candles had been lit beside Jack's bed and the atmosphere was hushed when she entered his ward. Nurses glided in an out to check on him. His breath rasped as he clung to life. He muttered Victor's name and repeated it again. His anguished expression seemed to be demanding answers, assurance. She dabbed his chapped lips with water and told him she had evidence that would put Victor away for life. She had no idea if he could hear her yet she noticed a change in his breathing.

'Go to Madelaine.' Tears stung her eyelids when she spoke her mother-in-law's full name. 'She's been waiting such a long time for you.'

His features relaxed. Did he smile as his breathing became softer, more irregular? Finally, after one last stare at Luke from his eye, so luminously blue that it seemed impossible to imagine it dimming, he gave a final sigh and died.

CHAPTER THIRTY-NINE

Isobel

At first, it was easy to be brave. Hyland Hall was no longer a Fear Zone and Jack was going to fly straight into Maddie's arms. She could see them running in slow motion towards each other through a field of golden corn. The image was perfect but Julie insisted on transferring her tears to Cordelia and the whiny, hiccupping cries set Isobel's teeth on edge.

'Stop that,' she ordered Julie. 'It's gross and inappropriate.'

'It's Cordelia.' Julie voice sounded thick, like she was chewing sticky toffee. '*I'm* really glad Jack's going to be out of pain and at peace.'

At *peace*? Isobel hated that phrase. Most of the time people had no idea how others felt in *this* world. Why should they assume they know how they would feel in the *next*?

'Jack had a vision once,' she said. 'Will I tell you what he saw?'

Julie peered out through her fringe. 'Is it creepy?' she asked.

'Kind of,' Isobel admitted. 'But beautiful, too.'

Cordelia fell to one side and was forgotten as Isobel described how Jack had flown above the world. Just the good parts, like being inside a kaleidoscope of colour and Maddie waving to him. Julie fell asleep as soon as the story ended. Isobel's sleep was restless and she awoke instantly when she heard the front door open. She checked the time on her phone. It was too soon for her parents to have returned from the hospital. The only other person with a key was Victor.

She listened to the sounds from the hall. Thuds and scraping noises, as if heavy objects were being moved. He went into the den also, and the music room. The front door kept opening and closing. Finally, he went upstairs. She opened her bedroom door and checked the hall. The walls were bare, the paintings removed. She didn't need to check the other rooms to know that they, too, had been ransacked. A crash came from Jack's living room, like a shelf had fallen or a lamp had been knocked over. The sound rippled across her scalp. She should return to her bed and pull the duvet over her face. She should plug her ears and hold her breath until he left yet she was too angry to do any of those things.

She climbed the stairs and entered the living room. The roll-up top on Jack's bureau was up and the desk had been pulled out. All the drawers were open, their contents scattered. She was right about the lamp. It was smashed to pieces on the floor. He saw her at the door and said, 'Isobel Kingston, I see you're haunting the house again. Why aren't you asleep?'

'I'm waiting for my parents to come back from the hospital.'

'Ah, yes. My poor uncle is soon to be released from his misery. Go back to bed, immediately. I've important business here.'

He smiled as he waited for her to obey him. His smile used to be the nicest thing about him. Now it was the nastiest. She looked at the broken lamp and the scattered documents, the cushions all upended, even the old trunk had been opened and the lid left up. She knew so much about the history of the house now. The plans Jack had made for its future.

'You stole my father's painting and now you're stealing the ones that belong to Jack. You've no right to take them.' She walked over to the bureau and folded her arms. 'He wants to make the music room into an art gallery so that the people looking after the horses can see them.'

'The junkies, you mean? And the ex-cons?' He laughed, as if he had heard the funniest joke ever. 'Their appreciation of art must never be underestimated. But, you're wrong. This is now my house and everything in it belongs to me. Stop being such a tiresome child and go back to bed.'

'I'm *not* being tiresome.'

'You've always been tiresome,' he snapped. 'And I've tolerated your moods for long enough.'

'I can't believe I ever thought you were a nice person.'

'Isobel, I'm busy.' He flapped his hand at her. She might as well have been a wasp that had flown too close to him. 'Do as I say and leave me alone.'

'No, I won't. Jack didn't want you here—'

'Jack this, Jack that.' He waved his hand from side to side. 'Since when did you become such an authority on my uncle? Don't be under any illusions that you meant anything to him. As of tomorrow, you'll have no right to be here and I'll see to it—'

'He's my grandad so I've as much right—'

'What the fuck did you just say?' He grabbed her shoulders and shook her so hard her teeth clacked together. The words had come so fast from her mouth that she could hardly remember what she had shouted at him. Everything around her seemed to have slowed down, like in films when people were walking slowly through mist. Her heels lifted off the ground as he pulled her closer to him.

'What right?' he shouted. 'Repeat what you just said.'

'It was *just* a joke.'

He didn't believe her. She could tell by the way his eyes bored into her until all she could see was a blue glitter, like ice catching the sun, only there was no warmth in them, just an awareness that she had revealed a secret she was not supposed to tell. He had turned pale, even his lips seemed drained of colour as his mouth fell open and his face froze in the same expression that she had seen earlier in the Hobbit Hut. As if she was a specimen in a jar, something oozing and evil that needed to be contained.

'You've a strange sense of humour.' He sounded breathless as he lowered her. 'Some would call it sick. Let's see what your parents have to say about your little lie.'

He released her so abruptly that she staggered backwards and crashed against the bureau. She would have fallen only for the desk. She thought it would come away from the bureau when she leant on it but it held firm. He hurried from the room and down the stairs. She watched from the window as he ran towards his jeep.

She had to ring her mother and warn her that Victor had been in the house. A zombie voice told her Sophy was not contactable. She heard the same message when she rang her father. They must have their phones switched off. Thinking about it, that wasn't surprising. Phones ringing when someone was dying was unacceptable but that did nothing to lessen her anxiety.

Unable to settle, she tidied Jack's room. She picked up the papers Victor had flung from the bureau. She swept up the broken lamp and replaced the cushions where they belonged. Apart from the dark patches on the wall where paintings once hung, and the broken lamp, the room looked the same as always.

She slid the rollout desk out of sight. As she pulled down the lid of the bureau, she realised that something was different. An ornate panel of wood that was only visible when the edge of the desk was sitting flush against the bureau was slightly out of kilter. It was a fake drawer. She had tried to open it once when Jack asked her to find his phone. Although it had a brass handle like the other drawers, it was solid wood – or so she had always believed.

The chink in the panel was barely noticeable yet it was enough to break its symmetry. She knelt down and placed her hands beneath the panel. The wood was smooth under her fingertips until she felt a slight bulge. Unable to tell if it was a knot in the wood, she pressed hard on it and after a few seconds a hidden drawer opened. Her collision with the bureau must have affected the mechanism that concealed it.

Jack Hyland's Last Will and Testament was written on the front of a sealed envelope. She had found what Victor sought. The words on the paper were simple, easy to understand. Quickly, she replaced it in its hiding place and closed the drawer. She sank down on Jack's armchair. Peeper had entered the room while she was tidying it. She lifted him onto her lap. His purring rippled against her knees and made it almost possible to believe that no harm could possibly come to her family.

CHAPTER FORTY

Sophy

Time passed. She and Luke were swept along on the procedure of death. Documents were signed by Luke and his father's body was removed from the ward. She would contact Tina Bracken in the morning. Tina would know how to look after him.

She was waiting in the family room for Luke, who had gone to the coffee machine for takeaways when Neil Nelson, the doctor who had been on night duty, came into the ward.

'Sophy, can I have a word before you go?'

'Is something wrong?' She stood to greet him.

'Not wrong, just difficult.' He leant back against the wall and sank his hands into his pockets. 'As you know, Jack left strict instructions with us that he did not want to see his nephew, Victor Coyne, at any time, even when he was dying. He also insisted that his nephew was not to be provided with information on his progress or, sadly, in his case, lack of progress.'

'I'm aware of that. They had a difficult relationship.'

'Families.' Neil smiled, ruefully. 'Can't live with them, can't live without them. Jack's insistence that Mr Coyne was not to be informed of his death was unusual but we've respected his wishes. However, you should know that his nephew created quite a scene earlier at reception.'

'Victor was here?' The knot of fear that she had carried in her chest for days tightened.

'Unfortunately, he was.' The doctor hesitated and frowned, his eyes red-rimmed from lack of sleep. 'Mr Coyne demanded to see his uncle's body. Unfortunately, he became very abusive to the night receptionist when his request was denied. He insisted it was his right, as Jack's nephew, to take care of his uncle's remains. Unfortunately, the receptionist is new to her position and was so intimidated by his attitude that she eventually admitted he is no longer listed as Jack's next of kin.'

'What else did she tell him?'

'Nothing else, apart from identifying your husband as Jack's next of kin.'

The room seemed to move, the sudden swoosh causing her to sit down abruptly. 'When did this happen?' she asked.

He checked his watch. 'Shortly after Jack died. About an hour and a half ago.'

'Thank you for telling me, Doctor.'

The doctor was leaving when Luke arrived back to the room with two takeaway coffees.

'Sustenance for the journey home,' he said. 'You look like you need this.' He held one out to Sophy but she was already switching on her phone.

'Victor's been to the hospital,' she said. 'He knows.'

'Knows?' His question resonated with her own dread.

'The receptionist told him he was no longer Jack's next of kin.'

'Oh, Jesus…' He choked back a cry as he set down the coffees on a nearby table and switched on his own phone.

'Isobel's been trying to contact me,' she said.

He stared at his screen. 'She was trying to contact me as well.'

Sophy was already ringing her daughter. An automated voice informed her that the number could not be reached for the moment. How many moments? The journey back to Hyland Hall would take an hour. They left immediately, running towards the car park, fumbling change into the parking meter, waiting impatiently for the barrier to rise. Luke drove behind her until he reached an all-night petrol station, where he stopped to fill the tank.

Each time she rang Isobel, she received the same automated message. *The number you have called is not in service at this moment.*

CHAPTER FORTY-ONE

Isobel

Dawn was creeping over the woods, the crowns of trees visible in the murky light when she heard the clang. Faint enough to have been imagined, it still startled Isobel awake. She crossed to her bedroom window. The gate in the wall was open and he was coming towards the house. She could tell by looking at his head, the way he pushed it forward, that he was in a rage. She shook Julie awake.

'You have to hide until Mum and Dad get back,' she told her. 'Victor will hurt us if you don't.'

'Why will he hurt us?' Julie's eyes were so wide, so frightened that Isobel wanted to pretend it was just a joke. But that would be a reckless lie and Victor must be crossing the courtyard by now.

'Cordelia…' Julie began but Isobel shook her head.

'Not now,' she said. 'I've a safe hiding place for you but Cordelia won't fit into it.'

They held hands as they ran up the stairs and into the bathroom. Isobel pressed her finger to her lips when she opened the closet door and showed her sister how to crouch up against the boiler.

'Will Cordelia be okay?' Julie was fighting tears.

Isobel pulled sheets of toilet paper off the roll and shoved them into her hand. 'I'll hide her too. I promise. Dad and Mum will be back soon but we just have to hide until then. You stay here and don't come out for any reason. Do you understand?'

Julie hunched her shoulders and whispered into her knees. 'Why is Victor bad?'

'I'll tell you later. Mum and Dad are driving as fast as they can. We *must* lie low until they get here.' She was about to close the door when she remembered something. 'Don't be frightened if you hear sounds. They travel along the pipes from Jack's room. No matter what you hear, stay where you are.'

Julie nodded and pressed her face deep into her knees. Isobel loved her so much, it hurt.

Victor was in the hall. He was so quiet she wouldn't have known he was in the house if she hadn't seen him coming across the courtyard. She stopped on the curve of the stairs and watched him. He was using his phone torch for light and was standing on top of the old table. The grandfather clock blocked her view and she was unable to check what he was doing. But she didn't need to see him to know he was unlocking the gun cabinet. No one was supposed to have the key. He had told Sophy it had been lost years ago and the gun was just an ornament. That was a lie. He used it to shoot Caesar. She had been right that evening when she thought she'd noticed the empty cabinet. He must have replaced the gun when no one was looking. He didn't make a sound as he jumped down from the table and moved silently past the grandfather clock. She had to warn her mother.

She tiptoed back to Jack's room where she had left her phone. She would hide in the room with the dust sheets and ring her parents from there. The creak on the stairs alerted her. He was already on the bend of the staircase. The trunk with the curved lid was her only option. She hunkered down inside it and lowered the lid. It was dark as a coffin and as silent. She was aware of her chest rising and falling, her moist breath, her heart doing somersaults as she swiped her phone. Still no answer. It was the same on her father's phone. Sweat oozed under her arms and along her spine.

She tried Kelly's number then remembered that her friend always left her phone off at night because of cyber bullying. Ringing 999 was something adults did in an emergency. She hesitated, afraid whoever answered would think she was a kid making a hoax call then hit the numbers.

The woman who answered was called Louise. She said she could hear Isobel clearly, even though she was whispering. Louise didn't sound frightened when Isobel told her about the gun. Instead, she asked questions in her calm voice but Isobel was breathing too fast to answer properly. She would suffocate if she didn't open the lid. She pushed it just a little and, after taking a long, deep breath, she was able to whisper that she was hiding in the trunk. Sweat was slick on her palm as the weight of the lid bore down on her and banged closed.

'Speak to me, Isobel,' said Louise. 'Tell me where you live. Can you give me your address?'

Light flooded into the trunk as Victor lifted the lid. He shook his head, like she'd done something deliberately to displease him and took her phone from her. He put it on the ground and stamped on it so hard it broke into pieces.

'Please, stand up, Isobel,' he said. He sounded polite, the way he used to do when he stayed for dinner. Somehow, that made her even more frightened. He waited until she was standing in front of him before asking her who she had been phoning.

She had to lick her lips before she could answer him. 'My Mum.'

'Ah, sweet Sophia. Will she be here soon?'

'She's not coming back here. She said she was staying at the hospital with my dad.'

'You're a bad liar, Isobel,' he said. 'Unfortunately, it's a problem that runs in your family and needs to be eradicated.' His hands were shaking. It couldn't be from fear, no one with a gun could feel fear, so it had to be fury that charged his voice as he ordered her to move before him down the stairs.

'Where's your sister?' he demanded.

'In bed.'

He didn't speak until they reached the bottom step.

'Open the bedroom door,' he said.

The room was still dark but there was enough light when he twitched the curtains for him to see Cordelia's blonde head on the pillow, the long fringe hiding her eyes.

He nodded and closed the door quietly behind them. 'Go to your play room,' he said and nudged the gun into her back. The thought of Julie crouched in the closet steadied her nerve as they entered the den.

It was brighter outside and the bushes her father had planted in the courtyard glistened. Spiders had spun their webs between the stems and the early morning dewdrops trembled on the delicate spirals. Fairy dust falling over a new day. A different day to any other.

CHAPTER FORTY-TWO

Sophy

As soon as Sophy opened the front door and switched on the light she knew. Fear had a taste, as tangy as blood. Her senses quivering, she moved forward into the hall. Dawn filtered through the fanlight window on the front door as she searched for signs of his presence. The faint, woody scent of his aftershave was barely detectable yet she drew it into her nostrils and recognised it. Somewhere in the house, he was waiting for her. This knowledge was instinctive, stomach-clenching. She wanted to believe he had come and gone, a thief in the night, but the glass door of the gun cabinet was slightly ajar. The gap was barely noticeable yet it drew her gaze to the vacant space behind the glass and forced her to a standstill.

She had passed the cabinet so many times without ever really noticing it. Like the paintings that had hung from the walls of Hyland Hall or the grandfather clock with its sturdy pendulums, the gun cabinet was just something ornamental, easily ignored. She imagined the gun with all its deadly power in his hands as she moved silently down the hall and into the girls' bedroom. Julie's bed was empty. She must have stayed in Isobel's bed but a quick glance at the smooth skin with its unnatural glow and the silky blonde strands of Cordelia's wig banished that hope.

Fear had feelers that crawled over her skin and lifted the hairs on her arms, the back of her neck. It slithered down her spine in a chilled sweat and broke beads on her hairline. This rush of adrenalin demanded that she fight or flee when, really, there was only one option open to her. She must concentrate and not give way to the petrifying fears that crowded her mind. Hyland Hall was filled with nooks and crannies, unused rooms and cubbyholes. The sheds and storerooms in the backyard also offered opportunities to hide, and the wood with its sheltering trees was only a short distance away. Thinking of such possible escape routes cleared the fog in her brain. She checked her jacket pocket for her phone. Luke had planned to be with her when they told the girls that Jack had died. He was only a few minutes behind her and must be prevented from entering the house. Unable to find her phone, she searched her second pocket. In her panic to reach the house she had left it in the car.

She returned to the hall. The steady tick-tock of the grandfather clock was the only sound to break the silence yet she sensed it was laden with menace. It waited to be broken by a command, a threat, maybe, even, a gunshot. Her legs weakened. She gripped the edge of the hall table for support but, like everything in this ramshackle house, it bore the brunt of time and the fragile legs vibrated when she leant on it. She straightened and moved swiftly towards the hall door. Her hand was on the latch when Isobel called out to her from the den.

'You have to come in here,' she shouted. Her voice, though shaky, was proof that she was alive and Sophy braced herself for what she would find when she entered the room. The scene that she had refused to contemplate on that frantic drive from the hospital – to do so would have caused her to scream and crash the car – was now unfolding in real time.

Victor stood close to the window, the gun aimed directly at Isobel, who was sitting opposite him on a straight-backed chair. Her fingers were linked together on her lap, her pyjamas tucked into her Uggs. Her eyes brimmed with tears when she saw Sophy but she sank back into the chair at a sharp command from Victor that she remain silent.

'Welcome home, Sophia,' he said. 'You look tired. It's been a long night for us all.' He sounded concerned as he tilted his head to one side and studied her.

'What are you doing?' she asked. His intentions were only too obvious but asking such an inane question steadied her nerve.

'I'm taking control,' he said. 'You've made it impossible for me to do anything else.'

'I don't understand—'

'Stay where you are.' He held the gun confidently in both hands as she came forward into the room.

She forced herself to concentrate. One step at a time. First, she needed to get her daughter out of his way.

'Our problems have nothing to do with Isobel,' she said. 'Let her go back to her bedroom and we'll talk.'

'Talk?' He raised his eyebrows, as if amused by the prospect. 'Since when did talking solve anything for us?'

'Please, let her go.' Their eyes locked. She forced herself to endure his stare. To give way would weaken her position.

'You're right, she should be in bed.' He nodded dismissively at Isobel. 'Go to your room and, this time, stay there. If you attempt to leave the house, you'll have to deal with the consequences. Do we understand each other?' To emphasise his point, he moved his finger fractionally on the trigger.

Isobel half-rose from the chair then slumped back down again. 'Can I bring Peeper with me?' she pleaded.

The cat, on hearing his name, leapt down from a shelf in the alcove where he had been dozing. As always, Peeper was unfazed by the happenings around him.

'Take him and get out before I change my mind,' Victor replied.

Isobel's legs buckled as she bent down to pick up her pet. Hunched over, she seemed incapable of rising until he roared at her to move.

The headlights on the pickup truck flooded the courtyard and were then switched off. Seconds later Luke's footsteps sounded in the hall. Victor, still pointing the gun at Isobel, walked backwards towards the door and opened it.

'Ah, Luke, you've finally arrived,' he said. 'Your father took a long time to die. Jack Hyland never made it easy for anyone. But *Sop-hi-a* kept me entertained, as she did so often in the past, while we waited for you.' He sounded courteous, a genial host drawling her name affectionately and smiling as Luke entered the room.

She had basked in that smile, been charmed and deceived by it, and had only seen the brutality that shaped it when it was too late. She wanted to run at him and claw his face until she reached bone. She would have turned the gun on him without hesitation, used a knife, a hammer to strike him down. Anything to wipe it from his face.

Luke's expression reflected her own dread as he glanced from the gun to Sophy, then at Isobel, who was risen with Peeper in her arms. Sophy could imagine his thoughts, his flight or fight reaction and how, like her, he knew there was only one choice open to him. The gun Victor held to her head was loaded. It must be the same gun that had ravaged Caesar. She forced the image from her mind. Thoughts of the old dog and his final moments would further weaken her.

'Get out of here.' He nodded at Isobel. 'Just remember what I've told you and stay in your room.'

'Let me say goodbye to Mum.' Her shoulders bowed as she hugged Peeper to her chest. 'Please let me say goodbye. Please... *please*?'

'Be quick about it then.' He kept the gun trained on her as she ran towards Sophy.

So many questions to ask her but, for now, only one needed answering. Where was Julie? Isobel shook her head, an almost imperceptible gesture that warned her not to ask it. Sophy bit down hard on her lip as she acknowledged her daughter's warning.

'Dry your tears, Isobel.' She took her hand and spoke softly into her ear. 'We've no time to be afraid. You must be brave and trust me.' How trite her reassurances sounded but Isobel's terrified expression eased a little. 'Victor is angry right now but we're going to sort everything out between us. You know he's not going to harm us—'

'Leave now, Isobel,' he shouted.

'I want to say goodbye to Dad.'

'Do that and they'll be the last words your father will ever hear.' He trained the gun on Luke and Isobel, stifling a cry, veered away from her father and ran from the den.

He ordered Luke to lock the door and throw the key on the floor. He appeared calm but Sophy was only too aware that his composure masked a chaotic rage. Land, inheritance, death and life, all would be decided in this house where she had hoped briefly that a new beginning with him was possible.

'How could you possibly have believed you'd get away with it?' he asked.

'I wasn't trying to get away—'

'Next of *fucking* kin. You owe me an explanation, Sophia.' He glared at her but kept the gun on Luke. 'You, of all people, know what this land means to me. When were you going to tell me the truth?'

'What truth, Victor?' she asked. 'Just tell us what this is about?'

'I had to find it out what was really going on from Isobel. The hospital receptionist confirmed it.'

'What did you hear?'

'Enough to know that I'm not Jack's next of kin.'

'A next of kin doesn't have to be a relative,' Luke said. 'Jack trusted me—'

'Don't lie to me, you fucking bastard.' He swivelled his gaze back to Luke. 'Yes, bastard, that's what you are. His long-lost son. You crawled out from under a stone and ingratiated yourself into my uncle's affections. You and your wife…' He levelled the gun at Sophy then smoothly swung it towards Luke. 'You took advantage of his senility and planned all along to steal my inheritance from me.'

'Take it,' said Luke. 'Take everything. I don't need any of it. All we want is to leave here with our children. We'll go right now. If Jack has left me anything, I'll sign it over—'

'You really expect me to believe that? I spent years nursing a slobbering old fool who disinherited me when his twin turned up out of nowhere. I've no intention of letting it happen again.'

'Victor, *please* stop.' His fury had the force of a boulder on a downward slope. Soon it would be out of control. Somehow, she must force him to listen to her. 'Luke will keep his promise. He can sign over everything to you—'

'He beggared you and your children, and you're asking me to trust him?' He laughed contemptuously. 'We both know what his promises are worth. This is your fault, Sophia. Jack would still be alive if you'd heeded my advice and written that report. Now, I understand why you refused.' He raised the gun higher. His eyes were fixed on Luke, his hands steady, the butt resting against his shoulder.

'I'm sorry I didn't do what you asked.' She knelt down and joined her hands together. 'You were right. Jack was crazy. I should have listened to you.' She moved closer to him, her knees scraping against the carpet. 'I was in love with you but Jack told me so many lies. Victor, please, *please* stop and listen to me.'

She was unable to see Luke but she knew from the position of the gun that it was aimed at his head. Victor's finger was on the trigger and the only weapon she could use to protect her husband was the slim blade of a letter opener. Somehow, Isobel had laid her hands on the knife and hidden it in her Uggs. After lifting Peeper from the floor, she had pulled it out and slipped it into Sophy's hand when they hugged. It was a derisory weapon against the gun but Sophy held it steady as she crashed against Victor's knees. She plunged it into his thigh in the same instant as he pulled the trigger. Her hope that she had knocked him off balance faded when she heard Luke cry out. The floor vibrated when he collapsed or, perhaps, it was her own body shuddering as Victor lashed his foot into her chest. She fell backwards, her ears still ringing from the shotgun's blast. He kicked her again, this time making contact with her face. She heard Luke screaming – or was it Victor's pain that ricocheted through the room? Then, she realised the screams were hers and Luke was silent, his body crumpled sideways on the floor.

Every breath she took as she crawled towards him caused her to gasp aloud. Her ribs had been fractured and yet she continued moving, even when Victor ordered her to stop. Her vision was blurred, the skin swelling around her eyes, but she was able to establish that Luke was still breathing. Part of the shot had entered his shoulder, which was bleeding, and other fragments were embedded in the wall behind him. He had hit his forehead off the side of the mantlepiece as he fell and was unconscious from this blow, rather than the shot. She needed to stem the flow of blood from both wounds. She pulled off her jacket and sweater. Twisting the sweater around his shoulder, she used it as a makeshift bandage. Her action had saved Luke's life but for how long? No second chances, Victor's aim would be true the next time. He had pulled the knife from his thigh and stabbed it into the sofa. He tried to rise but, unable to put pressure on his injured leg, he fell back again. Having removed the knife, his wound was bleeding more profusely.

Isobel's bedroom door banged as she rushed towards the den.

'What did I tell you about leaving your room?' Victor yelled. 'Go back there at once or I'll—'

'Let me in, let me in!' She was crying loudly as she tried to turn the handle on the locked door.

'Do as you're told or you'll only make things worse for your parents.'

'Isobel, go to the kitchen and bring me back the first aid box.' Sophy raised her voice above his. Horror had a safety valve. It was called courage and she needed every fibre she possessed to save her family. 'You know where I keep it. Victor has a cut on his leg. I need to bandage it. Leave the box outside the door and go back to your bedroom.'

He was attempting to stand again. Despite the pain of his wound, he still held the gun steady as he faced her. He pointed to the blood saturating his trousers.

'You started this, bitch. Now, fix it.'

Isobel banged again on the door. 'Is Dad okay? I heard the gun.'

'The gun went off by accident,' Sophy replied. 'He's got a scratch, nothing more. Go quickly and get the first aid box then go back to your room. I'll be in to see you as soon as I've tended to him.'

When Isobel came with the first aid box and returned to her bedroom, Sophy carried it towards Luke.

'No, you don't,' Victor said. 'Let him rot in his own blood.'

'I need that first aid box for both of you,' she said. Years of training to deal with emergencies were coming to the fore. Forget the situation that led to the injuries, just deal with the crisis as it was playing out. 'Don't try to stop me using it.'

Knowing there was no time to lose she used the scissors from the first aid box to cut the leg of his trousers. The temptation to bring the scissors to his throat came and went with dizzying speed. Too much was at stake for mindless gestures. The wound was sterilised and bandaged when she turned to Luke.

'I told you—'

'Go to hell,' she retorted. 'I'm doing what I'm trained to do and you're not going to stop me.'

'But this will.' He heaved himself upright and levelled the gun at her. He took one step, then another, his face contorting with pain as he limped across the floor towards her. He stopped abruptly and moved back from the nearest window when the room was engulfed in an unearthly shriek.

Banshees, Sophy thought, childhood memories resurfacing. Harbingers of death. Who else could scream with such unrestrained ferocity and blast the leafless trees along the avenue with blue, spinning whorls of light?

CHAPTER FORTY-THREE

Southern Stream FM

This is Gavin Darcy interrupting Morning Stream with breaking news about the besieged teenager and her mother. According to exclusive information received by Southern Stream, a fleet of squad cars have been dispatched to the location in an effort to bring a volatile situation under control. A spokesperson from the Garda Press Office admitted that lives could be at stake but refused to comment further, apart from stating that the gardai are hoping to contain the situation before it deteriorates. A media blackout remains in force. Names of the hostages have still not been released, nor has the location but Morning Stream will continue to bring you all the latest developments as soon as they become available.

CHAPTER FORTY-FOUR

Sophy

The sounds broke apart and became earthly, recognisable. Isobel must have managed to contact the gardai before Victor caught her.

'Pull those curtains closed on both windows.' Cursing loudly, he collapsed back on the sofa. 'Your husband is a dead man if you as much as breathe in the wrong direction when you speak to them.'

She swished the curtains across the windows just before the squad cars turned into the courtyard. The sirens were switched off and the sudden silence was a warning that gardai were assembling outside. No shots would be fired while they were within earshot. Victor was coldblooded but he was not stupid.

Defying him, Sophy loosened the bloodied sweater from around Luke's shoulder. His face, drained of colour, was contorted with pain. His pulse was still steady but this did nothing to ease her panic. How long before his oxygen levels dropped. She had tended to gun wounds when she was nursing and knew that victims whose vital signs were steady when they were brought to theatre could deteriorate rapidly. The speed with which events had unfolded was balanced by the feeling that everything was happening in slow motion. She could be dead within the next few minutes yet she worked efficiently under Victor's glowering gaze.

The silence from the courtyard continued. She could have imagined the gardai's arrival, but even as she thought this, the doorknocker banged. Four sharp knocks that caused Victor to limp closer to Luke and point the gun directly at his chest.

'Answer the door and get rid of them,' he told her. 'I've nothing to lose now. If you attempt to bring them in here, I'll finish what I started.' He nodded towards Luke. 'Just keep him in mind when you're talking to them. Now, wipe that gunge off your face and hands.'

In the mirror above the fireplace, she stared at her reflection. Blood was smeared on her forehead and her eyes were barely visible. If she could signal to the guards… But how would they respond? Any sudden movement would alert Victor. She believed his threats. If he went down, he would take Luke with him. Her mind screamed warnings and possible solutions as she wiped the blood from her face with sterile wipes then walked to the front door.

A man and a woman in uniform stood outside. 'Are you Mrs Kingston?' The woman spoke first. Beyond her shoulder, Sophy could see two squad cars.

'Yes, I am. Is anything wrong?'

'I'm Sergeant Moynihan.' She produced an identification card. 'And this is Garda Williams. We received an emergency call that someone in this house has a gun and is threatening a young girl. Did anyone here make that call?'

'No, of course not. There's no one here but us.'

'Us?' The sergeant raised her eyebrows.

'My children and my husband.'

'Do you mind if we step inside?' asked Garda Williams. 'The caller gave her name as Isobel. I believe she lives here.'

'She's my daughter. Isobel has been in bed all night. I've no idea why she would do something as foolish as that.'

'We'd like to speak to your daughter, Mrs Kingston.' Sergeant Moynihan took a purposeful step forward. 'Will you awaken her, please?' The 'please' was a pleasantry that did nothing to hide her determination and Sophy, nodding, opened the door wider.

'If you'd like to wait in the hall, I'll bring Isobel directly to you,' she spoke loudly enough for Victor to hear.

Isobel was sitting up in bed, her knees drawn to her chest. 'Are the police going to arrest Victor?' she whispered.

'Not yet.' Sophy shook her head and rushed the question that had been tormenting her since she returned to the house. 'Where's Julie?'

'She's hiding in Jack's bathroom. I told her not to come out until I tell her it's safe.'

'My two brave girls. Now, you have to continue to be brave. The guards want to talk about the call you made.'

'Victor stopped me talking to Louise. He broke my phone. I'm going to tell them what he did.' She flung back the duvet, almost knocking Sophy aside in her eagerness to speak to the police.

'Stop it, Isobel.' Sophy grabbed her and held her still. 'Stop and listen. Victor won't let you do that. He still has his gun and Dad is his hostage. You mustn't do anything to make the guards suspicious or Victor could hurt him again. We must do everything possible to protect him. Do you understand what I'm telling you?'

'But you said Dad was okay.'

'He's okay as long as we don't antagonise Victor. We must play for time and wait until the police can work out their plan to rescue us.'

'How will they do that if we're lying to them?'

'They're experienced at doing this kind of work. We have to trust them and convince Victor that he can trust us. Will you be able to do that?'

'I think so.'

'I know you can do it.' She squeezed Isobel's hand as they walked together towards the two guards.

'Why did you make that call, Isobel?' Sergeant Moynihan asked. 'Are you in some kind of trouble? If you are, don't be afraid to talk to us about it. We're here to help you.'

'I'm sorry... *really* sorry... It was meant to be a joke.' She stumbled through excuses, apologies, promises never to do anything stupid like that again. She had been so bored, she explained. Nothing exciting ever happened here.

'We heard about Mr Hyland's death. Is that not enough to cure your boredom, Isobel?' Garda William's severe tone caused her to hang her head.

'I'm *really* sorry.'

'Why would you do something so irresponsible at such a difficult time?'

'I don't know...' She shrugged, the picture of a petulant teenager, except for her eyes. That was where the terror pooled but the light was murky in the hall and the younger policeman sighed, resigned to the antics of a teenager.

'What happened to your face, Mrs Kingston?' Sergeant Moynihan had turned her attention back to Sophy.

'An accident. I fell off a ladder when I was removing cobwebs.' Her hand shook as she raised her index finger and jerked it towards the wall.

'A nasty accident, from the look of your injuries.' The sergeant's gaze was steely as she stared upwards at the gun cabinet. An old spider web was still stuck to the front of the cabinet but the viscous fibres had split into two, dangling hanks. 'I believe your husband lives in the gate lodge?'

'Yes, Sergeant, he does.'

'We were hoping to speak to him on the way in. He's not there.'

'He's spending the night here.'

'Forgive me for asking, but I was under the impression you and he were estranged?'

'We've had our difficulties but we're fine now.' Their concern unhinged her. Any second now, if the questioning didn't stop, she would lose control. The pressure Isobel was exerting on her hand warned her that she, too, was finding the strain intolerable.

'You have another daughter, I believe. Where is she?'

'She... she's sleeping.'

'Is there anything we can do for you, Mrs Kingston? You can talk to us in confidence—'

'All I need at the moment is to go to bed. I've had an extremely stressful night at the hospital, as you can imagine. I'm sorry Isobel made that call. It won't ever happen again.'

'We're sorry for disturbing you.' Sergeant Moynihan's brisk voice rang through the hall. 'We won't delay you any longer.'

Sophy closed the door and pressed her flushed forehead against it. She was panting, each breath sharp and painful.

'Julie's been in the hot press for ages,' Isobel whispered. 'I have to see if she's all right.'

'I'll look after Julie. Don't worry—'

'Stop telling me not to worry. Dad's in there—'

'I know, darling, I know.' She straightened and turned to Isobel. 'He's going to be fine. Victor just wants to frighten us. I'm determined to get us out of here, I promise.'

'Victor wants to kill us. I know he does.' Isobel's voice was feverish, her colour high. 'This is all my fault. I told him Jack was my grandfather and now he's going to kill us all—' She stopped and fell to her knees, her hands pressed to her ears as two shots fired in quick succession rang out from the den. Glass shattered in the same instant.

'Run!' Sophy pulled her to her feet and shoved her towards the front door. 'I'm going to get Julie.'

Isobel's hand was on the latch and Sophy had reached the foot of the stairs when Victor's voice commanded them to stop.

'Get back in here.' He stood in the hall, the gun still in his hands. He was shaking violently but smiling, as if amused by their efforts to escape.

Sophy veered away from the stairs. No matter what awaited her in the den, she must not antagonise him any further.

'Let Isobel go back to her bedroom,' she whispered. 'She did as you asked. She has nothing to do with any of this.'

'Oh, *really*.' He directed the gun at Isobel and spoke directly to her. 'Who brought the fucking cops to the door? You did. And you can take responsibility for what I was forced to do. Now move before I change my mind and blow your head off, you stupid little bitch.'

He was elated, his eyes darting, their blueness glittering. He was speaking fast yet coherently. His hands shook from a mix of recklessness and fear. All these signs increased the chances of him inadvertently pulling the trigger. The longing to stay outside the den was overpowering but Sophy was already moving along the hall, past the grandfather clock and in through the open door of the den.

She squeezed Isobel's hand. 'Be brave,' she whispered. 'Trust me, trust me...'

The curtains billowed gently as a chilly morning breeze flowed through the broken window. Victor slumped on the sofa and eased his leg out. He was in pain but the gun remained steady. Luke lay on his back, his eyes still closed. The shots she had heard had been fired through the window at Sergeant Moynihan and Garda Williams.

'He's alive,' she reassured Isobel, who was sobbing uncontrollably as she hunkered beside her father. Sophy spoke softly into her ear. 'Dry your tears. We've no time to be afraid. I'm a nurse.

You stay with Dad while I talk to Victor. I know how to deal with people like him.' She pulled gauze from the first aid box and handed it to her. 'Keep it pressed to his forehead. I want him to see your face as soon as he opens his eyes.'

Thoughts of Julie hiding in the closet added to Sophy's anguish as she approached Victor. To her relief, she could hear sounds from outside, raised voices, car doors opening and closing. The shots he fired appeared to have missed their targets.

'What have you done, Victor?' She sat beside him on the sofa. The letter opener, she noticed, was missing. 'I did what you asked. The police were going away.'

'You did an excellent job,' he said. 'Bravo, Sophia.'

'Why did you shoot at them? You could have killed them.'

'I know how to shoot and I know how to miss.' Shards of glass lay on the floor and there was a slight gap in the drawn curtains where he must have stood when he fired the shots. Had they caught a glimpse of him, photographed him? Wishful thinking. Sergeant Moynihan would not have been prepared for the attack.

'You deliberately missed them?'

He nodded. 'No casualties, yet.'

She ignored his inference. 'They'll have called for reinforcements. What are you going to do then?'

'I'm going to wait. The next move belongs to them.'

'No, it belongs to you. You can escape before it's too late. Once they storm the house—'

'You'll be dead by then, all of you. End of story. Don't you get it yet? It's not the first time a betrayed husband took matters into his own hands when his life was about to be destroyed. The gardai are already aware of that fact, thanks to your *excellent* performance—'

He was interrupted as Sergeant Moynihan's steady yet commanding voice reached them through a megaphone.

'This is Sergeant Moynihan. I don't want to conduct a conversation through a megaphone but I need to know if Sophy Kingston and her daughters are safe.'

'Go to the window and show yourself,' he said. 'I'll be behind you the whole time. Don't speak. If you say one word, I won't hesitate to act.'

Throughout their conversation, he had kept the gun trained on Isobel, who was sitting cross-legged on the floor, her back against the wall, her eyes on her father. Luke was still motionless, except for the slow rise and fall of his chest.

Victor stood unsteadily. The wound on his leg was his only weakness but his ruthlessness, aligned with his gun, made them powerless. Glass crunched under Sophy's feet as she walked to the window and opened the curtains wide enough to frame her. The sun was a white sphere, dazzling in the wintery morning light.

'Sophy, is there a phone number that we can use to speak to you and those who are in the room with you?'

The sergeant waited for a reply. When Sophy continued to stand silently by the window, she called out a helpline number that could be used to make immediate contact with her. She called it out again, more slowly this time.

'Stand back and close the curtains.' Victor's voice, calmer now and filled with purpose, came from behind Sophy.

She stiffened when he poked the gun into her back. He waited until she was sitting down before speaking to Isobel.

'Take your father's phone from his pocket and bring it over here,' he said.

She glared at him but did as she was told before returning to her position by the wall. He told Sophy to key in the sergeant's number.

'I can't remember…' Her fingers fumbled with the keypad, her mind blank until he called it out.

The knowledge of what he had set in motion was devastating, inconceivable. All she knew was that it would unfold with petrifying speed, just as everything else had done since she had entered the house.

'Send this message,' he said when she had added the sergeant's number. Clumsily and with tears streaming down her cheeks, Sophy finished the text and pressed 'Send'.

Fuck off out of here or I shoot again. If you send in reinforcements, my family will not leave here alive.

CHAPTER FORTY-FIVE

Isobel

Sometimes, Isobel found it hard to believe in God because of all the famine and melting icebergs but not now. She began to pray when she saw Victor coming through the gate in the wall and she was in the middle of the Lord's Prayer when the idea of hiding the letter opener in her Uggs came to her. Her prayers had been answered but only slightly. Even though Victor was limping badly, he was still able to move and give orders. He wanted them to move into the kitchen. The noises from outside were growing louder. It was possible to catch a glimpse of the courtyard every time the wind blew through the broken window and flapped the curtains. The den was icy cold. More squad cars had arrived but it was impossible to see any guards. Isobel guessed they must be hiding from the gun.

Going to the front door and telling lies to the sergeant had been agonising. The sergeant kept staring at Sophy's face and listening to the way she was breathing. All those sharp, short gasps, like she had a pain in her chest, even though she kept pretending she was okay. Had the police followed her clue about the gun cabinet? It was subtle yet Isobel had been attuned to every gesture her mother made, every word she spoke. The clue didn't matter now. The guards definitely knew there was a gun in the house and they seemed to believe her father was holding it.

'How can we move Luke?' her mother asked. 'He's still unconscious.'

'You'd better figure out a way to do so,' Victor replied. 'Otherwise, I'll shoot him now instead of later. That should solve the problem, don't you think?'

What Victor didn't realise was that her father had already opened his eyes and stared straight at Isobel. She read his warning. *Don't react. Don't listen to Victor when he talks about murder-suicide. Stay brave and we can defeat him together.* Sending signals and asking her to be brave was not enough to stop her stomach lurching every time Victor gave another order. In the end, she helped her mother to half-carry her father to the kitchen. Each time he tried to walk on his own, his legs wobbled so much he was in danger of collapsing.

Victor told her to fetch a rope from the annexe room. She considered escaping that way. She even opened the door but the knowledge that her parents' lives – and Julie's – were in her hands stopped her. She couldn't do anything that would add to the danger they were in. When she brought the rope into the kitchen, her mother knelt on the floor beside Luke and tied his hands together. She then tied his ankles to the legs of the chair. The bump on his forehead was huge. His mouth kept clenching, like he couldn't stand the pain in his shoulder but he never made a sound when he was being tied up. He reminded her of an animal who knew there was no way of escaping from the snare that had trapped him. His phone bleeped with messages from the police and her mother was forced to send horrible texts about how he was holding them at gunpoint. Although they could no longer see the courtyard, sounds still reached them, engines and sirens and the megaphone.

Victor turned on the radio. Southern Stream used to be Jack's favourite station. He could have listened to any station in the world but all he wanted to hear about was Clonmoore. Gavin Darcy was talking about the siege. He sounded more excited than usual and called the shooting at the gardai a 'sensational development'. Victor laughed out loud when he heard that.

During one of the advertising breaks, Victor forced her to use his phone to make contact with Southern Stream. He had a direct number to Gavin Darcy, who took the call immediately. She had to hold Victor's mobile to his mouth while he spewed out lies about how he was in Cork organising his uncle's funeral. Trying not to scream into the phone and interrupt him made Isobel's throat ache. If her hate had heat, Victor would be scorched to a cinder, just as Jack had been. He said there was speculation on Twitter that the siege was taking place at Hyland Hall and implied that her father had moved into the gate lodge so that he could stalk her mother. Gavin said he would definitely be asking some very pointed questions at the press conference.

She needed to pee. It wasn't urgent but she had to make Victor believe she would go on the spot if he didn't give her permission. She jigged from one foot to the other and cried out loud that she wasn't pretending.

He nodded and said, 'You know what'll happen if you try any funny tricks.' He swung the gun from her mother to her father. 'Be quick about it and bring your sister back with you.'

Sophy's mouth quivered when he mentioned Julie. The hope that he had forgotten her existence had been a faint one but now it was gone.

'Let her sleep, Victor.' Sophy batted her swollen eyelids at him. 'She's going to be one more person for you to handle. You might as well leave her in bed for as long as possible.'

'Do as I say, Isobel.' Victor ignored her mother and did that terrible thing with his finger on the trigger. 'Don't take long or I'll be forced to shoot your mother's lying head off.'

No matter how often he repeated that threat, it always sent a shock wave through Isobel. She didn't want to look at her mother because that would show her all scrunched up and helpless, the way she was on their first night here when she cried those big, glassy tears.

'Please, Victor...' She bent forward, like the pain in her chest was getting worse but Victor ordered her to stop annoying him.

Isobel sprinted up the stairs. No time to lose. If he came out of the kitchen, he would demand to know why she wasn't using the downstairs bathroom. Julie almost fell to the floor when Isobel opened the closet door. She had pins and needles in her legs and Isobel had to help her to stand up straight. The back of her nightdress was wet. She sounded embarrassed when she whispered that she'd peed in the closet. She looked so tiny and helpless. Isobel couldn't let her go downstairs – she just couldn't – but Victor had his finger on the trigger and there was nothing else she could do but obey him.

She hugged her sister and told her that Victor was playing games with them. That he was crazy but their mother knew how to deal with people who were sick in the head like him. She wanted to stand there forever, the two of them holding each other so close, but it was time to go. Isobel tried to pee on the throne toilet but nothing came. It was as if everything inside her had shrivelled up with fear.

She could see out the little window as they turned the bend on the stairs. The sun looked as if it was peering through gauze and a helicopter was flying across its face.

Julie ran straight into her mother's arms. She kissed her father's face over and over again until Victor told her to sit down or *else*. Now, he had another head to shoot off, Isobel thought. If only Caesar was alive and could tear him apart.

Ignoring the sounds from outside, he ordered Sophy to make breakfast. She cooked scrambled eggs with bacon, mushrooms and tomatoes.

'Can I bring Julie into the bedroom so she can take off her night-dress?' Isobel copied the wheedling voice her mother used when she asked Victor for favours. 'She needs to change.' She gestured towards the nightdress and Julie blushed crimson with embarrassment.

'Do it quickly,' he said, 'or—'

'You'll shoot us.' Isobel didn't know what made her say that out loud but he laughed like she'd said something hilarious.

'You're a quick learner,' he said and nodded at them to go.

When Julie was dressed in her leggings, top and jumper, she pulled the duvet down and stared at Cordelia. Isobel knew how much she wanted to empty out all her fears through Cordelia but she spoke in her own voice.

'Victor's not pretending, Issy. I heard him saying terrible things to you in Jack's room.'

'He *is* pretending—'

'*Stop* saying that.' Julie stamped her foot. 'He'll shoot us dead if we don't escape.'

'What's keeping you two?' Victor roared from the kitchen.

'Julie's vomited all over the place,' Isobel yelled back. 'I'm just cleaning her up.'

'Dress Cordelia in this.' She grabbed the hoodie she had been wearing yesterday and flung it towards Julie. 'Be quick. I'll be back in a second.'

She dashed into the den where blood and broken glass were grim reminders of the terror surrounding them. The smell of bacon frying wafted towards her. It was strange to smell normal things like food over the smell of fear? She grabbed the first aid box and ran back to the bedroom.

The hoodie had been pulled over Cordelia's head and Julie had wound the pink feather boa around her neck.

'Oh, for fuck's sake, now I've got five hostages to look after,' he said when Julie carried the mannequin into the kitchen.

Sophy had set the table. She smiled when she saw Cordelia and added another place. How she could pretend that it was just a normal breakfast was beyond Isobel's comprehension. Nothing made sense anymore but she would follow her mother and play along.

Victor sat at the head of the long table and ordered Sophy to fill his plate. He held the gun in one hand, a fork in the other. No matter how much her mother pleaded with him, he refused to take off her father's gag. She said it was important to eat and keep up their strength but even she put down her fork after one bite of scrambled eggs.

When her father's phone rang, everyone except Victor jerked with fright. 'Answer it and put it on speaker,' he said.

The woman who spoke was a siege negotiator called Miriam. She wanted to know how Luke was. His eyes rolled backed in his head when he heard Miriam using his name instead of Victor's. Everything could be solved if Luke would just talk everything through with her, Miriam said.

Sophy told Miriam that Luke had a gun trained on them. She made a gulping noise, like she was trying to get air into her mouth, before she could continue.

'Luke has no intention of speaking to any negotiator, 'she said. 'He insists that all negotiations must be done through me.'

His face turned from pale to furious red but he couldn't speak because of the gag.

'Can I speak to Isobel?' Miriam asked.

'She's here beside me.' Sweat trickled down the side of Sophy's face as she passed the phone to Isobel.

Miriam's voice reminded her of Louise from 999, so calm and certain that she knew how to handle everything.

'I'm not hurt at all,' Isobel said. It seemed unbelievable that Miriam and Sergeant Moynihan would think her father was threatening to shoot them. She wanted to yell out the nice things he did for them before he started gambling. Like the Valentine's Day when he erected a sign in the back garden that spelt out, *I LOVE YOU SOPHY* in flashing lights. Or when he told Isobel and Julie that they were going to stay overnight with Maddie at her house. Instead, he drove them to the airport where Maddie was waiting to go with them to Disneyland Paris. So many happy occasions before the sad, bad time after Maddie died. She was unable to tell Miriam about them because Victor's cold, deadly eyes held a warning she could not ignore.

Julie said she was okay too. Then Victor put his finger on the phone and ended the call.

'Well done, Sop-hi-a.' He said it exactly like he did when he used to praise her lasagne, only with much more emphasis.

Her mother's lips puckered. All those lies she'd had to tell. The taste in her mouth must be sickening. But when she looked across at Luke, and he looked back at her, it was like they were remembering that big, flashing sign in the back garden and it didn't matter what lies she told because they knew the truth and that was what would save them.

CHAPTER FORTY-SIX

Southern Stream FM

'Good afternoon everyone. I'm Chief Inspector Wallace. I'd like to begin by extending my thanks to the assembled press and media for exercising restraint on the reporting of this incident. I ask that you continue to do so. Rumours that gardai were injured in a shootout are untrue. Shots were fired from the scene of the siege but, thankfully, there were no injuries.

'The names of the hostages are Sophy Kingston and her daughters, Isobel, who made the emergency call, and Julie, aged ten. The siege is taking place in Hyland Hall, which is located just outside the town of Clonmoore.

'Reinforcements have been sent to the scene and a trained siege negotiator has made contact with the gunman. He's refusing to speak directly with our negotiator but is doing so via Mrs Kingston. I'll take your questions now.'

'Chief Inspector, I'm Gavin Darcy, Southern Stream. Is it true that this is being viewed as a domestic incident?'

'I've asked the media not to speculate on information that has not been verified by the gardai. Next question, please.'

'Coral-Anne Shields, Clonmoore Weekly. Is it true that members of the emergency response unit are on their way to handle the siege?'

'The Garda Press Office will keep you abreast with the latest information as the siege progresses. As of now, it is being handled sensitively by a team of experienced and highly skilled local gardai.'

'Chief Inspector, if this is a domestic incident and the gunman is heavily armed, when will an order be given to rescue the family?'

'I've asked you not to speculate, Gavin—'

'But is the Garda Press Office aware that details of the family's personal history have been released on social media and the father of the children—?'

'As a responsible reporter, we expect you to stick to the facts as they are being relayed to you today. Next—'

'Chief Inspector, you keep refusing to answer my questions. Southern Stream is the most listened to radio station in the region and our listeners are entitled to the full story. Recently, there was a tragic, work-related accident on Hyland Estate when Mr Charlie Bracken died while removing sections of a barn. Is there any connection between today's siege and that unfortunate incident?'

'No connection whatsoever.'

'Can you confirm that the estranged husband of Mrs Kingston has not been seen—?'

'You are totally out of order, Mr Darcy. Please sit down and give other journalists an opportunity to ask questions that are relevant to the progress of this highly volatile siege. Next question...'

CHAPTER FORTY-SEVEN

Sophy

The radio was loud, the questions unrelenting. Sophy checked her watch. Five minutes had passed since the last time she did so. A nervous tic that she was developing to deal with the dragging pull of time. Her dread that the police would storm the house and panic Victor had eased with Miriam's reassurances that that would only happen if the situation deteriorated. In effect, if the assembled police surrounding the house heard the gun going off again.

A narrative was being played out at the press conference. Nothing subtle about Gavin Darcy's questions. Hearing the chief inspector's efforts to hold back the insinuation that came with every question the presenter asked, the shape of Victor's intentions crystallised.

To escape alive and unharmed – she refused to contemplate any other option – she needed to be inside his mind. He would not hesitate to kill them when it suited him. Murder-suicide. He had tossed the term at her and Luke, knowing the petrifying images it conveyed. To defeat him, she had to visualise how he would carry out such an atrocious crime.

The basement was his only option. She remembered the musty tunnel and the steps leading to the overgrown labyrinth of shrubs, brambles and the neglected orchard. It would provide him with perfect cover for his escape. When the time was right, he would force her to free Luke from the bonds that she had tied and herd them into this dank grave. Her mind recoiled from the image of Isobel and Julie clinging to her but she forced herself to follow this horrifying train of thought. The gunfire would be muffled and could even cause a delay before the house was stormed. In that gap between decision and action on the part of the police, he would have time to flee. She had forced open the tunnel door when she explored the basement and knew it would yield easily under pressure. Or perhaps not. Was it possible he didn't know of the basement's existence? She clung to this hope as she devised one escape ruse after another. Every time she looked towards him, then towards Luke, who was bound and helpless, she felt her chest constrict so violently she feared she would suffer a heart attack.

If she could distract him enough to knock him out… The cast iron frying pan could work but it hung from a hook above the cooker and would take too long to unhook. Longer than it would take for him to fire. A knife, if she could reach the block that held them in position but Victor, anticipating potential danger, had pushed them far back on the dresser counter.

Miriam Gleeson rang again. She showed no signs of impatience when Sophy told her that Luke refused to engage with her. The siege negotiator's calmness suggested that she would wait indefinitely until he was ready to take her call. Sophy knew the negotiator was listening to her tone, charting every inflection, analysing every word she uttered.

'Luke will not harm us,' she said and winced as Victor moved the gun closer to her husband's head.

'I'm ready to listen to his side of the story,' Miriam said. 'Every problem has a solution but he needs to tell me how he feels.

Luke, if you're listening, and I hope you are, we can bring this situation to a safe conclusion without anyone being hurt. We can work this out between us but you are the person in control. Your children love you and I know you're devoted to them. Sophy trusts in you. She knows you won't harm her or the girls so please take the phone from her and talk to me.'

She made it sound so easy. How could she believe her own words? But, then, was it possible to be a siege negotiator without that belief in the powers of persuasion?

Julie was whimpering but directing the sound through Cordelia.

Miriam, hearing her, said, 'Luke, you don't have a quarrel with your children. I can hear how upset your daughter is. Can you confirm that she's safe?'

Victor shrugged, his silence challenging Sophy to respond. He seemed to enjoy watching her struggle to answer Miriam's questions. Occasionally, he would scribble a reply on a sheet of paper and Sophy would robotically read it out. Whenever he removed one hand from the gun, she would prime herself for an opportunity to lunge at him. Anticipating her thoughts, he never relaxed his guard for an instant.

'They must be getting impatient out there,' he said after he signalled to Sophy to end the call. 'There's nothing they'd like better than to storm the house, all guns blazing.'

Isobel moaned and pressed her knuckles to her mouth. She had pulled a chair close to Luke and had one arm around his neck. His legs tensed, as if his calves had cramped. Ignoring Victor, Sophy knelt and began to massage them. She noticed, as he tensed again, that the chair leg moved marginally. She had chosen that one deliberately when she had been ordered to bind his legs. Luke's eyes warned her not to react when she noticed that the rope holding him had slackened slightly.

'Now, now Isobel, this is not the time for tears.' Victor's voice was deceptively gentle as he chided her. 'I need cheering up. Let's listen to what Cordelia has to say.'

'She doesn't want to talk to you,' said Julie.

'Why not? She never stopped talking in the past. Prattle, prattle, prattle. What's wrong with her now? Cat got her tongue?'

'I'm going to kill you with a knife.' The squeaky voice drove like a nail through Sophy's head.

'That's enough, Julie,' she warned. 'No more talking.'

'It's not me—'

'I said that's *enough.*'

Julie stood up and plonked the mannequin on the chair furthest from Victor. Her face was flushed, her expression mutinous as she removed the feather boa and adjusted the hoodie. She spoke in a monotone to the mannequin and told her to be brave. The police were coming to rescue her. Julie would mind her until then.

Sophy was unsure why she was unnerved by Julie's behaviour when everything around them was laden with terrible danger. Her instincts warned her that Julie was unleashing another force. Even Isobel had taken her arm from around Luke's neck.

'Stop it, Julie,' Isobel shouted. 'Stop… *stop*—' but the young girl's face was livid with fury as she ran towards Victor.

Sophy was unable to see what she was holding until the overhead light flashed on a shard of glass. Stiletto sharp on the tip, it must have been taken from the den and hidden inside Cordelia's hoodie. Isobel's frantic expression confirmed her suspicions that a plan hatched between them was going dreadfully wrong.

She was too far away to reach Julie, who had raised her hand, as if to plunge the shard into Victor's body. She seemed oblivious of the danger she was in as he limped towards her. When Sophy shrieked her daughter's name, Julie staggered, as if the sound of her mother's terror had knocked her off balance. In that instant of pandemonium, Sophy felt, rather than heard the impact of wood straining. Luke's body lurched in a frenzied movement as the leg of the chair loosened and broke. The chair collapsed and flung him forward into Victor's path. Caught off-guard, Victor stumbled and struggled to control the gun. That allowed Sophy enough time to grab Julie around her waist and out of his range. The glass fell from Julie's hand and shattered on the floor. Unable to recover his balance, Victor skidded on the tiny shards. Moaning from the pain Sophy had inflicted on his thigh, he collapsed to his knees. Isobel, running at him from behind, pushed him forward and added to the momentum of his fall. Luke was frantically wriggling to free his ankles from the bindings and Sophy, knowing that every second counted, screamed at the girls to run.

Propelled by Sophy's screams, Isobel grabbed Julie's hand and pulled her towards the door. Victor lifted himself off the floor. Splinters of glass were embedded in his clothes but he still held on to the gun. Luke's efforts to free himself were futile and were, Sophy realised, aimed at drawing Victor's attention away from the girls.

Their footsteps pattered off the wooden floorboards on the hall as they ran towards the front door.

'I'll shoot your parents if you dare leave this house,' Victor roared after them. He pressed his back against the table and steadied the gun, aimed it at Luke. 'Stop moving or I finish you off here and now,' he said.

Blood from Luke's shoulder wound had seeped through the bandage and he looked shattered from the superhuman effort it had taken him to break the chair.

He's afraid to shoot, Sophy said to herself. She needed to stay inside his head. To follow his every diabolical thought. Firing the gun would stop negotiations and force the gardai to move too soon on the house.

'Tell them to come back here at once.' Victor towered over her as she knelt to assist Luke.

'No.' She straightened and faced him defiantly. 'I'm not subjecting my children to your madness.'

'We'll see about that.' His limp was more pronounced as he waked backwards towards the open door, the gun levelled at her. 'Your mother will die if you leave this house.' He shouted into the hall. His threat was met by silence.

Bluster, Sophy thought, *that's all it is*. This realisation brought no comfort but it gave the girls breathing space to escape.

'Bring them in here immediately or your husband takes the next bullet,' he said.

The grandfather clock boomed noon as she entered the hall. No sign of the girls anywhere. They could not have opened the front door without being heard. She glanced towards the staircase. Only Peeper, who was sleeping on the windowsill at the bend on the stairs, was visible.

For a blistering instant, she wondered if she could make it safely to the front door. Her brain whirred as she measured the distance with her eyes. If Luke could free himself sufficiently to tackle Victor… But the idea faltered before it could take shape. Weakened by his injuries, he would be shot the instant he moved.

'I don't know where they are.' She returned to the kitchen and sensed rather than saw Victor's indecision grow.

'I'll find them.' He gave a dismissive shrug and glanced down at Luke on the ground, his legs still entangled in the rope. 'Tie him up again and do a proper job this time.' He ordered her to wind the rope around the leg of the table. A sturdy structure that stood flush against the tabletop, there was no chance of it loosening.

The chair leg was just out of her reach. If she took a few steps forward, she could bring it down on Victor's head but he grabbed it before she could move and flung it on top of the dresser.

Luke's lips were parched and blue when she removed the gag from his mouth.

'Put that gag back on again!' Victor ordered.

She ignored him and filled a glass with cold water.

'Do what you're told, bitch.'

'Go to hell,' she replied and held the glass to Luke's mouth. 'I'm not putting that gag back on him again and I'm going to change his dressing. Shoot me if that's what you want to do but don't think for one instant that the police won't respond.'

She held her back straight as she lifted the first aid box from the counter. If he called her bluff and fired, that would be the end of everything.

'You do realise there's only one way that this is going to work out,' Victor said when she finished attending to Luke's wound. He walked to the wall and banged his fist off the indentation he had made on the night of her arrival at Hyland Hall. 'What a shame you didn't listen to me then.'

Before she could respond, he swung the gun in a wide arc and brought the butt down on her head. Stars exploded and spun in a frantic circle before she lost consciousness and the world turned black.

CHAPTER FORTY-EIGHT

Isobel

Fear was like a wave that kept rolling and tossing Isobel under the surf every time she tried to surface. She wanted to throw up and her stomach was swollen because she needed to pee but she was afraid to stop when they ran up the stairs and past the throne toilet, only stopping when they reached Jack's room.

Julie was sobbing and saying, 'Sorry... sorry for spoiling the plan with the broken glass.' Isobel was supposed to take the shard out of Cordelia's hood and stab Victor with it but Julie hated him so much she'd been unable to wait any longer.

Leaves had fallen from the tree outside the window. Some still clung to the branches but they must know their time was over. It couldn't be over for her or Julie, or for their parents. They were being held prisoner in their own house. Hyland Hall belonged to them. She hadn't understood some of the words she'd read in Jack's will but that much had been clear. Luke and Sophy Kingston, heirs to his possessions, and that was why Victor was determined to kill them.

She was unable to see the police, just lots of squad cars and vans. They must have been hiding behind the trees and cars in case Victor shot at them again. If she and Julie could manage to stretch from the outside ledge onto the nearest branch, they could climb down. Julie nodded and agreed it was a good idea, even though she was scared of heights.

Isobel pushed open the window. As soon as she looked at the distance they would have to stretch, she knew it would be impossible to escape that way. She might just be able to reach the nearest branch but Julie was too small. She imagined her sister tumbling like a rag doll to the ground and slammed the window closed. A policeman stood up from behind a car and stared up at her. He was holding a gun and wearing a helmet and a bulletproof vest. She needed to signal to him that Victor was the gunman.

It was Julie's idea to make a sign and display it from the window. She tore the sides off the cover from the Trivial Pursuits box. She found a red pen in Jack's desk and wrote the words VICTOR COYNE HAS THE GUN!!! in letters so large they covered all the white space. Isobel would need to put it up high so that the policeman would see it above the branches.

She shoved the coffee table under the window and stood on top of it. She had to concentrate on attracting his attention. When Julie handed her the sign, she stretched her arms upwards to display it. Leaning too far forward, she lost her balance. She tried to grab the window frame to steady herself but it was too late. The sound she made as she crashed to the floor was like a roll of thunder. The sign flew from her hands and landed at Julie's feet.

Footsteps crossed the hall. Victor was coming to get them. What had he done to their mother? He wouldn't leave Sophy on her own. She would grab the nearest weapon and strike him dead if she had a chance to do so. Isobel clenched her teeth at the thought of Victor aiming the gun at her mother. That couldn't have happened or she would have heard the shot. The wave of fear was rolling higher than ever as she grabbed Julie's hand and ran towards the trunk. No – that would be the first place he'd look. He was climbing the stairs as they fled across the landing and into the bedroom with the dust sheets. That first night she had spied on Jack, it had seemed like a haunted room. Now, it had become their refuge. They wriggled under a bed and held on to each other.

He entered Jack's living room and came out again. The *sign*. She had left it on the floor. She thought it fell face down but she couldn't be sure. He opened the door. She could see his shoes. He was standing perfectly still. He could move so silently yet at other times it sounded as if he was marching with an army behind him. Dust gathered in her nostrils. Decades of dust. When she sneezed, it must have been the loudest sound in the world.

He grabbed one of her legs and pulled her out. She tried to hold on to the bedpost but her fingers slid away. She lay on the ground and tried to stop sneezing.

'Julie's not here!' she managed to gasp between sneezes. 'She's escaped.'

He bent down almost teasingly and pointed his gun under the bed.

'Out you come, crazy girl,' he said and laughed loudly when Julie crawled out. Once, Isobel believed she knew him. He was wearing a mask then, one that showed affection and interest in her as a person. In reality, she had been nothing to him. His real face was set with hate. It told her everything that he intended to do to them. When she screamed it was impossible to stop. Even when he threatened to shoot her if she didn't control herself, she was unable to do so. Julie bent and picked up Peeper. He wriggled and tried to escape because he was only used to Isobel handling him. Without speaking, Julie shoved him into Isobel's arms. The rub of his fur, his nose nudging against her hand, forced her to concentrate on what was most important. Courage. It was the only way they would win. When she had caught her breath and fallen silent, Victor walked them down the stairs in front of him.

The hall smelled like Clonmoore Superfast Garage. Then she saw it: a can of petrol beside the door of the den. It hadn't been there earlier. Isobel would have smelled it before now, especially as the top was off. That meant Victor had left her parents alone while he brought it into the house. How could he have done that, unless… She felt the scream coming again and held tighter to Peeper.

'Keep moving!' He sounded as if he was talking to himself. They continued on down to the end of the hall and entered a corridor. She had never been in that part of the house before. He walked past them and opened a door. They stared into darkness until he switched on the light. The bare bulb was covered in cobwebs and kept flickering. Wooden steps led downwards. He stood back from the open door and beckoned with the gun towards the steps.

'Get down there,' he said to Isobel then nodded at Julie. 'You stay here with me, crazy girl.'

Peeper ran down the steps but Isobel had to hold onto the rickety railing as she descended into the basement. The air was heavy with her terror when Victor bolted the door behind her. Even though she was holding tightly to the railing, she had a sense that she was falling. Where was he bringing Julie? And where were her parents? The air was clammy, damp on her cheeks or, maybe, that was just her tears.

Shelves ran along one wall and trestle tables stretched along the centre of the basement. This must be the storeroom where Jack's mother had made her jams and preserves. It had also been a wine cellar. A massive wine rack, empty of bottles, stood against one wall. Spiderwebs clung to her fingers like glue as she searched for an empty bottle that she could use as a weapon. Victor had to return. The thought of being left here on her own was unbearable. Peeper rubbed against her ankles and reminded her that she was not totally on her own but it made no difference to her terror.

She ran up and down the length of the basement in an effort to stop thinking. The second time, she noticed a door at the far end. It was set into an archway and padlocked. She shoved against it with her shoulder and when it failed to budge, she flung her whole body against it. Unlike most things in Hyland Hall, it was not riddled with woodworm and she was forced to give up. Then, she heard the basement door opening. Her father was standing with Victor on the top step, and Julie was squashed between them.

At Victor's command, Julie descended the steps but her legs buckled when she was halfway down. She sank to the steps and bumped the rest of the way down. Isobel ran towards her and helped her to stand.

Their father's legs were free but his arms were still tied and the gag covered his mouth. He followed Julie down the steps. Unable to hold on to anything, he looked as if he was going to fall until Isobel steadied him and guided him down. Once again, the door was closed and the dank, musty air settled over them. He had a fever. His face was hot when she touched his forehead and he was breathing fast. She removed the gag and untied his hands. Julie rubbed the pins and needles from them.

They sat on the floor, one on either side of him. Victor never did anything without a reason. Bad things had yet to happen but for now, Isobel only wanted to know one thing.

'Is Mum... is she okay?' She squeezed her arms across her chest as she waited for him to answer.

He kept swallowing and clearing his throat.

'I saw her when I was untying Daddy.' Julie laid her head on his lap. 'Victor's tied her up but she can breathe.'

'Is that true, Dad?' Isobel asked. When he was able to nod, she joined her hands together. This time she recited the Lord's Prayer to the end.

Their father hugged them close. They were amazing daughters, he said, brave, wonderful, loved all the way to the moon and back. He had every intention of beating Victor and rescuing them. It was almost possible to believe him – and kinder to pretend that they did. Victor was holding their mother as his hostage. As long as she was alive, they could do nothing to endanger her.

CHAPTER FORTY-NINE

Southern Stream FM

This in Gavin Darcy bringing you the latest update from the siege at Hyland Hall. We now have confirmation that the sighting of the teenager at the window of Hyland Hall is the person who made that dramatic call for help. Isobel Kingston's brief appearance will be a relief to the police, who have been playing a waiting game with the gunman after hours of failed attempts to speak to him directly.

Since details of the location were released, the media have been gathering at the entrance to Hyland Estate. Gardai are manning the gates and ensuring that only personnel involved with the siege are allowed to enter the grounds.

The small gate lodge where the children's father lives is empty and locked. Earlier, it was raided by the gardai who removed a laptop and various other items.

Sophy Kingston had been employed as a private nurse to the late Jack Hyland, who passed away in the early hours of this morning at St Philomena's Hospital. She was last seen with her husband at the deathbed of Mr Hyland. They can be seen on camera leaving the hospital together. Since then Luke Kingston has been unavailable for comment.

Stay tuned to Afternoon Stream for the most up-to-date information on this unfolding family saga.

CHAPTER FIFTY

Sophy

The grandfather clock was still booming. That was her first thought when Sophy opened her eyes. Booming non-stop and so loudly that she needed to cover her ears to drown it out. She was unable to move and, slowly, as consciousness returned, she realised that her hands were tied. The booming was inside her head and the last sound she remembered hearing were the receding footsteps of her children.

She almost passed out again when she moved her head to get her bearings. She was lying down, her face close to one of the table legs. The broken chair lay on its side and the slivers of broken glass glinted on the floor. Tears flooded her eyes as she visualised Julie's frantic dash across the kitchen towards Victor. *Please God, keep them safe. Please protect them, and Luke... Help us... help us.* How long since she had prayed or believed there was someone who existed beyond her earthly grasp? A vision who could hear her voice above the multitudes? Rationally, that was impossible yet she prayed as if the God she used to worship as a child was standing before her in radiant splendour and with a perfect plan to rescue her.

Her legs were also tied and her mouth gagged with the elastic bandages from the first aid kit. The box was also in her line of vision, its contents scattered. She recalled giving Luke a drink of water and her determination to bandage his shoulder. Had she done so? She closed her eyes and saw Victor, his arm lifting. Stars scattering. A black hole opening. He must have bound and gagged her when she was unconscious.

She was alone in the kitchen. Her head ached but the boom had faded to a dull thump. Had the girls escaped? Where had he taken Luke? The basement – where else would Victor bring him? She became aware of a smell. Fumes sliding across the floor. Petrol. Her whimpers were muffled behind the gag as she tried to drag herself into a sitting position. She was still struggling to do so when the door opened. Victor moved quickly as he cut through the ropes binding her legs then dragged her to her feet.

'Move,' he said and gestured towards the open door.

The Persian rug that ran along the centre of the hall had been doused with petrol and the wooden floorboards were slick and slippery.

'This is it, *Sophia*,' he said. Even now, when she was totally under his control, he mocked her name. 'This kip is a piece of kindling. I'll enjoy watching it go up in flames.'

She fell to her knees, powerless to move any further.

'Get up,' he said. 'Keep moving if you want to say goodbye to your family.'

He was looking ahead to the completion of his plan. He had the girls and Luke in the basement and that was where it would end. She wailed without sound as the clock tolled again. How was it possible for another hour to pass while she remained frozen in the moment? Her mind worked feverishly for solutions and would continue to do so until he put a shot through her brain.

She had found it difficult to open the bolt on the door leading into the basement when she entered it the first time. Now it opened easily when Victor slid it across. He had prepared this grave for them and she was sure he had done the same to the exit door that led onto his property.

'They're hiding,' he said when he looked down the five steps into the empty basement. 'And wasting time that would be better spent saying goodbye to you.'

She stumbled and was in danger of falling until he grabbed the rope that he had looped around her wrists and steadied her. Once, she had responded with passion to his touch. Now, it was hatred that gave her the strength to force her body forward towards the steps and allow herself to fall. The rush of air against her face and the knowledge that he was falling with her filled her with wild exhilaration. Stunned and breathless from their clumsy tumble, they lay together in an obscene embrace on the basement floor. She could see boots, well-worn and familiar, coming towards them but Victor had grabbed the gun that had clattered to a stop beside them. He was on his knees, the gun raised, his hands shaking from the shock of his fall. Gagged and with her hands bound, she could only use her eyes to plead with Luke to stop his forward dash, for surely the shot Victor was preparing to fire would bring him to the ground.

Victor shook so violently that the shot went wide. She recoiled from the blast and could only watch helplessly as he took aim again. Blood splattered and spilled before her eyes but Luke was ducking out of sight behind one of the presses. He was holding something in his hand. The jagged remains of a bottle that had shattered from the impact of the shot, and it was wine, Sophy realised, that was spreading its ruby stain across the stone floor.

Victor was preparing to fire again when the basement exploded with noise. Wood splintered as the exit door was forced open. Boots clattered, voices roared, bodies, so many of them filling the space that had been empty seconds ago. Guns were aimed at Victor, who had dragged Sophy to her feet and shoved her in front of him. The girls were crying and calling out to her. They struggled to reach her as they were carried from the basement and Luke, emerging with his hands up, was calling out to her, his face contorted as the gardai surrounded him protectively and helped him away. Those who remained moved into position as Victor, forcing Sophy to stand before him, moved backwards up the steps and out through the open basement door.

'The hall is soaked in petrol,' he yelled. 'I won't hesitate to set it alight if anyone makes an attempt to shoot. If you take me down, she comes with me.'

CHAPTER FIFTY-ONE

Isobel

A snake with slithery eyes that could see everything at once. That was the only way Isobel could describe Victor. The negotiator nodded as if she could visualise him as Isobel did. That was not possible. No one except Julie and her parents could share Isobel's tormented images. She struggled to banish them and pay attention to the questions the negotiator asked. It was imperative, Miriam said, to understand the mind of the snake who was holding Sophy captive. Could Isobel give her a more factual description of Victor Coyne. Only one word came to mind. Merciless.

Her mother had fallen deliberately down the steps and brought him tumbling with her. They had been tangled up together on the floor when Isobel looked out from behind the big cabinet where she and Julie were hiding. Victor was calling Sophy the C word and grabbing his gun so that he could shoot their father. The bullet shattered the wine bottle. It was so well hidden under cobwebs that they almost missed it when they were searching for weapons. He had planned to smash it over Victor's head but a bottle was no match for a gun.

The guards had dragged them from the basement and into an orchard filled with weeds and brambles. Her father was strapped down on a stretcher to stop him struggling to get off and go back to rescue Sophy. No matter how often the police told him they had the situation under control, he refused to believe them. No one was able to control Victor. He had spilled petrol over the hall. All it would take was one match and the house would burn to a cinder. He would escape in the smoke, the way he did when he set fire to the stables, and leave her mother behind, tied up and locked in a room.

They had reached a fence of barbed wire that had been cut and rolled back to allow space for them to return under cover to the courtyard. An ambulance was waiting behind trees and her father was taken immediately to hospital. The courtyard was empty, or so she thought, until she saw the word *Garda* written in yellow across a policeman's back. He was hiding behind the tree under Jack's window and then, like a sky without stars until the first one is spotted, she saw dark shapes sheltering everywhere around the courtyard.

They ate chocolates and answered Miriam's questions in the back of a garda van. Her serene expression matched her voice. She didn't act upset when she heard how Victor had fooled her. The only time she reacted, and that was just to flutter her eyelashes, was when Julie described how she had tried to stop Victor with the broken glass. She said it had been an extraordinarily courageous thing to do. So was Isobel's decision to hide the letter opener in her Uggs. Their mother would be all right. Those were Miriam's last words to them before she left the garda van and went back to negotiating. They were not injured like their father but the paramedic who examined them said that not all injuries were visible. Despite their protests, they had to go in a car ambulance and have their invisible injuries checked at the Clonmoore Medical Centre.

The reporters shouted questions when the gates were opened. The driver ignored them and blasted the horn to move them out of his way. The back windows were covered with a black film that made it possible to see out but no one could see her or Julie. She recognised Gavin Darcy. He came to The Queen of Angels to do a news feature on cyber bullying shortly after she started there. She opened the window on her side and when he shoved a furry microphone towards her, she shouted, 'Tell Mum we love her and the guards are going to rescue—' That was all she had time to shout before they moved out of earshot.

Photographers ran alongside the ambulance. Television vans were parked outside the gates. Isobel was amazed at the cars and motorbikes parked along Hyland Lane and on either side of Marsh Road. She had assumed that only Gavin Darcy knew about the siege but it seemed as if the world's media were covering it. People with binoculars were standing on cars and some had even climbed trees in an effort to see what was going on. *You don't want to know*, Isobel felt like shouting at them.

After being examined by a doctor, they spoke to a counsellor. The questions she asked were different to the ones they'd answered for Miriam. No matter how long it took, the counsellor was willing to wait for answers every time Isobel or Julie began to cry. She believed a reason could always be found for things going wrong if the right questions were asked. She was interested in Cordelia. Isobel was glad the mannequin wasn't with them. She didn't want Julie pretending she was coping but saying she was terrified in that so-real squeaky voice. She pictured Cordelia sprawled on the kitchen chair, her bright red lips smiling, her vacant eyes staring Victor down. The only one of them who wasn't frightened of him.

They were discharged into the care of Tina Bracken, Kelly's mother. She collected them in her car and Kelly, who was waiting for them in the back seat, hugged them so tightly they could hardly breathe.

CHAPTER FIFTY-TWO

Southern Stream FM

Breaking news from the siege at Hyland Hall. In a dramatic move by the gardai, the two sisters and their father, who have been at the centre of the siege, have been rescued.

Luke Kingston is suffering from a bullet wound, blood loss and extensive injuries to his head. He has been transferred directly from the scene to St Philomena's Hospital. Isobel and Julie Kingston are unharmed physically and are helping the gardai with their enquiries. Southern Stream are happy to refute the scurrilous rumours online that implied that this was a domestic incident. Luke Kingston has shown tremendous bravery during this horrifying ordeal when he was held captive by an as yet unknown and vicious gunman.

Isobel spoke exclusively to me as she was driven from the scene. 'Tell Mum we love her and the guards are going to rescue—' Unfortunately, that was all she had time to say before she was out of earshot but it is indicative of the courage shown by the Kingston family as they endure this extraordinary ordeal.

Sophy Kingston is still being held hostage by her abductor. So far, all attempts to negotiate with the gunman have failed. It's believed that petrol has been poured over the entrance hall and the gunman is threatening to set it alight if there in another forced entry into the house.

This siege has now entered an extremely dangerous phase. Stayed tuned to Southern Stream FM for the latest updates of this tense and ongoing incident.

CHAPTER FIFTY-THREE

Sophy

Death waited in a space that measured the length of a gun barrel. It breathed between her shoulder blades, her spine, the back of her neck, yet Sophy was beyond terror. The rescue of Luke and the girls meant that she was no longer responsible for anyone but herself and this release from a greater horror allowed her rage to surface. Rage was dangerous. Skyrocketing adrenaline, palpitating heart rate. It could unhinge her and cause her to act recklessly. She needed to consider her options rationally but every prod from the gun increased her fury.

She heard birdsong as he walked her from the basement to the kitchen. The bird feeder she filled in the mornings with nuts and berries was empty now but that had not stopped the trilling, twittering, piping melodies. How was it possible for such an exuberant chorus to remain undisturbed by sirens, guns and squad cars?

'Blackbirds, robins and finches,' said Victor as he pushed her into the kitchen and kicked the door behind him.

Was this an extension of his power over her? How could she outwit him if he could read every thought that entered her mind? The gag on her mouth made swallowing difficult and Victor, hearing her gasp, pulled at the knot and removed it. She controlled her breath, inhaling and releasing it on the count of ten until she could think beyond her fury.

The background music playing on Southern Stream was interrupted by Gavin Darcy with the latest news update. Luke had been removed to hospital and the girls had been helping the gardai with information on the siege. His voice had a frenetic pitch as he shouted above a background of revving engines and the repetitive click of cameras. One voice sounded above the babble, a shriek that could only belong to Isobel.

Her voice faded and was replaced by Gavin repeating her message, along with the information that the girls were on their way to Clonmoore Medical Centre for counselling.

'Such a thoughtful child.' As if he was sharing the moment with her, Victor stroked the back of her neck with the muzzle of the gun, a light touch, almost a caress.

'She's safe from you,' Sophy replied. 'That's all that matters to me.'

Cordelia slumped on a chair, the feather boa dangling over the edges. The hood where the shard of glass had been hidden hung limp and empty. Sophy's skin tingled then and the tightness in her chest intensified as she battled for self-control.

'Sit down there.' He nodded towards a chair and untied her wrists when she was seated. He was forced to lay the gun on the table to do so but it was out of her reach. The vividness of her surroundings had an almost hallucinatory sharpness, her life compressed into this space she was forced to share with him. He had taken the brunt of the fall down the basement steps, his body cushioning hers as they landed. That shock, combined with his injured leg, gave her a certain advantage but, as yet, she was unable to figure out how to use it.

He ordered Sophy to check the backyard. She moved the window blind fractionally and peered out. The backyard appeared empty.

The gardai were obviously staying out of range, patient and watchful, behind the outhouses. She heard the chuffing reverberations of a helicopter. It must be flying low over the house. Was it bringing reinforcements? Would it make the slightest different? Her need to pee was becoming impossible to ignore. Her mind could fly to terrifying places but her body was responding to its basic functions.

He shook his head when she told him she wanted to use the bathroom. He knew, as she did, that the window would provide her with an escape route, but he, too, was feeling the effects of this long-running ordeal. He stood in the open doorway of the bathroom and, although the gun remained on her, he kept his eyes averted. She washed her hands, splashed cold water over her face. He was watching her again, his eyes reflecting back at her through the mirror. He gestured towards the window beside the toilet and waited until her face was pressed against the glass before he relieved himself. Their forced intimacy should have embarrassed her but she had gone beyond false modesty, her life pared down to one motivation— survival.

Luke's phone rang when they returned to the kitchen, the breezy, techno beat of its ringtone startling them.

'Answer it and put it on speaker,' he said. 'I'll do the talking from now on.'

'Sophy, are you safe?' The composed voice of the negotiator filled the room.

'She has a gun pointing at her head and it could go off at any moment,' he said. 'Does that answer your question?'

'Thank you, it does. Who am I speaking to?'

'I imagine that should be obvious by now.'

'Are you Victor Coyne?'

'Got it in one. Now, fuck off.'

'Can I have a word with Sophy?'

'She's got nothing to say to you.'

'I know you've been injured, Victor,' said Miriam. 'Are you in pain?'

'It's bearable.'

'Is there anything we can do to ease it?'

'Drug me, you mean.'

'Victor, help us to understand how this situation has spiralled so far out of control?'

'Is that what you think happened?'

'I believe so.'

'Are you speaking from experience?'

'I've spoken to people in siege situation in the past. We can handle this without it becoming more dangerous.'

'Nice one, Miriam. Empathy. Should work but it doesn't. What I need to know from you is how you're going to save Sophia's life when I decide I've had enough of this conversation?'

'We can—'

'I'll tell you exactly what you *can* do. I want a car brought to the courtyard with a full tank and the key in the ignition. I'll sit in the back seat and she'll sit in the driver's seat. My gun will be positioned at the back of her head, exactly where it is right now. In case anyone is foolish enough to track me, I won't hesitate to shoot her. Am I painting a clear enough picture for you, Miriam?'

'Yes, Victor, you are. I can't give you an answer until I discuss—'

'It's non-negotiable. If that car is not here within the next hour, this conversation is closed. You can deal with the fallout when her remains are removed from here. Imagine what that will do to your career as a negotiator.'

'All that concerns me is that both of you come safely out of this situation—'

'Then you'd better get that fucking car organised,' he snapped. 'Minutes are ticking by and you're wasting them.'

'Victor, let me speak to Sophy—'

'Cut the call,' he snapped at Sophy, who did so while Miriam was in mid-sentence.

How could he possibly think the gardai would agree to his request? The car would be under surveillance from the instant she drove away.

'Can you imagine the publicity that will follow if the gardai give into your demand?' she asked.

'Can you imagine the publicity if they don't?'

'If they refuse, what then?' she asked. 'Are you prepared to spend the rest of your life in jail? That's if you're not shot dead when the police storm the house. Don't look for mercy when my body is on the floor.'

'They won't let that happen.'

'Collateral damage must be built into any siege negotiation. If I'm dead, you'll have played your trump card and lost. Why not look for a deal? You could ask for a shorter jail sentence if you cooperate.'

He could pretend he was still in control but Sophy had grown used to reading expressionless faces. She could see his desperation, his awareness that time was running out on him.

'There'll be no deal,' he snapped. 'As you've discovered, gambling is the family curse. I'll stake my freedom against a prison sentence.'

Her face was puffy when she touched it. The pain in her head came in dizzying flashes. The rest of her body was one enormous bruise. She was conscious of minutes ticking by and, yet, she was always startled when the grandfather clock rang out another hour. She made sandwiches when Victor demanded food and ate with him. She needed fuel to keep going yet each time she swallowed she felt as though she was forcing a stone down her throat. He also must be in constant pain. The knowledge that she had inflicted his injuries on him added to her fear. Miriam was doing her utmost to keep him calm, but he was growing increasingly jittery.

'Stand up and turn towards the door.' He steadied his hands on the gun and kicked back the chair he had been sitting on. 'Take the radio. We're going into the music room.'

Fumes stung her eyes as they crossed the hall. A slant of wintery sunlight flowed through the fanlight and caught the shimmer of dust mites. The curtains on the two windows in the music room were open. On his instructions, she closed them and shoved an armchair in front of the nearest one.

'Bring the piano stool over and leave it behind the armchair,' he said.

When she had arranged the configuration to his satisfaction, he ordered her to open the curtains and sit down in the armchair. He positioned himself behind her on the stool. She did not need to feel the gun on her neck to sense his closeness. He could only be brought down if a bullet fired by a garda went through her.

Her body, fragmented as it was behind squared panes of glass, was plainly visible to all those watching eyes. She sensed a charged energy in the empty courtyard that could at any moment be shattered by boots and commands. She was a prop on a stage that Victor had set. If the audience, poised and waiting, made one wrong move, the curtains with their frayed edges would descend on her. So many ways to die. Gun, flames, car crash, heart attack; all as random as the numbers on a wheel of fortune.

CHAPTER FIFTY-FOUR

Isobel

Tina Bracken's kitchen was busy with women preparing food for the gardai and media. They fussed over the girls and set soup, sandwiches and smoothies before them. The three S's for survival, Tina joked as she encouraged them to eat up. A shower had revived Isobel. She had changed into a pair of Kelly's jeans and a thick, woolly jumper but the trembling didn't stop until she sat down to eat. She missed Peeper's rhythmic purring. She had glimpsed him streaking up the basement steps when the police arrived and he must still be trapped in Hyland Hall.

Kelly said the picture on television of Isobel leaning out of the car ambulance window and yelling at Gavin Darcy was really cool. Isobel knew she was lying. She looked like she was acting in a horror film and had just seen the face of a vampire. Julie's head began to droop. Her eyelashes flickered as she tried to stay awake but Tina overrode her protests that she wasn't tired and lay down beside her in the spare bedroom until she fell asleep.

Watching the same images over and over again on television was unbearable. Photos of Charlie were all over the house and that was also difficult. Her mother had been crying a lot since he died, Kelly said. She hadn't cried once, even though she felt like doing so when the grief washed over her. Crying would break an oath she had made to herself when she heard her friends were calling her 'Freak' behind her back.

Isobel went outside with her to her den at the bottom of the garden. Charlie had built it for her when she became a teenager. They wrapped rugs around themselves and curled up on an old sofa. Their friendship felt special because it had travelled along a difficult path to reach them, Kelly said. If only it had happened when her gramps was alive.

'Sergeant Moynihan is Tina's friend,' she said. 'She's tough. She'll have your mum free soon, I know she will.'

'You don't know what Victor is like.' Isobel had felt emptied out after talking to Miriam and the counsellor. But everything she had endured since she saw Victor coming through the gate in the wall was muddled again in her mind. It was difficult to remember what happened and when. Fear had exploded like a grenade in the pit of her stomach when she was in her bedroom and heard the first shot from the den. One shock had followed another and it seemed impossible that their ordeal could get worse until they were forced to leave her mother behind in the basement. Talking helped. Kelly was a good listener and didn't become impatient, even though Isobel kept going on and on about Victor.

'He burned down the stables because Jack was going to save horses and he shot Caesar with the same gun he shot my dad with. He even blamed Dad for your gramp's death but it was his fault because he kept ramming the bull bars on his jeep into the barn to loosen the wall that fell on top of... of...' She stopped, aware, suddenly, from her friend's confused expression, of the impact of that information on Kelly.

'Gramps death was an accident,' Kelly said. 'What have bull bars got to do with it?'

Unsure of exactly what she had blurted out, Isobel shook her head. 'I don't know. It was just something I overheard my mother saying. It was probably nothing, honestly.'

'Tell me every single word you heard,' Kelly demanded.

For once, Isobel had not been snooping on adults when she overheard the conversation between her parents. It was the day before Jack died and her father had arrived back from a shift at the hospital. He was sitting with her mother at the kitchen table when Isobel opened the door. They were talking so intently that they didn't notice her. Her mother kept going on about bull bars and how hard it would be to prove that Victor was responsible for loosening the barn wall foundations. She talked about Caesar, too, how she knew who shot him and started the fire in the stables. Isabel hadn't heard her mention a name but she could only have been talking about one person.

She was reluctant to tell Kelly yet, somehow, it was impossible to stop until Kelly pressed her face into a cushion and began to cry. They were tears of rage, she admitted. Some oaths just had to be broken. The crying stopped when they heard a helicopter. They went outside and watched it passing overhead. Was it heading to or going away from Hyland Hall? The uncertainty was agonising.

'I'm going crazy not knowing what's happening to Mum.' Isobel banged her fists against her thighs.

'We can get into the estate without anyone seeing us.' Kelly's tears had dried. Her eyes reminded Isobel of Peeper's green-eyed stare when he was stalking a bird. 'Gramps showed me all the shortcuts.'

'That's a mad idea,' Isobel said. 'You've no idea what it's like there.'

'We don't have to get close,' Kelly said. 'I know a place where it'll be safe to watch what's going on.'

Kelly's idea was dangerous, as dangerous as her mother's decision to deliberately fall down the steps and drag Victor with her.

Kelly's phone bleeped with an update from her Southern Stream app. She read it quickly then held it out so that Isobel could see it.

'Victor has your mum in a room at the front of the house,' she said. 'Someone took a photograph. Look, she's okay.'

A photographer had managed to slip beyond the cordon and had taken a long range shot of the house. Her mother was just visible behind a window in the music room. No sign of Victor. He must have been hiding behind her. Isobel knew exactly where the gun would have been pointed.

'I don't want to watch what's going on,' she said. 'I want to get close enough to distract Victor so that that police can rescue Mum and shoot him dead.'

The road running along the back of Kelly's garden was a cul-de-sac that was used only by people who lived on Marsh Road. It was too narrow for cars and most of the time they forgot it existed. But not Kelly Bracken who seemed to have an internal map of her surroundings imprinted on her mind. She knew how to enter Hyland Estate, veer into the woods, emerge again and cross a rickety bridge over a ditch. She opened a gate so woven with bindweed it was indistinguishable from the reeds and bracken growing around it.

'Gramps showed the gate to me,' Kelly said. 'It used to be a short cut from the Gallops back to Hyland Hall.'

The zigzagging trail they entered was so narrow they had to walk in single file. Kelly stopped suddenly and pressed her finger to her lips. 'We're being followed,' she whispered.

Isobel heard it then, an anxious, breathless cry, immediately recognisable.

'Wait for me, Issy. You're going too fast.'

'Oh, my God, it's Julie,' she whispered.

Kelly looked equally horrified. 'She can't come with us,' she said. 'It's far too dangerous.'

The rustling sounds grew louder as Julie emerged into view. 'You left without me.' Flushed and dishevelled, she stared accusingly at Isobel. 'Are you going to save Mammy?'

'Julie, you can't come with us.' Kelly took her by her shoulders and turned her around. 'Go back the way you came and say nothing to anyone. Tina will go ballistic if she knows where we're going.'

'She thinks I'm in your den with you and Issy.' She wriggled out of Kelly's grip. 'You can't make me go back.'

'I can.' Isobel forced authority into her voice. 'You have to do what I tell you. I'm in charge until Mum comes back.'

'What if she doesn't come back... Issy... what if Victor...'

'Stop... stop!' She hugged Julie. 'Miriam will make him come out with his hands up. You'll see.'

'I want to be there when that happens. You can't make me go back.' Her hair swished behind her when she broke free and ran ahead of them.

They reached the site where the stables had stood and crouched behind the rubble that had yet to be removed. Staring across the paddock at the wall bordering the back of Hyland Hall, they could see gardai moving about the backyard, their heads and shoulders visible. They had shields, helmets and bulletproof vests to protect them. Their purposefulness added to Isobel's awareness that she and Kelly had acted on an impulse. They had no clear plan of action once they reached Hyland Hall. And she now had Julie to protect. They needed to stop right now but Kelly, followed by Julie, was already running from the rubble to hide behind the dismantled walls of the barn that had been stacked for collection. An open space remained between them and the entrance to the annexe where a guard stood on duty outside the door. A second guard was speaking into a walkie-talkie. He gestured towards his companion when he finished the call. They both moved away from the entrance and hurried along the L-shaped side of the house.

The gardai waiting in the backyard had moved position. Even at a distance, Isobel could see how tense they had become. Something was definitely changing. The two men guarding the annexe must have been called to reinforce the front of the house. Had something else happened to her mother?

'Wait here,' Isobel said. 'I want to check something.' They could enter the house through the annexe if the door was still unlocked. She ducked low and ran towards the cobbled path outside the entrance and sighed with relief when the door opened. She waved across at Julie and Kelly, who sprinted towards her. No authoritative voices ordered them to stop as they stood on the threshold, shaken by the enormity of what they were about to do. Kelly took the first step and the others followed. Isobel closed the door quietly behind them.

The annexe had always felt separate from Hyland Hall. As long as they stood there, Isobel could pretend that they were not actually back at the scene of the siege. The room was full of clutter; anything that broke in Hyland Hall ended up being dumped there. Ellie was always planning to clear it out but never got around to doing so. A zinc tub balanced on top of a high stool swayed as Julie's shoulder hit against it then settled back into position. The realisation of what would have happened if it had hit the ground forced them to a standstill. Even Kelly looked frightened as she glanced back at the door they had just entered.

'Don't go in there.' Isobel grabbed Julie's arm as her sister started tiptoeing towards the kitchen. 'It's too dangerous Julie.'

'I want to talk to Cordelia.'

'I'll talk to her for you.' She forced Julie to a standstill. 'It's your job to keep watch in the annexe and warn us if the police come back.'

'I'm the only one she can hear.' Julie wriggled free and opened the door that led into the back of the kitchen.

Kelly shrugged. 'It's safer to stay together,' she whispered.

They listened for sounds beyond the kitchen but they were unable to hear anything except the ragged flow of their breathing.

The kitchen smelled of congealing food left too long on plates. Broken glass was still on the floor. Everywhere Isobel looked she could see signs of the horror they had endured. Running through the woods she had felt elated. The decision she had made with Kelly had diminished in her mind the true awfulness of what was going on inside the house. She must have been deranged to forget, even for an instant, what Victor was capable of doing.

Cordelia still sat on the same chair. Her wig was slanted to one side and shielded half of her face. Julie knelt before her and straightened the wig, all the time whispering softly to her. It was impossible to make out what she was saying. Her words were interspersed with kisses on Cordelia's cheeks and forehead.

They whispered plans to each other. They could use the sharpest kitchen knife and stab Victor from behind. They could batter him over his head with the frying pan or the heaviest saucepan. The chair leg could be used as a weapon, also the sweeping brush. Everywhere they looked in the kitchen they saw weapons but none of them had the power of the gun. Cordelia remained mute; her blank, blue gaze fixed on Julie.

CHAPTER FIFTY-FIVE

Sophy

The evening sun flamed the clouds. Its radiance bathed the courtyard and flashed off the surface of a police shield. Until that instant, the gardai had remained out of sight but the movement of one, and the sudden visibility of the shield, signalled that they were preparing for action. The effort to sit still required all her willpower when she heard the latest update from Gavin Darcy. The girls were missing. They had not been seen near the estate and initial fears that they would have returned to the scene of the siege had been discarded. Sophy had to believe him. The thought that they could be anywhere near Hyland Hall would snap another strand of the fragile thread that was preventing her from losing her mind.

The sky darkened. She could see her reflection in the window. Her disjointed image, broken apart by panes of glass, her agony segmented, seemed as surreal as the unseen shotgun pointed at her spine. Miriam's tone was steelier when she asked how Victor could ensure Sophy's safety if a car was made available to him. No decision was forthcoming as yet, she admitted. Many factors had to be considered. The decision to accede to his demand would be made at the highest level. It was obvious the gardai were playing for time as the deadline Victor had demanded passed.

'I'm not prepared to discuss anything except the car.' His voice was louder, more aggressive. 'It's your decision whether Sophia Kingston lives or dies.'

Despite his belligerence, Sophy sensed his tension rising after each conversation with the negotiator. She was wired to his thoughts, his gun a dowsing rod that twitched to his shifting moods.

Spotlights were switched on in the courtyard. Her reflection was no longer visible. If the girls were in the woods, there would be no light to guide them. The thought of them being lost drew an involuntary moan from her. Miriam rang again and tried to reassure her. The gardai were keeping watch on the grounds and had no reason to believe the girls were anywhere near the estate. Still no word from her superiors about the car but she now had the authority to negotiate a deal with Victor. A reduced charge would be brought against him if he was prepared to lay down his gun and surrender Sophy unharmed.

In reply, he fired at the ceiling. 'Next shot goes through her spine,' he said. 'Bring me my car.'

Plaster dust settled on her hair. Looking up, she saw that the bullet had gone through the cornicing. She had once climbed a ladder to examine the delicate images. A Greek woman holding a lyre, she remembered, and now reduced by Victor's shot to a scattering of white flakes.

CHAPTER FIFTY-SIX

Isobel

The gun shot was so loud, so unexpected, that Kelly dropped to the floor and covered her head with her hands. Isobel froze, unable to move until she realised that Julie was running towards the door leading into the hall.

'Julie, *stop*...' She reached her sister in time to prevent her opening it.

'He *shot* Mammy. I have to go to her... let me *go*!' Tears streamed down Julie's cheeks as she struggled to free herself but Isobel held her tight.

'We don't know what he's done,' she hissed. 'He shoots his gun for no reason and he won't hesitate to shoot you if you go out there.'

'Listen,' Kelly whispered. 'I can hear someone talking.' She carefully turned the handle and eased the door open. The words were inaudible yet Isobel slumped with relief when she recognised the familiar pitch of her mother's voice.

'It's Mum,' she whispered and Julie, nodding in agreement, wiped her eyes.

'I think they're leaving the music room,' Kelly whispered. 'Can you hear footsteps?'

Isobel nodded. Two sets, one loud and confident, the other hesitant, lighter. Victor was shouting at the police that he wanted a car. Her mother would be forced to drive him away. He would escape and never be punished for shooting her father… and Charlie's death, and Caesar too, and the fire in the stables. She could smell the petrol. It was still as strong as earlier when Victor had dumped her in the basement.

Julie had hunkered down in front of Cordelia and was whispering to her.

She stood up but kept her hand on the mannequin's shoulder. 'Cordelia hates Victor just as much as we do,' she whispered.

'That's not possible—' Isobel began then stopped. What was the sense in trying to reason with Julie when nothing made sense anymore?

'She wants to save Mammy.'

'We all do,' Isobel whispered back.

'We have to let Cordelia do it.'

That expression on her face – her determination as she had rushed at Victor with a shard of glass in her hand– was back again and Isobel, frightened by the thoughts going through her sister's mind, shook her head.

'Leave Cordelia out of this,' she hissed. 'You shouldn't be here at all.'

'Cordelia's not frightened of him. She'll be able to play tricks on him.'

'How?' Even as she asked the question, Isobel could feel her skin lifting in goosebumps. A plan was forming. It shuddered through her in all its brilliance. Cordelia, the decoy. Then, just as quickly, all she could see was its madness. It was as crazy as the glass shard plan and the decision they'd made to come here.

'He'll shoot her,' she whispered.

'We have to do this to save Mammy.' Julie lifted Cordelia from the chair and laid her on the table.

'But you love Cordelia—'

'I love Mum much, *much* more.'

Isobel knew her sister was right. Cordelia was the only one who could survive the danger surrounding them.

Julie stroked her bottom lip in a gesture that predicted what was to come and the voice resonating from the kitchen table made Cordelia's whispered words sound even more gruesome.

'I want to save Sophy.' Her smiling face stared up at them. 'I don't mind the bullets, not one little bit.'

CHAPTER FIFTY-SEVEN

Sophy

The fumes were stronger. A dense gathering of deadly, invisible vapours. She swallowed hard and fought back a swell of nausea. A spark, that was all it would take for them to combust. Victor was good at creating sparks. The wires in the barn; how easy it had been for him to start an inferno.

'There's been enough stalling.' He yanked her up from the chair by her hair. 'Walk to the hall,' he said. 'It's time they discovered that I mean what I say.'

The old grandfather clock struck six as she walked before him from the music room. Her eyes were drawn to its shining pendulum as it swayed back and forth behind the glass door. The steady ticking had marked her stay at Hyland Hall and she could be hearing it for the last time.

'Open the door,' he said. 'Make sure the police can see you.'

Her legs threatened to fold beneath her but she managed to keep walking. No longer separated from the police by panes of glass, she shrank back when she opened the front door and faced into the barrage of spotlights. Standing directly behind her, Victor was out of range for a sniper but he was more vulnerable to an assault from the back of the house. He was aware of the danger and knew also, as she did, that it would be impossible to make such an approach without the creak of a floorboard or an unoiled hinge alerting him. He took the cigarette lighter from his pocket. She heard the click as he switched it on. He was playing with fire, literally. One stray spark would set the hall ablaze.

'Remind them that the next shot is for you,' he said. 'Shout it out, loud and clear so that there can be no misunderstandings. If anyone attempts a rescue, Hyland Hall goes up in flames.'

When she had finished delivering his warning, he ordered her to walk backwards. Having exposed her to the waiting gardai, he was drawing her back step by step towards the rug in the centre of the hall. She whimpered when she felt the brush of fur against her ankles. Peeper. Earlier, in the basement, still dazed from her fall, he had streaked past her up the steps and out through the door. The impression had been fleeting and instantly forgotten in the mayhem that followed the storming of the basement. Now, he rubbed his sinewy body around her leg and meowed in distress when Victor kicked him out of the way. Instinctively, Sophy turned her head to see if the cat was injured, and, in that brief glance before Victor yelled at her to keep looking towards the front door, she noticed a movement behind the grandfather clock. As startling as the flash of a bird from a bush, it was gone just as suddenly. In her heightened state, it could have been imagined yet it caused the bile in her stomach to rise in a sudden gush. Victor appeared not to have noticed anything unusual but the impression stayed with Sophy. A white shoulder patterned with tiny, gold stars visible for an instant, then abruptly wrenched back out of sight. Julie's favourite sweater was patterned across the shoulders and down along the arms with stars. She was wearing it when she came back into the kitchen after changing out of her nightdress. And wearing it when she tried to attack Victor. The image of her fierce little virago, running towards him with the glass shard, constricted Sophy's throat. It wasn't possible... her thoughts raged… how could it have happened that her younger daughter, and probably Isobel, too, had entered Hyland Hall? She had to dismiss that nightmarish possibility. Otherwise her heart, unable to bear any more strain, would falter and stop.

'Victor is going to set fire to the house,' she shouted. Her voice was filled with authority, a mother-voice that demanded instant obedience. 'Do you hear me? The hall is saturated with petrol. Anyone who tries to rescue me will be burned in the flames.'

'You've already delivered the message,' Victor said. 'No need to overstate it. Our negotiator is well aware of my intentions.'

She had reached the Persian rug. The cloying fumes made it difficult for her to breathe when she stepped onto it.

'Victor Coyne, I'm going to kill you with a knife.' Julie's quavering threat sent shockwaves through Sophy but the hall looked empty when she spun around.

'You're going to die,' Julie continued. 'You're a horrible, wicked man and I hate you *so* much.'

Victor's attention was no longer fixed on Sophy when he raised the shotgun. She had no time to call out a warning, a plea, a prayer, before he took aim and fired at the grandfather clock.

The shot passed through the frame and set off the booming mechanism. The gongs reverberated through the hall as Julie fell forward, her blonde hair visible for an instant, that familiar, provocative swirl that always remined Sophy of sunshine. She opened her mouth but even the power to scream had been taken from her.

Victor fired again and the hall – as if it was responding to the madness – echoed with shouts and trampling boots. Peeper screeched an unearthly dirge as a whooshing noise turned the hall to flame. The flames did not take Sophy by surprise. What else could she expect when she was in hell?

Victor had used her name as an endearment, a taunt, a possession. It was the last word she heard him utter as he turned to fire at the advancing gardai and tripped over Peeper. He staggered backwards. As he struggled to regain his balance, he fell against the grandfather clock and brought it down with him. The cat's high-pitched keening rebounded against the walls; a cry that was as primal and fierce as Sophy's anguish when she finally found the strength to cry out. The body of her child was lying beneath a shattered grandfather clock that was, somehow, continuing to toll an echoing, relentless boom. She continued to scream as rough but capable arms held her firmly, and rushed her outside.

CHAPTER FIFTY-EIGHT

Isobel

Flickering sprites in bright blue shawls danced along the hall. Their sputtering growl grew louder when Isobel opened the kitchen door. The grandfather clock where Isobel had positioned Cordelia earlier lay on its side and had turned into a pillar of flame.

After Julie had thrown her voice, they had dashed for cover under the long, wooden table. They had heard the warning Sophy called out to them but it was too late to heed it. They scrunched even deeper into their knees when the shots rang out. Had Victor shot through Cordelia's plastic skin or had their plan failed? That possibility could not even be considered.

They had still been crouching out of sight when they heard voices yelling and boots pounding off the hall floorboards. Then there was silence until Isobel opened the kitchen door and realised the hall was blazing. The flames had not reached the back hall but they were running in a straight line towards them.

'Run!' she shouted at Julie and Kelly, who were still crouched under the table. They dashed towards the back door and discovered it was locked. It wouldn't open, even when Isobel turned the key. The gardai must have blocked it from the outside to prevent Victor escaping that way. She pulled across the curtains and looked out the window. A metal grid had been placed across it and the yard where the gardai had been standing with their guns and bullet vests just a short while ago was deserted.

Kelly scrabbled in her pocket for her phone. They were at the worst side of the house for a signal and she banged it against her forehead in frustration when she failed to reach Louise at 999. They ran into the annexe when a thin line of smoke began to seep under the kitchen door. This door was also locked and the window had been barricaded from the outside.

Isobel closed the door dividing the annexe from the kitchen, where the smoke was rising in a plume. It stung her eyes and charred her throat. Kelly had pulled the front of her sweater over her mouth and Julie was coughing. Their voices became hoarser every time they called for help. They were reliving every terrifying moment of Jack's experience. Smoke was as merciless and murderous as Victor Coyne's gun.

The noise from the flames had died down and been replaced by a low hiss. Isobel's mind was becoming cloudy. The oily smell was making it hard to breathe properly. Jack was speaking to her. She could hear his voice as clearly as if they were back at the lake and he was telling her what to do. They had to go into the shower room. She had always avoided that part of the annexe. It was too disgusting, all those stained shower stalls and urinals, yet she obeyed him when he told her to open the door. It dragged against the floor and the scraping noise it made helped her to concentrate.

The room was dark and when she pushed the door closed, the cratered face of a silver moon shone down through the skylight. That was when Isobel remembered the words she had read in Jack's journal. She understood, then, why he did not need to be in this world to hold out his hands to her. *Laurence knew the ways of our house. He found the hidden chinks and unguarded openings that gave him the freedom to leave and return at will. His favourite was the skylight in the shower room.*

The solidness of the shower door was keeping the smoke out for now. The skylight offered their only chance to escape but there was nothing in this empty space that they could use to reach the ceiling. How had Laurence managed? Isobel studied the top frame of the shower unit below the skylight. It was rusted in places and would break if she or Kelly put their weight on it. Julie had stopped coughing and was sobbing quietly when Isobel told her what she had to do.

'Julie is our only hope.' Jack was telling Julie to be brave and take on the challenge, or, maybe, it was Kelly who was speaking. The oily smell was forming into a cloud and confusing Isobel. She had to fight it off before it descended over them and blotted everything from their minds. She helped Kelly to hoist Julie into the air. They had to do it twice before Julie was able to grab the bar. She swung like a trapeze artist until she managed to swing one leg over the top of the shower frame. It bent and creaked from the strain of her weight as she straddled the bar. It held steady as Julie stretched upwards to open the handle and catch the full-bellied moon in her hands.

CHAPTER FIFTY-NINE

Sophy

'Stand back, Sophy.' She was pulled back when she tried to run towards the steps. The garda's arms were strong and her struggles easily contained. They were wearing fire-resistant suits and a fire engine was moving into position in front of the house. A guard, a woman this time, emerged from the house with the body of a child in her arms. The same scene Sophy had witnessed at the lake on that misty afternoon was being repeated. Unable to look, she hugged her chest and collapsed to her knees.

The woman laid the limp body with the star-patterned sweater on the ground beside Sophy. Arms held her. A voice, puzzled and commanding, asked her to look. Unable to ignore the woman, Sophy opened her eyes. Where was the blood? It should be spilling over her hands as she touched her child? A slow awareness penetrated her horror as she stared at the scorched but flame-resistant remains of Cordelia. The hole in her cheek had torn apart the fragile membrane but her red lips were still smiling, her blue eyes open and staring at the sky. A second shot had pierced her shoulder and shattered the gold stars. She had been a decoy. It was the only explanation and it had worked. Sophy staggered to her feet and ran towards the entrance. The flames had been quenched but smoke still billowed across the courtyard and carried the sickening stench of burned fuel.

'The children are still inside the house,' she screamed at the gardai, who were emerging through the smoke.

They dispersed immediately, some entering the hall, others running to the back of the house.

'Everything is under control.' A woman came to her side. Her face was unfamiliar but Sophy instantly recognised her voice. Miriam's unruffled tone belied the facts. Her daughters and Kelly Bracken were trapped inside the smoldering house. The negotiator and Sergeant Moynihan surrounded her like kindly but determined guardians as she begged to join the search.

Two paramedics carried a stretcher down the steps. Unaware and uncaring whether Victor had escaped or been consumed by fire, she looked away but not before she noticed that his face had been covered. An ambulance siren wailed as his body was driven away. He had died with her name on his lips but her terror allowed her no room for hate, shock, or pity. Her gaze remained fixed on Hyland Hall. Smoke still streamed from the entrance but the old house stood strong, solid and enduring.

Gardai came into view from the side of the house. Spotlights pierced the drifting plumes as Sophy watched the group break apart and then there was nothing left to do but reach out her arms to the three girls, who broke free and ran towards her.

CHAPTER SIXTY

Sophy

What did it take to mend a marriage? A near drowning, an unexpected inheritance, a siege? Each one should have been earth-shattering enough to drive her into Luke's arms but the issues that had broken them apart remained unresolved. Trust, when lost, was as arid as a desert. Where to root new beginnings?

After he was discharged from hospital, they met with Jack's solicitor. Benedict Hancock's offices were located on Upper Main Square, two doors away from Victor Coyne Property Analyst. The building was for sale. Sophy kept her face averted as she walked past the sign.

Two weeks had passed since the siege. She had not attended Victor's funeral and, according to Ellie, only a small number of people turned up to pay their last respects. The fire he had started, and that had led to his death, had not spread beyond the hall. Apart from smoke damage, the rooms were intact. The restoration that Jack had envisaged was now taking place. Until then, she was living in Clonmoore in a rented apartment with the girls. Luke would remain in the gate lodge to oversee the repairs.

Lost, she had said when Jack asked her for a word to describe her husband. It no longer applied to Luke. He had found himself when he came to Hyland Estate. An ancestral call, perhaps. She had no way of knowing the depth of his thoughts as he struggled into a new identity. The son of the late Jack Hyland.

Benedict Hancock made no secret of his curiosity about the siege as he escorted them into his office. He had known Victor all his life and he, like the rest of the town, was shocked by the fact that one of their own, born and bred in their midst, could commit such a heinous crime.

The document he laid before them was the same as the copy Isobel had found in the hidden drawer. Jack's wishes were clearly stated but he had offered them an option to sell their inheritance if they did not want to establish the Hyland Equine Foundation.

'You have a free rein, no pun intended, to do what you like with the estate.' Benedict chuckled dryly at his wit. 'Take your time to think about your options. Let me know your wishes when you decide.'

The Coffee Bean was quiet when they sat down at a table.

'Same as usual?' Jessie, the owner, called across to them. They both nodded as she busied herself at the coffee machine.

'Are you still having nightmares?' Luke asked.

'Waking or sleeping, they come, regardless,' Sophy replied. 'What about you?'

'The same.'

'After Julie almost drowned, I kept having flashbacks. Jack told me once to let them play. That's how you conquer them. I don't know if that's true.'

'He had a lot to conquer.' He shrugged and winced. The pain in his shoulder remained acute. 'I still can't take it in. Two lives breaking apart and never coming together again. It's like a Greek tragedy.'

'Only if that's what you decide it should be,' Sophy said. 'Maddie's life overflowed with love. Not just from us but the love Jack carried for her in his heart until he drew his last breath.'

'That thought comforts me,' he said. 'But then I think of how that love was squandered. All those missed opportunities. Only for Maddie's chance encounter with Olive Coyne, she and Jack would both have gone to their graves without ever discovering the truth. The randomness of fate, I find it terrifying.'

Jessie came to their table. She must have sensed the heavy atmosphere as she set their coffees down and left them staring at each other.

'Do you want to sell and move on?' he asked. The question was direct, abrupt. Shades of his father, perhaps.

'Do you?' Sophy replied.

He shook his head. 'No, I'm staying here. From the moment Jack shared his plans with me, I knew I had to take on his project.'

'You'll be working with addicts—'

'I *am* an addict.'

'I know but—'

'Sophy, I realised that fact when I was eighteen. My mother knew it, too. I couldn't understand why she was so devastated when I started playing the slots. That's how it began. I was out of control and had no idea how to stop. Maddie knew, of course. I'm sure she believed I was Laurence's son. What a torture that must have been for her.'

'If you'd only told me about that stage of your life—'

'It belonged to my past, or so I believed. But when she died…' He struggled to continue. 'It was as if I'd been possessed once again. It took such a short time to overpower me and devastate the people I love.'

'You make it sound like an alien force?'

'No, not alien,' he said. 'It's part of me. I own it.'

They drank their coffee in silence. The café would soon be filled with lunchtime customers, who would recognise them instantly. They had become celebrities for all the wrong reasons yet Sophy felt the warmth and support of the town behind them.

'Whatever you decide to do, Sophy, I won't stand in your way,' Luke said. 'All I ask is that I have equal custody of the girls.'

'That could be difficult if I return to Dublin.'

'If that's what you want to do, we can work it out.'

'My other alternative is to remain here.'

'Is it possible for us to get past all that's happened to us since Maddie died?'

'I don't know, Luke.' She shook her head. 'Do you remember the night you came out of Jack's room and told me you'd found yourself?'

He nodded. 'Yes, I remember it well.'

'I need space to find out who I really am.' She looked across the square towards Victor's office and felt the by-now familiar surge of guilt. So many thoughts to haunt her. And questions she must ask herself. She needed the space and strength to answer them. Luke, understanding that she was struggling with her own demons, reached into his pocket and laid a coin on the table.

'Jack gave me something that night,' he said. 'He told me to use it as a reminder that he'd made me walk through fire and back again.' The coin he displayed had the sheen of polished gold. Twin heads were finely etched on its surfaces. He made no effort to toss it as he passed it over to Sophy. 'He was speaking metaphorically, of course, and, in the same way, we've survived the flames of all we've endured. Would you…?' He hesitated, his fingers linked, clenched. 'If there is a chance of saving our marriage, is it possible for us to take our future one day at a time?'

EPILOGUE

Isobel

Her parents had a 'one day at a time' marriage. All that time they spent together, their two heads bent over plans that had so much space to grow. Why could their love not grow the same way? No sense asking her mother that question. Sophy would just go on about love not being a tap that could be turned on and off. Her father said it was a commodity that had to be earned and that was not always possible. They claimed there were not enough hours in the day to handle Jack's legacy, and said it ruefully, happily.

Two abandoned racehorses, Caballero and Making Whoopy were settling into their stables. Hyland Hall had a new face but one that was still craggy with age, which suited it very well, her father said. The days kept rolling on and summer came. A record-breaking scorcher, said the weather forecasters.

The sun was shining on the afternoon they took a boat to Withers Island. They stepped ashore on a shelf of rock and climbed upwards towards the stunted trees with their wind-stretched branches. How fragile they looked compared to the stalwart woodland trees on the estate yet they formed a green canopy above them as they carried the picnic basket to the centre of the island. Isobel laid the rug over a carpet of spongy pine needles. She had made it exactly as Jack had described in his memoir. Her parents agreed that she had prepared a wonderful spread. After they had eaten, Julie nodded at her sister. It was time for the two of them to explore the island.

There wasn't much to see. Lots of scrub and clumps of flowers growing from fissures in the rocks. Ducks and moorhens dived back into the water, alarmed no doubt by strangers trespassing on their domain. She sat with Julie on a rocky ledge overlooking the lake. They held hands and made a wish that had to come true on this island where Jack and Maddie had once loved deeply enough to make a son.

A swan swam towards them. A cob, his silky neck as curved as a question mark. He lifted into the air, a clumsy upwards lurch, and for an instant, it seemed as if his webbed feet would drag him back. He continued to rise and fly directly towards them, skimming so low they could see his yellow bill and steadfast eyes. In the distance, rooks looped the sky, cawing and calling faintly to them. The ducks and moorhens chattered but their clamour was unable to drown out the rumble of an old man's laughter. Louder and louder, that gravelly rasp. It chased the breeze, bent the water reeds, flurried the feathers on the swan's magnificent wings.

Their parents were standing on the shore. They turned their heads to watch the swan as he flew around the island before descending into the water and gliding into the reeds. The sun was sinking in the sky, its rays streaking the clouds and reddening the lake. It shaped their parents into cut-outs, black and stark until they moved together to form a single silhouette.

'It's time to go back,' Isobel said. 'They've made up at last.'

A LETTER FROM LAURA

Thank you so much for reading *The Silent House*. If you enjoyed it and would like to hear about when my next book is out, sign up below:

www.bookouture.com/laura-elliot

When I began to explore the opening chapters of *The Silent House*, a story that would culminate in a siege, I had no idea I would write it under the siege-like conditions imposed upon us by Covid-19. Usually when I begin each book, I head off on imaginary pathways that promise to be challenging, shadowy, fascinating and forked. On this occasion, I had to add another pathway: one studded with unfamiliar terms like coronavirus, social distancing, stay safe, airborne particles, hand sanitising, mask-wearing and lockdown.

Some writers have reported on the difficulties they experienced as they struggled to be creative during the pandemic. Personally, as I settled into this new Covid-reality, I enjoyed the slow sameness of drifting days. I was used to wheedling precious hours from my busy schedule and had often dreamed of establishing a writing routine without interruptions. Suddenly, for tragic, unforeseen reasons, I had that freedom. All my holidays and short breaks were cancelled. Outside commitments that had seemed unbreakable were jettisoned and there were no excuses to avoid the discipline necessary to pile word upon word until I reached those two definitive ones that signal The End.

I explored the terror of my fictitious family in tandem with my own Covid anxieties. Hyland Hall, the old house that inspired such fear in Isobel and Julie, personified the dark alleyways of the pandemic. The Recluse and his desire for isolation signified our retreat into lockdown. Marsh Lake, with its dangerously deceptive shoreline, reminded me of our changed world where we had to tread carefully for fear of sinking into the mire of the coronavirus. Confined within the privet hedge of my surroundings, the analogies came thick and fast as my story progressed.

I could understand Isobel's rage over losing all that was familiar to her. In the blink of an eye, or so it seemed, my local pub, coffee shop, restaurant and bookstore had closed. My friends and family had retreated as they obeyed the lockdown restrictions but, like the Kingston family, I was adjusting to my 'new normal'. I stopped panicking and attributing my every cough, sneeze and blocked nose to Covid-19. I became accustomed to Zoom and acquired the ability to stop staring critically at my face while others were speaking. I rediscovered the joy of baking and took up Tai Chi, which I did with my neighbours in the mornings on the green outside my house. We stood at a social distance from each other yet we experienced a closeness that time and our busy daily routine usually did not allow us to enjoy.

Sometimes, hearing stories about people who had discovered some new and wonderful creative talent that had remained hidden until the coronavirus flushed it out into the open, I wondered why I was passing those lockdown months doing what I always did. I had an editorial deadline to consider, but I suspect that there is only space in my creative sphere for one passion – and that will always be the written word.

Dear Reader, I hope you enjoyed reading *The Silent House*. Thank you for purchasing my new novel. If you would consider posting a review online on any of the book review sites, I'd be immensely grateful. Also, if you would like to contact me, it would be a pleasure to hear from you.

With warmest regards,
Laura Elliot

lauraelliotauthor

@Elliot_Laura

www.lauraelliotauthor.com

ACKNOWLEDGEMENTS

As I wrote in my author's letter, *The Silent House* was written during the turbulent months of the Covid-19 pandemic. It was a period of solitude mixed with uncertainty and anxiety. Familiar faces were missing from my daily life or, if seen, were reduced to a square on Zoom. New online relationships were formed during this strange Twilight Zone so, as well as acknowledging the support of my husband and family, I'd like to thank those who enlivened the lockdown in new and innovative ways.

Thank you to my neighbours and, in particular to the ever-resourceful Barbara McDonnell, who, in all weathers, voluntarily gathered a group of neighbours at a safe and social distance on the green outside our houses in the mornings to teach us the harmony of body and mind through Tai Chi.

A special nod of thanks to my friends from Scotland, Wales and Ireland, who were unable to gather with us for our annual holiday in West Kerry but who came into my living room via Zoom every Friday night to fill it with laughter and good conversation.

Thanks also to the Zoomers from the Irish Chapter of the Historical Novel Society. And a special shoutout to my good friend, Larry Okun, otherwise known as 'Pres', for his encouragement and mischievous sense of humour.

Grateful thanks to Sean, my friend and husband, who kept my coffee cup filled when our favourite café was shuttered, and who had his hand behind my back every time I faltered while writing *The Silent House*. To my family, Tony, Ciara and Michelle, and their spouses, Louise, Roddy and Harry, for their invaluable support during lockdown. My beloved grandchildren are my delight, so special thanks must go to Romy, Ava and Nina. Something wonderful happened this year and I would like to acknowledge my new grandson, Sean, whose birth we celebrated in September 2020. He has brought excitement and joy into our lives. Thank you to my extended family, those who live abroad and those nearby. Distance and separation make no difference to the bonds we share.

To my many friends whose company I missed during lockdown, and still miss. Thank you for the many emails, WhatsApps, jokes, quizzes, Zooms and invaluable good cheer that we still share online.

No acknowledgement would be complete without thanking you, my readers. Sometimes, it can be difficult to muster the creative energy necessary to begin a new chapter or rewrite a previous one. Reviews and letters from readers provide me with that energy. I wish to extend my gratitude to everyone who has contacted me over the years. No matter what the weather is like outside, hearing from you brings a ray of sunshine into my writing room.

As always, my sincere thanks to my editor, Claire Bord, for her insightful advice and suggestions while I was writing *The Silent House*, to Alexandra Holmes for managing the editorial and production process, Natasha Hodgson for her keen-eyed editing and Claire Rushbrook for proofreading, to Henry Steadman for a fabulous cover, to Kim Nash, Noelle Holten and Sarah Hardy for devising a busy promotional tour and to Alex Crow and the Bookouture marketing team.